KINGSWRAITH

and the

VADHAKA

Derek E Pearson

First published 2023
Published by GB Publishing Org
Copyright © 2023 Derek E Pearson
All rights reserved

ISBN: 978-1-912031-15-3 (paperback)
978-1-912031-33-7 (eBook)

Cover Art © Wendy Kimberley Art

GBP.
GB Publishing Org
www.gbpublishing.co.uk

To Sue

There is a place. Call it a dimension if you will, but it has no proper name and no measurements as we understand them. It is a place of contradictions, both infinite and no thicker than the skin on fresh, flowing water. It is the wellspring from which the spark of life cascades into every living thing, so we are all connected to it. But most of us will never see it, although all of us must travel through it. One day we must all traverse this shadowless plain.

At its heart is a flowing trail of ghost light travelling from featureless horizon to featureless horizon. It looks like a bright pulsing artery of crowded mist; an artery stretched taut below a colourless sky. It contains a torrent of freshly released souls travelling from life to afterlife. At one end of that trail is a person's last breath, at its end, eternity.

The nameless dimension is still as a frozen moment, an unplace of eternal breathless calm, a fistula that splits the fabric between life and death. A departing spirit needs no breath during its brief voyage through the nameless dimension. Nor does the dimension's sole inhabitant.

All alone, watching that artery of souls huddles the naked, emaciated form of a murdered boy. He sits quivering, his skeletal arms wrapped around his bony knees. Consumed by a sick and ravenous hunger, he never drags his gaze away from the stream of spirits. As he searches the stream his mouth waters. His immense eyes weigh the value of each and every soul as they cascade past him on their way to damnation or redemption. His eyes are black, inky wells of pain drawn from deep and ancient rivers of grief – and hatred.

The energy that now animates the boy's wasted form had never felt or seen or smelt anything before it snatched the murdered boy's soul from the ether. It had never sat at table and tasted a dish, never smelt snow nor heard the wind soughing through the forests. Now it revelled over every pallid experience it could suck from its host's wasted senses. Even the rushing ghost light seeping from the artery of souls was a banquet for its starved spirit. It relished everything it could glean from its bleak, featureless home.

It chuckled as hollow whispers fluttered down from the fresh souls swirling along above the bony dome of its skull. It listened with fascinated curiosity to the last mortal words uttered by the surprised dead, those few words that inked the last full stop at the end of a life. Every statement told a story.

What happens when I do this?

Is it safe?

I'll be fine, soon be up and about.

Lean forward and you'll see, there's a great view from up here.

Please, don't hurt me.

Oh yeah? You and who's army?

It looks like gin to me; I'll try it first.

Don't be an idiot. This cliff path's solid as a rock, been here forever. Follow me.

Look out!

Squirming behind the cage of slender ribs where his beating heart had once measured each new second of his life, the boy's helpless soul fluttered like a trapped songbird. He had been imprisoned in his cage for so long that he no longer remembered anything different. He had forgotten so much over the long years.

In the early days the parasite energy had gorged on memories of his mother's delicious cooking, the sweetness of creamy milk still warm from the udder, the soft pressure of a beloved cheek. It had devoured the scent of fresh mown hay, the warmth of the sun's heat on the boy's face, his wonder at the shining stars and the moon at night. The energy had devoured all of it and had eventually drained the boy dry.

The boy had been held so long in his captor's realm that everything else was lost – drifted away beyond recall. Everything was gone, everything except his fierce hunger for revenge and his soul's yearning to be free. Thousands of years before he had been brutally hacked to death by a berserk warrior on a drunken rampage. His small family home had been razed to the ground with his parents still inside it. The terrible slaughter had happened in the small hours and there had been no witnesses.

No witnesses that is, except the victims. Wise elders had decided that the child must have seen who had killed him and conjured his spirit back from the ether. They then asked him to name his killer so that justice could be done. His words had been recorded during the complex Spiritus Iudicii ritual and the

6

guilty warrior had finally received his just reward, slow strangulation by garotte.

But at the end of the ritual something had gone terribly wrong. A gifted necromancer had stolen the boy's soul before it could be returned to the afterlife. He had twisted the boy's innocent spirit into a tool through which he could focus a killing curse. The boy's soul had been fashioned into a pathway, a spirit needle through which the black magician could pour poison into the veins of a popular and noble king.

Afterwards the boy's spirit was discarded, left to wander lost and afraid in the dimension between this life and the next. But his torment was only just beginning. He was eagerly snatched up by one of the starving twists of leech-like energy that exist between this world and the next.

It had pounced on the boy's soul and used him as its gateway to a fresh new universe of memory and sensation. The nameless energy took possession of everything the boy had to offer, while, in the process, carefully turning itself into a shell with which to imprison the captive soul. It devised for itself a distorted and wizened mockery of the living body the boy could barely remember.

The parasite energy couldn't understand everything it dipped from the fresh experiences as they flowed into its newly expanded mind. It couldn't understand notions of justice or love, and memories of comfort and warmth were too alien to be appreciated. But it latched onto and fed from the boy's thirst for revenge like a leech siphoning rich heart blood.

The boy's soul had been left abandoned and vulnerable and he wanted revenge for that. Not against the gentle elder who had first drawn him forth, but against the dark necromancer who had twisted him into a weapon.

He had been touched by the mind of that evil necromancer. While everything else slowly drifted away he would never forget the coldness of that venomous intellect. He remembered the man's overpowering arrogance, his hatred for everything fine and decent in humankind, his insatiable lust for power. A noble King had to die so that an odious royal puppet could take his place and serve the necromancer's malignant will.

The necromancer had flung away the boy's broken soul as a thing without value, discarding him into the shadowless dimension. Now, countless centuries later, the boy crouched gazing up into the pulsing stream of free flying souls.

He yearned to fly with them, but his spirit had become fused with the ravenous twist of immortal energy. There was no hope of escape, but there was something he could do. He could hunt.

The boy could feel the energy's hunger, it was bone deep, sharp as a wolf's tooth. But the boy had so completely infected the energy with his hatred that it too had changed. It could only take one unique form of nourishment. The simple souls flocking past overhead held no sustenance for it, no, the energy could only stomach richer, more complex fare. Darker meat.

A select few of the living could draw power from the place between worlds and shape it to their will. They were thaumaturgists, practitioners of the magical arts. Some worked as forces for good and their spirits were bathed in a pure bright light that would be poisonous to the starving creature huddled on that shadowless plain. They were beyond its reach.

But there were others, black wizards like the necromancer. They used magic for their own ends, and when they died their souls were cloaked in darkness, standing out as tenebrous scraps of night swimming along in the stream of light. They alone could satiate the energy's cravings. When one of those rare delicacies came into his pale realm, he would snatch them from the stream and tear at their shrieking souls with his needle-sharp teeth.

He would feed, slowly gorging himself on the rich spice of evil, sucking the meat from that black soul until the final screaming mouthful was devoured. The necromancer who had condemned the boy's soul had been one of the very first dishes the boy had shared, much to the parasite energy's delight as they consumed every last shrieking mouthful.

In the belly of the lost soul the necromancer's eternity had been stolen away, excised as completely as any chalk marks wiped from the teacher's blackboard at the end of the lesson. He had since been followed by countless others, all condemned to vanish from the ether.

Just recently, however, they had found a new delicacy. The energy had snatched down a strange soul from the stream. It was unlike the previous dark meats which had once been human souls and although they had seen these unusual spirits in the stream before they had never thought to sample one. But it had proved delicious and they were hungry for another.

It seemed that evil had somehow fashioned itself into living shadows, the Umbra, and they provided a very satisfactory dish indeed. Haven Slighe had been quickly wolfed down and the starving boy wanted more. He gazed up into the artery of souls and sniffed, his black eyes sparkled with anticipation and his mouth widened into a creamy, razor-edged grin.

'Soon, my love,' the energy whispered to itself. 'Soon, we shall feed again.' His voice was tight with anticipation, 'They are the darkness in the stream of light, the darkness of the guilty. Guilt is the spice of death. Let us feast on them; let us feast on the shadows.'

The colourless sky rang to the sound of its insane laughter, and it rocked back and forth on its emaciated haunches. But all the while its eyes never left the stream of souls, they never even blinked.

2

On the high southern shoulder of a remote Turkish mountain there is a boat-shaped depression almost six hundred feet long and over one hundred feet wide. The depression is older than everything around it except, perhaps, the mountain itself. Its stones have been weathered by millennia, smoothed by unimaginable age and water. If they could speak, those time-worn stones would have whispered about the era of the great flood and the massive wooden ship that had come to rest there when the flood waters had finally receded.

In the dead centre of the depression stood nine slender figures, each standing within the outermost edge of a precisely drawn circle or zisurrû. It had a diameter of exactly nine feet. The original zisurrûs had been drawn with flour or ground cereals, this one had been cut into the ground using a silver dagger called an athame.

They had chosen that place to meet because it was one of the seven most sacred sites on Earth. It was protected by ancient and powerful wards, which meant that no wicked deed could be performed there. When evil such as theirs comes together it must armour itself with equally powerful charms. Their zisurrû provided an unbreakable wall between the nine and the mundane world, and it could only be entered or exited when one of them cut a portal to the east of the circle using the same athame that had fashioned it.

They made a striking group. They were so similar that anyone looking at them might suspect they were brothers and sisters, which, in a way, they were. But, in fact, none of them had been spawned by the same parents. Like many families they didn't trust each other. Beyond the wall of the circle their brutish guardian thralls waited for their master or mistress to emerge the circle. They snorted at each other, stamping at the ground like buffalo, and they smelt much worse. They could sense their owners' deep distrust. It unsettled them.

Such a gathering was almost unprecedented, the nine rarely saw each other unless there was a pressing reason. That this call to assemble had come so urgently had raised their suspicions, and they studied each other warily. They all held their hands stiffly down at their sides and made no sudden gestures that might be misconstrued as a threat.

Only one person knew why they had been convened at that particular spot at that particular time. Madame Cymbeline Fleischer, which we shall describe as a woman because that if how she had fashioned herself, very rarely left her tall elegant house in the heart of Paris. But then, she had reasoned, unprecedented times call for unprecedented actions.

Madame Fleischer coughed lightly to draw her colleagues' attention, and strode into the centre of the circle. With her rod-straight posture and cold, haughty demeanour, the 'woman' looked as if she might be impervious to any emotions. An observer might wonder if she could have ever known fear, but that observer would have been wrong. She was afraid.

She held her hands clasped firmly together at her waist but there was no mistaking the trails of blue light that seeped from between her long white fingertips. To her 'family' of living shadows, the Viventem Nominis Umbra, that seepage clearly indicated that she was extremely nervous. The Umbra only leak energy when they sense danger and their tissues prepare for defence, building up a lethal charge with which to destroy any foe.

The steel heels of her high boots clanged against the stony ground, sending ringing bell tones out into the night. She came to a halt with a final metallic reverberation which echoed around the vast, boat-shaped space, and she paused while she studied the faces of each of those disturbingly similar men and women. She had seen their likeness before, of course, most often in her mirror.

They were all different colours, different ages, and sported different hairstyles, but they might otherwise have been pressed from identical moulds. All had high cheekbones, lean faces and narrow eyes, and their slender figures were all robed in cultural variations on the theme of expensive, albeit slightly dated, jet-black fabric.

These nine were the surviving members of the family of living shadows. Until recently they had numbered ten, and it was regarding the loss of that single fellow Umbra that Madame Fleischer had called this 'unprecedented' conclave.

'Haven Slighe has gone.' Some people's voices can shatter crystal, Madame Fleischer's sharp tones could engrave bone, while it was still embedded in its owner's living body.

'We all do at some time,' responded the sepulchral tones of a black man called Emmanuel Flight, 'and Haven was getting old. He was reluctant to go, it is a great inconvenience as we all know, but surely it was time for him to open a fresh chapter. He'll be in touch soon enough, parading his fresh youth like a peacock once more. Slighe was a popinjay, he had a streak of vanity a mile wide. You know him, he always does. Eventually.'

'No,' barked Fleischer, 'you fool! Listen to me, I didn't say he'd passed through. I said he's gone, vanished, and so has his house. The house was burned to its foundations. It can be rebuilt, but Slighe can't. He... has... GONE! Now we have no-one in London, which means we have lost England. Can you not understand what I'm saying? We have lost the whole of Great Britain. We have lost ancient Albion! That cannot be allowed.'

The next speaker's voice sounded very much like the high-pitched whine of an insect, 'Be sensible, he can't be gone. He's one of us! Darling, we don't just vanish like smoke! Cymbeline, he's simply where you can't find him. Remember, my dear heart, he's a shadow. Have you looked into the darkness? We all of us hide in the shadows, our beautiful webs to weave, you know that. Slighe has merely faded away into the night and will surely return to us as a completely restored man when he is good and ready.'

Fleischer nearly spat her reply at the angular blond speaker, whose name was Titres Chambers, 'If any you idiots had enough sense to test the ether instead of swilling wine like peasant pigs, you too would have seen what I have seen. Slighe has gone.'

She held out her hands, 'All of us here are linked, we can sense each other. Even when we pass through, we remain in the weave of the Umbra. We are woven into the very fabric of the shadows. Even under the brightest light we touch the darkness. Try it now. Feel for Slighe's vibration now, at night when we are at our most powerful. Then tell me I'm wrong.'

The circle bowed their heads and became utterly still. They began to hum, a sound so deep that the stones around them vibrated, boulders jumped and rattled in the rocky soil. They looked up and shafts of phosphorescent light erupted from their eyes and flooded to where Madame Fleischer stood at their centre.

She flung out her hands in a cruciform gesture, palms facing outwards, and she pushed with all her might. The light sprayed out of the boat-shaped hollow like a shower of living fire and arrowed away into the night. It circled the Earth seven times in less than a second before returning to splash into the family group.

They all gasped with shock and staggered slightly when the wave of light, both burning hot and cold as ice water, roared back into their extended talents.

12

It spoke of secret knowledge, but it disclosed nothing of the missing tenth member of their family.

Fleischer was right after all, Slighe had vanished from the world. He had left no echo, no trace, no path to follow. There was no clue as to his whereabouts. But, they reasoned, that was impossible. A shadow can't vanish! Where there is light there is shadow, where there is shadow you will find the Viventem Nominis Umbra poised to pounce on the unwary.

They had always been able to feel the slightest vibration of threat and respond like the great venomous spiders they all admired so much. They were strong, strong enough to survive the apocalypse itself, they were much better at survival than cockroaches. They did not fear the four horsemen, they feared nothing, except, perhaps, each other.

Flight rumbled at Fleischer, 'What have you done with him, Cymbeline? How did you bring Slighe down? What have you done with our brother? Have you found a way to defeat us? Have you tested it on Slighe? Is that it? Did you gather us here to destroy us, also? Do you feel strong enough to face all eight of us, Cymbeline? Because I can promise you, you won't. You will not survive the attempt.'

Fleischer threw his words back at him, 'Bring Slighe down? Vanquish you? Are you insane? Listen to yourselves, will you? Don't you understand? Something has killed one of us, no, more than killed; something has erased one of us as if he had never existed. Wiped him out. If it can be done to Slighe it can be done to any of us. I beg of you, think about that.'

She jabbed a long finger at each of the circle in turn, 'It could be you next, or it could be you, you, you, you, you, you, or you.' She touched her breast, 'Or it could be me. I don't want to vanquish you, you idiots. I brought us here to work together! You must understand me, we have an enemy, a common enemy; and we must stand together and fight it! Slighe died because he was alone, but together we are strong! So, are you with me? Are you?'

Her razor-sharp voice lashed at them like a whip, chastised them, and they recoiled from her as if stung. Only one stood firm and examined Fleischer with intense concentration. She was a woman so pale and white her skin glowed like crystal in the darkness. When she opened her lipless mouth, it looked like a pink wound in her narrow, flawless face.

Her voice frosted the air. 'Cymbeline, I have answered your call to come here, and now I will answer your question. We are the Umbra, the shadows in the forest, the shade in the cave, the darkness from the deep. We are things of fear, we are the reason for nightmare, we are the footsteps following in the dark. We are creatures of power without equal.'

She drew herself to her full, commanding height, 'And now, you tell us we that have an enemy? You say there is an enemy that has destroyed one of our sacred number? You insist this impossibility to be true?'

Fleischer clasped her hands as if in prayer and nodded, 'Yes, Makrut, that is exactly what I'm saying.' She was astonished, the venerable white woman of Scandinavia had never spoken at any of their rare meetings. It was as if the stones themselves had found a voice.

'Very well,' said the crystalline woman. 'Then Makrut Wyndsyster stands beside you,' she paused for effect. 'As will these fools who still think they have a choice.'

A rapier thin, olive-skinned man wearing a black frock coat and a stove-pipe hat also stepped forward. He said nothing, but he pulled something out of his pocket. It wriggled until he popped it into his mouth, sucking the struggling, hairy legs between his lips. He crunched, then nodded at Cymbeline. Frossard really liked spiders, the fatter the better.

Fleischer smiled, coldly, 'Good, welcome Frossard. We three shall meet in London. We all have arrangements to make first. Slighe died alone, but nothing on this earth could defeat three of us. We shall find and crush this enemy and avenge our brother.'

The murmur of approval was marred by the waspish voice of Titres Chambers, 'May I just say that I never really liked Haven? I know he was one of us but really, he was far too full of himself, I'm just saying. That's all.'

3

A few miles upriver from the great sprawl of London, just beyond West Molesey and a good walk from Hampton Court, the Thames was clean enough to support fish. Cabel Brewster enjoyed the art of fishing almost as much as he enjoyed taking his catch back for his good wife to cook and they'd share a fine, fresh fish dinner fit for any lord.

A fat trout pan-fried in butter with wild garlic, served with fresh bread, sweet butter and some hedgerow greens, why, such a meal would be the envy of any fat judge at his high table; or even an ermined Earl in his great hall. And sometimes there was a salmon. It was a rare treat, true, but he had caught one or two over the years.

Cabel cast his home-made fly with an expert flex of his hand-made bamboo rod. The line was shop bought and had cost him a pretty penny, but it had paid for itself several times by putting a good meal on the table. That made it a sound investment.

His father had taught Cabel the art of fishing when he was still a boy, telling him, 'If you give a man a fish, he'll be hungry again in an hour. But if you teach him how to catch a fish, you do him a good turn, and he'll never go a' hungered.' It was a lesson Cabel never forgot.

What could be better, he thought, than to sit quietly in the shadows under an old oak tree beside the great river, breathing fresh air and the green scented goodness of mother nature, listening to bird song, and appreciating scenery as fine as any toff's fancy oil paintings?

Buying a picture of something that a man can see for free, now that was a poor investment. Where was the value in having a landscape in a frame on your wall when all you need do is look out of your window? That's just throwing money down the drain.

Portraits, there was another waste of money. A man buys a portrait of his wife; what for? She's there, ain't she? Look there, she's the other side of the dinner table smiling prettier than any picture. Cabel smiled to himself. He was proud of Edda, his lovely wife. She had the nature of a saint and she was easy on the eye. She was always glad to see him and she didn't begrudge a man the odd glass of cider. Why, she was partial to a little drop or two herself.

Cabel's marriage was the perfect partnership. He caught their meals on his line or in his traps and Edda dressed and prepared his catch for the pot. She could gut, skin and joint a coney ready for cooking in a few minutes, prepare a trout just as fast, and she knew her way around nature's garden as well as any wood Sprite.

Edda knew what was good to eat in the forest and what would do you harm; she only picked the best from her hedgerow larder. It was one of the many things Cabel valued about her. He certainly wouldn't risk eating any herbs, leaves, flowers or mushrooms he'd brought home. But Edda knew what was dinner and what was poison, right enough. And she knew how to prepare anything he brought her; trout, rabbit, fox or badger, blackbirds, pigeon, quail or grouse, all of them ended up tender and delicious on his fork.

His cork float bobbed; the fly was caught. It was a bite! Cabel already had three good fish in his basket, four would be champion. He would sell two to his friend Nevis, for his supper. Nevis had a hearty appetite. For all he was a skinny specimen he knew how to eat and enjoyed his food, but he was no hunter. His dinner came from the farm, the shops, or Cabel.

Fish had no respect for Nevis. They treated him like the gentle hearted soul he was, and had completely ignored his lure that one time he had tried his hand with Cabel's rod. Cabel's patient advice seemed to go in one ear and fall straight out the other without touching anything in between.

You can't teach a soul as won't learn. Nevis was the senior woodsman for the manor and could turn his hand to carpentry as would charm a stout stool out of a bit of discarded oak. His hands couldn't handle the fishing rod but they understood wood as if born to it.

It was as if he had splinters in his blood and his eyes were green as holly come yuletide, but he was clumsy as a new foal when it came to hunting and fishing. But there it was, that was the way of it. That was fine, that was dandy. Nevis always had a few coins in his pocket to buy Cabel's spare bounty, and he never said no to fresh provender.

The fourth fish slipped into Cabel's net slick as a thought and he quickly dispatched it with the heavy hardwood priest Nevis had made for him. Cabel would never let an animal suffer longer than it had to. God put plenty on Earth for Adam's children to eat, but he didn't put it there for man to torment. A fish out of water is drowning, same as a man in the water would do. Put the fish to sleep fast and painless and the Lord might smile on you, with a bit of luck.

It was the same with his snares. Some as use wires that bite into an animal's flesh causing great pain and suffering. He had found a poor coney once that had near torn off its own leg because it was caught in a wire noose, and the poor beast was still alive. He killed it with a single stroke of his knife to release it from its misery, but he didn't take it home.

'Pain spoils an animal's meat,' Edda had told him once. 'Leave it there for those as hurt the poor beast. Only bring home they creatures as died gentle-like, and you'll feast as fine as any King in his parlour. That's my promise, Cabel Brewster. The good Lord guides the hand of a kind hunter and turns his face away from the wicked, you'll see if I'm not right.'

Four fat trout, beautiful as rainbows in spring, their eyes bright as any star. He smiled at the trove in his basket. Edda would kiss him when he handed over the brace they would have for supper, and kiss him again when he handed over the money he would get from Nevis.

Then she would get busy in the kitchen while he went out and smoked his pipe in the orchards where he would admire the plump fruit on his trees, fruit he could either sell in the local town market on a Thursday, or press for his justifiably famous cider.

Brewster's cider was celebrated in the locality as the finest in Surrey. It was bought by most of his customers as a celebration tipple for when the nights drew in and the yuletide garlands were on the wall. It took a few weeks for the yeast to turn the clear juice into the magic potion that cheered the winter soul. He also added sugar to some of the juice to make the apple perry that Edda and the other ladies preferred. 'Apple Champagne,' she called it.

Soon it would be time for the harvest. The day before he had cupped and gently twisted one of the fruits and it hadn't come away in his hand. But the branches were laden, pregnant with bounty. He would start harvesting that weekend with Edda and Nevis giving him a hand. Nevis always lent a hand in exchange for a few free jugs when the season's brew was ready, and he was a hard willing worker.

Cabel thanked the Lord for his generous hand. He felt blessed with a life that anyone would envy. He had his wife, a good stout cottage he called home, and he was beholden to no man for his keep. Nevis worked for his wages and that

17

suited him, but Cabel walked in his own shoes on his own path and paid his way with money he'd earned from his own orchards. Any way you spun that wheel on its axle, it was a good life.

He and Hedda also knew to look after the Sprites on his land. A cider jug hung from the branch of a tree would be empty by morning, and whatever he could spare by way of food would be gifted to the elvish Sprites that looked like children but could only ever be seen from the corner of your eye. It was bad luck to see one face-to-face, but share what you could and your orchards would bloom and bear fruit. A gift freely given is rewarded with gratitude.

Thanks to the Sprites his fruit rarely spoiled on the branch, and his apples, pears and plums drew crowds in the market. One day a regular customer brought him a large slice of warm apple pie in a China bowl. It rested under a mounded dollop of clouted cream.

The man marched proudly up to Cabel's stall, held it out, handed him a spoon and said, 'You taste that. What my missus does with your apples she can't do with no others. It's like a taste of heaven. And I thought to myself, as 'ow them 'as grown they apples should 'ave a taste as what gets done with 'em. Enjoy it, that's by way of me saying thank-you for whatever it is you do, that others don't.'

It was a good pie, and the cream was fresh as the morning. Cabel thanked the man by giving him a bag of Bramley apples, which he tried to refuse but Cabel insisted, saying, 'Them's by way of saying thank-you to your missus for treating my apples proper, the way they deserve; and I know what I'm saying. My missus is no slouch in the kitchen but that pie was as fine as her best, and you tell your lady I said so.' They shook on it.

Cabel's thoughts returned to the riverbank and settled back into the here and now. His mind would often wander hither and yon while he was relaxing in the peaceful silence. He looked down the river where he thought he caught a glimpse of a kingfisher, a flash of bright blue darting down for its dinner. He touched his knuckle to his forehead in respect, one fisherman to another, and then he started to gather his gear together for the walk home.

He had just picked up his laden basket and dusted the leaves from the seat of his trousers when he noticed what looked like a strange tidal bore rolling down the river towards him. It was an arrow shaped wave nearly a foot high. He had never seen anything like it before. He wondered if some great sea fish had swum up the river. He'd heard tell of it happening but had never seen it for himself, and, in truth, he had never really believed it.

He stood entranced for a moment, and then realised how silent the scene had become. Even the birds had stopped singing in the trees. The whole riverbank seemed to be holding its breath and crouching down as if trying not to draw attention to itself. Cabel stepped backwards into the shadows until he felt the bark of the oak tree press against his spine. He suddenly felt a cold knot of fear tighten in his belly.

Whatever was carving its way up the Thames looked unnatural to him. It was as if the water was being sliced by a great invisible knife. Cabel had never seen a shark's fin cutting through the sea towards its prey, but some primal memory rose up in him and alarm bells jangled in his mind. That watery vector was a predator on the prowl, of that he was certain.

And then the point of the wave curved round to the right and headed straight towards the section of the bank on which he stood. He became frozen with fear. His legs had turned to stone and he began quivering with terror, unable to run away. There was something there under the water, something long like a dark eel. But it was not swimming like a fish, it flowed like a dart thrown at the board.

He realised he hadn't taken a breath since first seeing the wave and sucked air into his lungs. As he watched a pale woman rose up out of the water, long and lean with narrow eyes in a narrow, fine-boned face. She was dressed in black but her exposed skin glowed like the moon and her hair reminded him of silk. It was the colour of polished silver. She seemed almost translucent, as if the sun was shining right through her.

She spoke. Her voice was cool and dry with an accent he didn't recognise, and her mouth seemed shockingly pink against her pale complexion, 'Where is London from here?'

He pointed downstream. 'Back there,' he said, 'back the way you came. It's a big place, you can't miss it. You won't want to swim there, though. The water's not clean, it ain't healthy like this stretch is.'

She looked at his basket, 'What were you doing?'

'Fishing, I'm catching fish for me supper. It's good eating. Trout, you know?'

19

She shook her head. 'I don't eat fish,' she said, and stepped up out of the water, reaching for him with fingers like steel. Cabel's last coherent thought was that he would be letting Edda down so badly, leaving her all alone. But his thoughts were swept away in waves of agony as the strange, crystalline woman took her time with him.

4

The Sprite called Whipple was the first to stumble across the site. There was no body, but the tree trunk and trampled grass were spattered with a lot of blood. At first Whipple thought a rabbit must have been caught by a fox, but when he saw Cabel's fishing rod and the basket with its four, glossy, rainbow coloured fish, he got a sick suspicion that twisted in his gut like a screw in a plank. The fish were only just beginning to taint the air with their odour, so whatever had happened must have happened very recently.

Cabel Brewster was well known to the Sprite family. They respected him as a good friend to the forest folk and in return they helped him with his fruit trees. They also admired his skill with his home-made fishing rod, and the gentle way he treated any animals he had snared for his larder. He was that rare person, a good man; and a follower of the old disciplines who understood the importance of sharing and respect for others.

Whipple felt sick. He had to know what had happened and whether the good man Brewster was in trouble, or worse. He pressed his hands against the bark of the oak and whispered 'Witness'. Trees have no eyes but they can register events around them and sense emotions. The tree gave up its secrets and Whipple staggered back. So much pain there, so much pain.

He pressed his hands back against the oak. Yes, it had been Cabel Brewster, the tree recognised him as the gentle fisherman. It surrendered the sequence of events, and Whipple felt it as the living flesh was being torn from his own face and hands, as it had Cabel's. The tree had recorded every second of the man's agony while the meat was chewed from his bones and torn from his throat. It was savage, a brutal attack.

Whipple looked around to see if there was any sign of a dog or a large fox. He couldn't think what else it might have been. Whatever it was must have carried Cabel's body away, and that took a lot of strength. There had been rumours of a giant wild cat in the area, but no-one with any sense believed it. Where could a big cat hide that the Sprites couldn't find it?

Wolves had been gone from the forests for a long age, as had bears and wild boar, but big dogs like a mastiff or a wolfhound would sometimes attack a person. Was that what had happened? The tree couldn't tell. Whipple realised that he couldn't deal with the situation on his own and carefully circled around the bloodied site to press both his hands against the unmarked side of the oak. He called out for help and the forest whispered for him.

Then he sat where he could keep an eye on the site of Cabel's murder and he waited, his knees drawn up to his chin and his arms around his legs. Just by being there he would help deter the wild things that would lick at the blood. There was already enough movement in the undergrowth for him to know that the freshly spilt gore was sending out its invitation to an army of scavengers. The minutes ticked by, time passing slow as thick resin running down a pine. Whipple had never felt so alone in the forest before

When he finally heard the welcome sound of running feet, he leapt to his feet and hurried forward to greet his friends, relief flooding through him. The waiting had provided plenty of time for Whipple's imagination to become seriously inventive. He was jittery as a rabbit set loose in amongst hounds, tormented by a mixture of fear and confusion.

He was afraid that whatever had killed Cabel was close by and still peckish. He feared that it might slink back to find him all alone, just perfect for an after-dinner snack. And he kept picturing ever more fantastic beasts that might have done such a wicked thing to a poor gentle soul like Cabel Brewster. For sure, it would be nothing that had ever stalked his forest before.

Five of the child-like Sprites burst out of the undergrowth and sprinted towards him. Whipple was relieved to see that Morwen was the in the lead as usual. Tree Sprites, also known as the family of Epimeliads, were too capricious to countenance the idea of 'leaders', but Morwen was the closest thing to a leader that Whipple's clan had accepted. When she spoke, the family listened. She was beautiful, intelligent, and hard as her native oak.

'You sent the tree threat alarm?' said Morwen. 'Why?' She looked around, 'Oh.'

Whipple blurted, 'Something's happened to Mr Brewster, him from the orchards, you know, the cider man. I saw all this blood and got the tree to witness. Then I stayed until you came. I didn't want anything messing with the place, did I? I couldn't leave, it didn't feel right. You ask the tree; you see what it says. He was a good fellow, he made proper cider, but you'll see. Poor Mr Brewster got chewed up like a dog's bone. It ain't right.'

Morwen crouched by the blood-spattered grass but didn't touch it, then she reached out with the palm of her left hand and pressed it to the oak. While she listened to the tree's witness, she traced the shape of the spatter with her fingertips. Her breathing became laboured and she almost fainted. At last, she slowly stood up and stepped backwards, returning to the midst of her little group of friends.

She addressed the tallest, 'Acer, please, would you go and fetch Mr Nevis. Bring him here. Tell him its urgent, tell him it's about his friend Mr Brewster. Hurry now, quickly, quickly.'

There was no need for Acer to ask where Nevis was, after all this was their forest. Each Epimeliad knew where everything and anyone could be found within its borders. The designated Sprite scurried away into the trees.

Morwen faced the remaining four members of her tribe. She said, 'Something terrible has happened here, something wicked and wrong. It was done by a dreadful powerful creature. But, truth to tell, I've felt a presence like this before, I have. But that was a long, long time ago, a true forest's age, and that was over in old London town.

'You four stay here and wait until Acer gets back; I'm going to the conference tree. We've got to let Penelope and the London tribe know what's happened, warn them that the ancient evil has returned. I'll be quick as I can.'

The conference tree was a giant, sprawling wych elm at the heart of the wild forest, a woodland now reduced to a shrinking island of green surrounded on all sides by cultured fields and human dwellings. What had once been thousands upon thousands of square miles of trees had been reduced to the few dense acres screened by the vicious thorns of tangled bramble and briar, protected by the Lord of the local Manor.

A keen but unfortunately untalented romantic poet, the Lord preferred to leave nature untrammelled by civilisation wherever possible. He had employed Nevis for his skills as a woodman, then sat back and enjoyed the view without getting his hands dirty. Unlike true men of the earth such as Nevis and Cable, he had never learned the old customs, and couldn't understand the importance of earning the goodwill of the Sprites.

Nevis knew about the elf-like Epimeliads in the woods and respected them. Like Cabel, he made offerings in exchange for their blessings. It was after sharing such wisdom over a few pots of cider that the two men had found their kinship, becoming firm friends.

23

Like Cabel, Nevis had always believed that one should never look the Sprites directly in the eye, it was disrespectful, so he was surprised when one of them stepped lightly from the bushes directly in front of him and strode out onto the path just a few feet away, blocking his passage. He nearly fainted when the child-like creature addressed him by name.

'Mr Nevis, please, you must come with me. It's your friend Mr Brewster. Something terrible... See, I'm to take you there where it happened. Please, Mr Nevis, follow me, we must hurry. Poor man, he's been...'

The sentence was too brutal to finish, so the Sprite spun on his heel and sprinted down the path towards the river. Long-legged and slender Nevis barely had to trot to keep up, but his heart began pounding in his chest as if he was running a marathon at full tilt. With a mounting sense of sick dread, he believed he knew full well what the Sprite was about to show him, and he wondered what he might have to tell Edda. What could he say?

In the heart of the forest Morwen was stretched out at full length on one the stoutest boughs of the conversation tree, her naked arms and legs pressed against the grey-brown bark. The wych was not her tree, that was a massive oak close by, but even so it welcomed her familiar touch. She felt it grow warm against her bare skin and its fissures softened, opened and sculpted themselves around her.

She sank into its gentle embrace and surrendered herself to its spirit. There is a time-honoured synergy between Sprite and tree. Although it was a falsehood that a Sprite might die if their tree was felled, it was true that any tree nurtured by the elf-like people would flourish. The giant wych was almost regarded as a beloved grandparent by Morwen's tribe, and it had been gifted with their attention like no other. It was beautiful.

Any tree can whisper to any other tree within the boundaries of the forest, but no further. That was how Whipple had been able to send out his threat alarm from the oak by the river. Yet every clan's forest has a single conversation tree through which they can send a message to anywhere else on Earth, and that message can be precisely directed towards the 'pattern' of a fellow Sprite clan. How it worked was a mystery, its origins were lost in myths and old stories about veins of gold and dragon lore, but it worked, and that was all that mattered.

24

In her mind's eye Morwen pictured a giant Roman reservoir sunk deep beneath the foundations of the Tower of London. She allowed her vision to sweep to the centre of the reservoir where a slender girlish figure sat on a small stone throne that had once graced a palace in lost Atlantis. She saw that the girl was in close conversation with a young human male. That surprised her and she looked closer at the young man.

Even through the light touch of the Wych tree Morwen could feel his power, and realised with shocked surprise that the London Sprite was not only acting as his mentor, she was teaching him the deepest secrets of her craft. The two were absorbed in what was evidently an intensely private moment, an intimate moment as if between two lovers. Human and Sprite lovers? That was impossible. Well, almost impossible.

But there was no time to wait, Morwen's message was much too urgent to worry about the social niceties. 'Penelope, Epimeliad sister!' she sent. 'I'm sorry, but I must speak with you. I have terrible news, news that will shock you. Please, send the human away.'

In her mind's eye she saw Penelope look up in confusion, startled by the interruption. The young man also looked concerned and evidently wondered what had just happened to break his tutor's concentration.

Penelope held up a hand to him, signalling that he must wait a moment, then she said out loud, 'No, sister, Kingswraith can stay. He has been accepted by the oak. He is one of our family now. So then, what news have you to tell me, Morwen of the woods?'

Morwen almost lost her train of thought, the human was a tree brother? Why, that hadn't happened since, well, since the fabled Pendragon many forest ages before. Who was this Kingswraith? But there was no time for questions, she had news to share.

'Very well, so be it, he shall stay if he must. Penelope, there has been a killing here. A simple man of the orchards has been murdered; his body has gone, perhaps stolen. I read the traces of the act and felt the vibrations of the tree witness. I recognised the taste of it, the style. See what I've seen.' Morwen sent her tree witness impressions along with mental images of the copious blood at the riverside site.

Penelope gasped in horror, 'Morwen, you understand what this means?'

25

Morwen sighed, her fears confirmed, 'Yes, my sister, I too thought it to be the mark of the living shadows. A new Umbra has come to Albion. But why has it come here to our little forest. We have nothing it might want. Ours is but a small community.'

Penelope felt sick and she turned haunted eyes on Kingswraith. 'I think I know why,' she said. 'I believe it must be hunting for someone.'

She launched into a long explanation covering events during the autumn of the previous year and Kingswraith's involvement in the death of the Umbra Haven Slighe. Even from her place on the communication tree Morwen felt Penelope's fear for her friend's safety, and understood that the young human had become more than just a lover. Much more. He was family and must be protected at all costs.

By the time Morwen returned to the river and stepped out onto the riverbank, she found Nevis sitting beside Whipple, both their faces a picture of abject misery. Nevis sat fidgeting, compulsively rubbing his palms together and gazing at the blood. Morwen sat by his side and rested her hand on his arm. She said nothing but she looked into his eyes with all the warmth she could muster.

There was nothing she could say to comfort the man, but she could lend him her ears if he needed to unburden some of the horror that weighed so heavily on his heart.

Whipple said, 'Mr Nevis, sir, this is the Lady Morwen. She is our sister and she has a thoughtful head on her shoulders. You must tell her what you told me. She will listen.'

The woodman shivered as if the words were too cruel and painful to utter. He said, his voice a barely audible rumble, 'I've seen the signs left by everything that has ever chewed on anything in this forest. I've seen signs left by dog and fox, pig, cat, all the things that eat meat. I knows them like I knows the back of my hands. But what left those marks, that weren't any wild animal. I'll swear on any Bible that 'tweren't no wild animal.'

The Sprite's response was gentle and coaxing, she knew the answer before he spoke 'So then, Mr Nevis, what do you think it was? Where have you seen marks like that before?'

He turned his head to look hard into her eyes, 'I'll tell you, Miss. I see 'em on every pathway and on every road. I see 'em on the floor of every house. Those are shoe prints. They come out of the river there and they go back in

26

again. And Cabel follows on, into the water. I tell you that horror was done by a man, Miss Morwen, by a man, and he took Cabel with him. I don't know how, but that's what the sign tells me, clear as any writing on a page.'

He wiped at his lips with the back of his fist, tears clouding his eyes, 'I can't almost believe it meself, but that's the truth of it. That dreadful crime was done by a man who ate poor Cabel while he was still alive. By a man who et 'im raw as an onion. You say they chewed his face off and sucked the meat from his hands before they ripped out his throat. But then, how could he walk after them into the river. How could he follow them as killed him? How can that happen? Miss, do you know?'

5

Kingswraith had been spending more of his time with Penelope in the Sprites' Roman reservoir since his patron, the Professor Lord Whitekirk, had married Clare Winter in a ceremony for which Kingswraith had stood as best man. It had been an intimate service attended on the groom's side by the domestic staff from Owl's Tower, the Professor's Chelsea home in Cheyne Row, and the recently promoted Detective Inspector Chandler who stood next to his happily weeping wife. 'Mrs Chandler do love a wedding,' he explained

On Clare's side of the nave was her immediate family, mother, father and a brother, and the two girls she described as her 'caged birds' Phoebe and Regan, whom she employed as shop assistants at Scheer's, her highly successful bookshop in Russell Square.

The Professor and his bride had then honeymooned for a month, taking a grand tour of Italy, a trip that featured the cultural splendours of Venice, Milan, and Florence. During the tour Clare had also been introduced to the senior European members of the Lux Texentes, the convocation of white wizards to whom the Professor, Kingswraith, and now Clare belonged. The circle of Lux Texentes was steadily dwindling, and they welcomed a new practitioner to their ranks, especially one as lovely and intelligent as the new Lady Whitekirk.

The Lux lived in secret for fear of the 'Conflagration' of shadow creatures known as Viventem Nominis Umbra. Any company of dark practitioners, whether the Umbra themselves or the growing number of Necromancers who emulated them, was categorised as a 'Conflagration', although the Professor believed that to be too fine a description for the vile practitioners. He opined that they should best be labelled a 'Murder' like a flock of crows, or a 'Skulk' after any band of foxes.

During their time away the couple had sent postcards and letters to Kingswraith, the Professor's ward and closest friend, and they had also discussed between themselves how the young man was an essential member of their family, but what should be done about his ongoing education, and what would his place be within their marital home.

Oblivious to the couple's concerns Kingswraith had happily accepted all of these changes to his life and had eagerly looked forward to the messages and cards his patron sent him. He shared the latest news regarding the couple's cultural adventures in Italy with Mrs Vermont the housekeeper, her general handyman husband Wills, and Shelagh, the live-in maid.

Problems only arose once the newlyweds had returned home and carried with them into the house an atmosphere of such tender intimacy that Kingswraith began to feel very much the prize gooseberry whenever he was around them – which was most of the time. He was still meant to be in training with the Professor acting as his mentor, but now his patron was also training his wife, whose wild natural talent had to be reined in before she became dangerous.

It became increasingly awkward for the young man to share a room with them, they seemed almost in thrall to their love and constantly touched each other or exchanged lingering glances and not so secret smiles. Kingswraith felt himself to be surplus to requirements but he couldn't make his feelings known for fear of offending his friends.

There was another problem, a much more important one. In order to fight the London Umbra known as Haven Slighe, Kingswraith had begun his transition to a new level of thaumaturgical power. He had already achieved a level of magical arts far beyond the Professor's ability but could say nothing about it. He had vowed to Penelope that he would keep his latest advances into the most arcane arts as a complete secret.

He worked hard to disguise the way the world answered to his every whim as if he had his own personal genii in an invisible lamp. If he thought about fetching something it would instantly speed to his hand; gas lamps flared into life at his approach, and he could even fly – after a fashion. His environment had become his very own well trained and obedient pet.

If he walked in the rain, he remained dry, and he could see in the dark thanks to the living blue light the Sprites called pneuma, a loyal fluid phenomenon the Sprites used to illuminate their sunless tunnels, and which only allowed itself to be visible to the 'family' of the Epimeliad into which Kingswraith had recently been adopted.

He had learned how to render himself invisible, and had access to an almost limitless source of magical energy. He wasn't yet fully cognisant of all his abilities and was still learning what his 'transition' to a new state might mean; a transition through which Penelope was doing her best to guide him – with the occasional aid of Garth, the venerable steward from the Halls of the Dead whom Kingswraith only visited at night in spirit form.

The young wizard was constantly stumbling across new ways in which his abilities had been enhanced, but what he believed he lacked were the correct words with which to perform more complex carmini, or what the general public might naively describe as either 'spells' or 'cantrips'. His reliance on verbal charms deeply frustrated his Sprite mentor.

Penelope told him she had never needed to, 'Fiddle about with spoken enchantments and mumble at the magic as if begging it to perform.' As a magical creature she wove her magic as naturally as breathing. She suggested he either learned to do without words altogether or talk to the Professor, his human mentor, about improving his command of Latin.

'You don't ask your heart to beat or plead for your eyes to see, you don't try to wheedle your hands into grasping a cup or your feet to walk, well, do you? Then why do you have to find words before you can make your enchantments? They are as much a part of you as any of your limbs, and they will do your bidding when you learn how to reach out and use them properly. That Professor of yours has led you down a right wrong cul-de-sac, and you need to find a way out.'

And there lay another problem. The Professor had fully intended to begin Kingswraith's advanced training once he'd reached his sixteenth birthday, an important year in magical circles, but there had been two major stumbling blocks. First, the Professor had been weakened the previous year when he was very badly treated by Haven Slighe, mentally and physically. He had barely survived their encounter.

While he had been imprisoned in Slighe's cellar the Umbra had drained most of the magical life force from the Professor's body, and any advanced thaumaturgical practitioner depends on magical energy to survive. After his dreadful ordeal the Professor, Lord Whitekirk, had been rendered an invalid for several months. Then, as soon as he was fit enough, he married Clare and they departed for their grand tour of Italy with no further thoughts about his talented young ward's training.

And then, a few months after the Whitekirks' returned, Kingswraith's fifteenth year had come and gone. His sixteenth was a day celebrated with good food, fine gifts, and warm wishes, but afterwards Kingswraith had received precious little of the advanced training his mentor had promised. He was made very welcome if he wanted to sit in with the Whitekirks and help guide Clare's nursery steps towards becoming a full white practitioner, but constantly revisiting his old and familiar lessons soon palled.

There was some excitement to be had. The sheer strength of Clare's wild talent meant that Kingswraith witnessed some hair-raising displays of seemingly brute magical force. During one session the Professor's Thaumatograph – which registered magical activity – almost shook itself to pieces while Clare was attempting a lux spiritus carmini, which was only meant to create a simple floating ball of coherent light.

Unfortunately, she was all too successful. Kingswraith and the Professor threw themselves to the ground when the glowing ball began to spin in her palm, leapt into the air, whirled around the room three times then launched itself through one of the study's skylight windows with a shattering crash. When Wills repaired the window, he quietly observed that it was unusual for a bird strike – which was the excuse he had been offered – to scatter so much broken glass on the outside. And also, for the bird to make its escape afterwards.

Despite such brief moments of domestic excitement Kingswraith felt himself increasingly drawn to the peace of the great Roman reservoir and the generosity of the Epimeliad clan. Outwardly the lady Penelope looked like little more than an urchin child, perhaps as much as four or five years his junior. But she wore her slight, gamine adolescent body as a disguise, as did all her family. She was in truth very much an adult.

Sprites were long-lived, many remembered the dark forests that had once cloaked Britain. Kingswraith's companions entertained him with stories of great woolly mammoths that had once loomed tall and strode like giants through their forests. That was at a time when great glaciers covered the land. And they also remembered the fall of the Doggerland bridge that had once linked Eastern Prydain, the ancient name for Britain, and Northern Gaul, the equally ancient name for France.

It was across that land bridge that great toothed cats had come to stalk their prey through centuries of dark winter; and hairy rhinos shouldered their massive path through the icy woodlands. It was by walking across that bridge that man had arrived from the east, at first the slope faced Neanderthals and then the taller, straighter-backed homo sapiens. Both burned the forests for heat and to cook their food. Humankind began to alter the landscape.

A Sprite called Porewit, who had appointed himself the unelected leader of Kingswraith's companions, offered him a rueful smile, 'You humans came here before the big warm melted the ice and flooded Doggerland. You hunted just about everything that wasn't hunting you, and then you started to build houses. Then it was villages you built, communities of farmers, then it was towns, towns became cities, until one day the world was made in your image. It was your world then. The great forests were gone and we had to learn how to live in your world as best we could. And here we are now; down here instead of in our forests. Times, they do change, don't they?'

Kingswraith asked, 'But when London first started to get as big as it is, why didn't you just move out into the country? There are still large areas of woodland even now. Why didn't you just follow Watling Street north? Scotland would be perfect for you, wouldn't it?'

Porewit looked around at the dozen or so companions seated in a relaxed circle around them, and raised his brows and shoulders in a heartfelt shrug that said, 'Should I tell him? What do you say? Should I?'

The companions urged him on with nods and smiles. He said, 'We can't do that. That would be like people from down the street moving into your house. We're from the trees of the lands that later became London. Our roots are here, only here, and they run deep.'

His friends chuckled; it was evidently an old joke but one they still appreciated. Kingswraith grinned with them.

Porewit smiled at his own wordplay, then his face grew sombre, 'Old Doggerland, that had forests once, and they've been drowned, lost under the sea for nearly nine thousand years. The spirits of those forests have been living down there with the fish all that time. They've changed, they're marine people now. You've heard of mermaids and such? That's what happens when forests sink beneath the waves. Same thing happened when the great flood made the Mediterranean, ain't that right, boys?'

The group muttered their agreement, nodding to each other and at Kingswraith. 'That's right,' they said, 'that's true an all.' And they shuddered at the thought.

Porewit spoke for the group, 'We've heard them, haven't we? We've heard them singing in the Thames. They don't come up too far because they can't survive in the water up here, it's too dirty. They say it's like walking through the worst London fog to swim up here, but worse. It chokes them, see?'

Kingswraith grimaced, he could imagine.

Porewit pulled a sad face, 'But that's the other thing, see. They still sing about forest clearings and sunshine in the glade. They sing about the sound of the wind soughing through summer leaves, and the dark silence of a winter's night under stars so bright it's like nature spent all summer polishing them until they were just perfect. They don't have that anymore, see, but they remember it well enough. Those songs would break your heart.'

Kingswraith remembered his companions' tales of sea Sprites when Penelope had told him what had happened to Cabel Brewster, and he impulsively asked her if it might have been one of the spirits of the drowned forests that had climbed up out the river and attacked him.

'Like you did with those evil men when you drained all the minerals from them. The "depleted men" the police called them, remember? Might it have been something like that? Was Cabel Brewster a wicked man made to pay for his crimes? Was it a punishment?'

A flash of anger burned behind Penelope's large black eyes, just for a moment, then Kingswraith watched as she reined in her fury and calmed herself with an effort.

She took a deep breath before she answered, her voice steady, 'No, master Kingswraith, the answer is no. I understand the reasons for the question and, true enough, it angered me, but I forgive you for it, and no. We Epimeliads are guardians of light, much like your good selves. We punish the wicked, but none of us would think of eating raw flesh, not even from an utterly evil man's face. Not while he still lived. It's a horrible idea.'

She clasped her hands in her lap, 'The sunken lands. There are stories about forests that were half drowned and half remained on dry land, about loved ones separated from their families, about madness and despair. Whole swathes of the East Anglian coastline were levelled when spirits surrendered their life energies back to the soil. They chose to take the long path, but they never became wicked and cruel. Not like that.'

'It sounds terrible, those poor desperate souls.'

'Oh, Kingswraith. You mortals live and die in the time it takes to grow a small copse of wych. You have no idea what it means to lose a love you have shared for thousands upon thousands of years. You people jump from spring to midwinter in just three score years and ten, if you're lucky. You no sooner find love than it becomes dust and ashes. Yet your passions burn so hot in that hasty time. Still, you are a young race.'

She touched his cheek with the tips of her fingers, 'Listen to me, you have so much to learn and we waste time talking about things that the world has forgotten, and perhaps that's for the best. So, no. The killing Morwen told me about was not by one of us, not even by one of the marine spirits. But Morwen tasted the killing in a tree's witness, it's a thing we can do, and she recognised the traces left by his killer. She said they tasted very like Haven Slighe.'

'Haven Slighe?! But surely, he's dead?'

'Yes, oh yes, he's gone, we killed him. But he was one of ten, the old steward Garth told you that. As I said, the trace was like Slighe, but it wasn't him. No, it was another of those creatures, the Umbra, and we believe it was hunting for something, or someone.'

'Hunting for what? Have they developed a taste for man meat now? Is that it? Do we have to protect mankind from an evil tribe of cannibal dark wizards? That sounds like something from Mr Allan Poe's strange imagination. Oh, no, this is too vile. It can't be that.'

Penelope shook her head, 'No, my dear Kingswraith, not that, but we believe they are hunting, in fact we believe they are hunting for you. Poor Mr Brewster was just a man in the wrong place at the wrong time and they used him for their foul practices.'

Kingswraith blurted, 'Me? They are looking for me? But why?'

Penelope looked sombre, 'You killed one of their number, well, we did, they can't allow that. And we have no more time to waste hoping the Professor will wake up and begin your advanced training. Let's leave him to his love-play, your training is now in our hands.'

She reached out and took his hands in her slender fingers, he felt a thrill of electricity at her touch, 'So, then,' she said, 'shall we prepare your defences, sharpen your weapons? You are like a powerful cat that still has its baby teeth. Strong but not enough bite, not yet. Together we shall work to make you the perfect enchanted warrior, only then will you be ready. So, let's hope they don't find you before then, eh? Let's give you some teeth like those great cats that once stalked the ice forests of old Prydain, teeth strong enough to bite the shadows.'

6

The Professor referred to Penelope and her family of Epimeliads as Kingswraith's 'charming little friends'. He suspected that there might be more about them, some secret that attracted so much of his ward's attention, but he didn't know that they were ancient beings and directly responsible for the strange case of the 'depleted men'.

He found it easier to accept the evidence of his own eyes, and what he saw was a group of street urchins who had gained a certain notoriety for caring for the homeless and vulnerable multitude in an area stretching from around Leicester Square and Piccadilly to Limehouse and the Thames Basin.

He'd heard that they did good works, that the 'urchins' provided a bit of food here, some few pennies there, a kind word for the lonely. How they were funded he didn't know – he didn't want to know, he suspected it might not be strictly legal – but the ends justified the means. But why, he wondered, did they cause a mental itch in his memory that he couldn't reach to scratch? What was it that haunted him so much?

In fact, he remembered practically nothing of his rescue from the prison in Haven Slighe's cellar, which had been performed by a small group of Kingswraith's Sprite companions. Nor had he learned about Penelope reactivating the oak floorboards in Slighe's parlour, their branches bursting forth like long fingers to rescue Kingswraith who had been trapped in a lethal spinning cage of burning gold. Kingswraith's rescue had ignited the fire that totally destroyed the Umbra's house. The young wizard had barely escaped with his skin intact.

Clare knew more about the Sprites than her husband, but even she would have been amazed to learn the complete truth; just how ancient, and powerful the 'children' truly were. They walked openly through the streets of London disguised as a ragged band of street Arabs, helping the innocent whenever they could, but they lived in their network of tunnels at the centre of which was an immense Roman reservoir, far below the Tower of London.

Many of the Sprites remembered Albion and a time of heroes, of rough yet noble men who had since dissolved into myth. They spoke with familiar smiles of Bran the Blessed, Finn McCool, Merlin, Arthur Pendragon and his warriors.

The Sprites had watched the glaciers retreat and witnessed the arrival of the Roman legions who turned a riverside settlement into a city. And over the centuries they had watched the city grow until it had become the greatest collection of buildings in the world; with some of the meanest slums.

In her accustomed street Arab guise Penelope resembled a skinny, raven-haired girl. She knew how to cast a glamour that would entrance any human – when she needed to – and she had the power to take a man's life using a painful process that drained the minerals from his body while also forcing him to relive every second of his wickedness, to suffer as his victims had suffered. She gave the evilest, the basest, vilest sinners a taste of hell, and much more.

Kingswraith had seen the woman behind the child, and she had needed no glamour to entrance him. Images of her physical perfection haunted his dreams and coloured his waking hours. She had tried to protect him from her charms, but it was too late, the damage had been done. In all his sixteen years Kingswraith had never seen anyone like her, she was unique.

While she was training him in advanced thaumaturgy, Penelope would only appear in her true form. She claimed it was too difficult to maintain her urchin persona while she needed to manipulate magic to the high degree necessary to support Kingswraith's development and guide him through his complex transition. She didn't know what her student would finally become, but she understood how important it would be to avoid unnecessary distractions.

And yet, she was a distraction. Her true self was a taller woman, lithe and long-legged with slender curves. Her eyes flashed hazel, emerald and gold under hazel curls, and her firm cupid's bow of a mouth curved under an exquisite nose. She was sublime, and all too often Kingswraith had found it difficult to drag his eyes away from her and concentrate on his lessons.

Since taking part in his first ceremony of transition, which had involved him spiritually and physically bonding with Penelope's guardian oak tree in Green Park, Kingswraith had also taken on some of the corporeal aspects of the tree Sprites. He had become taller and his features more striking. His physique had been well honed before, but under Penelope's tutelage he had developed into a model of broad-shouldered yet lean athleticism.

He had always been a good-looking young man, but now he had become startlingly handsome with an elegant, fresh-faced ruggedness that drew attention wherever he went, and that was beginning to prove troublesome at times, both amongst the general public and in his home, Owl's Tower.

Shelagh the housemaid had once accidently walked in on him when he was naked in the bathtub, but lately she seemed to lose the ability to breathe properly when she entered any room and found him there. Her cheeks took on a rosy glow and her pretty eyes gleamed. The Professor had previously maintained that the young servant had an exquisite taste for fine art, but now, he quietly observed to his wife, he believed the poor smitten girl had placed Kingswraith on a pedestal and was treating him as a living masterpiece.

The other problem was Clare, who never missed an opportunity to tell him how well he was looking. Kingswraith couldn't miss the hint of resentment in her voice. The Professor had been a beautiful, almost pre-Raphaelite example of manhood before he was captured and tormented by Slighe. His ordeal had ravaged both his health and his appearance. He was still a fine-looking man, but his tawny mane was now silver and his eyes looked haunted.

Kingswraith too had been mentally scarred and physically diminished during his encounter with the Umbra, but a year later he had not only fully recovered he was evidently flourishing. He suspected that Clare believed he was keeping some secret therapy from his patron, that he had found a way to heal himself and that the Professor could also be returned to his former vigour and aesthetic glory, but for some reason he had chosen to withhold it. Why would he?

She never made an open accusation, but her suspicions sat between them like a black wall, her unspoken questions festering in her unquiet mind. Kingswraith had raised the question of the Professor's condition with Penelope, but she had shaken her head in resignation. 'Part of your recovery is thanks to your successful melding with my tree. You already had the strength of an oak in your tissues before you met Slighe, and that helped you recover and bloom, I'd say that "bloom" is a very apt word in your case.'

She added, 'Your roots run very deep into the reservoir of natural energy, and we could draw on that strength to heal you and help you grow. Your patron has been damaged to his roots; sadly, he is a broken vessel. Unfortunately, that means he cannot draw from the reservoir as you have, and that locks him away from the deep healing. Perhaps...'

Then she brightened, and to Kingswraith it was as if the sun had suddenly burst through thick clouds. 'But wait, there might be a way,' she said, 'yes,

38

there might be a way. But we shall need some materials.' She was suddenly very excited, 'Yes, why didn't I think of this before? Yes, it calls for magic from the elder craft but that doesn't mean it won't work.'

She gazed up into his eyes and shards of emerald glittered in the gold. He felt his stomach lurch, 'My Lord Kingswraith, can you fetch me two rods of purest silver? They must be at least as thick as my thumb if not more, and both must be three feet long. The silver must be as pure as spring water. It is essential that there must be no contamination with iron or tin, no taint of base metals in the cast, they must be completely pure. Can you do that?'

He nodded, while also wondering where he would find such things. 'Why, what are you going to do with them?' he asked.

She smiled like an angel, yet with a mischievous hint of the devil in her gold-flecked eyes. 'That is for you to find out, but I think it will please you. Now go, and be quick about it. The sooner we have the materials the sooner the cure can begin.'

Kingswraith did what he always did when he wanted a sound answer to a practical question, he turned to Wills, the goodman of his household. Wills listened to his request and then regarded him with questions burning bright in his deep-set, intelligent eyes. He said nothing but ran his muscular fist through his thick, pepper and salt thatch of tight curls.

The young man continued, 'It's for the guvnor, Wills, so cave's the word. Can you help me? Or might you know someone else I should ask?'

The big man shrugged his powerful shoulders, 'Ay, yes, I know summat, but I'll have to be goin' with 'e young sir. Yes, I know a place in Candlewick. It's near the tall Monument to the great fire. I'll just let my missus know that we're on a job for the master and we'll be on our way directly. You'll need a fair parcel of money; we'd best fetch that first. I'll take my lead weighted stick along, just in case a wrong 'un takes a fancy to 'un. A smart knock on the head helps settles any question about who owns what, if you see what I mean, young sir.'

After visiting Kingswraith's bank and withdrawing a considerable sum of money they flagged down a growler that took them from the King's Road to Candlewick, one of the twenty-five ancient wards in the City of London. Wills directed their driver to Clement's Lane off Lombard Street, a narrow path under the tall shadow of the Monument.

From there he led Kingswraith along a covered alleyway then out into a cobbled courtyard, where he rapped on what looked like a stable door fronting a windowless brick building that crouched down on its foundations, its fabric grimy and low, squat and weighted with great age. It looked as if it was the hub around which the courtyard had grown.

After a few moments a boy as grimy as the bricks drew the door open a mere crack, but he grinned when he recognised Wills and quickly dragged the protesting door open wide enough to allow his visitors entry to the premises.

'Well, bless my soul if it isn't Mr Vermont,' he said in a voice that seemed far too old and refined for his age and appearance. 'It's a pleasure to see you again, sir. You'll be wanting Mr Taylor I presume? Please, please step in. Give me a second, I'll just shut and bolt the door first then I'll go and fetch him. We don't want all and sundry wandering in here, do we?'

Kingswraith looked around in wonder. The interior of the building was sooty but bright with light from big skylights set in the ceiling. A smithy's forge filled half the space. It was tamped down but glowed, warm against the early autumn chill. Thick pots of all shapes and sizes were racked on shelves, and metal working tools were mounted on neat brackets, each according to size and type.

This workplace was hushed as a cathedral and Kingswraith could feel the craft reflected from the walls, and more than a hint of wild magic. The youngster re-emerged from a room at the back followed by a well-built, bearded man wearing a stained leather apron and a beaming smile. His skin was as dark as good chocolate and his eyes black as ebony; but his smile was white as freshly washed linen and broadened with genuine pleasure when he recognised Wills.

He strode forward, wiping his hands on a cloth, and then stuck out a big paw for Wills to shake before he turned to face Kingswraith. He seemed to hold his breath for a moment while he studied the young wizard. A knowing light danced in his eyes and he nodded his head as if a whispered voice was whispering a great secret in his ear. He spoke, and his tone was deep and rich as finest velvet. Kingswraith thought he must have a wonderful singing voice.

'Any friend of Wills Vermont will always be welcomed to Jeremiah Taylor's workshop. So, then gentlemen, what can Jeremiah Taylor fashion for you today? Is it to be another fine engagement ring for a beautiful lady? Or perhaps

40

a pair of wedding rings to seal two heartstrings together in the Lord's holy matrimony?'

For a profound moment the silversmith looked into Kingswraith's eyes and the young wizard felt as if he and Taylor had somehow shared a silent confidence; then the smiling man continued. 'Or shall this be a challenge to the smith's craft that will open windows onto stranger horizons? Are we looking at something other than beckoning the good ship wedlock to a happy future? What shall you ask of me, young sir? Jeremiah Taylor is at your service.'

Kingswraith repeated Penelope's request, underlining her insistence that the rods must be wrought from the finest, unadulterated silver. He asked for them to be at least as thick as his thumb, which was thicker than Penelope's. Taylor took a deep breath and mentioned his price. Kingswraith took a pouch from Wills and counted out one hundred and twenty guineas.

It was the largest sum he had ever transacted for a single purchase. Taylor handed the coins to his assistant, 'Master Kingswraith,' he said, 'I shall fashion your rods in silver so pure you could use them to shoe a unicorn. Please, might I ask that you come back in three days?'

As they shook hands the black man leaned forward and whispered, 'Come back alone. I would talk with you of old times and of the lords and ladies who lived amongst us back then. I believe we have something in common do we not?'

Kingswraith responded, 'And, what might that be, good sir?'

'Jeremiah, please. A man of the craft will always recognise another practitioner, you know that. I've spent a lifetime working precious metals and I've made my obeisance to the nature spirits who keep my tools sharp, my materials sweet, and my eye sure. I'm talking about magic, master Kingswraith, of course, I'm talking about magic.'

7

Three days later Kingswraith returned to the forge and resumed his conversation with Taylor, who had sent his boy away on an errand. All the better, he explained, for them to have an 'uninterrupted chat'. But before Christopher had left the forge, the jeweller had asked him to fetch Kingswraith his silver rods. They were perfect cylinders of bright metal, identical in every dimension and surprisingly heavy for such fine workmanship.

Christopher had let Kingswraith examine the rods before he carefully wrapped them separately in sheets of fine leather followed by layers of soft hessian, then he bundled them together in cotton duck and finally rolled them in two layers of brown paper which he tied with strong twine.

It was important to protect the silver, he explained, 'And anyway,' he added, 'you'll not want to walk through London flashing solid silver around. It would be a temptation to a devout churchman, and there's some around here as daren't step into a church for fear the water in the font would start boiling and the lead on the roof melt away.'

He grinned mischievously, 'They'd have you with a knife in your ribs and be away on their toes with this fine booty quick as "how's your father". Be a shame to waste all that hard work, wouldn't it? Best hide it in plain brown paper until it's where it needs to be.'

His father nodded his approval, 'Pure silver is soft, that's why most smiths adulterate it with copper. It hardens it and makes it easier to work. It's right and proper to wrap it with kid leather and hessian, and, Kingswraith, my friend, try not to bash it around or knock it on anything. Even wrapped like a new-born you'll bend it into all sorts of shapes, and whatever you intend them for, I suspect they must remain straight as Christ's true path to glory.'

Kingswraith had learned that the youngster was, in fact, Taylor's only son, and he couldn't hide his surprise upon hearing it. The black man smiled. 'You'll be asking yourself how a Nubian like me can sire a Christian white boy? It's a good question. You see, I am descended from slaves stolen from the Ivory Coast and shipped to plantations in the West Indies. Generations down the line we poor slaves have finally won our freedom, but as with so many there is now a touch of milk in my African coffee. Christopher takes after his mother. My wife is as pale and beautiful as a winter's dawn. He has my eyes though, don't you think?'

Once they were alone Taylor could no longer contain his curiosity, 'Tell me, friend Kingswraith, which of the spirits has tasked you with creating two such rare devices as these rods of yours? I know some of us prize the purest silver for its monetary value, but, in truth, sterling silver is stronger and almost as beautiful. It is only the secret folk who value the purest metals because they act as a funnel for magical energy, and you have asked me to fashion two such funnels. I must know, which of the secret high born commissioned this?'

They were sitting on bentwood chairs in the back room sipping at excellent tea, for all that it had been served in white enamelled mugs with a fine blue rim as the only decoration. Unlike the larger forge area – where every surface was covered with a layer of fine black soot – the back room was Taylor's workshop where he meticulously crafted his intricate jewellery. It was spotlessly neat and clean, with every tool in its place.

The young wizard was cautious, 'Very well, but, quid pro quo, Jeremiah. Will you also tell me which of the elementals guides your hand? You call them "high born" "lords and ladies" and "secret folk", and yes, they are secret, it's true. But surely, such secrets can be shared between we practitioners? So, please, master craftsman, if you would, you first.'

Taylor paused, and then smiled in acquiescence, 'Very well, when I was younger and first apprenticed, I was taught to bow to Hephaestus, also known as Klytotékhnēs. And to Vesta who tames fire and to Vulcan who makes it hot enough to forge the hardest metal. But since I have mastered my own workshop there's a beautiful girl called Brigid who visits me. It was Brigid who blessed my forge and my hands. She appears as a child, but she's not childish, and in return for her protection she accepts my humble offerings of metal and food. So, now then, what about you? Quid pro quo?'

Kingswraith answered, 'For me there are tree Sprites, the first of whom is called Penelope. I think she has other names, but I call her Penelope. It was she who asked for the silver rods but I don't know why. I'm sure I will learn soon enough. Their clan is the Epimeliad. Like Brigid they choose to appear as children, as street Arabs, but that is merely their disguise.'

'But why should your Penelope and her clan need such a disguise? Are they so very strange looking that they might frighten people?'

'No, quite the opposite, they're very beautiful. People would lust after them and they might need to defend themselves. You see, they're all extremely powerful practitioners, born to the arts, so they might accidently hurt someone. No, not strange or frightening, they simply disguise themselves to protect others from their strength. Nobody looks at street Arabs twice, which means they become practically invisible. They're fine people.'

It was time for Kingswraith to leave, but Taylor first elicited a promise that he would come back, saying that he was welcome to enjoy London's finest cup of tea whenever he was in the area. Then Taylor held his hand up as if he had just remembered something.

'I hope you don't mind,' he said looking a little embarrassed, 'but I had some silver left after the rods were finished. I greatly admired your ring when you came here with Wills, so I made some cufflinks to go with it. Just a little token from one practitioner to another. Please, accept these, and please, you must also make sure that you let me know what Penelope does with the rods. I'll admit my curiosity's burning hotter than my forge. You know how 'tis, my young friend, so little happens in the workshop and I spend most of my time in my own head. Anything strange is like a magnet to me and my mind is full of iron.'

The cufflinks were breathtakingly beautiful. Each consisted of two carefully shaped flat discs chased with a subtle dragon motif that wound around in a curving circle. Just as on Kingswraith's ring the dragon was biting its own tail, and yet it also seemed to be moving, as if flowing in sinuous arcs. Taylor was obviously a true magician in his craft.

The young wizard didn't hesitate to replace his current gold cufflinks with the new silver ones. Each pair of dragon discs was held together by a short and robust chain, and they fitted through the holes in the fabric of his cuffs perfectly. Kingswraith greatly admired the way the links sparkled at his wrists, but he protested that they were far too fine a gift, and made as if to take them off and return them.

But Taylor insisted, 'One day perhaps you might do something for me in return; but today we have shared the bounty of friendship, and I believe there is no greater gift that one man can give another. Wear them with pride, as I made them with pride, my friend. Perhaps, sometimes, you might think of your fellow practitioner and his forge when you put them on.'

44

Taylor unlocked the street door, they shook hands once more, and then Kingswraith slipped out into a thick and sour tasting fog. He heard the sound of the big key turning behind him, flipped up his collar against the chill, and made his way back to Clement's Lane before turning right towards Lombard Street in the hope of finding a growler that could take him to Brompton Cemetery and the secret door to the Sprite's tunnels.

He had to admit that his curiosity was also burning hot as any forge, and he was eager to find out what Penelope planned for the pure silver rods he had tucked under his arm. What marvellous magic could she fashion that might bring some comfort to the Professor and Clare? His imagination spun a fine web of possibilities.

He was thus distracted by his thoughts when a brutish voice broke into his reverie, 'You can turn around slowly and 'and over that bundle sharpish or I'll blow the 'ead clean off your shoulders. Gentle now, this ain't no toffee apple I'm holding but it will give you the pip. I knows you've seen the black fellah at his place of business, and I knows but that means metal 'as changed 'ands. So, come on nah, 'and it over sharpish, and you might just go 'ome in one piece, and your old mum would thank me for me kind 'eart.'

The man loomed over him and thrust a pistol in his face. Kingswraith was assaulted by the nose curling reek of rotten teeth, cheap tobacco, rank sweat and stale beer that exuded thick as the fog from the thief's body. The thief had evidently spent many nights in low taverns, and across the front of his grime encrusted Dutchman's pea coat Kingswraith noticed the horizontal scar left by the 'drunkard's rope' or 'hangover'. This was a device like a thick washing line strung between two walls over which boozers who couldn't afford a bed could pay a pittance to hang by their armpits until roused in the morning.

The pistol looked small in the thief's fist, but to Kingswraith's eyes it seemed to grow until it filled his vision. He had been practicing some defensive carmini with Penelope, and they all used short commands, but he found it difficult to concentrate when a stinking, drunken bull of a man was thrusting a gun in his face. He was trying to calm his fluttering nerves and prepare a lacta or throwing charm, when the brute barked again.

'Oi! I'm talking to you, cully! If you can't 'ear me you ain't got no use for no ears, have yah? So, I'll blow 'em orf your 'ead, then I'll blow the 'ead orf yer shoulders. So, 'and over the goods. I'm thirsty and so's me uncle. Time's a' wasting, boy.'

He thrust the gun out and reached for the package. Sudden fury boiled up in Kingswraith's belly. What right had this oaf to steal someone's property? He threw up his free hand and snarled lacta!

The big man grunted in surprise and staggered several feet backwards. But he was made of sturdy stuff. He squealed in fury and aimed his pistol directly at Kingswraith's chest. But he was too late, the young wizard had already gathered his energy for another spell. Cultro, he snapped and watched a line of blood slash across the thief's bluntly porcine features.

His attacker roared and made to aim his pistol at his victim once more. Kingswraith heard him cock the hammer back, priming the revolver to fire. There was no time for mercy. The wizard braced himself and thrust forward with both hands, one of which was holding the bundled pair of silver rods. He felt power surge along his arms and he shouted stupefaciunt! Energy flowed through him and hit the big man like a poleaxe.

The thug reeled backwards, fell and bounced just once. His head hit the cobbles with a solid crack! Kingswraith ran forward and checked the brute was still breathing, but hastened away from the vile reek of the man's sour breath, deciding that the brute was lucky enough to be alive, and that he could sleep it off where he lay.

He spun at the sound of a new voice and saw two child-like figures emerge out of the fog. 'The streets ain't safe for innocent footpads with the likes of you prowling about in them, Boss. We were waiting to see if you needed a hand, but you managed the big lump just fine. I've never seen that cultro knife charm before, you'll have to teach it to me. So then, shall we go see the lady? Penelope wants to see you safe and sound, and best get there before you throw another wrong 'un into the gutter, eh?'

Kingswraith recognised two of his companion Sprites, Porewit and Yarrow. He paused for a moment to catch his breath and stop his limbs from trembling. He couldn't disguise the quiver in his throat when he said, 'I'm off down to Lombard Street to find a Hackney. You're both welcome to join me. We don't want to walk to Brompton in this filthy pea-souper.'

Porewit grinned, 'Fair enough, Boss, we hear what you're saying. But civilised folk like us don't want to be walking these streets in a London pea souper, now do we? Come on, you follow us and we'll soon get you out of this horrible weather and away from the likes of sleeping beauty there.'

As if responding to his name the unconscious mound of humanity on the cobbles uttered a loud snore followed by a long, ripe, flatulent raspberry. The foul air became fouler still.

Porewit theatrically wafted an open hand across his grimacing features, 'Hardly a breath of fresh air, is he? Look here, Boss, shall we get out of here before we get gifted with another rude comment from the horizontal local? Personally, if we must have a musical accompaniment, I'd rather have a bit of Mozart, not Brahms and Liszt. Let's be gone before his guts rip him a new one, eh?'

They turned up Clement's Lane and walked to King William Street, crossed diagonally right to Abchurch Lane and then down until they reached the shoulder of St Mary church. The Sprites looked around, then dashed over to a paving slab which they lifted to disclose a flight of worn stone steps.

'After you, Boss,' grinned Yarrow. 'We'll be right behind you.'

8

The steps led down to a wide ledge beside a running sewer which was every bit as foul as his attacker's breath. Thankfully the ledge was wide enough to walk along dry shod, without any need to wade through the dank, stinking water. He followed his companions' guidance in the darkness, walking along the ledge until they halted him beside a shallow arch. Yarrow leant down and pressed two bricks inwards and the arch swung open like a well-oiled door.

Kingswraith gratefully stepped through the arch into the much sweeter tunnel, and the now familiar blue pneuma blazed up and illuminated their path ahead. The arched door closed on the sewer's reek. He wondered how the air under London's streets could smell so much cleaner than the streets themselves. Along the Sprites' underground pathways there was always a fresh green perfume that reminded him of forest clearings, cut grass, and mown hay.

'Our fragrant friend back there can't be all bad,' he said, 'at least he's looking after his family. He was going to share his loot with his uncle, or at least buy him a drink.'

Porewit stifled a guffaw, 'Boss, first you carve a man up like a joint of beef then you come out with something like that! You astound me. The farting felon's "uncle" would be his fence, his receiver of stolen goods. There's nothing about family there. Now come on.'

They swiftly made their way towards the Roman reservoir at the centre of the labyrinthine network of Sprite tunnels. Eastcheap was closer to the Tower than Brompton, so they reached one of the arrow straight bridges across the black water of the reservoir that much sooner.

Kingswraith questioned his guides, 'If it's so much faster to get here from elsewhere, why, until today, have I always come down into the tunnels from Brompton Cemetery?'

Porewit answered, 'Why? Because that's the entrance nearest to your home, Boss. The faster you're down here the sooner you get here, wherever you started from, if you see what I mean? We've never intended to inconvenience you in any way. We're got gates all over the city, but Brompton's the only one out near Chelsea. That's almost at the edge of civilisation.'

Yarrow agreed, 'Our tunnels cover the place underground, but we've had to close some of them down when men start digging everything up, as they do for sewers or trains or whatever else. It's always the same; when men get their hands on something, they can't stop from fiddling with it. They always go changing things and filling the place with buildings. I'd say that before we know it, the only trees in London will be locked up in parks or surrounded by garden fences. Men put nature in a corset, no offense intended.'

His normally cheerful voice took on a bitter edge, 'Lord knows what they'll do with the world in the long run. They'll put a wall around it and charge people by the hour to visit the fresh air. Look at that fog out there, that ain't no sea fret, that's man-made filth from all the chimneys. I feel proper sorry for mother nature, I do. They'll have her trussed up like a Christmas goose and throttled on the muck they make – you mark my words.'

Porewit voiced his sympathy with his friend and Kingswraith felt guilty and embarrassed for his species. Previously he had felt quite proud of man's achievements. The world had become a smaller place thanks to steam travel, and the windows of the cathedral of science had been flung open to new horizons of incredible potential. But the natural world was shrinking, and what might that mean to these ancient spirits?

He wondered what defences human logic and science might muster against the Sprites if they decided to fight back? Kingswraith shuddered at the thought of humanity going to war with Penelope and her family. The Sprites might be outnumbered, but they had sunk their roots deep into the Earth's heart and could call on thousands of years of experience. They would be hard to budge if they chose to make a stand.

Man could bring his bayonets, his cannon and his guns; but would they prevail? Could they? Or would they end up like the thief who had faced Kingswraith with a gun in his hand and been left stretched out on the cobbles, stricken by magic.

Look at the way Penelope had brought Slighe's oaken floorboards back to life and made them obey her will, made them remember when the sap had flowed through their veins. After the branches had burst from the hardened wood the powerful Umbra had burned to death.

Who could stand against such power? Who could stand if the very trees themselves leaned down to pluck rifles from the soldiers' hands? What could soldiers do if the wooden wheels of their cannon woke up, took bud, rooted themselves in the ground and refused to turn? Who could stand firm in the face of such puissant magic and mystery?

Would it have to be him who fought the Epimeliad? Would it be the Professor, or Clare? Who else could do it? Would it be the Umbra? He looked up, dragging his mind away from the dark images poisoning his thoughts, and he saw Penelope on the platform waiting for him in her adult form. She smiled at him, and in that moment he knew.

If man ever goes to war with you, he thought, then they will be at war with me too. And that certainty settled in his heart, hard as a diamond. He realised how much he loved her, and his stomach knotted with the sheer madness of that love, she wasn't even human. And then he remembered why he was there, and he held out his bundle to her, and she received it in her slender hands.

The other Sprites clustered around. Few disguised themselves as children in front of Kingswraith any more, many stood as tall and graceful as Penelope. He compared the memory of the tubby, red faced and aging royalty and aristocracy of Britain he had met, with the elegance and poise of the tree Sprites chattering and whispering around them while Penelope unwrapped and admired the gleaming silver rods. What human could match them?

There was the Professor, known to polite society as the Viscount Lord Henry Rupert William Cecil Clarence Cubitt Hiram Menzies Whitekirk. Yes, he could take his place amongst this magical throng, even in his present diminished form.

And as for himself? The Baronet Lord Martin Alexander Simon Kingswraith? He had already been accepted into this family of tree spirits. His eyes had been opened with Penelope's kiss, and he was still trying to come to terms with all the changes he had experienced since his arms had been held firm in the meat of her oak tree and his body taken into her arcane embrace.

She had never been so close to him since, but he would never forget the heat of her body pressed against his. What next? he wondered.

Unaware of his wandering thoughts Penelope held up the two rods of silver, one in each hand. She began to chant in her people's sweet and musical tongue. The other Sprites joined the song, and from somewhere music washed over them and added its hypnotic rhythm. Kingswraith was caught up like a snake before the charmer. His blood responded to the exotic enchantment with a primal urgency.

He felt as if all his senses were being heightened at once. The cadence seemed to tear away a secret veil that had, until that moment, dimmed his sight and muffled his hearing. He had never felt so vibrant, so exquisitely alive. He heard his own voice join the choir, caught up in the sweet, pulsing sound which was both exquisite and yet, somehow, primitive.

The crescendo peaked in a note that would break a song thrush's heart with envy, and blue fire splashed and surged from the tip of each of the silver rods. It was the blue of a clear summer sky, the blue of pure ice under the winter's sun. It was the blue that called to some forgotten race memory, and Kingswraith gasped in awe. Every nerve in his body yearned to bathe in that crystal light and be cleansed of everything sordid and petty.

No evil thing could survive in that light. It would be shrivelled, burned away and cast into the shadows as dust. The light bloomed brighter; it shone into the furthest corners of the reservoir scouring away the grime of centuries to reveal pure white stone and clean red Roman brick in a variety of sizes and shades.

Kingswraith felt his spirit swept out of his body and up into the light, soaring higher and higher. From the highest point he hung poised like a kite in a breeze and looked down at the black water with its arrow straight bridges and central stone platform.

And he saw a great black eye looking back at him. The reservoir was in the shape of an eye? In that moment the light winked out and he tumbled helplessly back into his body. He staggered back to life, shaking his head in confusion and trembling like a leaf in a gale.

Penelope's expression was one of utter elation, her eyes glittered with bright splinters of emerald. She breathed, 'Lord of all creation, but that felt good. I must quickly craft these wonderful fingers of bright silver as I promised, or the temptation to keep them will become too great. My Lord Kingswraith, who made these for you? What is he, craftsman, or god?'

Kingswraith scrambled to gather his wits, still thinking about that great black eye. What just happened? What is this place? Then he answered, 'He is a man, a black man. His name is Jeremiah Taylor. His wonderful talent has been blessed by a spirit called Brigid; like you she appears as a young girl, but I haven't seen her. She blessed his forge and his hands, and Jeremiah is a true practitioner; I sense deep magic in his work. Look at these.'

He showed her his cufflinks. All of the Sprites pressed closer and a hum of excitement buzzed through them. Penelope delicately touched the discs of bright metal, and instantly drew her fingers away as if she had been scorched.

She studied her reddened fingertips with evident curiosity. 'Blessed indeed,' she said. 'Brigid, you say? Very well, very well. So then, where does this craftsman ply his trade?'

There was nothing soft in her voice now, her intense curiosity had transformed her into a figure of bladelike authority. Kingswraith wondered what fresh mystery had awakened in her brilliant mind. He touched one of his cufflinks, and felt only the thrill of the pure metal.

He looked to his companion Sprites, 'Porewit and Yarrow met me by the alleyway that leads to his workshop. It's just off Clement's Lane. Didn't you, lads?'

They nodded their agreement, 'We did,' said Yarrow. 'That was where the Boss flattened a big stinker. The filthy bugger had a loaded pistol in his hand but never got a chance to use it. Boss used some sweet carmini. One was a knife spell that cut the stinker's face. Then he knocked the big fellow down. It was done fast, and over neat as you like.'

Penelope's eyes narrowed and she pointed one of the rods at Porewit, 'I thought I told you to keep an eye on him?'

Porewit backed away looking nervous. He stuttered 'W, w, we did, we were there and ready, right enough. But the Boss was having such a good time trying different stuff out on the bloke that we didn't want to interrupt. The big bugger didn't know what hit him, did he, Yarrow? Went down like a stunned ox he did. It was over faster than the telling of it, weren't it, Yarrow? Yarrow, ain't that right, eh?'

It hadn't seemed that fast to Kingswraith, but he saw the storm clouds gathering on Penelope's brow and decided that discretion was the better part of valour. He held his tongue, preferring to keep his companions out of hot water, or at least, not to push them any further in. They were already up to their chins in trouble.

Penelope met his eyes with a steely gaze, 'What charms did you use?'

He shrugged, 'Lacta, cultro, and stupefaciunt. All as you taught me.'

52

She nodded, 'Throw, knife, and stun. Very good. You didn't try shield, fire or ice, nor did you lock his muscles?'

'No, he had a gun and I had no time to think. He said he wanted to steal your silver rods. I couldn't allow that. I wanted to push him back then knock him down. They were the first carmini I thought of.' And anyway, he realised, I was beginning to enjoy myself. After all, I did it; I faced the armed bully and I brought him down.

Penelope grinned and the storm clouds broke open and the sun flooded out once more. She turned to the assembled Sprites, 'I must work with Lord Kingswraith alone for a few hours, and then we shall eat together before he leaves us for his home. Yarrow will tell us the tale of the thief brought low, and he shall leave out none of the details; including the two brave heroes hiding in the fog while Kingswraith fought alone.'

She beckoned to the young wizard, 'Now, you must come with me, please, my Lord. And bring your wits with you, you're going to need them. All of them.'

9

Mackenzie discreetly studied the two women seated in the stern of his boat and a quiet voice in his numb brain kept asking how on earth they had got there. He ran a little ferry service from Ham to Teddington, but he couldn't remember picking up this particular fare. And he had to admit that he didn't like the look of these two very much. They were both thin and dressed in black, and while one seemed to shimmer as if she was made of glass, the other was olive skinned, dark haired, and studied him through cold and narrow, slit-like eyes.

They looked like twins cast from different materials. He couldn't imagine what their parents must have been like, but a chill rolled off them that made him very nervous, and when he was nervous Mackenzie did what every boatman has always done – probably since the first caveman had hitched a lift in a stranger's dug-out canoe at the dawn of time – he began to talk. Words spilled out of him in an incontinent rush.

'What about this fog, eh? Mind you, I've seen it worse than this. I been on this river for over forty years and I've seen the fog so bad you can't see past the end of your own nose. You got to feel your way about. It's like being a blind man when someone's nicked 'is stick, poor covey. It's enough to give you a dose of the morbs. Still, London and fog, eh? Go together like beefsteak pie and oysters, don't they? One's dimmer, the other's dinner, eh?'

Neither woman answered. Their expressions didn't alter. Must be foreigners, he thought, over for a bit of culture. He changed tack, 'Vouley vous over 'ere from foreign parts, are you? Parley the English, do you? Tricky langwidge the English; I'm still learnin' and I was born 'ere. Must be terrible hard for you foreigners. Don't blame you for not knowing the mother tongue, I mean, what can you say when you don't know the lingo, eh, eh?'

The glass woman gazed at him as if she had suddenly realised there was a man handling a pair of oars in the middle of the boat. The other one, whom he thought of as 'the dark haughty bint', regarded him with an expression of utter disdain. She looked down her nose at him, as if he was something very unpleasant, something she had just discovered on the sole of her shoe.

The glass one opened a surprisingly pink mouth and reeled off a list of questions, 'So then, my man, what do you do for a living? Are you one of those street beggars we've heard about? Do you drink gin and carouse in public houses? Are you a glutton at the table or are you abstemious? Do you frequent women of easy virtue? How much does it cost for a threepenny knee trembler? Am I talking too fast for you? Try to keep up.'

Before he could answer any of the questions, she turned her face away and stared out at the river as if she had completely forgotten he was there.

'Here,' he protested, 'hang on a mo', you can't talk to me like that. I'm a proper boatman I am, man and boy. I'm no glutton, and I don't know what the other word means, but I don't think I'm one of them neither. I don't rightly know what a threepenny knee trembler is, but I reckon it's going to cost you threepence on current evidence.'

The dark woman sniffed loudly as if she had just caught the stink of the mess on her shoe. Then she snarled, 'Who asked you, man? Get on with your job. Do you smoke, by the way?'

'She asked me, her there, your mate. She did, you heard her. She asked me if I drink gin and if I go with tarts, well I don't and I don't. And I don't smoke neither. Boatman can't smoke, it weakens the lungs and you can't row proper, though there's some as puff on a pipe when the fancy takes 'em. I don't do that neither. Where are we a going to, anyhow?'

The glass woman said to the fog, 'You'll know when we get there.' She faced him once more, then glanced at her companion, 'He seems clean. Tell me, are you hungry after such a long journey?'

Mackenzie answered, 'I must admit, something like a hot beef pie would go down very well about now.'

The glass woman frowned slightly. 'I wasn't talking to you.' She pointed over his shoulder. 'Tell me, what's the name of that bridge over there?'

'Bridge? There's no bridge here!' Mackenzie turned to see what she was pointing at, and two pairs of steel hard hands dragged him from his seat. He never got the chance to scream. Later when the boat bounced its way down a weir and the women had to concentrate hard, using their talents to avoid it tipping over and dumping them in the water, the glass-like Umbra sighed.

'Cymbeline, perhaps it would have been wiser to let him get us where we are going before we ate him, don't you think? He was very useful on the oars, wasn't he?'

The dark-haired woman chuckled and licked blood from her fingers with a long narrow tongue. It coiled around her dagger-like fingernail. 'Makrut, my heart, are you really saying that we need any aid from one of these cattle? You always were the wit, my dear, you really do amuse me. And his French! It was simply terrible, unforgivable. He had to go.'

The humourless expression on the bland, glass-like face flickered slightly, and with long teeth she gnawed the last little scrap of meat from Mackenzie's fleshless hand, like someone nibbling cherries from the stalk. Then the boatman's corpse rose to its feet and rolled into the river, smooth as an otter. It joined Cabel who was swimming underwater, chasing after his crystalline mistress. They swam side-by-side. Soon, others joined them, a swarm of shadows arrowing through the Thame's murk.

…

Penelope led Kingswraith away from the platform and took him along a bridge he had never crossed before. She walked tall with her head high and her back oddly stiff, holding the two rods of silver vertically in front of her, one in each hand, as if they were symbols of state. Her steps were carefully paced and her face solemn. The air was very still. Kingswraith felt if the whole world had become caught-up in the moment and, like him, was waiting to see what incredible thing could happened. Time seemed frozen.

He couldn't escape the feeling that he would soon have to take part in yet another strange Sprite ceremony, undergo an induction into yet another arcane mystery. His life had always been unusual, but since meeting Penelope, he had found himself wandering along increasingly obscure and sometimes dangerous pathways. There were no signposts that he could recognise, no maps, and no compass; he just had to trust that his guide knew her way.

His civilised veneer had been slowly stripped away, and his guise as a modern man of natural science – a passion he had shared with the Professor since his childhood – was slipping from his shoulders like an unwanted and unneeded skin.

As a practitioner of the Lux Texentes he had been brought up to think of himself as heir to an ancient convocation of practitioners, a group of white wizards whose roots stretched back into the mists of a bygone age. What he was learning now came from a much earlier time, a time of legend, an age before human history had begun.

He surreptitiously glanced sideways at the regal figure pacing like a tall cat at his shoulder and experienced a sudden desire to touch her, to feel her warmth again, as he had once before when imprisoned by her oak in Green Park. That had been the most shatteringly intimate moment in his life, and yet it had taken place before an audience of Epimeliad urchins in a public park. What had really happened there? And why was Penelope the only female Sprite?

His head was bursting with questions, yet for the moment he felt compelled to hold his tongue. Something important was about to happen, and the silver rods would be an essential part of it, but he couldn't imagine what it might be. He could never be sure what the unpredictable creature by his side might do next. She was a quicksilver spirit who all too often confused him with the mercurial shifts in her mood.

They approached what, at first sight, appeared to be a solid fence of glossy evergreen leaves growing on a mat of tightly woven roots. Penelope didn't even slow her steady pace but strode towards the wall as if it wasn't there. Kingswraith felt a nervous hollow sensation ballooning in the pit of his stomach. What now? he wondered, is she in some kind of a trance? Then, just before she walked into the dense growth, it irised open and flowered around her.

They entered what seemed to be a living cave, but before Kingswraith could take stock of his surroundings the roots closed behind them, binding tightly once more. They stood together in complete darkness; not even the blue pneuma illuminated this space.

Penelope said in a hushed voice, 'Can you make a light, my Lord? But be careful, it must be a cold light. We dare not risk sparking a fire in here.'

Kingswraith barely raised his fingers and gratefully whispered, 'Lux spiritus'. Something about that stygian darkness filled his heart with deep foreboding. He wondered if some race memory of this arcane place was where a child's fear of the monster under the bed had first originated, and the shadow in the wardrobe, the ghostly figure in the mirror, or the slippery eldritch creature haunting the slick green weeds in the black waters at the bottom of a lake. He took a shuddering breath and cast his carmini.

The ball of cool silvery light burst into life above his shoulder. He was shocked to see how the walls of the cave had silently crept closer during those few moments of pitch blackness. They were almost touching Penelope now and had creaked much closer to him. The Sprite looked oddly drawn and pale in his Lux light, but her eyes were huge and she seemed to vibrate with barely contained excitement. He thought she had never looked more lovely.

She held out the silver rods to him, and said, 'You must take a firm grip of the naked silver. Hold the rods, place your hands directly above my hands. For this to work our skin must be touching. Whatever happens you must not let go; it will be very dangerous to both of us if you do. Do you understand?'

He breathed, 'I do, but... what's happening?'

'You must trust me, Martin Kingswraith. Remember, we are doing this for you, and for your Professor. Whatever happens, no matter how strange it might seem, don't fight it. You have to promise me, you must not fight it.'

'I promise.'

And then his Lux light winked out, plunging them both into total darkness once more. He could hear the walls of the cave as they contracted. They rustled and crackled like dried leaves under softly padding feet, creaked like the shrouds of a ship. The pressure of bony fingers pressing against his back became irresistible and he found himself being pushed forward until he was firmly pinned against Penelope's yielding body. She was the only soft thing in a world filled with scratching briars and thorns.

The silver rods began to burn his palms as if a stream of boiling liquid was coursing through them. He could hear Penelope panting and he felt her heart pounding hard against his ribs, just as his must be beating against hers. They were locked together at breast, belly and groin, he could feel every inch of her. And still the cave wound itself tighter and tighter until he could barely breathe.

Something pressed against his lips, and with a shock he realised it was Penelope. She was kissing him, just as she had that time when he was held fast, trapped by her oak tree. Once again, he was held firm and couldn't resist. But he didn't want to. He closed his eyes and opened his mouth to her. Her long tongue flickered and explored across his teeth then pushed through and flicked over his tongue, probing and touching like a living creature.

He had to fight hard to keep his hands gripped on the silver rods instead of taking her in his arms. He felt his body responding to the pressure of her touch and her intimate heat burned him until he trembled with a desire so fierce that he began panting like a dog under the desert sun. His hot breath filled Penelope's mouth. He groaned.

In his mouth her tongue stiffened, he felt it lancing into the tissues at the back of his throat, sharp as a fine needle. His body convulsed with shock as the burning in his hands flooded up his arms and seemed to fill his veins with fire. He took a great involuntary gasp of air. His eyes flew open.

10

He blinked as unexpected shafts of pearly light flooded down from a white sun in a silver sky. He and Penelope were still clasped closely together but the bindings of the cave were gone and they were standing in the centre of what appeared to be a forest glade. She was gazing up at him with a curious expression on her face, as if seeing him for the first time. They were no longer pressed lip to lip, but he still thrilled at the intense feeling of warm intimacy between them.

When thinking about the careless heat of her touch he found it difficult to breathe. Without pulling away from him she smiled archly, and distracted his errant mind with a strange question, 'So then, which of these silver rods feels most comfortable in your hand?'

The question was so far away from where his thoughts had wandered that Kingswraith mumbled a confused, 'Sorry, what?'

His response sounded dull and stupid to his ears, more like the bray of a dumb animal than the voice of a talented and sophisticated young wizard about town. He felt overwhelmed by recent events; and deeply embarrassed by some of his physical reactions which were proving very difficult to hide.

She smiled again, mischief dancing a seductive jig in her eyes, 'I said it's time to wake up, Lord Kingswraith, and tell me which of these staves feels as if it belongs to you? They will both talk to you if you care to listen, but one of them will be louder. So, tell me, which one?'

He took a firmer grip on his mind and the silver, and then he realised what Penelope had just said, which jolted him completely wide awake. 'Staves' she had said, and at that moment he realised that both of the precious metal rods felt very different to his touch. He reluctantly dragged his eyes away from Penelope's face, and then gaped at what was grasped in both his fists. Each of the silver rods had been transformed into something new and wonderful.

They still had the heft of silver, but where once there had been two long and slender bars of beautifully tooled and bright metal, he found instead two intricately woven lengths of what looked like pale golden wood. He could see that fine tendrils of organic material had been knitted around the silver to form a fine sheath, including the sections under his closed fist. How could that have happened?

Penelope whispered, 'Which one of them is yours? To find out you must first let go of both of them, then you must step away, not too far, just a few feet. Then I'll ask you to close your eyes and relax, because only then will you be able to hear your chosen stave calling to you.'

Kingswraith released both staves and stepped back. Penelope continued, 'At first the stave will feel pain at being separated from you, as, I'm afraid, will you at being separated from it. At this early stage in your relationship the pain of separation grows worse with distance, but it is the only way you will discover what a true wizard's stave can do. It is also the only way you can discover which of them belongs to you, exclusively to you. It will call to you.'

When he released his grip from the strange new devices Kingswraith's heart suddenly felt bereft. The further he walked away from Penelope and the staves the more he was filled with a terrible sense of loss. It was as if a loved one had died and left him completely alone in the world. The glade became drab and grey. He desperately wanted to hurry back and grab the rods once more, but he obediently shut his eyes as he had been ordered, held out his right hand, fingers wide, and called veni ad me. Nothing happened.

He repeated the carmini, 'veni ad me', 'come to me', his voice driven by every ounce of the pain he felt in his soul, and suddenly he heard a responding sound. No, he realised, not a sound as such. It was more like the silent echo of the reverberation after a great bell has been struck. The hushed resonance after the chime ends.

A stillness filled the air with sweetness and sang a single silent note of crystal clarity. It was a vibration just beyond hearing that touched something in the ether and temporarily translated Kingswraith to where he could experience the sacred poetry woven by silence.

The silence posed a question in answer to his carmini. It asked, 'Are you calling to me?'

This time he replied with a welcome in his voice, an invitation rather than a command, 'Yes, you. It must be you, veni ad me, please, if you will. Come to me, my beloved.' No sooner had he said it than something slapped into his palm as hard as a cricket ball flying from the bat. His fingers snatched shut and he opened his eyes once more.

61

One of the fine-grained staves now nestled in his grip as if it belonged there. It was firm to his touch, solid as steel, and yet somehow it also emitted a soft sound. He was almost reminded of a cat purring. A few feet away Penelope was gazing at her now empty right hand with an expression of utter shock on her lovely face. Her jaw had dropped open.

She gasped, 'It was torn from my hand. I couldn't hold it back. I've never before felt such power. Lord Kingswraith, I've never seen anything like that before! It was only meant to call to you until you reached out and took it, not fly to you like a trained hawk.'

She turned her attention to the other stave and almost giggled, 'And what about you? Are you going to behave yourself? Or must I fit you with a leash, jesses and anklets?'

She looked askance at Kingswraith with widening eyes, 'You might need to curb some of that energy, my Lord. Too open a display of such power might draw too much attention. As you know all too well the simple human folk with whom we share our great land are easily alarmed, which is why we Epimeliads have chosen to become such a secret breed.'

Kingswraith couldn't wipe the smile from his face; it was as if an emptiness that had been festering away at his core for his whole life had just been torn open, cleansed, and filled with immense joy. He felt complete for the first time. He placed his stave point down on the ground and took a deep breath. He gazed at Penelope and began grasping for the right words with which to tell this incredible woman what she had just done for him; and he failed.

'Penelope, I don't... you see... oh, this is so stupid. Words escape me. Look, how can I possibly thank-you for everything you've done? I don't understand what you've done, but I know you've done so much. I've never... Penelope, may I ask, what just happened to me?'

Although his words faltered and died away his voice had gained new depth and greater confidence. Even as he stuttered away into silence Penelope drank in the sight of the glorious man he had become. His eyes shone and he stood tall and straight. All hint of the youth had been washed away and the adult had been left behind. She realised that through the stave they had finally completed his transition; and at that point she became terribly afraid for him.

Her heart trembled, and she struggled to keep the smile on her face. She said, with a quiver in her voice, 'You have come into your inheritance, my Lord

Kingswraith, as the true scion of Pendragon. Yours is the blood and spirit of Arthur, the once and future King.'

She stepped forward and touched his cheek. She added, 'Forget the stories they told in the old days, forget the legends. Arthur doesn't sleep in some hidden tumulus like a hibernating badger, nor is his sett filled with rows of slumbering warriors. No, he lives on in your noble veins, my Lord, only in your sacred blood. And now, here you are. You rise at the time of Albion's greatest need, just as the prophesy foretold.'

Kingswraith lifted his gaze to the sky and he squinted against the bright sunlight. The air was so pure it washed his lungs clean of London's taint and he felt more alive than he had ever felt before. All of his senses stretched out to touch the horizon. He heard birdsong like never before, saw the beautiful balance of nature that shaped the trees. His drank in the silver arc of the sky and he felt as if he could reach out and take the sun in both hands.

He grinned down at Penelope, 'You know something? I still remember that wonderful elixir you gifted to me once when I was a sadly beaten creature in need of a friend. I remember being the poor ragged fellow you cared for after my companions had rescued me from Slighe's trap. I would have died then, I know that, but you called me back. Whoever I am today, you have made me. Whatever I do next is in your hands.'

She opened her mouth to protest but he stayed her with shake of his head, 'No, I'm no hero, my Lady Penelope. I'm just a simple fellow who knows what he owes to those who lead him by the hand. But even so, I promise I shall fight at your side, and I'll be right proud to do so, except...' He paused as if he had run dry of words.

'Except what?' Penelope tilted her fine head at him, and he admired the simple and artless elegance of the gesture. The emotions sweeping through him were far too complex for his naïve mind to grasp properly. He might be the scion of a King, but he was also a fifteen-year-old boy with a massive crush on a beautiful woman. He would happily have stood there in silence forever, glorying in her exquisite beauty. But she wouldn't let him.

She frowned and repeated, 'Except what? My Lord.'

He grinned awkwardly and flushed slightly, 'Except I haven't a clue where we are, nor how we got here. Some great and immortal hero I am, eh? A hero who doesn't know where he is? This place looks as if it has never known a moment of danger, except to the fieldmouse spotted by the hungry owl. This place is evidently somewhere in England's green and pleasant land, not on some battlefield calling a warrior to arms. How do we get back to London from here? Do we fly?'

Penelope laughed then, laughed with all the artless charm of fresh water chuckling along a pebbled stream. She quickly moved closer until their bodies were pressed together once more. Kingswraith was startled but he didn't try to draw away. The sensation was far too pleasurable.

'How do we return to London?' she breathed. 'Why, we never left. Close your eyes or you might get dizzy, this will only take a matter of seconds. It might feel a little strange at first, as if the world had tilted to one side for a moment, but please, trust me. Close your eyes.'

Kingswraith wondered if she might kiss him once more, but instead he felt the pleasant warmth of her and the pressure of her firm, lithe body against his. And then he felt a chaste peck brush at his cheek.

'You can open your eyes now,' she said, and he felt her move away. He blinked his eyes and found it was pitch dark once more. He heard a rustling sound all around him that sounded like the dry leathery fluttering of bats, and the floor seemed to suddenly buck a little to the right. He steadied himself with his marvellous stave and felt the entire length of it tremble like a living thing at his touch. He would have a lot to get used to.

The rustling grew louder, and then the cool blue light of the pneuma seeped into the cave as the binding limbs irised outwards once more. He stepped out onto the bridge that stretched like an arrow across the black water of the reservoir, and with a touch of sadness he saw that the family of Epimeliads were already clustered and waiting for them on the raised central platform. His intimate time alone with Penelope was over.

'Welcome home,' said Penelope, and she led him back across the bridge. Kingswraith heard the excited buzz of the Sprites building as the pair approached and he wondered what incredible event must have happened to get them so excited in the short time he and Penelope had been away. But he quickly discovered that the family were simply voicing their surprise at how much he had changed since entering the cave. They gathered around him.

Alone in the throng stood Okeanus, who had once been Penelope's most constant companion. He believed Kingswraith had stolen her from him, and pressed his lips together in a sneer. He didn't choose to join the fuss over the cursed human. Instead, he drank deep from the bitter cup of jealousy and felt the acid burn of growing hatred. With all his ancient heart he wanted the human to be gone, whatever it took. Only then, he thought, would he get his Penelope back and life would return to normal.

He skulked at the outer fringes of the Epimeliad family. His mood was so foul that his friends could feel it and edged away from him, which created a clear space all around him. His clan understood the cause of his frustration; a few actually sympathised with him. Okeanus had been Penelope's favourite, but she had practically ignored him since beginning her work with the young wizard, which, to some, didn't seem fair.

But even his closest sympathisers couldn't comprehend the depth of Okeanus' misery – nor realise the truly malevolent heat of his loathing for the human.

11

Despite his surname Oliver Quaker was a devout Methodist. He believed that he walked in the light of the Lord, and, so long as he kept his hands clean and his soul free from sin, he would one day die peacefully in his bed at a grand old age. He had always pictured his dignified end with sunlight shining down on him while he gently breathed his last, passing away peacefully while surrounded by his grieving and devoted family.

He expected to enjoy every decade of his three score years and ten, and as many more as the good Lord granted; but when he met the stony gaze of the two strange women waiting for him under the portico of Arcadia House, he was no longer quite so sure. Truth to tell he just wanted to survive the next hour and get home in one piece.

'Ladies, welcome, welcome,' he said, with a false bonhomie and the sick certainty that such haughty and cruel looking creatures had never been truly welcomed anywhere. 'I understand from your message that you are looking to acquire a substantial property with good grounds, high fences, and plenty of rooms. I hold in my hand the keys to Arcadia House,' he indicated the tall stone frontage of the handsome building behind them, 'which I think you'll find will fit all your needs to the very "T". Shall I escort you around the property? There is much to admire.'

The woman with oddly translucent features opened an impossibly pink mouth as if she was about to speak, but then closed it again and remained silent. Her companion offered a twisted attempt at a smile, and then concentrated her attention on something she had seen over Quaker's shoulder.

He turned and jumped with surprise when he found a rapier thin, olive-skinned man wearing a black frock coat and stove-pipe hat standing so close to his shoulder that he could smell the odd chemical reek of the man's breath, or was it something else, something on his clothes? Quaker recognised the odd fellow who had visited his offices that morning to silently put forward his mistresses' requests using hand-written notes.

He was the reason Quaker had decided to personally attend this property in the middle of the afternoon rather than send a lacky. Despite the slender man's chemical reek Quaker had also detected the welcome odour of considerable sums of money. Delegation had never been the policy at Quaker Esq. and Associates when the rewards were so promising, and these clients had itemised substantial requirements that were not to be sneezed at.

Arcadia House was the most lucrative freehold on his books at that time. It met all of these customers' needs and more, and, if the transaction proved successful, it would mean such a generous commission for Quaker's business that his palms itched. That was the reason he had ridden out to the premises on his bay mare, Orchid. But now he had met the strange women he wondered if he might have made a mistake.

Quaker and his firm acted as Receivers of the Rents, and Stewards, (Quaker always thought of the titles as capitalised) for a number of the landed gentry in London. He was authorised to transact sales, employ staff and generally administer such premises and estates that his wealthy clientele gave into his charge. Some properties had been left vacant for any number of reasons, most of which required absolute discretion. Quaker prided himself on his discretion. His clients' secrets were as safe as if they had been placed in a locked bank vault.

Discretion, however, was also the better part of valour, and when faced with these odd new 'clients' he suspected he should have taken more notice when his horse had shied nervously backwards when they had passed through the street gate and onto the long drive leading to the house. As they drew closer to the pair of women Orchid had come to a stop and stubbornly refused to move another inch. Quaker had been forced to dismount and approach his waiting clients on foot leaving Orchid lashed to a handy post halfway down the drive.

Orchid always had been a great judge of character, thought Quaker. She could smell a bad 'un from a hundred paces. If only she had been able to speak and had offered him a proper word of warning he would have listened and turned back.

But it was too late, and now the lean lacky smiled insinuatingly, his thin moustaches making a precise 'V' shape under his pencil sharp nose. His equally thin eyebrows echoed the odd black V-shaped tick. Quaker felt sick. That face, that expression! It would have curdled the freshest milk in the churn; probably spoil it in the udder if the cow saw him.

The man's cold black eyes were devoid of humour. When his lips parted in a grin, he seemed to have far too many teeth in his overwide mouth. Quaker swallowed, hard, trying to think of something to say other than a hasty 'Goodbye'. At that moment profit was the last thing on his mind.

He jumped again when a crisp, sexless voice insinuated itself into his ear like a serpent's tongue. The dark woman was leaning towards his other shoulder. She didn't even attempt a smile but regarded him with frosty dislike.

'Tour the property you say? No, I think not. Frossard here is our most trusted advisor, and a member of our family. He shall examine the interior of the building with you, as it shall be his task to administer the property on our family's behalf. He will be our guide as to its suitability. When you deal with Monsieur Frossard, you deal with all of us, don't you agree Makrut?' The crystalline woman tilted her head in acquiescence but remained silent.

Despite his discomfiture Quaker was annoyed at such presumption. As if any client would need to manage their own property when there was a Quaker to hand. What rot! He puffed out his chest and thrust his thumbs into the sleeves of his waistcoat, which made him appear every inch the image of a stout and disgruntled cockerel.

'Madam,' he said, 'I can promise you that we at Quaker Esq. and Associates (Ltd) pride ourselves on being the most effective Stewards for our clientele. Most effective. Mr Frossard can trust us to take care of the property for you, as we always have. May I assure you that you can place all your property administration requirements in our professional hands with the greatest confidence.'

The dark woman gave him such an offended look that she made him feel as if he needed a thorough wash, her nostrils flared as if she could smell him and it was an unpleasant experience. Which was silly because he'd had his regular hot bath the previous Sunday and it was only Wednesday afternoon. He had strict ideas about cleanliness and resented the idea that he might be regarded as yet another example of the great unwashed masses.

The oddly translucent woman seemed somehow to glide to her sister's side without moving her legs. Quaker was convinced they were sisters, for all that each of them was most singular in complexion. They were an exact match in bone structure and could also have been stamped from the same angular mould as their 'brother' Frossard. He wondered if the crystalline creature might be an albino. He had read somewhere in an almanac that albinos had pink eyes while this woman's eyes were almost silver, but she was certainly pale enough.

She regarded him hungrily, her pink tongue sliding around her thin, colourless lips. She hissed, 'He would make a fine fat platter, don't you think? What shall we do with him, Cymbeline? He is too dainty a dish to cook, so tender, so plump.'

The dark sister replied, 'Please, you always think of your stomach, Makrut. This good fellow is going to show Frossard around the house and outbuildings while we investigate the grounds. Frossard, please explain to him that we shan't require his excellent stewardship, and that we have ample staff on the way to meet our every need.'

Frossard bowed slightly and lifted his stovepipe hat. He grinned again showing his teeth, and silently shook his head. Quaker saw that his hair was glossy, parted in the middle and plastered to an egg-shaped skull. He realised with smug contempt that the man was the worst kind of foreigner, nothing but an oily popinjay.

There were far too many foreigners in London, he thought, all of them drawn by the lure of easy money, he was convinced of that. And they all seemed far too wealthy, ill-gotten gains no doubt. The man probably remained quiet because he didn't speak the Queen's English.

What's more the crystalline albino woman couldn't even speak sensibly. Her accentless comment was utter balderdash. Fine fat platter indeed! Dainty and tender? She was talking about him as if he was a joint of veal. Quaker knew he was a fine figure of a man, 'robust as John Bull himself' his wife said. He was accustomed to the admiration of the fairer sex, inured to it, but he wished the odd woman would use language properly.

'As you wish, ma'am,' he rumbled, grumpily tugging the tattered skirts of his dignity around his rotund form. 'Mr Frossard, after you, sir.'

Frossard proved a silent companion, but he got his meaning across with a few curt gestures, and he insisted on examining every inch of the fine old house from attic to cellars. Quaker was not used to so much exercise in a single day, but if Arcadia House had found new owners the thought of his commission maintained him as he puffed his way after the lean, mute fellow with all the pragmatic resignation that marked the best of the British breed.

At least, he thought, with so many acres of parklands attached to the property the odd women wouldn't have to disturb their neighbours, some of whom were also his valued clients. He wondered how they had travelled to the house, and remembered the way the albino glided to her sister's side. Maybe they flew here on broomsticks? He smiled at the image. He was noted for his arch tomfoolery, which Mrs Quaker described as 'dry as a Bishop's wit and the curate's sherry'.

But there it is, there was no sign of a chariot or a growler that could have carried the strange household to South Barnes. Perhaps they had arrived by boat? he thought. After all the grounds bordered the Beverley Brook and the Thames was near enough to smell its rank waters when the wind blew right. Yes, surely that was it. There was no fifteen-puzzle mystery that an intelligent man couldn't solve with a little application.

'I suppose you arrived by boat?' he said to Frossard. By then they were in the stables, which still carried a faint tang of horse dung and mouldy hay. The lean man said nothing by way of reply, but continued examining a fine spider's web he'd found in one of the stalls. Frossard blew on the web, causing the strands to tremble. Quaker took a step backwards when a fat and dusty brownish grey spider, some five inches across from foot to foot, scuttled out of the shadows.

It reared up, raising its front legs and waving its pedipalps with hungry curiosity. 'Come into my parlour,' it seemed to say. It was a Cardinal spider and was harmless for all its size, but like many pampered city dwellers Quaker couldn't disguise the arachnophobic shiver of fascinated horror that swept through him.

'Will you look at the size of that beast,' he gasped, 'it's almost as big as my hand!'

Frossard looked at Quaker's pudgy fists, and then at his own long and slender digits. He smiled that sinister pointed smile of his, and then his hand flashed out and took the Cardinal between fingers and thumb. The thing waved its legs in a desperate attempt to break free. Frossard's smile widened, and then, with almost loving tenderness, he squeezed.

Quaker felt a surge of nausea bubble up at the crunching popping sound that the Cardinal's cephalothorax and abdomen made as they burst. It would haunt his dreams for months to come. He swallowed bile, and then stared in numb shock as the lean man raised the twisted wreckage of the spider up to his face and opened his mouth.

Quaker blurted out in disbelief, 'Wait, you can't eat that! That's disgusting! What are you for God's sake, some sort of heathen?'

Frossard hesitated, showed Quaker his teeth in a cynical grin, and then shrugged and thrust the pathetic ruin into his coat pocket. He drew out a florid kerchief and carefully wiped his fingers, then indicated that Quaker should precede him out onto the cobbles of the stableyard. The Steward was glad to be back out in the sunlight, and was eager to conclude his business with this group of macabre foreigners.

He heard a soft crunching sound close behind him, turned in horror and watched the last, frail, multiply jointed limb as it vanished between the lean man's razor thin lips. Quaker had had enough. He put his head down and scurried through the house back to the portico where the two women waited, one looking like an icicle in a dress, the other like night made flesh. Did they all eat insects?

Frossard stalked after him, close on his heels. He said nothing to his sisters or Quaker, he merely nodded then folded his arms. Cymbeline turned her narrow eyes towards the trembling, plump man, 'Very good, we shall take it with immediate effect. The money and the necessary signed documents will be at your offices later this afternoon. You may go.'

Quaker didn't argue. He didn't smile, shake hands or bow as a gentleman should at the conclusion of a deal. Without another word he merely handed over the keys and scrambled down the drive to where Orchid was waiting. He hauled himself into her saddle and rode away as fast as was decent for a businessman. Once he reached the gates and dashed out onto the road he began laughing with relief. He felt as if he had escaped from a waking nightmare.

All the way back to Putney he wondered if he had done the right thing in letting the alien troupe have full access to Arcadia House without first putting the contracts and money in order. But he had been royally intimidated by the dark woman and her cadre of freaks, and as he rode further away, he became thoroughly ashamed at his display of utter funk.

If he had sent someone else on the business and they had handed over the keys without so much as a sniff of the cash, he would have reprimanded them, and likely given them a week's notice. Even so, he told himself, one would have had to meet the strange dark woman and her kin to understand her powerful effect. She was inhuman. The spider eating smiling man and the crystalline woman merely reinforced her grotesque potency.

When he reached his offices, Quaker was very relieved to discover that she had been as good as her word. A package of signed documents and a bank receipt for the full price took pride of place on his desk. He handed the documents to Price, his legal assistant, and told him that it was late and the Arcadia House deal could be ratified in the morning. He wished everyone a pleasant evening, closed the offices, and, his mind a whirl, let Orchid carry him homewards along roads so familiar that he could have travelled them blindfolded.

He was so deeply absorbed in his thoughts that he didn't see Frossard standing in the shadows on the corner of Lower Richmond Road. Nor did he see the snake-like gesture the lean man made with his left arm, as if striking towards Quaker's bowler-hatted head.

Quaker reeled in his saddle with a sudden attack of dizziness and became disoriented. Unaware of her rider's condition Orchid continued to follow her route towards her stall and some fresh hay. Quaker's nerveless hands loosened from the reins and he slumped forward in a faint. He might have slid to the ground on a more boisterous horse, but luckily Orchid was a gentle mount and he kept his seat.

After a few moments he roused from his stupor and gazed around, reeling giddily while wondering where he was and what had happened. By the time he got to his house he was recovered enough to leave his mount in the Irish boy's capable hands, he never was sure of the lad's name, and then hastened into the house to advise Mrs Quaker that they were to celebrate a fine deal on Arcadia House.

He explained over a glass of port that he had a riddle of a tale to tell her about the property's odd new inhabitants, and then discovered that his mind had become a complete blank. The entire afternoon had become a featureless blur. And yet, as he carved the tender platter of veal at dinner that evening, he winced, and wondered why, for the first time in his life, he should feel so much sympathy for a joint of roast meat.

12

As he climbed the short flight of stone steps up to his home's door, with the pair of freshly fashioned staves wrapped and held securely in the crook of his arm, Kingswraith had to remind himself once again that he wasn't dreaming. So much had changed over the last year that he felt as if he might have stepped through one door and out of another to a different world, as if he had climbed into a new body, and started a brand-new life.

And the way people had begun to treat him with greater respect was confusing enough so that he almost felt himself to be a fraud. There must surely come a time when somebody patted him on the shoulder and said, 'Sorry, old chap, but we made a big mistake. It isn't you after all, sorry for the confusion. The real fellow just turned up and he wants his ring back and the staves. Thanks for looking after them, but he needs them now. Sorry about the mix-up, we hope you understand.'

In his heart Kingswraith worried that he was wading into deep waters that were way out of his depth, and that when he was finally called to account and expected to act, he would let everybody down. Badly. He paused and caught his breath for a moment before he threaded his key into the lock and opened the door to his home. Home? He felt out of place there, too.

Where he had once returned to the familiar and more masculine atmosphere of furniture polish, good food, and soap, there was now a subtle bouquet of perfume. The Lady Clare Whitekirk, nee Winter, had scent marked her new married quarters with a fresh, floral aroma and the rich savour of good Viennese mocha coffee. She still ran Scheer's, her bookshop, but she had donned Owl's Tower like a cloak, and stamped her dainty feminine mark all over it.

As there was nobody in the picture gallery, or more correctly – according to the domestic gospel of the housekeeper Mrs Vermont – the 'downstairs parlour', Kingswraith made his way up to the first floor. The door to the kitchen stood ajar and a rich savoury steam flowed out. He put his head into the room and said hello to Mrs Vermont and the housemaid Shelagh, advising them that he would be home for dinner.

Shelagh gazed mutely at him, and her large ears turned the same shade of pink as her heated cheeks. Mrs Vermont looked from her to him and raised her eyes to the heavens, an exasperated look on her handsome face. Kingswraith read the question in the housekeeper's expression 'What shall we do with this moonstruck girl?' as clearly as if she had spoken aloud. Shelagh was visibly trembling, and her eyes glistened at him, large and dark.

Kingswraith smiled and nodded at both females, then quickly ducked back out into the corridor and hastened up to the second floor, which housed his bedroom, his patron's room, and the bathroom where Shelagh had once walked in on him, while he was soaking in the tub. That had been embarrassing to say the least, and she had acted oddly around him ever since. However, just recently she had become even stranger. He wondered what the solution might be. Might a carefully chosen carmini help the poor smitten girl?

He hung his coat in his wardrobe, washed his face and hands in the washbasin on his room's vanity cabinet, towelled dry with a soft white hand-towel, and only then did he make his way up to the top floor and the study where he and the Professor had once spent most of their evenings in easy companionship.

He had been adopted as the Professor's ward, but their relationship was closer to that of brothers than father and son. They were good friends. The Professor had welcomed Kingswraith in to his home when the boy's family had died in a tragic 'accident', as had the Professor's parents not long before. However, both knew the true difference between an honest accident and the ongoing systematic slaughter of the Lux Texentes.

Kingswraith felt the heft of the staves, which he carried in the crook of his arm like a brace of shotguns, and wondered if they might provide the leverage they desperately needed in their fight against the lethal machinations of the Umbra. The door of the study was locked as he expected, but he could hear two voices conversing in soft intimacy the other side of its solid panels. He knocked.

A gentle male voice called out, 'Yes, who is it?'

He answered, 'It's me, guvnor, Martin.'

There followed the tap of heels approaching the door, the click of a key turning in a well-oiled lock, and then he was confronted by Clare. She was beautiful. Still as beautiful as that first day at Scheer's when the Professor had been seeking books on the natural sciences, and they had struck up a friendship sparked by a mutual interest in the supernatural. Kingswraith had also been charmed by the comely young woman, but she only had eyes for his patron.

Kingswraith had since become much more enchanted by Penelope, but there was still no escaping Clare's appeal. She smiled at him and ushered him into the study as if he was a guest rather than a long-established resident of the house. He wondered if his sudden flare of irritated pique might not be due to his resentment that she had taken so much of his patron's attention and completely altered the once familiar atmosphere in his home.

She put her arm around his shoulders and steered him to the table where the Professor was just climbing to his feet. Apart from a slight stoop to his shoulders and his silver hair, which had once been a tawny silken frame for his elegant, pre-Raphaelite features, the Professor had almost recovered from his ordeal at the hands of Haven Slighe. Almost. Kingswraith could still feel the residual weakness in the man, as, he was sure, could Clare.

The Professor warmly shook his hand and clasped his shoulder, 'Martin, old love! We were wondering if we might see you this evening, weren't we, Clare? You have become quite the nomad since meeting the Epimeliads. But please never forget that this is your home. Wonderful to see you, and the timing is perfect as ever. We have something of a fifteen puzzle you'll surely find interesting. Sit down, sit down, take a bowl of coffee with us.'

Kingswraith answered, 'A cup of Clare's excellent coffee would be bang up to the elephant, thank-you. But first, guvnor, I have something for you. Penelope fashioned them for us. One is mine, I mean, only I can use it, but the other is yours. There's the two of you now so I suppose you might share it? I'm not quite sure how it all works yet, but let me show you. You'll find this interesting I promise.'

He placed his parcels on the table. The others drew close as he unwrapped them. He heard the Professor's sharp intake of breath as he peeled away the last layers of fabric to expose the sturdy looking rods with their intricately chased, pale patterning. Kingswraith thought they looked somehow thicker and more powerful, as if they had continued developing since he had wrapped them back at the reservoir.

He held his open hand out over the table and his stave leapt to his palm like an eager pet. Then he stepped away from the table, indicated the other staff, and said, 'It's a stave, fashioned from pure silver with something extraordinary added to the outside by Penelope. All I know is that it somehow does something to reinforce carmini. I believe they might somehow draw thaumaturgical

75

energy from somewhere else. I don't quite understand the science of it all, I'll leave that to you, but please, try it.'

Clare said, 'After you, my dear. I'm still the lowly student, you are the master here.'

The Professor grinned, 'I don't know about that. Leaps and bounds, my dear wife; you are coming along fierce and fast, becoming quite the adept. Still,' he turned to Kingswraith, 'I am your student here, old love. So, then what do I do? Shall I call to it? Will it fly to my hand? Or do I just pick it up? I've heard of these of course, but I thought they were just legendary trinkets, the subject of myths and old wizards' tales.'

Kingswraith was about to shrug his ignorance when he felt his stave trembling in his fist and a scene popped into his mind's eye, clear as life itself. He said, 'Open your hand over it, fingers spread wide; we don't want to crack any of your knuckles, do we? Then remain perfectly still.'

The Professor did as he was told. He stood still as stone with his arm rigid and his fingers stretched out to their fullest extent. His breathing was a little laboured as if he was nervous, and Kingswraith understood perfectly why that should be. But perhaps he was doing the man a disservice; instead of nerves it could be pure excitement roaring through his veins like a charge of Luigi Aloisio Galvani's electrical fluid.

The young wizard reached out with his stave and barely touched the end of its fellow with the tip. The result was dramatic. There came a flash bright as lightning and the table shuddered as if it had been struck by something heavy and powerful. The Professor shouted 'My God!' but remained still, while Clare reeled away, covering her face with her hands.

The whole house seemed to tilt to one side, much as the tree-root cave had tilted when he and Penelope had returned from the forest glade. A massive jarring thump rang through its walls. Kingswraith watched as the table's legs bowed in impossible curves, as if the sturdy piece of furniture was preparing to leap into the air. Instead, it was the stave that soared up into the Professor's outstretched hand with a resounding thwack!

'Good lord,' his patron cried, 'when you say things might get interesting, old lad, you certainly keep your promises. Cave, all of you, that row was enough to waken the dead, and it will certainly have alarmed the household. I think I hear the good Mrs Vermont on the stairs.'

He looked around to make sure there was nothing amiss, such as the Thaumatograph out in the open, but everything was secure. Then he asked, holding up his staff, 'Shall we hide these away, do you think?'

Kingswraith said, 'No, hang on to your stave, guvnor. They'll have to get used to seeing us with them. They are very much the latest thing in walking canes, totally the modern style, so they won't think anything more of them. Oh, 'ello, sounds like the troops are at the gates. I shall be doorkeeper this time, shall I?'

This was in response to a barrage of knocks at the door, and some shouting. Kingswraith turned the key and opened it. The housekeeper stood poised, with her fist raised as if ready to strike the door down if it hadn't been answered. When she saw everyone standing safe and sound and the room intact, she seemed to deflate like a punctured football bladder. Shelagh's pink face appeared around the door jamb, and Will's brawny form pounded up the stairs behind her to make the entire household complete.

Mrs Vermont gazed around at the unscathed Professor, Clare and Kingswraith. She was in a state of evident confusion, 'We thought the gas had gone,' she gasped. 'The 'ole 'ouse shook like a tree in a storm it did. We thought you was all blowed up and the ceiling was coming down on our 'eads, which was a shame, with dinner nearly ready an all. What was that bang, sir? You being a man of science, an all, do you know what it was? Pardon me for being so forrard an' askin' like.'

The Professor leant on his staff and looked up at the skylights, 'Yes, quite; you are right. We had something of a fearful flash, bang and more than a hint of a wallop up here too, Mrs Vermont. I would say it was electrical fluid earthing from a low cloud, literally a bolt of lightning striking the copper conductors on the roof. Thank the Lord Wills insisted we fit them, otherwise we might all be little more than a fine drift of ash by now. What do you say, Martin? Do you agree with my surmise?'

'I say after all that excitement we should take advantage of Mrs Vermont's excellent cooking and repair to the dining room. There's nothing that stokes an appetite like mother nature doing her best to blow us all to smithereens and tatters. You did say dinner was nearly ready, didn't you, Mrs Vermont?'

Shelagh gasped, 'Wait, wait, what, what are you sayin? That is, sir, are you sayin' that the sky will burn us all in our beds even if we say our prayers like proper Christian folk? That don't seem right do it? The sky taking people's lives into its own hands like that?'

Then she leaned forward and gazed at Kingswraith's stave, all her concerns about a vindictive sky forgotten. Her eyes grew round as pennies, and her mouth followed suit,

"Oooh, but, oooh, will you look at that! I do like your new stick, young sir. That looks like it's been growed in an orchard or fashioned by an artist who's clever with his 'ands. I see you got one too, guvnor, sir. Very fine, very fine. Like something growed in a fairy circle.'

She reached her fingers out towards Kingswraith's staff, but didn't quite touch it. Then she vanished from the doorway with a pattering of iron heeled boots. Mrs Vermont said, 'Well, I never did! And yes, young sir, dinner will be ready in ten minutes, beggin' your pardon. I'd best go and make sure nothing got scorched while I was lollygagging about up 'ere. I think I can smell the gravy catching. Excuse us, come on, Wills.'

Kingswraith studied the empty doorway and wondered what 'something growed in a fairy circle' might look like. Not for the first time he suspected that there was more to Shelagh than met the eye. Perhaps much more. He could swear he saw a flash of emerald in her brown eyes when she went to touch his stave, what might that mean?

13

Penelope lay in the branches of her tree. She had allowed her body to relax to the point that the sap pulsing through the meat of the oak was the only thing stirring her spirit. She was the tree, and the tree was her. She could feel its branches in her hair and its roots in her toes. The wind rustling through its midnight form caressed her body and the black rags of her urchin aspect fluttering around her like leaves was the only movement.

She always came here when she was troubled. Her tree would not judge her, nor try to protect her with lies. It held up a mirror to her thoughts in which she saw only the truth, no matter how painful it felt. The problem was that she had become confused when she needed certainty, she felt weak when she needed strength, she was afraid when everything she cared about called for courage. She felt too small for the mammoth task in front of her.

The stench of evil was flooding through the London streets, thick as the city's noxious fog. It made her skin crawl in much the way that a worm under the bark of a healthy tree will slowly steal its vitality, until all that's left is rot and soft pulp. She sensed evil's careless cruelty; she breathed the cold wind of its utter hatred for all things good.

Worst of all she recognised the siren call of its power, the allure of its complete and utter disregard for human life. Evil had no need for excuses. It knew what it wanted and took it, took it all, and if anything – or anyone – got in its way, it would hack them down without a second's hesitation. This force, this power, had no shame. She admired its purity.

Over the millennia Penelope had been tempted by the black flame of revenge, tempted to reward humankind for the chaos it had wreaked on her natural world. Her memory of an ancient Albion was still fresh, a lush green sea of forests where the Epimeliads had nurtured the trees and the animals that depended on them. The cycle of life was simpler then. That was before man had brought his stone tools and his fire; that was before iron.

Iron can kill a Sprite. Iron is the vampire metal that sucks the life and spirit out of their ancient bodies. Iron is pain, and men cover their homes in it. Iron is what makes men's blood red. When she drained a man's body of all its minerals the iron must be leeched away and passed from her as rust, or it would hurt her. Men are forged of iron, which is why magic escapes them. Except the rare few like Kingswraith, and Arthur and Merlin before him.

Sprites and humans had sometimes interbred. Not often, but it had happened. Any offspring was a hybrid, the iron in their bodies partly supplemented by copper. Instead of haemoglobin in their blood they used haemocyanin, which gave it a bluish tint. Their eyes might reflect green under certain light conditions, as did the Sprites'. It was the only outer sign. Kingswraith's eyes sometimes glittered green, she had seen it.

And that was part of her pain. She remembered Uther, the Bear, Arthur's warrior father. She remembered learning of a night in that very glade where she had taken Kingswraith, it was a place she would never forget, where her sister Lampetia, had enchanted Uther and they had lain down together. Lampetia never forgot that night, but Uther would never be allowed to remember it.

That single union had resulted in a baby, which had been presented to Igraine, Uther's wife. Igraine was wise in the elder ways and had made many offerings to the Sprites while begging them to help her bear a child. So great was Igraine's need for motherhood that it had been easy to provide her with false memories of her term of childbearing and of the long hours of a difficult delivery.

Her women were also made to remember the birth, and that it had happened while Uther was away in battle, as usual. He had been home at the right time for the conception, that was essential, and, he had always made full and passionate use of his nuptial rights. He wanted a son, and his beautiful, dutiful wife had delivered him with a son. The kingdom celebrated.

Soon afterwards Uther died at the hands of his enemies. His defeat threw the kingdom into darkness and put the infant Arthur in grave peril. He was heir to the crystal throne, but the Saxon barons who had butchered his father wanted Arthur dead too, because with him gone would die all dreams of Albion and Angleland could rise from its ashes.

Igraine gave her boy to a trusted advisor called Myrddin Emrys. It was true he was old, she thought, but he had always been old for as long as she had known him, and he was still hale and strong. When he accepted the care of the baby, his eyes had glittered green as any emeralds. Myrddin secreted Arthur away to a place of safety where the boy grew up to be a fine youth, ready to fight, to take back his birthright.

The rest of Arthur's story had since become a woven tapestry of half-forgotten truths, myth, and wishful thinking, the cocktail of stories compiled by mediaeval knights with a literary bent who had too much spare time on their hands. Penelope had met the young knight Arthur, and she had helped him much as she was helping Kingswraith, except that back then it was Myrddin who had received the stave.

Arthur had instead been gifted with a sword fashioned from sky metal. The sword had no name, not then, but it had power. The name came later with the stories. Penelope took a deep breath and opened her eyes. They glittered green and gold in the grey light of the dawn. Her impish features screwed into a resigned smile, and she muttered, 'The thing is, Kingswraith, when am I going to tell you that in fact, I am your great, great, heaven knows how many times removed, great aunt? How will you react to that bit of news?'

It was a genuine concern; it was becoming embarrassingly obvious how the young wizard felt about her. She climbed down out of her oak like a lithe cat, and stalked through Green Park, deep in thought. The Umbra were growing stronger all the time. She sensed that at least three of them had now roosted to the south west of the city in Barnes. Kingswraith, the Professor, and his wife must be made ready to face them.

But the Professor was still weakened by his ordeal with Slighe, Clare Whitekirk was an unknown quantity, and Kingswraith had not yet learned how to take a firmer grip of his talent. He must master his powers or he will fail.

The boy was so young. He looked older, but he was still a green shoot. He had not spent enough time under the sun to develop the toughness he needed to become a true warrior. A warrior must kill or be killed, quickly and without mercy. She could sense the mercy and compassion flowing from Kingswraith's heart. The sentiment was noble, but it would...

Rough hands grabbed at her from behind and pushed her to the ground. She smelt the harsh stink of an unwashed body mixed with the raw stench of tooth decay and poorly digested food. One of the man's hands held her down, pressing her into the damp grass while the other scrabbled to hoist up the hem of her dress.

He was panting with lust. In her urchin form Penelope looked no older than eleven or twelve. She looked like easy meat; a fruit ripe for plucking. She reminded the man of his own daughter, with whom he had his way whenever the fancy took him. He fumbled with his victim's clothes and gasped, 'Shall we go a dancing my pretty? Will you dance for me?'

All the anger and resentment that had built up inside her over the centuries swelled into her narrow breast. She felt the wolf howl in her blood and she barked, 'No!' Slowly, inexorably she turned around, and the man was helpless to stop her. She took his head in her hands and her face darted forward for a lethal kiss. Her tongue lanced into the back of her attacker's throat and she drained him of every mineral he needed to live.

All the while she fed back to him his memories of his victims, especially the poor defeated mouse of a woman he lived with, and his terrified, abused daughter. There were others. The man was a predatory rat who took relish in snatching innocence between his teeth and shaking the juice out of it. He was everything Penelope hated most about humankind; selfish, venal, prey to his own carnal urges, careless of another's pain while he used them, and he was an arrent coward – his victims were always weaker than him.

She took from his mind every detail of his sick cravings and cowardly assaults, and she poured them back into his diseased head until he was whimpering under her onslaught. She made sure he suffered every pain he had ever inflicted on others, magnifying the torture. She lashed at him with a pitiless crescendo of torments until finally he succumbed to agony and sought peaceful death. Penelope siphoned the last minerals from his tissues, every drop.

Then she spat his translucent face to the ground and pushed his gelatinous remains off her body to flop boneless as a puddle into the wrinkled nest of his filthy clothes. Even in death he stank of the sewer and stale sweat. She knew she would be tasting his rancid odour for days.

Penelope had once promised Kingswraith that she would stop punishing evil men and end those mysterious deaths that had been filed by Scotland Yard as 'The Depleted Men'. But this verminous piece of filth had attacked her, he deserved it. The city was cleaner without him. She had no regrets. She primly brushed herself clean of grass and wiped away a layer of greasy moisture, straightened her shoulders, and marched away with her head held high.

If any witness had gone to that place, they would have found the man's puddled remains in its litter of shabby clothes. His pallid, gelatinous skin shapeless as egg whites, and his mouth wide open in an eternal scream, round as a wheel in the centre of a flat, boneless face. Only his hair stood proud, stiff as the bristles on a wire brush, black as tar.

Our witness would have looked after the slight form of a young girl dressed in the night black tatters of a pinafore dress, her hair blowing in a breeze they couldn't feel. And they might have tried to understand everything they had just seen. Perhaps they would have sought the help of a constable, and together try to come to grips with the impossible, unworldly event they had just observed.

But no, the only witness that misty morning was a red squirrel. It investigated the remains of the depleted man. They stank so badly that the squirrel had urinated on them to try to freshen them up a bit. It hadn't worked, and anyway it was autumn, and in autumn squirrels had enough to do stocking their secret larders ready for winter. Depleted rapists were nowhere near so important. It bounded away and continued its hunt for acorns.

An hour later a constable sprinted towards the terrified shrieks of a young nanny who had stumbled across the remains, some of which had fouled the wheels of her perambulator. When he saw what had alarmed her, he raised his whistle to his lips and blew three long blasts. Then he waited for the support that he so desperately needed, and tried to calm the weeping woman. All he could think to say was, 'There, there, there, there, madam, it's alright, there, there...'

But it wasn't alright. After seeing that glistening obscenity, that mockery, that impossible soft, empty, jelly-like shell of a man, nothing could ever be alright again.

14

Inspector Chandler felt tired. It had been a good while since the last Depleted Man had turned up on his patch and he had hoped that the whole bizarre episode was finished, but now a fresh one had appeared in Green Park. The victim had a letter in his pocket, and as the senior Detective Inspector of the Metropolitan Police, along with a handy constable, Chandler had visited the address. It was a squalid pit, the thin walls only held together by the thick layers of grease and London soot that coated every inch of them.

There they found a world-weary mouse of a woman of an indeterminate age, and her nine-year old daughter. The girl gazed sullenly at the visitors with eyes far older than her years. The woman recognised the letter, although she couldn't read it, and she also recognised the other bit of paper that had come with the letter, though she didn't know what it was.

She said the letter had arrived late the previous day, 'For me 'usband, 'Enry, but what 'e's aht at the moment on business, or so 'e said. An what would a brace 'o mutton shunters want wiv an 'onest man, that's what I'd like to know, fanking you very much, eh?'

Chandler read the letter to her, and showed her the bank draft for nine hundred and seventy-six pounds, fourteen shillings and eleven pence. That was the sum passed down to her husband by his more successful brother, who had died of cholera in India. He explained that her husband was dead, murdered, which meant that the money was now hers.

Mrs Henry Cake had stared at the bank draft as if it might bite her. Chandler said, 'It's a tidy sum Mrs Cake. If you like, the constable and I will accompany you to the bank and explain what's happened. We'll smooth any little details and make sure the bank does right by you. Will that be alright?'

The woman's eyes brightened. She turned to her daughter who looked utterly dazed, and pulled her to her feet, 'E's dead?' she crowed. 'The dirty old devil's been done in! Gawd bless the covey what done for 'im. Give us a dance, Clara, that's what 'e says, eh? Give us a dance? Well, 'we won't any more, my lovely, never no more. You won't 'ave to dance for that dirty old sod, not never again. Dance 'e called it, dirty old sod.'

She squinted at Chandler, 'And 'oo are you to be 'elpin' the likes of us? What do you get aht of it? I've never known no mutton shunter to 'elp us. An what's all this about a bank? What do we want wiv any bank? What would any bank want wiv us, eh? That's what I'd like to know? An' are you sure that black-'earted bugger's really dead and gorn? You don't want to go putting ideas into me 'ead and the old bugger turns up drunk as always, do yiz?'

With an effort Chandler finally convinced the woman to accompany him to the bank, where he explained the situation to a surprised teller who had then carried the draft out into the daylight to make sure it was legitimate. The Inspector of police then watched the man like a hawk while he counted out the money to the last penny and presented it all to the widow Cake, who almost fainted.

The wild-eyed woman looked at the fortune in her hands and turned to the Inspector, her expression a mixture of fear and confusion, 'If I go 'ome with all this in me skyrocket, Clara 'n me will be dead before tea-time. If I 'ad a mattress I'd 'ide it in there, so I would, but I don't. And there's wrong 'uns in our gaff would cosh me over the 'ead and slit little Clara's throat for a just a sniff of sommat like this. What do I do, mister? What do I do?'

By the time the constable walked Mrs Cake back to her home she had a few handy pounds in the pocket of her apron and was the proud owner of her very own, brand spanking-new, bank account. Chandler had been surprised at the pride with which she had signed her name, saying with a bright, almost youthful lilt to her voice, 'They taught me my letters in the poor 'ouse, din't they. I don't sign with no cross like some!'

Two days later, on Sunday, the newspapers had got the story about the death in Green Park from the usual insider informant at New Scotland Yard, and the evening editions played around with variations on the same headline; 'London Ghoul Has His Cake and Eats Him too.' The press was describing Scotland Yard as a 'pack of tired old bloodhounds who had lost their sense of smell and didn't know where to turn next'.

And so, the self-confessed tired and confused Inspector Chandler, accompanied this time by Detective Sergeant Charlton who had been working on the Depleted Men case since the beginning, found themselves standing in Cheyne Row, at the base of the steps leading up to the gleaming black street door of Owl's Tower.

Chandler sighed, and growled, 'The Professor's the best man I know when it comes to a fifteen puzzle, but he's recently got married to a fine girl. You'll see what I mean, she really puts jam on the strawberry. Wait 'til you meet her. He might not want to be out on a cold afternoon when there's warm arms waiting for him at home. Still, can't do any harm to ask.'

Charlton said nothing. There were warm arms and a good Sunday roast waiting for him at home too, and his wife wasn't best pleased that her husband was out at work on the Sabbath. The best he would probably get now was congealed gravy, folded arms, and a frosty reception when he finally called it a day. Gilbert and Sullivan were right, he thought, a policeman's lot is not a happy one, and he is a slave to duty.

But there was no escaping the facts. Something strange was killing people on his manor, and it wasn't just the Depleted Men. There was the Face Eaters too, the latest entry in the catalogue of strange horrors. A trio of murdered men had been found in the Victoria Embankment Gardens. The meat had been chewed from their faces and hands and they were wet through, stinking of river mud. The medical examiner had thrown up his hands and declared himself completely-stumped, the evidence made no sense.

Charlton agreed, I ask you, he thought, what kind of a lunatic goes around chewing the faces off people and munching their hands down to the bone? Then he throws them in the river for a bit before he dumps them in a public park where anyone can find 'em. Whatever happened to an honest old-fashioned bit of domestic? What happened to the good old drunken row? Husband beats wife, wife clouts husband with a skillet and cracks his skull, Bob's your uncle! Just now, something as simple as that would be a breath of fresh air.

Chandler climbed the steps and pulled on the bell rope that hung from a pully between the door frame and an elegant coach lamp. Charlton stood just behind him, his hands in his pockets, suspecting that they were wasting their time. Nothing happened for a few minutes and Chandler was just reaching for another tug at the bell rope when the door opened to reveal a startlingly good-looking young man.

'Inspector,' he beamed, 'how good to see you again. If you need the facilities, I think I can assure you that you won't meet any girls in the bathtub this time.' Charlton looked at the back of the Inspector's head and caught the moment his ears and the back of his neck burned pink. Kingswraith shook hands with

86

Chandler, 'Come in, come in, where are my manners, leaving the force out on a cold afternoon? Feels like winter's come early.'

He reached for Charlton's hand, 'Good to meet you too, sir, always pleased to take the hand at the end of the long arm of the law. With whom do I have the pleasure?'

Charlton was still trying to work out if the fellow was twitting him and was carefully gauging his response when Chandler replied for him, 'Martin, this is Detective Sergeant George Charlton, George, this is the Baronet, Lord Martin Kingswraith. Don't let the titles fool you, he's the salt of the earth is Martin, much like his guvnor, the Professor.'

Kingswraith shut the door against the gathering mist and shook his head. 'Simple Martin or Kingswraith will do, I answer to both. But I suppose you're here to see the guvnor? Something interesting out there we can help with? I'm afraid the Depleted Men led us to a dead end, but at least that's all done with now. So, then, this must be something new?'

Chandler made a noise that could only just be interpreted as a rueful laugh, 'Something old and something new, I'm afraid. If we can just borrow your guvnor's wits, he'll make us boys in blue as happy as sandboys. If he could lend us the time that would be bang up to the elephant. We've got a fifteen-puzzle as makes no sense at all.'

Charlton was feeling out of his depth; why was the Inspector hob-knobbing like this with the upper-crust? In his experience these sorts wouldn't find their backsides with both hands a map and a compass. He had met a few knights he respected, men who had earned their peerage, usually from the military, but in his experience the aristocracy was rarely more than a chinless, hoity-toity type; living proof that cousins shouldn't be allowed to marry.

But then, this youngster didn't fit the bill at all. He had far too much chin and an intelligent light in his eye. Despite his hide-bound reservations, Charlton decided to give the chap the benefit of the doubt. He had never met a Baronet before, but weren't they commoners like knights? But Chandler called the bloke a Lord, that didn't sound very common. Charlton decided that he would just take each moment as it came, and roll with the punches.

He followed the Inspector and their host up to the third floor of the house and believed he understood why the young man looked so fit, if he had to climb all those stairs every day. He fought not to puff as they reached the rarefied air of the study. The door was shut. Kingswraith knocked and waited. A man's voice asked, 'Yes, who is it?'

Kingswraith replied, 'It's me guvnor, with visitors. It's Inspector Chandler and Sergeant Charlton, they say they need to talk with you, if you're free, sir.'

The study door opened to disclose one of the most dazzlingly beautiful women Charlton had ever seen. Of course, the good Mrs Charlton could charm the birds out of the trees when she had a mind to, but this creature had stepped out of a painting by one of the masters. He felt his mouth go dry and butterflies skittered around in his belly.

Her voice matched her looks, which Charlton thought was totally unfair. How was a man meant to hold his own against such feminine perfection? If she had been one of the three graces, she would have won the golden apple hands down.

She said, 'Welcome, gentlemen. We're just taking coffee and sandwiches. Please join us.' Kingswraith made the introductions again and urged the policemen into the room, locking the door behind them.

Charlton didn't like the idea of being in a room behind locked doors in a strange house, but Chandler seemed relaxed in the household's company so he resigned himself to the situation. Then he clapped eyes on the Professor and began to wonder if there was something special in the water of Chelsea.

The tall, slender chap had all the looks and elegance of a pre-Raphaelite painting, made even more striking by his silken silver locks which framed an intensely intelligent face and ice-blue eyes.

Charlton was a man who felt confident in his own skin, but these people made him feel shabby and almost unfinished, for all that he had been made to feel welcome enough. He accepted a large bowl of the best coffee he had ever tasted and took a plate filled with tender and dainty roast beef and mustard sandwiches. They were delicious. If he ever made it to heaven, thought Charlton, at least he would have somewhere decent to measure it against.

He waited while Chandler explained the reason for their visit and Kingswraith appeared uncommonly shocked to hear of the new Depleted Man in Green Park. The Professor had already heard about the pitiful remains left by the Face Eaters and had been discussing that case with Kingswraith, but he and his wife readily agreed to accompany the police officers to the Scotland Yard bone cellar, the mortuary, to examine the fresh depleted corpse.

Charlton noticed that the Professor walked with the aid of a particularly fine cane. The silver-haired man spoke quietly to his ward, who nodded and then reached for an identical cane of his own. The Professor said, 'Very well, gentlemen, we shall just fetch our coats and then we are yours to command.'

15

Kingswraith saw everyone down to the street door and waited until their chariot had clattered off south towards the river before he closed the door and made to return up to the study and get on with the task the Professor had given him. He found himself confronted by Shelagh, her bare legs in her unlaced yet carefully polished boots. She was attired in her 'relaxing dress' which she only wore on a Sunday when she visited her mother.

The maid was almost wriggling with embarrassment, her face and ears pink with her customary and rather endearing blush.

She spoke breathlessly, 'Young sir,' she said, 'thing is, I was hoping to take a bath in the downstairs facilities. I promise I shan't use more'n a spoonful of hot water! But, see, there's only us in the house which might not be strictly proper, with me down there in the raw, and us all alone, me in the same house as 'e. You do see what I'm getting at, sir?'

He smiled back at her, 'You've nothing to fear, Shelagh. Bathe away my girl and use all the water you want; drench the steeples and drown the cocks if you wish. I shall be up in the study if you need me, but please make sure you knock first. I shall be concentrating on some serious business. Have a lovely evening. I wish you goodnight, and I shall see you at breakfast tomorrow morning.'

He wondered if he had seen a touch of disappointment in her expression when he said that, but told himself he was imagining things and climbed the stairs towards the study. There he would set the Thaumatograph to spinning and weave a seeker to discover if there was any evidence of magic at work in the capital. Working alone he would have to drop the needle from his lips, but he had practiced the procedure and it had worked just fine, most of the time.

Behind him Shelagh grumbled to herself as she clomped in her boots towards the steep stairs that led down to the cellar bathroom and the water closets, 'I ain't taking no cocks into no bathtub with I, what does 'e think I am, a chicken farmer? An what does he mean by steeples? It sounds mucky. Whatever he means there won't be nothing in that water but what nature intended for I to scrub clean of a Sunday. I'm proper as a sermon in church I am.'

In the study Kingswraith opened the cover on the wall-mounted silk map of the London streets, then fetched the Thaumatograph from its place in the bureau and the inlaid wooden box containing the seeker's strands and the silver needle. In the cellar Shelagh had decided to take the young master at his word and filled the tub with steaming water.

To the rear of Owl's Tower, a lean shadow slid over the wall of the courtyard garden and dropped soundlessly into a flower bed.

The dark shape of Frossard crouched and looked around him, sniffing at the air like a hound on the scent. He emitted a hungry, whining exhalation, and started towards the Tower's back door. A leaf-shaped knife flashed in his hand. Shelagh had left the backdoor unlocked and Frossard chuckled, an oily, bubbling sound, as he pulled the door open. His steps made less noise than a soap bubble bouncing across a soft carpet.

The warm yellow light of the gas mantles cast his slick shadow across both walls of the narrow hallway, sharp as the knife he held out before him. His slender form flickered as if trying to repel the light. The hollowed planes of his narrow face were lost in shadow, its sallow skin bloodless and corpselike. He smelt soap, steam and the enigmatic yet instantly recognisable perfume of a magical creature floating up through the open door to his right. He slipped through it and paused, gauging his surroundings.

He was at the top of a flight of stairs that was steep and narrow with gas mantles every few yards. The steps descended to a narrow archway from which spilled yellowish light. He could hear a tuneless humming, then a soft feminine voice attempting the chorus to a popular music hall song. The smell of soap and lavender grew stronger as he crept down the steps, and his hunger to inflict pain redoubled as the arch into the cellar bathroom came ever closer.

Up in the study Kingswraith was losing patience with his seeker. The Thaumatograph was spinning like a complex steam turbine, its precious metal wheels a blur. Magic was happening somewhere, a lot of magic, but he couldn't quite manage the trick of holding the cat's cradle of the seeker in his fingertips while dropping the needle into it from his mouth. He kept losing his concentration at the last moment and the seeker's blue glow winked out, so that the needle just fell into the seeker's web instead of flying to its target.

He was tempted to ask Shelagh to help, after all she didn't need to understand what he was doing. But he could imagine the Professor's expression while he tried to explain why he had involved their maid in wizard's business. And then he had an idea. He lay the woven seeker on a footstool and took up his stave.

He pointed its tip at the silver strands and said 'resurgemus', but at his first attempt he managed to levitate himself several feet into the air.

He sighed and floated back to the floor. At his next attempt he touched the seeker with his stave and pronounced 'quaesitor resurgemus'. This time the seeker rose to head hight and hovered like a small flying carpet, gently undulating in the grip of magical energy.

Down in the cellar Frossard sensed Kingswraith's magical charm, paused in what he was doing to the terrified girl in the bathtub, and smiled his precise V of a smile towards the ceiling. You're next, he thought, then turned back to his task. Like any craftsman he always took great pleasure in his work.

Kingswraith dropped the silver needle onto the blue aura surrounding the floating cat's cradle of the seeker and watched it spin until it was almost invisible, becoming a shimmering metallic disc. Using his stave to funnel the command he muttered 'Ostende mihi viam, ostende mihi viam'. The blue glow brightened, and there followed a flash of light across the study, straight as an arrow. The needle struck the map and quivered in place.

Kingswraith plucked the seeker from the air and folded it back into its box, muttered 'Lux spiritus' with the casual air of a practiced adept, and used the ball of light that popped into existence at his shoulder to study the needle's position in the map. He squinted at the finely drawn lines, street names and shaded areas, then he blinked and gasped in pure shock and horror. The needle was embedded directly into the little square of Owl's Tower.

Something was in the house and Shelagh was alone downstairs. He took a grip on his stave and once again commanded 'resurgemus'. This time he flowed into the air and towards the study door. He blew it off its hinges in his haste to get down to the little maid. He didn't yet know if she was in danger, but there was no time to waste if she was in the grip of powerful black magic.

He rocketed through the house, careening down the stairs and along the narrow landings like a shell fired from a gun. He didn't hesitate when he reached the ground floor but spun through the opening to the cellar bathroom and accelerated down towards the yellow light of the archway at the foot of the stairs. He had no thought about surprising the little maid in her bath, his only concern was that something was in the house and she might be in danger.

His worst fears were realised when he swept into the bathroom and saw a lean and sinister black shape bent over the big tub in the middle of the room.

He flew at it and struck hard with his stave, swiping at the figure's stove-pipe hatted head. Something glittered as it flew from the man's hand and Kingswraith heard Shelagh scream – good, at least she was alive!

The man sprawled sideways to the floor. Kingswraith briefly saw that the little maid was sitting up in the tub, her mouth and eyes wide with terror and her body laced with ribbons of dark purple blood. She screamed again and pointed. The rapier thin man had sprung onto all fours. He crouched like a giant black cat poised to pounce on its prey. He opened his thin-lipped mouth to display an armoury of fang-like, needle sharp teeth.

Even as Kingswraith watched, the creature's finger's extended into wicked talons, and the narrow man hissed at him, a sound filled with evil cunning. Kingswraith felt the ice of terror chill his veins, which inspired him to point his stave at the shadowy nightmare and shout 'Combustio!' A jet of white flame arrowed from his staff and splashed into the creature's surprised face. His hat was instantly incinerated, falling to the floor as a smoking ruin.

The narrow man opened his mouth impossibly wide and he swallowed the flame, then he smiled and licked his lips, almost purring with pleasure. He blew a perfect smoke ring, and suddenly leapt for Kingswraith's throat. The move was so unexpected that Kingswraith reacted instinctively. He used his stave like a rapier and lunged at the man's chest, yelling 'Demorior!' The stave penetrated the man's body directly over where his heart should be.

This had a powerful effect. At first the narrow man grasped the stave in both his fists and then instantly tore his hands away. They smoked and his flesh made a sound like spitting fat in a pan. Frossard hissed with furious rage. Kingswraith had felt the surge of energy burn along its shaft as his stave rejected the stranger's unwanted touch using intense heat. Where the stave was thrust into the stranger's body the flesh had begun to crackle and smoke.

The stranger's mouth opened wide and he howled, a sound that ebbed away to a mewling note of pain, sounding almost pathetic. But then he began to push himself along the shaft of the stave, grimly reaching out for Kingswraith's throat once more.

Desperately the wizard shouted, 'Demorior!' again, and he saw how the carefully woven strands of Penelope's covering for the silver rod had thickened and were lancing up into the man's body as if trying to push him back, acting as a shield to keep him away from its owner.

93

The narrow man grunted with pain, but kept pushing forward, until one of his razor-sharp talons lashed out, drawing a hot bloody line along Kingswraith's cheek. The young wizard reeled backwards, barely keeping his grip on his stave. The stranger grinned in triumph and thrust himself closer to the wizard using all his considerable strength.

Then suddenly he flailed his arms wildly, staggered, and reared upwards, his expression a mask of shocked surprise. He shrieked, the sound rising higher and higher until it became an inhuman scream of feral agony. He seemed to diminish, to collapse in on himself.

Faltering and falling backwards he pulled himself away along Kingswraith's stave and whirled to face the naked Shelagh who glared at him with an expression of fury.

'You stay away from him,' she yelled, emerald light flashing in her brown eyes, 'I know what iron does for such as you! You brought your own end in here with you, you foul bastard! Cut me will you! I'll teach you to cut a fair maid, and learn you a proper lesson!'

Kingswraith spotted the silver handle of a knife protruding from between the narrow man's shoulders. He leapt forward and grabbed it with his free hand, wrenched it out, then hacked sideways at the stranger's throat with the razor-sharp blade. The flesh at the stranger's neck parted like an opening mouth; black, slimy blood oozed out.

Kingswraith struck again and again and again until the man's head fell from his shoulders. It thudded to the ground with a resounding crack and rolled away to fetch up against one of the lion's paw feet of the big bathtub.

The narrow man's headless body dropped, dissolving into a murky mess of crumbling bone and slithering internal organs. Even in death the vile creature's decapitated remains were writhing like a nest of venomous snakes cast into a furnace; and its claws were reaching out to tear and rend anyone within reach.

The shuddering pile quietened at last and only his stained black clothes remained, surrounded by a faint cloud of steam that stank with the vinegary taint of roasted insects. The man's face and head had caved in and melted away, leaving nothing behind except a sticky purple mess of ash on the tiles.

Shelagh began shivering uncontrollably and Kingswraith hurried to put his arms around her in an attempt to comfort her. Her quick actions had almost certainly saved his life. He didn't know what they had just killed but he was convinced it was something to do with the Umbra. 'It's alright,' he mumbled, 'he's gone.'

'No,' she whispered pushing him away, 'no, no, please.'

'Sorry,' he replied, stepping away, 'sorry.' He dropped his eyes to the ground.

Shelagh, touched his hand, 'It's alright,' she said, 'it's alright, but I do think I ought to get dressed first before we 'as a cuddle, don't you?'

He couldn't hold back the laughter, it was that or scream, 'Yes, I'll let you get on with it, sorry.' And he turned towards the stairs.

Behind him a small voice whispered, 'No, please, no. Don't leave me alone. I'll just be a minute, but please, don't leave me alone, not alone, not with that thing. Please.'

'I won't,' he replied, feeling his own body trembling with shock 'I won't, I promise.'

He could hear the sounds of fabric sliding over bare skin, then Shelagh's voice, 'I think we need to talk,' she said, 'I really think we should, don't you? Person to person, proper like.'

Meanwhile Frossard was floating through the place between worlds, caught up in the stream of light that would carry him towards reincarnation. The Viventem Nominis Umbra never truly died; death had little stomach for the venomous evil of the living shadows. He would be reborn and then he would return to Chelsea and take his time with that little hybrid bitch who had stabbed him in the back. He would skin her alive – making sure that she stayed alive – and she would feel every bite as he slowly stripped her flesh from her bones and swallowed every last tender mouthful.

His thoughts were interrupted when his passage to rebirth seemed to hit a wall. He bounced, jolted against something solid, then everything seemed to turn inside-out, and he fell from the stream of souls, tumbling out into a colourless, barren place. He landed hard.

At first, he thought the place to be uninhabited, that he was alone, but then he saw what he took to be a small child. As if hypnotised he stumbled towards it. As he drew closer his perceptions changed, it watched him with eyes like bottomless pits and for the first time in his existence Frossard experienced a sensation of profound terror.

He fell, helpless at the feet of the skeletal Spiritus Iudicii which smiled down at him and reached towards him with eager hands. He heard it giggle and say, 'I promised we wouldn't have to wait long, my dear one, I promised, and I always keep my promises, you know that.'

And then it began to eat, slowly and with great relish.

The relentless agony continued for so long that it felt as if it had lasted for an eternity, perhaps it had, time meant nothing in that place. Frossard's screaming didn't stop until it had torn out his throat. But, although the screaming might have ceased, the intense pain of being devoured like a succulent morsel persisted until the very last delicious mouthful of Frossard's black soul had been sucked away, after which the child licked its fingers. He turned his black eyes back up towards the stream of souls, and waited for his next black souled visitor.

'Not long,' he said to himself, for there was no-one else to hear him, 'not long now, my dear one, we shall feast again soon.'

16

Charlton and Chandler perched on the fold-down seats at the front of the chariot's cabin with their backs to the driver. The Professor and Clare sat on the buttoned leather bench seat. The pair of horses pulled the workaday transport along at a fair lick that would deliver them to the famous front entrance of New Scotland Yard in just twenty minutes. Clare felt the warm pressure of her husband's body jostle against her every time the chariot wheels bounced over one of the frequent potholes. She quite enjoyed it.

Since he had received the gift of his magical stave the Professor seemed to have regained most, if not all, of his strength. The stave somehow filled him with energy, and he was healing nicely from his terrible ordeal in Haven Slighe's cellar. There was still the occasional shadow that darkened his moods, and sometimes she saw his eyes become vacant as if he was looking out from a dark abyss from which, if only briefly, he couldn't escape.

She was profoundly grateful to Kingswraith for his gift of the stave. It had gone a long way towards not only restoring the man she loved but had also pushed open the door to her own thaumaturgical talents, which her husband had been ready and willing to help her master.

It was proving a wonderful journey of exploration into a new and exciting world of enchantment, one that she had always believed existed but to which she had never before had access. But she also knew that there might be a great price to be paid for her new adventure. It might cost them their lives.

She thought of their enemy, the Umbra, the family of living shadows. They sounded like demons risen from the deepest pits of hell; although, for all that, they looked human enough if Slighe was any guideline. And what of his dreadful beast men, the Drokhel Minai? What if they were still prowling the darkened streets? She shuddered at the thought. What could be worse? No, she thought, what could be worse? Her imagination ran riot.

The chariot lurched to a stop and the police officers climbed out onto the pavement under the great blue lamp of New Scotland Yard. Chandler offered Clare a hand out of the carriage, and she shivered at the cold bite of the late afternoon air. The Professor took her arm and steered her up the steps into the warmth of the Yard. Chandler waved a greeting to the sergeant at the reception desk before guiding them along a corridor and through two green painted doors inset with frosted glass windows leading to a wide flight of stairs.

They descended the stairs and walked along an echoing corridor until they reached another set of glazed wooden doors, passed through into a small lobby, and then on to yet another set of doors. There they found the familiar figure of medical pathologist Dr Kendal. As they entered, Kendal was standing over his porcelain autopsy table while carefully wiping his hands on a white cloth. He strode towards the Professor with his hand outstretched. A welcoming smile creased his broad, handsome features.

'My dear fellow, well met, well met. Glad to see you again.' He beamed at Clare, 'And who is this charming young lady? Might I say, without intending offence, that you brighten my humble offices, my dear? The sun don't shine down here, so you are a very welcome ray of light.'

The Professor introduced his wife to the doctor, who bowed and took her hand with an honest display of old-world gallantry. 'Proud and a pleasure to meet you, Lady Whitekirk. the Professor is a lucky man indeed. Most charming. But there it is, listen to me, I'm wasting your precious time with banter. Now then, let's to business.'

He reluctantly turned away from Clare and pointed at the Professor's weighted left hand. 'I see you've brought along your necessaries bag as always, my friend, good, good. So, let me introduce you to our latest clients. As I say, the sun don't shine down here, so I'd be grateful for any light you can shine on these odd cases. I'm fifteen stumped on the situation, can't make neither head nor tail of them.'

He indicated a group of three gurneys, each containing a sheet covered form, 'I ask you, what sort of strange cannibal runs around chewing people's faces off? Is it something you've ever heard of, Professor?'

'Sounds dreadful, Doctor. Inspector Chandler tells me you also have another Depleted Man? Thought we'd seen the end of those. But, as for your faceless victims, I must say this cannibal hunger for living flesh sounds more animal than human. Are you sure we're not looking at rat bites or something more mundane?'

Kendal replied, 'I'll show you, Professor. Perhaps your wife might prefer to wait outside? It's not a pretty sight I'm afraid. I'm sure Sergeant Charlton can find a nice cup of tea and a biscuit to nibble on while you wait, Mrs Whitekirk.'

Clare smiled charmingly enough, but the Professor spotted some familiar storm clouds gathering on the horizon. His wife didn't like to be treated as the 'good little lady', as Kendal was about to find out.

'Call me Clare, please, Dr Kendal, let's not be so formal. As for something not being a "pretty sight", I think I can study the corpora delicti and lend my weak feminine insights without fainting away. If I should feel a swoon coming on, I'm sure I shall find courage by gripping at my husband's good right arm; as any little lady would, yes?'

Kendal looked momentarily disconcerted. Carried on the edge of Clare's soft yet firm voice he felt the slight chill rolling towards him and his accustomed world view – which maintained women to be the frivolous and weaker sex – had been thrown askew. The Professor covertly observed the doctor while he inwardly digested Clare's words, and smiled to himself.

Kendal finally came to some kind of resolution and squared his shoulders. 'Very good, Clare, I shall value your thoughts regarding the matter. Our clients are over here on the gurneys. They are just out from the storage cabinets and quite cold. You might have already noticed that there is surprisingly little in the way of the usual odour of post-mortem decay. But if you need it, I have a strong liniment that you can apply to the nostrils. It will mask all but the most pungent corpse – and we've had some right stinkers down here in our time, I can tell you, eh?'

He drew back the sheets and uncovered three naked bodies, all male. Each had evidently been subjected to a stringent anatomopathological examination, evidenced by the long purple scars down and across their torsos that had been closed using neat, blanket stitch sutures. Kendal angled the lamps to better illuminate his subjects.

'I'd prefer to think of our clients as people rather than research cases. They each had a life, hopes, dreams, and a future, until they met their cruel fate. I'm used to death by blunt instruments, blades and firearms, poisons, and on some rare occasions, bare hands. Fists instead of cudgels. Then there's strangulation, deliberate drowning and even incineration. We are an imaginative breed when it comes to murder. But this? This is beyond comprehension.'

Clare paled slightly at the sight of the wickedly mutilated victims. The Professor opened his case and fetched out a magnifying glass. Leaning on his stave for balance he examined the nearest of the chewed faces. He tilted his head to one side the better to see what he was looking at under the best light.

He glanced towards Kendal, 'Doctor, have you made a cast of these bite marks? You say they are human, and I agree they are very like, but the grooves are narrow and there seems to be too many canines. See, what do you think?' He handed over his glass.

Kendal leaned closer to the body and squinted down at the magnified face, 'I never thought to make a cast, but I can see what you...'

The figure on the gurney lurched forward and snatched at Kendal's wrist with its fleshless, claw-like right hand. Its left hand levered it up into a sitting position. The other two bodies also stirred as if roused from sleep. They emitted inhuman hissing sounds as they climbed to their feet and moved quickly and smoothly, like exquisitely fashioned automatons, towards the stupefied group in the middle of the room.

They were fast, and their jaws swung open as they rushed towards their prey, yearning like starving predatory animals on the hunt. Driven by stark terror Charlton was galvanised into action. The doctor was struggling with the body that had a firm grip on his arm and was now trying to take a bite out of his throat. Its narrow, ruined head lunged and snapped at Kendal. Charlton grabbed the nearest chair and leapt forward, driving the chair's legs hard into the creature's body, screaming, 'Doctor, get clear!'

Kendal pulled his arm out of the thing's grasp and fell backwards, snaking along the floor with his elbows and heels pumping desperately. All three faceless bodies now reached out towards both the policeman and the scrambling doctor. The Professor stepped forward; his stave held in both his hands like a knight wielding a broadsword. He pointed it towards the gruesomely eerie attackers. They paused, very much like curious visitors to an exhibition that have spotted something new, and all three turned towards him. Their heads made a gristly, grinding sound as they pivoted on their necks, but then they returned to their original targets.

The Professor shouted, his voice electric with urgency, 'Get away from them, both of you get behind me! MOVE!' The doctor scrabbled across the room on all fours with a surprising turn of speed for a portly middle-aged man, but Charlton seemed numb with horror and stood transfixed by the approaching nightmares. His eyes rolled up into his head and his lips were flecked with foam. The first corpse to draw close to him hissed and examined its prey with almost delicate interest.

Charlton was trembling uncontrollably and only the whites of his eyes were visible, he was evidently in real trouble. At the Professor's side Clare flung out her arms and barked 'Percutiens!' Charlton and the animated corpse were swept apart, the police sergeant staggering back towards his colleagues while the faceless corpse reeled helplessly across the room and crashed into its dreadful companions.

The corpses' frustrated hissing sound grew louder and they turned all of their attention onto Clare and the Professor. Clare could swear their fleshless mouths were grinning. She moaned in fear when their heads swivelled towards her, squeaking horribly as they did so. It was too much to bear, she rallied her courage to the sticking place and commanded 'Demorior' but the killing charm had no effect on the three figures.

The Professor gasped, 'No, that won't work, they're already dead.' He took a firmer grip on his stave and spat out, 'Incendii!' The trio of dead men halted in their tracks, as if momentarily confused by the carmini. They faltered and lurched like puppets with some of their strings cut. The leader's mouth swung open once more as if ready to bite, but this time gouts of white flame erupted from between its teeth and from the holes in its face where its eyes and nose used to be.

The other two jerked and danced, slapping at their bodies while smoke began seeping from every orifice, their skin split open along the lines of their post-mortem scars. The stench of burning flesh filled the mortuary and the room became clogged with choking, acrid smoke. It became difficult to breathe. Doctor Kendal and Chandler each grabbed one of Charlton's arms and steered him away through the double doors that led out through the little lobby into the passageway beyond, all hacking and spluttering in the suffocating haze.

The Professor and Clare remained behind to watch as the bodies collapsed and were finally rendered down to twitching piles of ash and calcined bone. They had to be sure that the creatures had been utterly destroyed by fire, before safely joining the police officers and the medical examiner out in the fresher air of the passageway.

When they eventually emerged, they found Charlton sitting on the floor with his back to a wall, weeping softly. Kendal was massaging his wrists and talking gently to him in an attempt to restore the sergeant's scattered wits.

Chandler had broken the glass of the fire cabinet a few yards away, and stood poised with an axe, ready to strike down whatever came through the doors from that room of nightmares. He slumped and let the axe fall when he recognised the Professor and Clare, then broke into a paroxysm of coughing, before spitting sticky gobs of black phlegm into his handkerchief.

He wiped his mouth. 'Bloody smoke, it nearly had me I swear,' he spluttered, 'and I've no idea what just happened in there. Those, those things, they came alive! They nearly had poor Charlton and the Doc. I thought they must surely be goners and we were going to be next. We had no hope. It was a nightmare! What were they? How...?'

His eyes blinked blearily out at them from his soot smudged features. 'Then you did something, the two of you did something. What you did, I'm sure I don't know. You saved our lives. It was like we were living through a story by that Yank, Edgar Allan Poe. What just happened to us? Can you tell me? What happened in there?'

The Professor briefly considered casting the Obliviscatur carmini to wipe the Scotland Yard men's minds clean of recent events, but the smoking ruins in the mortuary would have to be explained, and anyway, Charlton was probably too stricken by terror for the spell to work. All of them were soot blackened and shocked, even Clare's amber eyes looked pale in her besmirched face. It was no good, only the truth would suffice.

He leaned forward on his stave and favoured Chandler with his ice blue gaze. 'Inspector, I know you to be a pragmatic man, practical and down-to-earth, with a sound grasp of reality, a firm hand on truth's rudder. Unfortunately, that is exactly why I fear that what I'm about to tell you might prove difficult to believe. Is there somewhere we can wash this filth from our faces and get a drink? Then I shall explain all, and I'll trust you to decide who else needs to know about this. Are we agreed?'

Chandler wiped his mouth with the back of his hand, smearing the greasy soot, 'Just tell me this, are those things in there finished? Are they dealt with? I mean they're not going to come running out here and pounce on some poor devil the minute we walk away?'

102

'I can assure you that they are quite harmless now. There's nothing left of the filthy creatures, just crumbled bones and ashes. But might I suggest that if you get any more like them, they must be instantly cremated without a moment's hesitation. It would be the only sensible course of action.'

Speaking from his place beside Charlton's shoulder, Kendal agreed, 'I'll second that, right readily, third it if you like. And I'd like to hear this explanation too. But first we need to get Sergeant Charlton where he can recover his wits, the poor fellow. He's had quite the fright, and we need to get him away from here. Will somebody help me?'

Chandler and the Professor stepped forward, while Clare looked down and examined her favourite tapestried jacket. She had bought it while she was on a tour of Florence with her father. It was badly smoke damaged and she wondered if Mrs Vermont might be able to save it. Then the events of the last few minutes hit her hard and she began trembling.

She could have died, killed by those impossible undead creatures. She had only survived because their attackers had been incinerated by her husband using the 'Incendii' carmini, which was practically forbidden to the convocation of Lux Texentes. She had herself attempted a killing charm. The polite rulebook of white wizardry – into which she had barely ventured as a neophyte – had evidently been torn up and flung away.

The state of her jacket seemed extremely petty by comparison. She fought back the tears that threatened to overwhelm her, swallowed bile and the bitter taste of burned flesh, and thoughtfully followed the men along the passageway.

17

Cymbeline Fleischer stood under the wide marble portico at the top of the broad sweep of steps and gazed down the driveway of Arcadia House, using much more than just her eyes to pluck secrets from the gathering gloom. Around her the recently arrived corps of her hierodule followers were putting the mansion house in order while desperately trying not to attract her attention. Mme Fleischer did not like her train of thought to be disturbed by the activities of her ape-like underlings.

Some of the creeping phalanx of servants walked oddly, as if still coming to terms with their rough, human shape. Some fell to all fours when climbing the stairs, others moved with an inhumanly snake-like swish that gave them a sinuous and sinister grace. None of them had been selected for their beauty or intelligence. All Fleischer required was their unquestioning loyalty, total obedience, and utter silence when in her presence.

Cymbeline felt someone join her on the top stair. She had no need to turn to know who it was. She said, 'Makrut, something is happening out there. Frossard went off to investigate that flare of magic we felt yesterday and he hasn't returned. I felt something else on the web too, those three magic trap corpses we created have woken up. Something eldritch set them off, something powerful. I felt that very strongly. At one point they were as loud as hounds on point but now I can't sense them at all. What do you think happened?'

Makrut sniffed, 'Frossard gets distracted by irrelevancies, he's like a puppy dog that goes chasing after butterflies because he likes the colours. He'll be back, or have you cast the searcher light? You sound as if you're expecting the worst. Frossard is an idiot it's true, but he's as strong as any of us. And we set those traps, you and I. Once they scent magic and wake, the manus mortuus will kill everything around them, nothing could stop them.'

'Not true, I could, my dear. So, could you. Yes, I know they're dead and impervious to almost anything but fire, but we could stop them in any number of ways, from burning them to tearing them apart. I wonder, might there be someone out there as powerful as us?'

The two women stood silently in the darkness for a moment, the only sounds the shuffling feet of the hierodules in the hallway at their backs. Then they burst into harsh, blade-like chimes of crystal laughter. The pale sister chuckled, 'Cymbeline, sometimes your waggish humour quite surprises me. No, but seriously, have you cast the searcher? Is Frossard corporeal and off playing his games, or is he a shade? You must tell me.'

The dark shadow woman shook her head, 'He is neither. Frossard has vanished from the ether as completely as Haven Slighe. Something or someone has erased him from existence. You realise, Makrut, that must mean that two of our company have been completely and utterly obliterated. We must find out who or what is doing this and destroy it, destroy it completely, obliterate it! I have called the Vadhaka Disputabo down from the mountain. He will arrive here soon. He will cut out this canker that afflicts us.'

'The Vadhaka! Are you sure you want to use him, Cymbeline? You know he will insist on payment in advance. He always demands a life for a life. Are you willing to die and be resurrected for the sake of this "canker"? Surely, we can go home and leave England to the humans, the rest of the world is still our oyster, all we need is a spoon. I value you too much to allow such a needless sacrifice. Cymbeline, my heart, I beg of you, don't do this.'

'Makrut, Makrut, do you mistake me for some footling sister of mercy? What on earth made you think I would sacrifice myself?'

The crystalline shadow drew in a sharp breath, 'Then would you sacrifice me? I'd like to see you try!'

'No, of course not. Really, think clearly, my heart. We are sisters as well as colleagues of the shadows, and anyway we have already lost too many of our precious family. Come, let me show you what I have to offer the Vadhaka when he gets here. That black-hearted assassin will be more than satisfied with his wage, I promise you.'

The women walked back into the great house to be surrounded by a whirling hubbub of servants all scurrying to clear their path. Cymbeline led her 'sister' down to the wine cellar and through a hissing crowded pack of manus mortuus then she took her into a vaulted chapel. An arched niche on one wall still contained a finely carved wooden crucifix, while another held a darkened stained-glass window that looked blindly out into the gathering night. Two tall, fat church candles in heavy wall sconces provided the only illumination.

A slight form crouched on the stone flagged floor. It stirred at their approach and whimpered, rattling at its iron chains. The chains were fixed to the wall by a thick iron ring threaded on an iron bracket. He was a child-like urchin dressed in black rags, and the iron in the chains was agony for him. His eyes glinted green in the warm candlelight, and his face was a mask of utter misery. It was Okeanus.

He pleaded with Cymbeline, his surprisingly deep voice barely rising above a hoarse whisper, 'Missus, why have you done this to me? I came here to do you a favour. I told you where he is, didn't I? And I didn't ask anything from you, did I? I do you a favour and in return you do this to me, is that fair? Please, just take the chains away, they hurt, they hurt.'

Cymbeline ignored his begging and said to Makrut, sounding as if they were discussing a new pet or an unusual recipe, 'He turned up here this morning and gave us the address in Chelsea that Frossard went to visit. It was obviously some kind of a trick, look what's happened to Frossard since. I had one of the servants chain the creature to the stone with iron. Who knows what mischief he might have got up to otherwise? I think he's a Dryad, and he tells me he's a prince. Well, good. Now he's a bribe.'

The shadow women walked out of the crypt without so much as glancing back at the wretched Epimeliad. Okeanus called after them, imploring, offering them anything they wanted if they would only release him from his terrible torment, release him from the vampire metal, iron. He didn't know it but the Umbra were as prone to iron as every other magical creature. Iron would burn as fiercely and painfully in their blue blood as it did in his.

Back out under the portico Cymbeline and Makrut waited and watched the skies. When they needed it, they had the patience of spiders and they would stand still as sculptures until they saw the need to move. Only their hair was lifted by the slight, warm breeze blowing in from mainland Europe. Cymbeline almost imagined she could smell her old home in Paris.

Makrut spoke, 'Why is Albion so important to you? You've never said.'

Cymbeline chuckled, 'Albion? Albion is nothing, my heart. It's just an island set away from everything really important. It's having its day at the moment, but that will only last until Europe wakes up and steps on her, squashing her like the arrogant little upstart she is. What's important is what's underneath her, what has been under her since the earliest times... Wait, there, see! See that falling star? It's him, he's here. The Vadhaka has answered my summons. The dark assassin comes.'

106

A great streak of light fell towards the grounds of Arcadia House, growing in brightness until it impacted, splashing into the ancient lawns with the force of a bomb. The foundations of the robust building jolted and the servants had to run around catching things that flew off the shelves. People up to a mile away looked up in alarm as the shockwave rippled through the streets. Dogs barked, cats yowled, birds took to the air and sly foxes slunk away into their dens, suddenly very cautious about being out in the open.

It was a mighty powerful introduction, but what stepped from the centre of that steaming crater had an even greater impact on the Umbra women than the detonation. It was a man, at least, it looked like a man, but he seemed to move without walking. The Umbra favoured all of the many shades and variations of black in their attire. The man gliding towards them was a poem in scarlet, from his wide-brimmed hat to his high, Spanish heeled boots.

He stopped in front of the two women with his head tilted down so they couldn't see his face, but they had enough time to examine his body. His shoulders were wide and his hips narrow. His legs were long and encased in tight, gas pipe trousers, all the better to enhance his athletic figure. Cymbeline thought him the most beautiful man she had ever seen, very like a bullfighter or a flamenco dancer. Makrut practically purred. Then he looked up at them.

Both women took a step backwards away from him. It wasn't just his lean, lupine features that had shocked them, which included a long jaw, chiselled chin, narrow patrician nose and a wide brow with thick, flaring, auburn eyebrows. Nor was it his high cheekbones or the deep grooves that ran down either side of his smilingly mocking mouth.

It was his deep-set eyes. They gazed at the world through almost invisible pupils from the centre of bone-white irises set in blood-red sclera, eyes that were bright red, red as a freshly opened wound. His eyes were cruel, cold as ice, and he seemed wickedly amused by his hosts. Makrut attempted to gather some semblance of dignity around herself.

'A gentleman removes his hat in the presence of ladies.'

His smile grew wider, showing large white teeth, 'If you wanted to call a gentleman there are plenty of clubs in this city full of the pointless, strutting peacocks. But no, you called me. So, tell me, who is going to have the final pleasure of meeting me?'

Cymbeline stepped forward, 'It is a boy, a young man. He is at an address called Owl's Tower in Cheyne Row, Chelsea. His name is Martin Kingswraith. He is very dangerous.'

Vadhaka chuckled, 'No, Cymbeline, I am dangerous, he is dead. Which is something I will happily explain to him at length when we meet. But tell me, I'm curious; why have the Umbra come to me? You've never called on my services before, you've always solved your own problems. What makes this Kingswraith boy so very different?'

Cymbeline was momentarily surprised that the Vadhaka knew her name, but she replied, 'I told you, he is dangerous. It seems he has erased two of our family. He has erased two of our brothers completely and utterly. They have vanished from the ether, leaving not so much as a shade to mark their passing. That too has never happened before. Kingswraith is a thorn we should like pulled from our side, and you are said to be the best thorn puller ever born. That is why you are here.'

Vadhaka blinked at the word 'born' and shrugged. What the shadows didn't know couldn't hurt them. He growled, 'You know my terms? Payment in advance.'

Cymbeline bowed, a curt movement of her narrow head on its long neck, 'Of course, when would you like to take your bounty?'

'I always say there's no time like the present. Which of you shall it be?'

Cymbeline chuckled, a dry sound without an ounce of humour, 'Us? One of us? No, no my dear fellow, we offer you something much more diverting than one of us! Please, come with me, you won't be disappointed I promise you.'

She led the stalking, red-eyed creature through the house, down to the wine cellar where he ignored the manus mortuus as if they weren't there, and took him on into the crypt. The candles cast their mellow light onto the childlike figure crouched in his chains. Vadhaka paused at the door and hissed, 'Get somebody to remove that superstitious object from the room, I will not enter while it is there.'

Cymbeline scanned the crypt, 'What superstitious object? I see nothing.'

Vadhaka pointed at the crucifix, 'Have that thing removed. He has seen enough; I will not have Him watching me while I amuse myself. And have those chains removed from my prize too. I will not touch them, and I will not need them.'

Cymbeline shouted her orders, and within moments the niche was empty. A little later Okeanus was released from his shackles and rose unsteadily to his feet. He rubbed at his wrists with a petulant expression on his face, almost groaning with relief to be free of the vampire metal at last. He squinted at the two figures framed in the entrance archway, their features swallowed in the shadows; it was as if they drained away the light cast by the flickering candle flames.

Free of the iron he felt his energy returning, and automatically he reached out to the trees just beyond the stained-glass window. One of the branches burst through a glazed representation of Eve plucking the apple from the tree, the serpent twined around her feet. The coloured fragments were scattered across the flagstones. Okeanus ran across and threw himself out towards the branch, urging it to snatch him away to freedom and out of the reach of his tormenters. He almost made it, but tormentors, like cats and the Vadhaka, love to play.

Something like a razor thin, whirling buzzsaw flew across the room. It ripped into the tree and slashed away the branches. In the process it sliced off Okeanus's right arm just below the elbow. The Sprite screamed in pain and shock, watching his purplish blood spatter across the chapel. He fell to his knees and pressed his left hand to the stump. This was impossible, it couldn't be happening!

Behind him he heard a gravelly voice growl, 'Leave us now, Cymbeline. I will savour my prize at my leisure. What happens now is between me and my little reward. We shall enjoy our brief time together, or, at least, I shall enjoy it. Traitorous little Okeanus will endure it.'

Okeanus was folded tight over his pain, and waited for the sound of approaching footsteps. None came. He was dizzy with loss of blood but fought to rally his will and call another tree to his aid. Then a firm hand took his shoulder and swivelled him to face a countenance that he instantly recognised. Those blood-red eyes had haunted the nightmares of the tree folk. With a sick certainty he realised that he would never live to see another dawn.

He was right, but only just. Vadhaka was very skilled at keeping his victims alive until agony had been piled onto agony; until he had drawn every last moment of exquisite pain from their screaming nerve endings. In his own twisted way, he thought his celebration of the fine arts of torture as showing respect for his victims. He made their final moments last as long as he could. It was an artform he had perfected over thousands of years on countless men, women, children, and magical spirits.

Vadhaka did not just take a life, he teased it away until the torment was so intense that surrendering it became a pleasure, a release, allowing his victim to find Elysium and peace. Almost gently he lay down the ruined thing that had once been Okeanus, bedding his corpse in a sticky pool of his own lifeblood. Peace at last, my little friend, accept the gift of peace. He stood and stretched, and now I must take Kingswraith. Will he make as fine an end as you, I wonder? We shall see, yes, we shall see.

He turned gracefully, light on the toes of his leather clad feet and flowed towards the archway, back through the silent manus mortuus and up the stairs leading to the outside world. In his mind he clearly saw his route to Chelsea and the house where his next performance must take place. He was eager for the kill, and knew that Kingswraith's fate was not only sealed but would also be a lingering poem to pain. Kingswraith's death would be the Vadhaka's new masterpiece.

18

The Professor and Clare had still not returned home by the time Mrs Vermont and Wills came back from their Sunday outing and found Shelagh drinking tea with Kingswraith in the downstairs gallery. The housekeeper's old-fashioned views on the subject of men and women spending time alone together out of wedlock saw her raising Cain for a few minutes, but she eventually calmed down when Kingswraith explained that the poor girl had had a fright, and he was only keeping her company until she and her husband had made their appearance.

'Shelagh didn't want to be alone,' he explained, working hard to maintain an air of complete innocence. He offered up the little fiction that he and the maid had agreed upon.

'She was walking back from her mother's house and some drunken fellow tried to get a bit too friendly, if you know what I mean. She gave him a good slap for his pains and ran for it, but it has left her a little shaken. She was worried the blackguard might have followed her back here, so I was looking after her while we waited for you.'

Mrs Vermont instantly changed her tune, 'Shame! Villains like that want locking up and the key throwing away. Flustering a poor innocent young chick like our Shelagh! Does she even look like that sort of girl? I've a mind to go find the brute and give him the sharp edge of my tongue. He'll steer clear of good girls after I've finished with him, I can promise you.'

Wills stood silent with his fists clenched and his brow knotted with anger. He and his wife had a strong parental attitude towards the young girl who slept under their roof, and the thought of some booze sodden wretch pawing at her was enough to make his blood boil. Mrs Vermont thanked Kingswraith for his 'kind consideration' then put her arms around Shelagh's thin shoulders and led her away towards the cottage they shared in the courtyard.

Once he was alone Kingswraith made his way down to the cellar bathroom with a dustpan and brush and a box he had found in the 'necessaries' cupboard under the stairs. He carefully swept up all that remained of their attacker, and then carried the surprisingly light box up to the study, intending to discuss what had happened with the Professor and Clare the next morning. He also needed to explore the mystery of Shelagh with Penelope.

He felt exhausted. That Sunday had proved a very long and confusing day. He prepared himself for bed and climbed under the covers, all the while listening for any suspicious sounds in the house. The silence was only broken by the creaking music of old architecture settling down for the night, its timbers getting comfortable in the cooling evening air.

The young wizard decided that it was time to have a conversation with an old soul who might provide some solid answers. He lay absolutely still with his arms at his sides and performed gentle tantric breathing exercises to release the tensions that had knotted his body since he had discovered the stranger with Shelagh, forcing the stress to flow away from his clenched muscles. Once he finally felt completely relaxed, he breathed, 'Garth.'

'At last, at last! I have been calling to you, shouting at you, screaming at you, but do you take any notice? No, you don't! I was tempted to possess some empty-headed delivery boy to pass you a message, but there are rules about that sort of thing. And once you start down the possession road it's a bit like biscuits, you'll always fancy another one. Still, here you are, my prince. And I tell you, you have to leave! You are in serious danger, unspeakable peril! Unspeakable, I say!'

'Leave? Danger? But, Garth, I've only just got here. What threat could there be here?' Kingswraith looked around the familiar Halls of the Dead before returning his attention to the ancient Steward, who was hopping from one gnarled foot to the other.

'Threat, threat? I'll give you threat if you don't listen. Something is coming and it will kill you; you and the entire household of Owl's Tower. It is the single deadliest creature you could ever meet. It is single-minded, merciless and utterly remorseless. You're not ready to meet it yet, not even with that fancy new stave of yours. Luckily just now it is entertaining itself with one of the Epimeliads, otherwise you would be here visiting me in person by now.'

'What is this mortal terror? Has it got a name?'

'Name, no, it needs no name, it was neither born nor christened. But it has a description. It is called the Vadhaka Disputabo. Have you ever heard of it?'

'No, that means nothing to me. And what do you mean by saying it's entertaining itself with an Epimeliad? How did it catch them? And which one is it? Not, Penelope!'

Garth was almost dancing in his frustration, 'What does it matter? You're in danger I tell you. Alright, alright, I recognise that stubborn look from your noble forebears. It has the one called Okeanus, the girl's companion. He turned traitor on you and told the Umbra women where you live and who you are. They sent a brother of the family to you, a nasty stick of malice called Frossard. What did you do to him by the way? He seems to have vanished.'

'Shelagh and I killed him. He was slicing at Shelagh with an iron knife, the handle is made of silver so he could hold it, but he dropped it when I hit him with my stave.'

'You hit him? Excellent, great news! Then what happened?'

'Yes, I hit him. He was torturing Shelagh; I couldn't allow that. Then, when he attacked me, Shelagh stabbed him in the back with his own knife, then I pulled out the knife and cut his head off. He crumbled to dust, so yes, in a way, he vanished. Is that what you mean?'

'Well done, that's good work, but no, it isn't what I mean. When I say vanished, I mean that he is neither there nor here nor in the middens of the damned. Like Haven Slighe of vile memory, he's gone, completely and utterly gone, like a puff of smoke, poof! I don't know how or where. You must look after that Shelagh girl, by the way, she's very important, or one day she will be, that's if she lives. Have you still got that Frossard's iron knife by the way?'

'Yes, I kept it, why?'

'Good, then this is what you must do. You will meet the Vadhaka one day, and you will need to be ready. Now, listen closely...'

It was mid-morning the following day before Kingswraith was able to follow Garth's urgent instructions and make his way back to Clement's Lane in Candlewick. Jeremiah Taylor was delighted to see him once more, and studied Penelope's work on the stave with great interest. Then he listened to the young practitioner's request regarding the iron blade with a sober expression on his broad face.

'I understand, this is deep magic. So then, you are going to war,' he said. 'In its current state, this staff of yours is a fine tool for enchantments, but if I do as you ask it will become a weapon. Is that what you want?'

'Jeremiah, I am being hunted by the Vadhaka. Does that mean anything to you?'

The metalsmith nodded, then called out, 'Christopher, come here, we need you.'

The young man appeared. He was close in age to Kingswraith and offered him a bright smile from his permanently grubby face. Then he said, 'Pleased to be of service, father. Good to see you again, master Kingswraith, what may I do for you?'

'Christopher my boy, what can you tell me about this?' Taylor carefully handed his son Frossard's knife. The boy studied the blade and held it up to the light. What he saw there took his breath away and he turned to his father with excitement in his voice.

'The hilt is fairly recent and pure silver, but if I'm right the blade is sky metal. By the leaf shape I'd say eighteenth dynasty Egyptian so that would make it well over three thousand years old. Nickel iron mix, sharp as anything I'd use to cut steak with, or this...' He pulled a handkerchief from his pocket, opened it, and flung it into the air. On its way down he slashed at it and the fabric parted, falling as two pieces.

He grinned, as would any boy with such a weapon, 'I wouldn't dare carry this without a sheath. Unsheathed, a blade like this might prove just as dangerous to its owner as it would to anyone else. It takes a fine edge but it will blunt quickly, you'd have to be constantly sharpening it, but someone likes it razor fine.'

He made as if to give it back to his father, but the smith held up his hand, 'No, my son. You know I am forbidden to forge base iron; it is part of the agreed contract for my art that I work with nothing but precious metals. Friend Kingswraith has asked that the metal from this blade be forged and inset to his stave, but only to the front half of its shaft. I say melt it in the clay crucible with charcoal and extrude it to make steel wire, then inset it to the wooden outer fabric of the staff. What do you think?'

Christopher asked to see the stave. He carried it to the light from the skylights and examined it intently, stroking the fine grain of Penelope's work. His eyes shone as he drank in the exquisite quality of the craftsmanship.

He gazed at Kingswraith with new respect, 'I will do my very best to match such work,' he breathed. 'This was never fashioned by man; I can see that. But if anyone can meld steel into such a beautiful creation as this, I can, with my father's blessing.'

'How long do you think it will take?'

Christopher raised an eyebrow to his father. The older man grunted, 'Shall we say three days? We have to forge the steel and then bind it to the warp and weft of the shaft. The end of the stave must remain open or it will act as a barrier to your talent, friend Kingswraith, and we don't want that.'

He added, 'By the way, if you are to avoid the Vadhaka you must remain in hiding until the stave is finished. Please, accept our hospitality, you are very welcome to stay here.'

Under a sudden impulse Kingswraith threw his arms around the smith's broad shoulders and hugged him. The man was as solid as the metal he forged. Kingswraith then shook hands with Christopher.

'Thank-you, thank-you, you are too kind. I would love to spend time with you, and one day I shall, but I'm afraid I can't, not yet. If he is only half as dangerous as I'm told he is, I don't want to bring the Vadhaka down on your house. And I have someone else I must see first. I shall return in three days.'

He listened to their protests for a few more minutes, but eventually he made his way out and away to St Mary Church. He made sure he was unobserved before he levered up the paving slab and climbed down the stone steps to the sewer, and then along to the secret door that opened to the Sprites' underground passageways.

He was surprised to hear a pattering of feet behind him and spun to face whoever was approaching, preparing the Lacta throwing charm. Any attacker's spirits would be thoroughly dampened after a ducking in the filthy sewer water. He relaxed when he recognised two of his companions, Melsh and Listener. They must have drawn escort duty that day.

Melsh protested, 'You move fast as a slippery fox running from the hounds, Boss. We thought you was gone before we could catch you, and that wouldn't do at all. The lady would carve her initials on our backsides with a blunt knife if'n she thought we'd let you out of our sight for so much as one minute, isn't that right, Listener?'

The other companion nodded eagerly, 'Blunt knife on our bare behinds, she would.'

Kingswraith held up both hands to calm them, 'Very well, I understand and you're right to chide me, and yes, I imagine she would; but you'll just have to keep up as best you can. I've important news for the Lady Penelope, and I'm afraid it can't wait just to save your bare little arses. So, come on, lads, let's go.'

19

The Vadhaka made his way through Owl's Tower like a scarlet blur, searching it from cellar bathroom to attic study in a matter of minutes. Locked doors fell open at his touch. When he found no-one in the house he stalked out to the Vermont's cottage in the courtyard at the rear. It was just as empty, but a little bedroom in the eaves stank of magic, much like every floor of the main house. He realised that the house must have been infested with practitioners as recently as that very morning, but for the moment they had escaped him. No matter, he had the scent, the hunt was on.

In the hall by the downstairs gallery lay the headless corpse of an importunate young constable who had observed the killer at work on the street door and had raced up the stairs from the pavement to find out what he was doing. He never got the opportunity to utter a single word. Even as the door opened wide and without a moment's hesitation the Vadhaka had flicked a spinning force blade at the unfortunate policeman.

The assassin had observed the surprised expression on the policeman's face as his helmeted head sailed in an arc across the hallway to bounce off a wall and then roll through the downstairs gallery door before it finally fetched up under the central display table. The Vadhaka flung the headless body into the house where it jetted a huge volume of blood across the hallway for just over three seconds. The policeman's stunned brain lasted a little longer and he gazed at the underside of the display table in perplexed incredulity for desperate seconds before his life finally ebbed away into a vacuum.

His killer apologised for his rapid demise. 'Sorry to rush you, my friend,' he said, 'but I'm looking for someone, you know how it is. There was no time to play. Maybe next time, yes?' But after his forensic search the assassin had found no-one. The Vadhaka wasn't angry that his prey had eluded him. Anger was a waste of energy. And anyway, he took no joy in plucking his prize from the branch like a piece of fruit. The challenge was in the chase.

He carefully locked the street door behind him as he walked back out onto Cheyne Row, there was no need to offer Kingswraith's home as an easy gift to thieves and vagabonds. He despised the professional criminal classes almost as much as he hated thuggish murderers and mindless violence.

He wondered, where is the poetry in slashing a throat with a broken bottle or crushing a skull with a cudgel? Where's the finesse in using brute force like that? It gives killing a poor reputation, as does drunken brawling and wife beating. There's no respect for death in such brutal acts. When you take a life, you should caress your victim, treat them to exquisite agony. Not bludgeon the poor creatures into a pulp of broken bones and splintered teeth.

He shuddered at the thought. Then he went to see what the neighbours might know about the missing household from Owl's Tower. Two hours later he was interviewing one of the botanists at the Chelsea Physic Garden. That lead him to Scheer's bookshop where the two young assistants could only say that the proprietor was not yet on the premises that day, although she had been expected.

He walked out into Russell Square and found a bench where he could sit and think. Autumn was painting the world in glorious shades of russet and gold, but his landscape might as well have been grey on grey for all that he noticed.

Surprisingly not one of the people he had spoken to had found anything strange in his appearance. He customarily cloaked himself in an illusion of normalcy until he plied his sinister art. Only then would he show his true face to his victims, which, he believed, heightened the artistic quality of their death experience. They would die knowing that they were in the hands of a true virtuoso and not some guttersnipe squib, drunk on gin and flailing about with a handy blunt instrument.

His researches to date had buttered no beans, so he must change his tack. The Sprite Okeanus had opened his heart to the Vadhaka while he was dying, at the end quite literally. He had been played like an instrument, the Vadhaka expertly plucking at his exposed nerves to maximise his torment. In the latter stages of such a performance he had often seen his victims enter an almost hallucinatory state, dancing on the wire between life and death.

The Sprite had babbled about his family of tree people who lived underground in a maze of tunnels but also roamed the streets of London caring for the dispossessed and the lost. They moved amongst the rough sleepers in Trafalgar Square, gifting a little money here, some food there, a smile for the lonely and a kind word to those lost to despair. That must be his next port of call. Okeanus had proved a fount of information, so, what might his family know?

A nanny in uniform who was pushing a perambulator smiled at the attractive man on the bench, his thick head of hair red as a fox's pelt. He smiled back. She was pretty enough; but with a shallow prettiness that throughout history could be found in any marketplace without need for any lantern. He was tempted to show her the truth behind the mask, to allow his dark red light to shine just for her. His alien beauty would haunt her lacklustre dreams, give them some colour, season them with fear.

But no, no time, he had a job to do. He waved his hat at her in salute and nodded. The woman blushed, her complexion rosy in that typically English strawberry and cream fashion so admired by foreigners. And she prinked at the curls of dark hair just visible under her cap, before trotting daintily away in her sensible shoes.

After a few yards she turned to see if he was watching her, but the handsome fox had already gone, vanishing like a ghost into the London mist. She sighed, not realising how lucky she had been, and turned her steps towards home.

He walked with the muscular, lithe grace of a big cat. People moved out of his way, even on the congested pavements of Charing Cross Road. Under the Vadhaka's uncanny influence one man stepped blindly out into the road, right in the path of a growler and almost fell under the horse's hooves. The cabby left him reeling after loudly making observations regarding the lack of the careless pedestrian's wits, the unlikelihood of any legal marital status for his parents; and advising that if he must throw himself under something, a train would be best.

In just twenty minutes the Vadhaka traversed the mile or so from Bloomsbury to the crowded stones between the National Gallery and Nelson's Column. He gazed out over a ragged sea of unwashed and unwanted vagabonds. A man was standing between two of Landseer's lions at the base of Nelson's column enthusiastically bellowing at the crowd, warning about the dangers of drink with the help of a loudhailer he didn't need.

He was surrounded by a small gang of well-fed placard carriers, their bovine faces pink and plump as well scrubbed pork. They were not the Vadhaka's prey, nor were any of the man's gaunt audience, who were largely ignoring his impassioned address.

The Vadhaka heard one of the street dwellers complain, 'Does he 'ave to use that flippin' Skipper's speaking 'orn? Cor blimey, that's the butter on the bacon that is. 'E's plenty loud enough on his own without any 'elp.'

His companion, a gaunt-faced woman with hollowed out cheeks under bones so sharp they could be used to fillet a fish, whined, 'Gorn, but 'e ain't the one talking about bacon is 'e? What you doin' talkin about bacon, eh? If we 'ad bacon we could 'ave a bacon sandwich, that is, if we 'ad any bread. Cor, you've set me guts to grumblin' just when I was settling down for a nap while that old flap-doodle's still yappin'. Now you done put it in me 'ead and I'd kill for a bacon sandwich.'

Vadhaka smiled. He was tempted to fetch the woman her salty treat and hand her a knife to see who she might dispatch first. But no matter, he had to get on. It was at that moment he felt light fingers insinuate themselves into his jacket, hunting for the bounty they expected to lift from his inside pocket. Vadhaka followed the line of the arm to confront a rat-faced unshaven man in a battered bowler hat.

The pick-pocket realised he had been caught fair with his daddles in the biscuit tin and made to back-slang it, but he found himself frozen to the spot. For all the crowds around them, he and his mark suddenly seemed to be floating all alone in a little bubble of silence. When he copped the geezer's dial, he near filled his trousers. The cove had the face of a wolf and eyes like open wounds, his iris's bone-white circles floating on puddles of fresh blood.

The Vadhaka knew the type of guttersnipe he was dealing with, and decided to address him using the street parley he would understand best. A 'toff' was a lot less threatening than a rough. The Vadhaka had had an amusing idea, and to make it work he needed to terrify his victim. It wouldn't be hard; the thief was already pale and quivering with fear.

When the mark's smile grew wider and ever more wolflike, the thief shrank down deeper into his boots. The stranger growled in a low voice that only he could hear. 'I've got your scent now, you skilamalink purse dipper. I can find you wherever you go, whenever I want. If I have to come after you, you know you'll cop more than a mouse. So, I'm going to make you a deal, matey. See that raw-faced woman there and her man, nod if you see who I mean.'

The man nodded enthusiastically but his face was a mask of terror, those eyes! The bloody orbs drew closer, 'Good, then listen. I want you to buy them both a bacon sandwich, with butter and plenty of bacon. Get them each a cup of sugared splosh too, and make sure it's as hot as your breath.'

The horror gripped him by the cheeks. 'Then you make like a butler and bring the wittles back here to them. I'll know if you let me down, and I promise you, if you do, you'll wish you hadn't. Are you hearing me? Nod if you understand.'

The finger dipper nodded, and then felt himself released from the strange hold. He gasped, 'But I ain't got no readies on me, guvnor, no moolah, see. You want me to steal all that gear I might get collared before I can get back 'ere. What's a bloke meant to do then, eh?'

Vadhaka laughed, and the raw sound froze the thief's blood in his veins. The wolf reached into a pocket and extracted a pound note from a thick wad of cash that brought a flood of saliva into the rat-faced man's mouth. Cor, look at the readies in that bundle.

The wolfman handed him the note, 'Look after my friends properly, and treat yourself with what's left. If you cut them on our deal then I'll cut you in turn, slow, an inch at a time. You know I will, don't you? You know I can.'

Fifteen minutes later the raw-faced woman and her partner were surprised by a total stranger who handed each of them a cup of hot sweet tea and a bacon and egg banjo, dripping with fresh butter. Their benefactor only squeaked, 'If your mate asks you, you tell him I kept to our deal fair and square, that's all I want from you. Alright?' Then he scurried away into the crowd and vanished, nimble as the rat he so closely resembled.

The Vadhaka was already long gone, following a black suited and ragged street urchin away from the square. The urchin looked the perfect pea popped from the same pod as Okeanus, and hopefully would lead the killer to his nest, and the rest of his family. And then they would all have a nice long informative talk.

The object was to find Kingswraith, his patron, and the new bookseller bride. Once he knew where to find them, the Vadhaka might let the Sprites live. He might, but, then again...

20

Early that morning Kingswraith had convinced the Owl's Tower household that remaining in Chelsea for as much as another single day would prove incredibly dangerous. He had shown the Professor and Clare the box of Frossard's ashes and told them the truth about the Umbra's attack on Shelagh. He then produced the knife and explained how he planned to follow Garth's advice and return to Jeramiah Taylor's forge for some added work on his stave.

He warned them that the Vadhaka certainly knew their address, and the entire household was packed and underway by hired Landau within the hour. Shelagh fell asleep just minutes into the journey. She was still in shock after the events of the previous evening and she dreamed of red-eyed monsters pursuing her through a dense forest. In her dream it didn't matter how fast she ran she could feel their hot breath scorching the back of her neck.

Mrs Vermont and Wills sat either side of her and felt her twitching like a nervous puppy whenever the Landau's wheel hit a rut or bounced in a pothole.

'Poor lass,' said Wills, 'that drunken sot must 'ave put the fear of God into 'er. I wish I could 'ave got my hands on the beggar, I'd teach him to keep 'imself to 'imself no matter how arfarfan' arf he was. 'Tain't right, a man like that shouldn't be allowed loose amongst decent folk.'

Clare passed a sideways glance to the Professor. They were both thinking of the young maid's courage in stabbing her molester in the back, and of the lines of blood drawn on her naked body with Frossard's iron blade. The fact that he chose iron for his weapon proved that the Umbra had expected to be dealing with magical beings. That he had started on Shelagh, gave the Professor pause for serious thought. And Kingswraith had explained that Garth had said she was important... What might that mean?

The Professor himself hadn't spirit travelled to the Halls of the Dead since his rescue from the clutches of Haven Slighe. He had come too close to becoming a permanent resident in the afterlife to feel comfortable about visiting, no matter how welcome the antique soul might make him feel. He preferred not to abandon his physical body to talk with Garth, not yet. But the question of Shelagh, who and what she might be, had him intrigued.

She had become a proper 'fifteen-puzzle', as Detective Inspector Chandler might say. Before leaving his Chelsea home the Professor had sent a note to Scotland Yard explaining that Owl's Tower would be empty for a while, and that he would send another message to advise the good Inspector when they had returned from their excursion.

He didn't explain where they were going nor why. What the Inspector didn't know couldn't put him in harm's way. And harm was coming. The Vadhaka. The Assassin. The name was new to the Professor's crowded lexicon of monsters, but Kingswraith had explained that Garth described him as neither born nor christened, but fashioned, much like a demon. Then how had he come into being? Had he been forged in the pits of hell?

Clare was thinking of the many ways in which Martin Kingswraith had changed during the previous year. He was no longer the naïve young man, still barely a boy, she had shared coffee with when he had visited her bookshop with his patron a scant twelve months previously. Back then he had been skittish as a young colt. There had been little sign of the steely resolve she had seen in his eyes when he explained how they must deal with this terrible new threat.

She wondered what strange chrysalis he had emerged from to become so wonderfully transformed? His once merry brown eyes, now amber and flecked with gold, would sometimes flash with emerald light. He still smiled, but there was no longer any sign of the heart pricking innocence she had liked about him. His voice was deeper, his athletic physique more poised. He seemed adult and much more capable. Dangerously so.

That was it, she realised, he had a dangerous edge to him now. Shelagh had stabbed her attacker, but Kingswraith had hacked off the man's head! If he had been a man. What kind of man crumbles to purple ashes when he's killed? And there was no blood, just blue-grey dust and fragments of petrified bone. It seemed likely that he was of the same family as Haven Slighe, but perhaps there were many variations to the Umbra species?

Unlike Frossard Slighe had sent out his beast men, the Drokhel Minai, to do his dirty work. She had personally fallen victim to their brutish strength, and had watched one of them burn to death while freeing her and the Professor from their deadly prison. The Professor had barely been conscious throughout most of it, but an image of the beast man's eyes melting from their sockets was scarred into her memory and still haunted her dreams.

Mrs Vermont, meanwhile was pondering her changing fortunes. She and her husband had always been properly looked after by the Professor, Lord Whitekirk, but things had become passing strange of late. When the Professor went missing the young master Kingswraith had taken up the financial reins of Owl's Tower and put her in charge of the house, and she had continued managing the day-to-day domestic minutia after the weakened Professor had returned. Nobody questioned her new role and she didn't raise the subject.

The Professor had been right poorly for a while and Miss Clare had been a constant visitor, without a chaperone, but by then they were betrothed so that was alright. But the young master didn't come home for another two weeks, and when he did, he looked different. It was like he had become his own older, more confident brother. He positively glowed with health and energy, while the Professor was a pale reflection of his former self. What had happened?

And now they were all running away to the sticks as if the hounds of hell were after them. She'd barely had time to pack her necessities. And the girl Shelagh! She might be in a daze, but she too had changed. She had always been a little odd, which Wills had ascribed to her youth, and it was obvious to a blind beggar that she'd been bitten by a fancy for the young master. But somehow, she too seemed more certain of herself; more womanly, more mature.

Shelagh had been gawky, awkward, shy, all attractive attributes in an innocent girl, but just recently something had brought her out of her shell and she had flowered. Mrs Vermont thought there were too many mysteries about for comfort. Where had the young master gone with that fancy walking stick of his, same as the Professor's? Why wasn't he here with them? And where was he spending so much of his time these days? She barely even saw him at breakfast. Something was up, that much was obvious.

Wills left most of the thinking to his wife. He believed that a Christian soul should stick to what they knew best, and while he was strong and could turn his hand to just about anything of a practical nature, anything involving brain sweat was best left to the missus. But even he was aware that Shelagh wasn't just a little dot of a thing running around the house with a mop and a bucket anymore.

She had taken on a disturbing sheen of femininity, as if she had taken to wearing her big sister's clothes and, suddenly, they fitted her just right. Like Ethel, his wife, Wills was honest right down to his marrow. He saw what was in front of him without need for fancy or frippery. Some folk felt the need to hold a coloured glass up to the world but Wills took pride in keeping a level head. Even so the events of the last year had made him wonder just what was happening in Owl's Tower.

He sometimes felt so mazed by the strange goings on that he worried that the butter might have slid off his noodles. But he was reassured by the sight of his beautiful and practical wife, sitting upright with her hands on her lap and her little necessities bag gripped in her gloved hands. She looked like a cannon shell couldn't knock her off her perch. Solid as a rock, my Eth', he told himself. If she's accepting things, then they must be alright.

And between them was the girl Shelagh, sleeping like a stone angel on a grave, albeit one that twitched and jolted as if she was being pinched by harpies. Whatever came next, Wills decided, whatever happened, he would die to protect these people. They were family.

When they finally reached their destination, what the Professor had described as his old family pile but was officially known as the Whitekirk estate, they found a fine drizzle shrouding everything in a pearlescent mist. The grey haze softened the outlines of the house and made it more romantic and mysterious than the Professor remembered. He had expected some sense of homecoming, but instead he was filled with an intense curiosity. So much had happened since he was last there, surely the old place must also have changed?

Whitekirk Hall still looked to the Professor like an overweight green cat crouching low on its lawns as if exhausted by its long centuries under the Oxfordshire sky. It was a jumbled collection of disparate architectural styles bound together by thick masses of ivy. Somewhere at the heart of it was the ghost of an original twelfth century great hall around which the rest of the building had accrued over the years, like shipwrecks piled on a reef.

As the Landau fetched up before the portico and marble steps leading up to an imposing front door a stout man wearing a collarless shirt under a bright red waistcoat, his legs encased in a tight pair of moleskin trousers, scurried out pulling a low top hat onto his head. He began bellowing at their driver to, 'Clear off out of it, this here's a private estate! We don't want no visitors! Go on, get out of it!'

When the Professor climbed down from the coach and grinned at the round, reddened face with its sprouting mutton chop sideburns, the stout man's eyes nearly burst from their sockets and he slapped his hands to his cheeks.

The Professor said, 'Marple, I do swear you never change from one year to the next. Good to see you, old chap. Is the house fit for a visit by a small party of five? Sorry to break your peace and quiet but we've come up for a breath of fresh Oxfordshire air. Is that practical, d'you think? Shall we decamp to the old house?'

Marple had been left in charge of a small brigade of retainers who had been tasked with keeping the manor fit for habitation should the Professor ever return. But this was the first time he had appeared in over seven years, and he had done so without any forewarning. And he had brought a retinue with him? It was all very peculiar. The other occupants of the coach climbed down into the grey afternoon light and stood blinking around at the silent grounds.

Shelagh was the first to be galvanised into action, she dashed to the Professor's side and whimpered, 'I have a desperate need of the facilities, sir, if I may be so bold? 'Twas a passing long journey and I have a pressing need.' She hopped from one foot to the other and urgently clenched her fists to her midriff.

The Professor gestured to his steward, 'Marple, please show miss Shelagh to the nearest WC. We shall fetch our luggage and get in out of this damp air. Get a move on, man, we don't want the poor girl having a misfortune, do we?'

Marple took Shelagh's arm and led her away at a trot. The rest of the party waited while the driver fetched everything out from under the tarpaulin on the Landau's roof and carefully passed it down to them. Everyone else marshalled the cases and trunks through into the house's entrance hallway and gazed around at the panelled interior in shy wonder while the Professor paid their driver and wished him a safe journey back to London.

He joined Clare and the Vermont's in the hallway and shut the great door behind him, saying, 'We need to get out of these travelling clothes and make ourselves more comfortable; then I think a spot of lunch would be just perfect.' He raised his voice, 'Hello, there, you have guests! Is anyone about? Hello the house!'

He was answered by a clattering of boots and two aproned women came up from below stairs, one wiping her hands on a tea towel and the other adjusting a neat little cap on her carefully styled chignon. She strode forward with a stern expression on her bony features, but as she drew closer, she slowed, leaned forward to better see the Professor, and raised her eyebrows. A gentle smile of recognition lit up her face.

'My lord,' she breathed, 'welcome home, sir. We've been waiting for you all this while, and here you are! You're right welcome, a sight for sore eyes indeed. You've hardly changed at all, sir.' Her eyes told the lie to her statement. She was gazing at the Professor's silken locks, once tawny as a lion's mane and now silver as mid-winter frost.

He strode forward and took her narrow shoulders in his long, elegant hands, 'Neither have you, Jenny, lovely as ever. And it's good to see you too, Millicent. You're looking fresh as the blossom in spring. Now, ladies, I'd like to present my wife, this is the Lady Clare Whitekirk.' The women curtsied to Clare and she felt her ears burn with embarrassment. Being the Professor's wife was taking some getting used to.

The Professor continued, 'We'll need to sort out our sleeping arrangements. Clare and I will be in the master bedroom, of course. I'd be grateful if you could please show Mr and Mrs Vermont to the blue room. Marple is looking after a young girl called Shelagh just now, she will be in the yellow room, once she has finished answering her call of nature. Can we presume on you for a bite or two of lunch in say, twenty or thirty minutes?'

Jenny bobbed and made a little bow, 'Shall we prepare the dining room, sir? I'd have to light a fire but it's no trouble.'

The Professor graced her with his most charming smile, 'Come on, Jenny, you know me better than that. Sort out the long table in the kitchen and join us for lunch. I want to hear your news and we have a few things to share with you too. Be best to tell all over a bowl of soup and a fresh loaf of your good white bread, don't you think?'

Jenny chuckled, 'You are you, sir, and no mistake. The zebra can't change its stripes nor the leopard his spots, and that proves it. You always did prefer your food hot on hot down in the kitchen. But what is it you've got to tell us, sir? And where's master Martin? He's normally by your side, glued to you like your own shadow. Isn't he here?'

'It's a long story and that's what we need to discuss. You see we might need to defend ourselves against a terribly wicked man who intends to do us harm.

We escaped from him in London, but we must prepare a reception in case he follows us here. You might want to be elsewhere for a while, at least until we've dealt with it.'

Jenny folded her arms, 'We never run away while your parents were here, sir, and I can't see us running away now you've come home. No, sir, don't think on it for one minute.'

She turned to her colleague, 'Millicent, if you would kindly help the master with his things and show Mr and Mrs Vermont to their room. I'll get lunch and set the table ready.' She almost wriggled with barely contained happiness as she made her way towards the stairs with a lightness in her stride.

From the top step she looked back at the Professor and shook her head as if she couldn't believe he was really there, 'It feels right champion to see you back where you belong, sir. Lunch will be ready in twenty minutes.'

21

Porewit made his way from Trafalgar Square to the squalid, crowded streets of Seven Dials and St Giles. He slipped through the noisesome mob of drunken rowdies congregating there, and headed into the dark chasm of Great Earl Street. All the while he was stalked by the Vadhaka. After a few dozen yards Porewit reached an alleyway that stank as if it had been used as a public toilet since its stones had first been laid in the early sixteen nineties.

When he checked to ensure he wasn't being observed he missed the faint scarlet blur as the assassin faded into the shadows. The Vadhaka watched while the diminutive figure darted off the main thoroughfare into the narrow lane, then, moving fast he gained the entrance to the passageway just in time to see the Sprite lowering a paving stone over his head as he vanished underground.

The Vadhaka slithered silently to the slab. If he hadn't seen it with his own eyes, he wouldn't have believed that the stone had ever been moved. All around him he heard the urgent rustling sounds of large rats as they scurried away from him. Rats recognise a dangerous predator when they see one. Whether it's a starving hound with a taste for rat meat, a feral cat that wants to play, or a scarlet demon risen from the pit, they run for safety.

He waited long enough for the Sprite to be clear of the entrance, then levered the stone up to reveal a narrow, worn stairway leading down into darkness. He stepped down and carefully closed the slab behind him, making no sound. Sprites find their way through their tunnels using the blue illumination of the pneuma, a living force that recognises and cares for them. It quickly spotted the Vadhaka for what he was, and plunged him into darkness.

The assassin allowed his senses to reach out into the utter blackness, and slowly, like dry tinder coming to life, the red flame of his eyes shone bright until he was able to jog along the tunnels with confidence. He heard a fluttering noise. It sounded as if flocks of small birds were winging around above his head but he could see nothing except the woven roots, compacted earth, and ancient rocks of the tunnel walls. He ignored the sound and carried on.

When he reached a fork in the tunnels, he always sought out the well-trodden path. He was a born hunter who believed he was hot on the scent, but for once he was wrong. The tunnels had been the home for the Epimeliad clan for long centuries. Like the pneuma the tunnels were also alive, and acted as a protective shield for the Sprites. In following the illusion of well-trodden paths, the Vadhaka was actually being led away from Porewit and the great reservoir at the heart of the underground maze.

Meanwhile, word of his arrival had been telegraphed to Penelope. The fluttering sound was not the wings of birds but the whispering voice of the pneuma which was passing information regarding the Vadhaka's whereabouts to Penelope's cave. She and the young wizard stood at the mouth of the cave and listened to the news that a crimson-eyed hell beast had entered the tunnels, but was being led a merry dance to buy them all some time.

Porewit burst out of an archway and raced across one of the arrow straight bridges until he reached Penelope's side. He was breathless and his eyes wide with horror and shame.

Panting he gasped, 'He followed me from Seven Dials! How could he do that? I didn't see him behind me and I swear I was looking hard as always. He was right behind me, the pneuma told me. Can this demon creature make himself invisible?'

He glanced at Kingswraith, 'After what you said he did to Okeanus, Boss, I've got to wonder what he might have done to me if he'd caught me.' He shuddered, 'What can we do? What are we going to do?'

Kingswraith sounded resolute, 'I've had an idea. My guvnor has a house out in Oxfordshire, it's the Whitekirk family estate. He'd welcome you there. The grounds have acres of unspoiled woodland where you can vanish until all this is over. Can you get there?'

Penelope was wearing her mature form. She was almost as tall as Kingswraith and beautiful as an autumn day. Her thoughtful eyes glittered with points of amber, gold and emerald. She nodded.

'Yes, I know of it. That is the home of my sister's clan. Eurynome might allow us haven there for a while, but we can't presume on her hospitality. I will ask her permission through the conference tree. Please, both of you, wait for me at the heart of our reservoir. I will need to abase myself to her, and I'd rather you didn't have to see that.'

Kingswraith followed Porewit back to the broad stone platform in the centre of the reservoir's black waters and took a seat on the marble sarcophagus that had been his bed while he was recovering from his fatal encounter with Haven

Slighe. Porewit hopped up beside him. The Sprite had recovered his breath, and with it some of his courage.

He growled unhappily, 'The Lady won't be happy about asking any favours from Eurynome, I can tell you that. Having to go begging, that's not her style, no it's not her style at all. This will leave a proper bad taste in her mouth an' all.'

Kingswraith replied, 'Why? Surely you are all family? Would any sister turn away her family at a time of desperate need?'

The Sprite leaped off the marble and turned to look up at the wizard, 'It's like bees, see? You can only have one queen in the hive, and for us there can only be one queen in a forest. That means there can only be one queen to any clan. Never more. The Lady Penelope has been queen of London since it was all trees and ice, since before the wetlands and long before the city sprouted up like weeds. Her roots are dug deep here; deep down to the heart. This is her home; it can only ever be her home. Surely you can see that?'

Kingswraith pressed his fingers through his chestnut curls, his face a mask of confusion. 'So,' he said, trying to think of a tactful way to ask his question. His mind was filled with the thought of Penelope as a queen bee and the clan of Sprites as her drones. 'So,' he repeated, 'how do you get baby Epimeliads?'

Porewit coloured slightly, 'Well, it's a secret,' he replied. 'But you know about the birds and the bees and the things they do?'

Kingswraith had read up on the subject, 'Well, yes.'

'Right,' said Porewit, 'well, it's not like that. It's more like acorns and trees than the birds and the bees. But,' and he lowered his voice, 'there have been times when we've been with humans, and then things get confusing. There've been hybrid births, six months after the act. Men have made children happen to the queens; and Sprites have left human womenfolk with offspring. It's passing rare, but we're close enough in nature for it to happen.'

'Six months? But surely childbirth takes nine months!'

'Not always, especially not when the baby shouldn't be there. The female passes the fully formed child as quickly as possible. She delivers a halfling, a hybrid, quick as she can. And that's the thing, see. That halfling blood, that never gets diluted. It gets passed down from generation to generation, see. Some never know it, but we do. We know the signs.'

He gave Kingswraith a sly glance, 'Yes, we know the signs alright.'

He spun at the sound of a measured step and they both watched as Penelope drew near. Complex emotions were chasing each other across her flawless face. Kingswraith held his breath, thinking that the Oxfordshire queen must have turned down her request. His mind was racing, trying to think of an alternative option.

Penelope sighed, then said, 'Porewit, there's no time to waste. Assemble the clan and gather everything you'll need for a journey. I don't want any of us left behind to meet the Vadhaka. You're going to the Oxfordshire Whitekirk glades, Eurynome has accepted my pledge. You will be made welcome in the old way; she has given her word. Get going.'

The Sprite scurried away at high speed. Kingswraith and Penelope watched him vanish back through the archway to the tunnels from where he would head out to muster the clan. The pneuma would ensure he didn't have to face any unpleasant, Vadhaka shaped surprises. It was only a matter of time before the wolf-like killer found his way to the reservoir, but before that happened London's Epimeliad clan must be far away.

Kingswraith asked, 'Does he realise that you're not going to Oxfordshire?'

Penelope didn't answer at first, then she said, 'I told him that the clan would be made welcome in the old way. That means that while they are there, they will be subject to Eurynome's will. I could not accept that and she would not expect me to. Long ago we declared war on each other, as humankind wars with itself. The old way was established to end such conflicts, but there can never be two queens in any forest. That's the way of it.'

'What will you do?'

She shrugged, 'I shall go to my tree, I will be safe there. You must leave here too, Lord Kingswraith. Until your stave is finished you will be as helpless as any rabbit in the snare. This Vadhaka is a powerful force, an evil creature forged outside nature. You will need all your strength and more if you are to have the slightest chance of surviving your encounter.'

'May I escort you to your tree? I don't want to leave you here alone, not now.' The young wizard's gaze explored her face as if trying to imprint every contour to his memory. He had never seen her looking so subdued, so grave. She seemed to be marshalling her energies. She returned his look, and something inside him grew cold.

'No,' she said, 'no, you are the lure. I will not dare be caught with you until I understand this hunter more clearly. I must discover more about this Vadhaka, and I have my ways. You are in danger, true, but you also bring danger to everyone around you. Find somewhere safe until your stave is ready. If you must, pull the world up around your ears and vanish. I'll find you when it's time, and then we shall wage battle in ways the world has never seen before.'

She reached up and touched his cheek, her smile was strained. 'This was not the way I would have brought you to your legacy, Lord Kingswraith. But if we survive this, we shall face the Umbra with greater confidence than ever before. They thought to bring ruin down upon your head, but, perhaps, they have brought you a lesson you needed to learn. As must I. Now, please, go. There are things I must do alone.'

Penelope waited until the young man had waved for the last time from the archway and entered the tunnels and she was alone in the reservoir. She walked to the edge of the stone platform and gazed down into the inky waters. 'Old friend and master,' she said, 'what must I do now? What can I do now?' And the still surface of the reservoir waters stirred, rippled and opened before her.

22

The Vadhaka finally decided to follow his nose instead of his eyes. The well-trodden path gambit had led him nowhere and his hunter's instinct told him he was being taken for a fool. It was time to gather the reins back into his own hands, to take control of his situation and be led by his nose, which was an incredible tool. The average human has about five to six million scent receptors and can differentiate between a trillion different smells. Humans can scent a forest fire from over sixty miles away, we are quite amazing. But we humans are nothing compared to him.

The Vadhaka's sense of smell was more like that of a wolf. He had approximately 280 million scent receptors, with the added bonus that he could 'scent' magical creatures. He also has preternatural hearing, can taste his prey on the air, and his blood red eyes have a layer behind the retina called the tapetum lucidum that sampled any light source twice, no matter how faint. This was then boosted by his talent so he could see quite well in total darkness.

As an apex predator he was more like a human-shaped throwback to the most evolved carnivorous dinosaurs than anything else on the planet; and although he had not one single ounce of mercy in his psychological make-up, he did the terrible things he did without conscious cruelty. The Vadhaka might think of himself as an artist who worked with pain, but he had been designed as the most superb killing machine ever to stalk the planet.

Only death would stop him, and he was very hard to kill. The hand that had fashioned him was now nothing more than cold dust blowing in the deep desert. The cellar workshop where he had been crafted had been ground to a fine powder in the mortar of time. Little remained of the great city where his creator had once lived; its stupendous stone walls were reduced to drifts of pale grey sand rolling across ancient dunes. It had vanished. He survived.

His were the last eyes to have explored that civilisation's wonders. Only the Vadhaka remained of those who had once walked those forgotten streets. He remembered everything, but he had no-one with whom to share those memories. He was unique – and utterly alone.

He was the quintessence of his deadly craft, and every death was a poem to pain – when he had enough time. In his hands, death became a release and the most consummate joy. Ending another's life well was his greatest gift, but those who stumbled across his victims afterwards might not agree. Even the hardest hearts shrank in horror at the bloody results of his work.

Down in the labyrinthine maze under the streets of London he knew he had been led astray by the Sprites' tunnels but he felt no frustration or anger. Such emotions would cloud the perfection of his mind. He dismissed the deceptive visual trails and followed the olfactory path instead. The tunnels were still attempting to impede his progress, but now, when he found himself in a dead end with his path blocked by tightly woven roots, he quickly cut his way through and continued to follow the scent of Kingswraith's magic.

At last, he stepped through an arch and found himself in a vast echoing chamber. It was a reservoir. Even his night-attuned eyesight could not quite fathom its immense dimensions. Slender pillars rose up out of black waters and finished far overhead in delicate arcs of decorated stone. He recognised the architectural skill of the Romans, a fairly recent empire.

Before him stretched a slender bridge, which barely rose above the level of the water. Its surface had been polished to a high gloss by centuries of footfall. The bridge ended at a platform on which was a stone bench. On the bench sat a young girl dressed in black. She was slender as a reed with a mane of sable hair, fine and glossy as a silk flag. Her prettily gamine head was poised on her elegant white column of a neck.

The Vadhaka had no real appreciation for female beauty, not even the fleeting butterfly beauty of an adolescent, but he recognised the aesthetic lines of a well-formed animal and she was a gem of her species. He started towards her making no attempt to quieten his footsteps. As he drew closer, he slowed slightly. The girl ignored him. Her eyes seemed focused on the distance as if she was lost in thought, completely immersed in a world of her own making.

She took no notice of his approach until he was standing directly in front of her and completely blocked her view. She raised her eyes to his face and tilted her fine head, first to one side, and then the other, as if she was studying him. She had a delicate, fragile air. For some reason she reminded him of a small woodland creature.

'How very sad,' she said, her voice as soft and seductive as the wind soughing through a forest. The Vadhaka felt it then, the charm calling to him. She was trying to enchant his mind with her subtle glamour. He shrugged it off.

'Does it hurt,' she asked, 'to have your eyes bleed like that? Are they as sore as they look? I have a tincture that might calm the inflammation and reduce the redness, if you like. I could administer it now if you take a seat next to me. You needn't be afraid; I won't hurt you.'

His smile would have given a tiger pause for thought, wolf-like and sharp as a blade. He spoke quietly with a threatening edge to his voice, 'Where's Kingswraith? I followed one of your people to this place and your talented maze tried to lose me in its tunnels; a clever trick. But I can smell him. He was here, you can't deny it. I can smell him. Over everything else I recognise his distinctive scent.'

The girl shook her head as if he was a silly child asking all the wrong questions. She shrugged, 'I don't know where he is. He was here, yes. But we knew you were coming and he's gone. He'll pick his own time and place to meet you. He's gone where you can't find him, and I'm afraid I don't know where that might be.'

She studied the back of her right hand as if admiring it, and giggled, 'You know, it might be better if you didn't look for him. He's very skilled and very powerful. It might be dangerous for you to meet him. That's just a friendly warning, by the way. Please, don't think of it as a threat.'

A new voice spoke from behind him and he turned to find himself facing a tall, slender woman, a glorious, more mature creature. She too was beautiful, and she shone with all the golden colours of autumn. But she was looking him straight in the eye. Like any predator the Vadhaka's hackles rose if another creature looked directly at him. He perceived it as a challenge and growled a warning from deep in his throat.

The woman maintained her gaze and said, 'I know what you are and who sent you. But there's no-one here you can harm, not anymore. My clan has gone to ground, and the Lord Kingswraith and his household have escaped you. Your hunt is finished before it begins, Vadhaka. You are beaten. Go now and tell your Umbra masters how you have failed them. You're an intelligent creature, surely you must realise when the game is lost.'

All the while her stare remained fixed on his, her large, slightly almond shaped eyes scintillating with bright shards of hazel, green and gold. The growl in his throat grew in pitch until it became a roar. This woman was mocking him, and that could never be allowed. He decided he would wring the truth from her if he had to pluck it from every nerve in her body. She must know where Kingswraith was hiding.

He flicked a force blade at her arm, snarling, 'Very well! Let's see how much you know once your blood starts spurting from your veins. I've seen you people bleed.'

He fully expected the limb to fall to the ground, to see purple blood fountain across the stones and the woman to cry out in shock. But nothing happened. The woman gazed at him for a moment longer, and then examined her arm with interest, lifting the flawless and undamaged limb into the air. She flexed her nimble fingers and gestured like a dancer. His head followed her movement as if hypnotised.

She said, 'I see no blood, but that was a neat trick of yours all the same. You twist space into a blade and throw it. Kingswraith can do something similar. He developed a carmini he calls Cultro. Perhaps one day you should swap notes with each other. That would be so much better than fighting like boys in the schoolyard, don't you think? Much more civilised.'

He scythed two more force blades at the impossible woman. Behind her he saw one of the stone pillars scored by a pair of deep gouges. It was obvious that his talent was working as powerfully as ever, but the woman remained unharmed. He reached out to grip her throat, but his hand passed right through her without so much as a ripple. With a roar he flung both of his fists into her face but his knuckles hit nothing but air.

The little girl giggled behind him and he turned on her, breathing heavily. It was not in his nature to harm children unless he had been paid to, but she might prove just the bargaining chip he needed. If he threatened to hurt the child, it might prove the lever he needed to prise the truth from the woman.

He lunged at the girl with all his strength, his fingers extended like claws to rend her tender flesh. Instead, they passed through her and struck hard against the stone of the bench with a terrible crunching noise. He fell to his knees pressing his hands into his armpits.

Three of his fingers had been badly dislocated by the strike, and the agony shot painfully up his arms like a jolt of electrical fluid. He groaned, got to his feet, and yanked the fingers back into place with loud cracks. He paused and quietly considered the two female shadows. They were taunting him. They returned his scrutiny with equal curiosity, as if waiting patiently for his next mistake. The older female was right, he was intelligent enough to know when he was wasting his time.

He snarled at them, and was pleased to see them flinch, 'You want me to think of you as illusions, but you are much more than that. You've answered me and responded to my questions without pause. That means you must be right here, in this place, somewhere.'

He took a deep breath through his nose and licked at the air, 'I can sense the traces of living things, the air is rank with it, but I can't find you. So be it, I don't have time for this, not yet. But once I've finished with Kingswraith I promise I will come back; and I will find you. Then I shall demonstrate my craft. There's little profit in revenge, but I shall make an exception in your case. I shall grant you the sweet pleasure of death, you've earned it.'

He grinned and offered them a mocking bow. His crimson eyes burned with the fire of pure malice. He raised his face to the ceiling and drew another deep draught of air into his nose, held it, and then exhaled, tapping his index finger against his nostrils.

'I have him now,' he crooned, 'his is a very distinctive scent. I could follow him as far as the walls of Timbuktu and tear them down to drag him from his hiding place, if I had to. But no, he is closer than that. Much, much, closer. His hour glass is almost empty. And when his last grains of sand have fallen, then I shall return to deal with you. Ladies, adieu.'

He strode swiftly back across the bridge to the tunnel mouth. From her hiding place Penelope watched him leave. It was a long time before she felt safe enough to emerge from the waters and climb back onto the platform. All the while her mind was racing. She desperately needed help, but she didn't know where to turn.

23

J eremiah Taylor ushered the red-eyed demon creature into his workshop as if he had been expecting him, and made him welcome. He offered him tea and bade him sit down so they could converse at leisure.

'You are lucky, Vadhaka. I have no pressing work at present, so I am entirely at your service. How may I assist you? Do you wish to commission something beautiful and exotic? I'll admit it has been quite a while since I fashioned something for a practitioner like you. So, pray tell me, how may I please you?'

The Vadhaka licked the air, 'You have been visited by Kingswraith, you cannot deny it.'

'My friend, why should I? I recently completed a commission for him, silversmith work. Very fine work too, just as I would for your gracious good self. What would you have me make for you? Challenge me, I enjoy a challenge.'

'Then, where is he?'

'I have his address here, somewhere.' Taylor opened a drawer in his desk and fetched out a beautifully tooled, leather-bound ledger. He thumbed through the pages, 'Ah, here it is, yes, Owl's Tower, Cheyne Row, Chelsea. Would you like me to write it down for you?'

'When was he here last? I know it was recent.'

'Why, quite early this very morning. He collected his walking stick. I had completed the silverwork on it. A very handsome piece. I can show you the drawings if you like. The core is pure silver, just as he insisted. I told him that the metal would be soft and might wear quickly, but he wanted the purest silver and nothing else would do. You know what young men of breeding are like. Once their minds are made up nothing can gainsay them.'

'Tell me, silversmith, why do I smell magic here?'

From the shadows of the forge a girl stepped through the workshop doorway and advanced into the light. Her eyes were large and tilted upwards in the Slavic manner. They were as iridescent as a Buprestidae or jewel beetle's carapace. Her hair was a wild mop of midnight curls, tousled around large and slightly pointed ears. The living embodiment of an elf, her slender body vibrated with barely contained energy, but she carried herself with sober dignity and feminine elegance.

She offered a brief bow to the room then went to stand at Jeremiah Taylor's side. At no time did she allow her gaze to challenge the assassin, keeping her eyes demurely lowered. 'I believe you have sensed my presence, Vadhaka. I protect this man and this forge. I am Brigid of the deep wells, and I mean you no harm.'

The assassin returned a respectful bow, whispered, 'My lady', and left the workshop without another word. Jeremiah Taylor took up his guest's abandoned enamel mug and sighed, 'Look at that, he didn't even drink his tea. I wonder why not? I make good tea.'

Brigid placed a proprietary hand on his broad shoulder, 'You're a good man, Jeremiah. He didn't come for your tea; he came for information. He would have tortured you until he learned what he wanted to hear or became convinced you had nothing to tell him. Then he would have tortured you some more until death came as welcome release. It's what he does.'

'Poor man, to live such a life.'

'No, my friend, no. He's not a man. You can no more pity him than you can pity the knife in a murderer's fist. He is a living tool that was fashioned for a single purpose a long, long time ago. He was created back when magic was unrestrained, feral. Before even the circle of Viventem Nominis Umbra set their toxic claws on the world. The Vadhaka is unique, and we must thank God that there is only the one of him.'

She touched the tips of her slim fingers to the tears rolling down Jeremiah Taylor's leathery skin, then gently kissed his heat scarred cheeks, 'I stepped from the shadows to save your great heart, my dear friend. And yet you mourn the devil creature that would have burst it with torments you cannot begin to imagine. You are the gentlest prince amongst men, Jeremiah Taylor. That you exist at all gives me hope that humankind might be saved.'

The silversmith's voice was gravelly with emotion, 'To create such a terrible thing. That, and only that was the crime. Can you blame the blade when the killer thrusts it into his victim? The steel is innocent. Metal is just metal after all. I weep that so much art was put to such a terrible use, and I weep for that poor creature all alone and still condemned to do its master's bidding after all these years. How could I not pity him?'

140

He pulled a surprisingly clean handkerchief from his apron pocket, blew his nose then dabbed at his eyes. He said, 'He says he is looking for Kingswraith. The day after tomorrow that young fellow will return here to collect his stave from Christopher. My son is weaving sky metal into the wooden outer fabric of the silver staff. I think nothing like it has been made since Myrddin Wyllt walked the mountains around Cadbury. I do hope that fine young fellow will stay safe until then.'

'Where is Christopher?'

'He's at the bell foundry in Whitechapel. You know I couldn't allow him to forge iron here, it would contaminate my workshop. The people at the foundry are happy to let him work there, in return he will do some chores for them. They are fine craftsmen; their bells sing with the voice of angels. See, look, I have a little one here.'

He handed Brigid a bell set to a wooden handle and she swung it. The peal was as pure as anything she had ever heard, and, in her mind's eye, she followed the sound's signature almost two miles to Whitechapel and found the workshop where it had first been forged. There she discovered Christopher weaving an intricate web of extruded sky metal wire into the outer fabric of Penelope's wooden sheath. Brigid carefully reached out and poured some of her own essence into the stave.

Christopher gasped when he felt the staff thrill with raw electricity under his hands. One of the nearby workers turned from his bellfounding when the boy leapt to his feet with both of his tingling palms tucked under his armpits.

The man asked, 'What is it, Christopher? That walking stick just bit you or something?'

Christopher shook his head and grinned, 'No, but I think it just got struck by lightning or was visited by a ghost. It was passing strange. I swear it felt alive; it moved.'

The owner of the bell foundry, a man called Malachi Jessop, laughed, 'You're turning into one of us, my friend. I'd swear on me daughter's life that the bells talk to me when I'm here on me own. That's a fancy piece you're working on there, fine work. It's just giving back a bit of the love you've put into it, mate! Giving a little something back, that's all.'

Over in Taylor's forge in Candlewick, Brigid clearly heard the exchange between Christopher and the bellfounder in Whitechapel. She chuckled, which

Jeremiah thought must be due to the charming purity of the bell she had rung, and he laughed with her.

She handed the sweet-sounding bell back to him, 'Bless you, and may God keep you and your son, Jeremiah Taylor. I must go now, but I will always come to you if you need me. Remember, I will always be at your side.'

As she faded away into the shadows the silversmith put his big, calloused hand over his heart, 'And God bless you too, my Lady, God bless you, too.'

Drifting up from the silversmith's workshop Brigid glided swiftly along in the wake of the Vadhaka. She knew that the creature's keen nose was capable of sniffing Kingswraith out and he had to be stopped. She caught up with the scarlet killer as he swept down onto the Embankment, his head in the air and his red eyes glowing with the excitement of the chase. He had clearly found Kingswraith's scent and was hot on the wizard's trail.

He turned north towards Charing Cross and then carved a path through the crowds on Trafalgar Square. People stepped to one side at his approach as if they sensed the deadly strangeness radiating from the scarlet-clad man in his wide-brimmed hat. He was moving faster now; he could taste his prey on the breeze and knew he was drawing closer.

He stalked along Coventry Street, entered Piccadilly, and came to a stop. The roads were a torrent of clattering horse-drawn traffic, and the pavements overflowed like swollen rivers, bursting with an endless stream of pedestrians. The Vadhaka slowed his headlong pace. Even if they wanted to people couldn't step out of his path without getting bowled over by a growler or stamped flat by a dray. His passage was blocked by their sheer weight of numbers.

Brigid could sense his growing frustration as he tried to push his way forward. That was when she struck. The Vadhaka suddenly lost Kingswraith's scent. It was as if it had been drowned by the rank miasma of fresh horse manure, unwashed humanity and rank city dust.

When he attempted to recover his bearings, he was buffeted by masses of pedestrians blindly pushing past him. Caught like a tiger in a stampede of buffalo, he turned and fled back towards Trafalgar Square, seeking to find the last place he had been certain of his line.

But he found no trace of his prey. Brigid had foiled the hunt by washing Kingswraith's scent from the air. Her element was to water as Penelope's was to the forests. And Brigid was much more powerful. The Vadhaka had abandoned Jeremiah Taylor's workshop because he had recognised her potency. In her he had felt the immense energy of the oceans and the deep waters of the Earth. Even he knew not to challenge the mettle of a god.

She had told Jeremiah that her name was Brigid, and it was; sometimes. But in truth she was Amphitrite, goddess of the sea. She knew about Penelope and all the Epimeliad clans, just as she knew their cousins, the water Sprites of the submerged Doggerland forests. They were good people. And she took special care of such rare souls, people who lived without selfishness or greed. Souls that shone like bright lanterns in the darkness; like Jeremiah and his son Christopher. She would never allow that light to be extinguished.

If Jeremiah cared about Kingswraith, Brigid/Amphitrite would care for the young wizard too. She waited and watched the Vadhaka as he wandered around the streets of Piccadilly and Pall Mall, snuffing and licking at the air like a lost hound, dashing in futile haste after the least trace of any promising scent. When she was absolutely certain he was completely confounded she followed her own lead to the heart of Green Park and eventually reached a fine old oak tree.

Brigid could not make herself invisible, but she could transform her substance into mist or a cloud. In such a form she had floated after the Vadhaka, and now, as a mist, she settled down into the oak's branches, before manifesting as a green clad elf perched on a bough.

She chuckled, 'If Penelope's tree allows you to perform magic like that while you hide in its branches, it must like you a lot. It shields the Epimeliad clan from harm as best it can, including from potentially dangerous invisible wizards concealed in its canopy. So, it must have welcomed you into its family. Is that true, Lord Kingswraith?'

A strikingly handsome young man appeared slowly on an adjacent branch. He came into focus like a glass photographic plate developing. It took a few seconds for him to become fully established, but soon he was as solid as the rough bark on which he sat. He studied Brigid with intense curiosity.

'You have me at a disadvantage, miss,' he said.

'Then we have much to discuss. You may call me Brigid, if you like. I am a friend of Jeremiah Taylor's. He is worried about you and I have just come from his forge to find you. Now, please, follow me. I shall take you to a place of safety, a place where you can sleep and while away the hours until you are

143

ready to face the Vadhaka. I should like to spend a little time with you, get to know you better if I may. But first let's get you down from this tree.'

24

The day after they arrived at Whitekirk Hall the Professor and Clare retired to the library and left the Chelsea and Oxfordshire households to come to their own amicable arrangements. Jenny had discovered a fellow cook in Mrs Vermont and they made their home in the kitchen; meanwhile Millicent took Shelagh under her wing and they twittered like songbirds as they set about making the Hall that little bit cleaner and more comfortable.

Marple and Wills had chosen to address a number of maintenance jobs around the house, things Marple had intended to deal with, but, he said, his other duties had always come first. He was more than happy to take instruction from the ever-practical Wills. Wills was a quiet man, he only spoke when he had something to say, and the garrulous Marple filled the silences with anecdotes about the Professor's family, including the mystery of their deaths.

'The present Lord Henry was away in Chelsea studying botany or something equally high-brow when the whole family here was taken in a single day. The old Lord Henry and Lady Charlotte were out for a ride with little Charlotte, their daughter. The Grandfather, Viscount "Billy" he was taking a nap in the garden. He was found dead when Agatha, she was the housekeeper before Jenny, Jenny being just a housemaid then, took him some tea.'

Wills realised that when Marple started talking he stopped working, and that he never stopped talking. Wills sighed and began repairing a broken sash window that looked as if it had been neglected for some considerable time.

Marple continued, 'We'll never know what happened to the family, the coach was found wrecked and overturned with the three of them dead underneath it. The horses were never seen again. That's the mystery, you see. What happened? It was a straight road, quiet like, and a fine day. But something must have spooked those horses into a mad dash, and that was the end of all of them, all but the young Lord Henry. Horrible.'

His voice became grimly confidential, 'But there's the mystery. The mutton shunter who attended the scene, an Inspector he was, he said that the traces looked as if they'd been cut. And he didn't like the way the coach had been broken up. He said it didn't look like a crash but more like it had been smashed up, deliberate like.'

Wills was only listening with half an ear, but he said, 'Might it have been wild boar? I hear tell they can be dreadful fierce.'

Marple shook his head, 'No, we haven't seen wild boar about here for many a long year. Gentry ate 'em all back in the day, and I'm told they made wonderful meat too. And anyway, who ever heard of a wild boar cutting the traces like that? No, the County Coroner recorded the deaths as murder by person or persons unknown. Horse thieves I shouldn't wonder, otherwise what happened to those horses? Neither hide nor hair was ever found of them.'

Wills was a simple man who had no taste for any mystery. He asked, 'The only question I want answered today, Mr Marple, is whether we're going to thread the new sash cords for this window. I need you to hold the window while I unscrew the stock beads, then we take the window out and I'll unscrew the panels to get at the weights. You ready to help? Or are we just here to chat? Just so's I know.'

Elsewhere Millicent was learning a lot about Shelagh's unique approach to the English language, which she considered charming and entertaining in equal measure. They were airing rooms that had lain vacant for a number of years and clearing great colonies of spiders from above cupboards and the corners of ceilings. Shelagh was only happy doing this when there was an open window through which she could release the spiders into the wild.

She was telling Millicent about the young Master Kingswraith, whom, Millicent thought as she listened, sounded like the perfect blend of a London gentleman and a Knights Templar. Unlike Marple, Shelagh was adept at working and talking at the same time.

'He's much like that David sculpture I did see once. It were a plaster cast of course, of a sculpture by Mr Michael of the angels and he's from Italy. That's Mr Michael who's from Italy of course, not David. David is him from the scriptures who was handy with a sling. Master Kingswraith looks like him, although I've never seen him with a sling, of course. No. But I did learn how to use one for catching coneys. It's easy enough when you know how.'

She shook a pan full of spiders and cobwebs out of the window, then said, 'He was in the altogether, that David fellow was. Naked as a new-born babe, all apart from a big leaf someone had stuck on him. I did see Master Kingswraith like that too, when he was in the bath tub. Without never no leaf, mind. He were raw as a plucked chicken, ready for the pot."

146

She giggled wickedly, "I tell you I was that shocked I ran right into the doorframe. But I've never forgotten him in there, lord no. It's alright though, for he saw I in the cellar bath tub when that terrible man broke into the house and tried to do wicked things, so that's alright. We's even and square now. I've seen he and he's seen I, and so did that police inspector that time. Lord, what a fuss he made. He yelled and near wet 'imself.'

Her head spinning, Millicent wondered at the strange goings on in Chelsea. She found it hard to imagine a house where everyone was free to walk in and out of bathrooms like that; let alone have regular visits by Inspectors of police who might also catch the maid in her bath. Millicent decided that she would always lock her bathroom door in future, just in case.

Millicent studied the girl while she chattered away about all things Kingswraith, and she realised that Shelagh was on the cusp of flowering into womanhood. The maid had great poise, for all her girlish innocence, and she would be striking, if not downright beautiful, when she reached maturity.

Millicent had never experienced such exhausting animation and energy in another soul before, and she liked the way Shelagh addressed every task with earnest intelligence, for all that her mind seemed as light and flighty as the seeds from a dandelion clock.

In the library Clare was studying the shelves with keen professional interest. Her husband grinned, 'Some of those tomes date back from before the reformation. We were protected by the Catholic church back then, of course; but the fiercer reformists would have burned the books and then the owners. It's only since we entered the enlightened age that we've been able to display them so openly like this. Now then, let me show you something.'

He reached up to a small, leather-bound book on the top shelf of the stack Clare was examining. He moved part of the shelf to one side then levered the book out of its place. With a rumbling sound the bookshelf first rolled forward and then slid smoothly to one side. Clare found herself gazing through a secret doorway into a room with two small windows. It contained a single bunk, a desk and a chair. The wall to her left was filled with shelves and there was a simple but exquisitely carved wooden crucifix on the wall at the head of the bunk to her right.

She walked in and looked around in wonder, followed by her husband. He explained, 'The Catholic church always looked after us, so it only seemed fair to look after them in turn. This is our priest hole, and our sub rosa library. You now join Martin and I as guardians of our clandestine history. The household must never know, for their own protection. What if the culture of enlightenment came to an end? It's best we keep our secrets to ourselves.'

'But, darling, there are no books on these shelves! What great secrets are we keeping?'

'This.' The Professor reached out for an ornamental knob at one end of the moulding at the top of the wall above the shelves. He turned it anticlockwise and pulled, also tugging at one of the shelves. The entire assembly swung open to reveal a steep wooden stairway. A thick lacework of cobwebs, that would probably have kept Shelagh and Millicent busy for a week, billowed and fluttered as a gust of stale cool air flowed up through them.

'Oh dear,' said the Professor, 'must be the maid's day off.' He lifted the stave that now never left his side and intoned, 'Adolebitque telas araneæ solus.'

Pale flame rolled down the stairway, searing away years of intricate work by a well-established colony of spiders. The fire cleared away the webs but seemed to slide over the architecture without scorching it. When it reached the bottom of the steps it vanished, but Clare could still see its glow while it continued its work.

She gasped, 'Careful, my dear, you might burn the house down!'

The Professor chuckled, 'No, not a chance. I was very specific. I told the carmini to only burn the webs. This stave Kingswraith gave me is really quite remarkable, it provides an extraordinary degree of control. I would never have tried that before.'

'Right,' said Clare, 'and of course you've limited its effects to just this stairwell and whatever's down there. That's extremely clever of you, my darling, dear Professor. Brilliant work and beautifully done!'

When her husband didn't answer Clare turned on him and saw the mortified expression on his face. 'Oh no! What have I done?' he gasped.

Shelagh and Millicent had the window of the Chinese room open and were just about to swirl up some more arachnids and their homes when the dense cluster of webs vanished in a white bloom of transparent flame. Shelagh jerked back, fell off the chair she was standing on, and rolled across the carpet until she fetched up against a bedpost. She leapt to her feet and joined Millicent in the centre of the room.

They watched the pale blaze circle and dance around their heads, scorching everywhere the spiders had practiced their weaving. Nothing else was touched, not even when the webs closely threaded along the fragile lace curtains were burned away. When it was over the two women raced from room to room and examined every nook and cranny where one might expect to find cobwebs, but even down in the wine cellars no trace of a web remained.

Millicent gasped, 'Well, I never did!'

Shelagh pulled a face, 'I think the master has been trying some new folderol of a folly fiddle to do with spiders' webs and such. He's clever like that. Took a lot of learning he did.' Then she gasped in alarm, 'Quick, oh, quick, let's take a look outside.'

'Why?'

'Why? Because spiders 'as got a job to do same as housemaids an all, and the world would be a poor place without the little darlings. What if the Master's folly fiddlin' has burnt up all the spiders in the world, eh? Who would eat all the flies then? That's what I'd like to know.'

They found the litters of web and its occupants still safe and sound in the shrubbery where Shelagh had dumped them. She put a hand to her breast and sighed with relief, exclaiming to Millicent, 'Thank the Lord, he's only set it off indoors. Well then, now we've cleaned all the webs from the whole house and all, with a little bit of help as I'll freely admit, I reckon we've earned a nice cup of tea and a bit of Jenny's seed cake, don't you?'

At dinner that evening, everyone around the long table in the kitchen was talking about the mysterious pale fire that had demonstrated such an appetite for spiders' webs, but touched nothing else. Shelagh cast mischievous sideways glances at Clare and the Professor, as if daring them to come up with some mundane explanation. The Professor rose to the occasion like a champion by describing a scientific phenomenon he called 'St Elmo's Fire'.

'I've heard it's been seen in the rigging of ships, and is actually quite harmless. Perhaps Millicent and Shelagh have worked so assiduously that they created a wild static charge with their polishing cloths and sparked the flow of electrical fluid that has only scoured away the filmiest fabric in the house, ergo, those spiders' webs.'

Everyone at the table nodded sagely at this; Jenny even suggested that perhaps the girls shouldn't polish quite so hard in future. Only Shelagh remained silent. She regarded the Professor with pursed lips and an arch expression under raised brows. She looked as if she was sharing an arcane secret with him. He noted the shards of green light glittering in her hazel eyes and he heard Clare whisper, close to his ear, 'That girl is a proper fifteen-puzzle.' The Professor agreed completely.

25

Chatting all the while Brigid led Kingswraith across London Bridge and then turned east towards Shad Thames. They passed under the rows of brick bridges linking the top floor of warehouses on one side of the road to those on the other, and then descended to the Downing's Road moorings by Reed's Wharf. Kingswraith noticed that the brickwork of the warehouses was stained white with flour. He could also smell a heady melange of exotic spices on the air.

Work had recently begun on a major new bridge across the river Thames, but just a short way upstream from the scars of construction work the eye was inexorably drawn – through the thicket of masts belonging to the great cluster of ships moored within the Pool of London – to the sooty majesty of the Tower on the other side of the river.

Brigid walked out onto a pontoon and called 'Hello the boat' into the cabin of a heavily built barge, that Kingswraith estimated to be over a hundred feet in length. A powerful looking man stepped out and instantly snatched the floppy round cap from his balding head when he recognised his visitor.

He bowed low, and then turned to examine Kingswraith with intense curiosity. A sturdy looking woman wearing a grey headscarf on her greying hair and swathed in a bulky light blue woollen dress, topped with a short, pale grey canvas jacket, followed the man out on deck. They both wore heavy boots.

The woman also treated Brigid like visiting royalty, but bowed to her rather than curtseying as an Englishwoman might have done. She called out a question in a tongue that Kingswraith thought sounded European, but he couldn't be sure which country. He wondered why Brigid had brought him there. If this was meant to be a hiding place it seemed very exposed. They were standing in plain sight on a wharf, out in the open, and right by the busiest commercial stretch of the river Thames.

Brigid indicated the young wizard and asked a question in the same sing-song language the woman had used. Her face was very grave and her voice low. The man turned to his wife with a questioning glance, she, in turn, studied Kingswraith with a calculating look. Then she nodded and beamed at him. Something important had evidently been decided.

The man stepped up onto the pontoon beside Brigid and followed her back to where Kingswraith was standing. He stuck out a dry calloused hand which Kingswraith shook without hesitation.

Brigid explained, 'Kingswraith, this is Lucas Bakker and the good lady over there is his wife, Mirte. This craft is their beautiful Schuyt (Kingswraith heard it pronounced as Shoo-it) sailing barge. She's named Nova, on which, as I'm sure your nose has already told you, they earn their living by fishing for eels. They're two of the finest people I know, and they have agreed to look after you. I warned them that there might be danger but even so they insist you are very welcome.'

Kingswraith protested, 'No, but wait! It's not fair to risk these good people for my sake. I'm a complete stranger to them. I can't allow them to put themselves in harm's way to protect me. Thank them, it's wonderful and more than generous of them, but no. I couldn't let them do it.'

Lucas grinned and shouted something back to his wife, and then he addressed Kingswraith in perfect English except for a slight lisping burr on his 'S's, 'I told Mirte that a true gentleman would say no, and here you prove me right. Sir, you are welcome on my barge for as long as you like, and anyway, Mirte insists that you join us. You will soon find, as I did very early in our married life, that you might win a fight with the sea but you will never win an argument with Mirte. So then, that's settled. Have you ever sailed in a barge before?'

Brigid explained that the plan was for Lucas and Mirte to take Kingswraith down the Thames towards the North Sea and keep him well away from the Vadhaka's hunting ground. Yes, they would be accepting a certain degree of risk, but they would also be minimising any danger for the young wizard. The assassin principally hunted using his sense of smell and even the best hounds lose their line over water.

Lucas studied the sky towards the east and shook his head, 'That looks like a mighty rain storm brewing. Is the young man going to be alright if we hit foul weather? It can take some fellows very badly if the weather is not, as they say here, "up to dick". Perhaps we should rethink our plans and stay put with the young fellow under cover. What do you say, Lady?'

Brigid grinned, showing an impish flash of humour that Kingswraith found enchanting. She said, 'No, my good friend. There are forces at work that will bring those thunderheads around in a great circle to the north. They'll arrive here in the city later this evening. They won't trouble you, but London will have a good downpour it very badly needs. Those filthy streets will be washed as clean as a Queen's dinner plate.'

She turned her smile on Kingswraith, 'People here in the city will have to seek shelter if they want to keep their heads dry, but you'll have fair weather and friendly winds. You'll find the journey very agreeable, that much I can promise you.'

Kingswraith bowed to the inevitable and took his place on board. Lucas found him some clothes to change into for the voyage. They were plain but well made, and more than a little large around the waist. But they fitted snugly enough once they had been cinched tight with one of Mirte's leather belts. With one of Lucas's floppy round caps perched on his curls the wizard looked every inch the bargee, if you ignored his neatly buttoned and well-polished shoes. None of Lucas's footwear would fit him, the big man had small feet.

Brigid wished them a safe voyage, plain sailing, and 'deep water', which set Lucas and Mirte to laughing as if she had just told the best joke ever. Then she left them and strode purposefully back towards the centre of town. It was not just Kingswraith who needed protection; with the Vadhaka and the Umbra loose in London she feared that any number of the people she valued most might be in jeopardy and might need of her protection.

Kingswraith helped the Bakkers cast off, and while he did so he asked them what was so funny about Brigid's comment about deep water? Lucas promised he would explain everything once he had the Nova underway, there was no time to waste. He poled the boat away from the wharf and it drifted backwards, out onto the wide river. Then he expertly lowered the sails while Mirte took the tiller and pointed the Nova's bows eastwards.

The sails bellied and they were soon picking up speed, passing sooty rows of docks, wharfs and warehouses, steering around clusters of moored transports, heading first towards Greenwich, then Erith and finally on to the sea. The fresh yet rank smell of the river filled Kingswraith's nostrils and the heaving motion of the deck seemed to settle into his blood.

The thrill of the barge slicing smoothly through the water sang in his muscles, and he felt strangely relaxed. It was as if the deck of the barge had been his accustomed home in a previous life. Mirte relinquished control of the boat and disappeared into the cabin and Lucas took her place in the stern.

The boatman invited Kingswraith to take the tiller, showed him how it worked, and then began to explain everything anyone could ever need to know about his beloved vessel. Kingswraith discovered that he'd have to get used to a whole new language, and it wasn't Dutch. It was barge lore, and as arcane as any carmini.

He learned that the boat was a flat-bottomed shoal-draught Netherlandish sailing barge. That's why Brigid's wish that they should have deep water was so funny, Nova had been designed to navigate the Netherland's shallow rivers and canals. She was rounded or 'bluff' at bow and stern, and gaff rigged, which, Lucas explained, was very efficient and, 'Highly responsive in changeable weather, even at sea.'

What Kingswraith had at first thought to be spare rudders mounted on either side of the sturdy craft were in fact a pair of 'leeboards' which could be quickly raised and lowered into the water using an arrangement of blocks and tackles. These devices looked simple enough, but when Lucas explained what they were used for and why, it turned out that they were, in fact, a much more sophisticated arrangement than their plain appearance first allowed.

'You see, Nova has no keel. So, as a flat-bottomed boat she has poor water resistance, which means she can be blown sideways by the wind,' Lucas explained. 'If the wind catches her from either side, it will push her off course. We call that "leeway", and, that's why we call those things "leeboards".'

He rubbed his broad chin thoughtfully, 'Except, in fact, in the Netherlands we call them "Zwaarden", which in English means "swords". I don't know why we do that. They look nothing like swords, do they? I think they look more like big flat spoons.'

They both considered the carefully shaped wooden devices, and Kingswraith agreed, yes, they were nothing like swords.

Lucas continued, 'Anyway, see, if you drop the leeboard on the lee side, it acts as a keel and stops the wind blowing us off course. You have to be quick, but it works fine, and if the wind rolls the boat the leeboard goes deeper into the water, which makes it even more effective at controlling leeway.'

Kingswraith learned that the Schuyt's original design dated back to before the time of the English Queen, Elizabeth Tudor; and in the right hands they were fast enough to race. Traditionally, Lucas said with a fond smile, Schuyt sailing matches were held on the IJsselmeer and on the Wadden Sea during the calmer, fairer weather in May. He and Mirte had taken part when they were younger. But all that fancy stuff was behind them now.

As if conjured by the sound of her name Mirte appeared with three steaming mugs of strong sweet tea and a linen bag filled with large, hard, honey flavoured biscuits which the couple dunked in their tea until they were soft enough to eat.

Kingswraith refused the biscuits but welcomed the tea. He needed one hand free to concentrate on steering the blunt-nosed barge through the interweaving traffic on the Thames. Lucas kept a close eye on his protégé, and sometimes reached out and nudged the tiller when he suspected that his new steersman was cutting too close to another vessel, or, more often, when the other vessel obviously hadn't realised that there was a novice at the rudder and threatened to ram him.

Some of the great ships that passed them dwarfed the Nova. Their hulls loomed over her, large as floating cathedrals, and their wake rocked her like a toy boat on a pond. But Kingswraith was reassured when he saw that his hosts were unconcerned, even when something the size of a great fort brushed past them and the barge rolled like a drunken sailor in a barrel.

Once Kingswraith had gained sufficient confidence with the tiller Lucas was happy to leave him unsupervised for the time it took him to use both hands to stuff and light his pipe. Mirte fetched a flat wooden box from her pocket from which she extracted a neatly hand rolled, liquorice-coloured cigarette. She too lit up, and the couple quietly enjoyed their smokes while Kingswraith gazed around him at a London he had never before seen from such a vantage point.

He compared the relative freedom of the waterway to the crowded pavements and pell-mell, traffic-choked roads he had become accustomed to on land, and contrasted the slightly tainted water smell of the river with the constant harsh stink of ordure, smoke, soot, people, food, and horse manure that so permeated every street of the town that a Londoner either ceased to notice it or choked to death.

The Thames wasn't entirely free of the city's pollution, the water was dark, glossy and ripe with effluent, but even so he felt he could breathe more freely on the river. And it was easy to be quiet with his hosts. There was no pressure to be entertaining, no need to fill the silences with empty chatter. He had joined the Bakkers on their boat out of necessity, but he was beginning to realise how relaxing it was to share their easy company.

155

Lucas drew his pipe from his lips, blew a stream of sweet smoke at the sky, and observed, 'I think Nova likes you. She can be skittish with strangers, but she's settled to your hand very well. I also think the Lady is helping us a little, but you're doing fine, a natural bargeman. Let's see how you do when we reach Erith, and then, perhaps, we go out onto the open sea.'

'That sounds like a challenge, what shall I see there? Will there be seals, whales and dolphins? I should very much like to see dolphins.'

'Seals? Yes. Dolphins? Perhaps, if we're lucky. Whales? I've seen them, but they are rare. And if we're really lucky we might see the strangest and rarest sight of all.'

'Really, what's that?'

'Why, mermaids of course! What else?'

26

Later that day, at almost exactly the same hour that Kingswraith was steering the Nova into the Thames Estuary, and several hours after Brigid had watched Christopher at work on Kingswraith's stave, the young smith was still carefully letting the iron wires into the woven wooden fabric. It was slow and meticulous work and he was concentrating hard in the hope of getting the job done right and on time.

It was at that moment that something happened that stopped the young smith in the middle of his work and he cried out in alarm. It made him jump up from his seat and scramble several long steps away from the workbench. The one remaining bellfounder, Jessop, the foundry's owner, came to stand at his side and joined him in gazing at the staff. It was late in the day and the man was feeling more than a little tetchy. He was missing his wife and already late for his dinner. By the time he got home it would also be too late to read his daughter her bedtime story.

'What's going on there, now, Christopher? What hobgoblin have you brought into my foundry? Bells are sensitive to all sorts of vibrations, you know that. They're like hot house flowers, for all the brass in them. I tell you; you'd better not have brought some evil spirit into this place to queer the work or I'll have strong words with your dad. I will an' all.'

Christopher protested, 'No, no, it's nothing like that. I don't know what it is but it's nothing like that I promise you. Just take a look at that thing, master Jessop! Just look at what it's doing. I've never seen anything like that before, have you?'

The smith and the bellfounder stepped forward in unison and leaned over the stave. The bellfounder gasped, his eyes bulging from their sockets, 'Well, I never did. I'd never 'ave believed if I 'adn't seen it with me own eyes. That's witchcraft that is; proper burn 'em at the stake and duck 'em in the pond witchcraft. What is that thing you're meant to be making there anyway, young Christopher? And don't pretend it's no walking stick cause it ain't and that's a God afeared fact!'

Before their startled gaze the metal wires that Christopher had fashioned from the ancient Egyptian blade were weaving and embedding themselves into the fine wooden fabric that sheathed the pure silver rod. The unsupported stave was floating several inches above the workbench and the metal strands were flowing and spinning in intricate patterns along the length of it in a way that made Christopher think of ivy growing up a tree – but at high speed.

Jessop pushed his hand through his bronze-coloured hair, leaving it sticking up at odd angles. He spoke in hushed tones, 'I'll say one thing, young fellow me lad, you were doing a fine job before, but whatever that is, it's doing a better bit of smithing on its own than any beading I've ever seen. Look at it! As you say, it's like it's alive! How's that even possible?'

Christopher said nothing, his mind a blank. What could he say? His knees buckled and he knelt before the workbench, putting his hands together as if in prayer. He couldn't drag his eyes away from the impossibly intricate craftwork.

His words softened to an awed whisper, he said, 'Thank-you, Lady. If that's you, you'd make a right marvellous master smith. That work is better than any jewellery I've ever seen.'

When he heard a familiar voice behind him, he leapt to his feet and spun to face the great doors of the foundry. Brigid walked into the workshop as solemnly as if she was entering a church and drew close to the two men.

That evening was becoming all too strange for Jessop. There was the magic happening on the workbench, and that was plenty odd enough for any single day. Now this strange young girl calmly walks into his foundry as if she owned the place. She was the crazy cherry on the cake, more than enough to make a stuffed bird laugh. He wondered what might happen next.

Part of him was beginning to wish he'd risked the torrential rain and gone home at his usual time instead of staying behind to keep Christopher company. After all the deluge was all but over now, the thunderheads drifting north west towards Wales and taking the storm with them. He might have got away with little more than a slight dampening. He'd be home and warm by now. He'd have had little Jessica's story read, and there's be a nice plate of dinner in front of him while Agatha was telling him about her day.

But no, he'd stayed, and he had found himself caught up in a tale as would give Mr Charles Dickens serious pause for thought. Magic staves floating about in mid-air, wires weaving themselves as if they were alive, that was mad enough. But now in walks in this mysterious girl that Christopher was treating like a visiting Archbishop. If he didn't know better, he'd think himself the worst for the Chinese curse, drugged by the smoke from a happy pipe in a Limehouse den. The butter must have slipped right off his noodles and dripped onto the floor.

Then he asked himself, in all honesty, would he really have wanted to miss all this? No, he admitted, he wouldn't. And while he didn't recognise the visitor, a gifted bellfounder like Jessop was as sensitive as any of his creations. As she drew closer, he felt her energy resonating deep in his bones. It felt as if the world had tilted at an insane angle and this slight wisp of a girl had become his new centre of gravity.

Brigid nodded at Jessop and smiled, 'I promise you that Christopher has brought neither hobgoblin nor sorcery into your workplace, bellfounder. He has brought me, and I bless you. I bless your hands, and your foundry. If you remain true to your craft, your craft will always be true to you. Your wonderful bells will always ring to the welkin, alive with joy.'

Jessop felt the hair on the back of his neck stand on end as a strange sensation crept up his body from his feet to his scalp. At that moment he was truly glad he had worked late after all, and thought he understood why Christopher had felt it right to fall to his knees in prayer. 'Thank-you, Lady,' he replied, unconsciously echoing Christopher's words.

The girl nodded again, then directed her gaze at the young smith, 'I'm afraid we have no more time to wait for you to finish your work, my young friend. As I have in the past for your father, now I must do so for you. See, the work is done, the beading is complete. The sky metal is woven into the fabric of the staff.'

She reached out her hand and the stave leapt to her palm, 'With your consent I shall take this to the place where it is most needed. And trust me, I will justly praise your craft in the beginnings of it. Please, give my greetings to your father. Tell him I shall see him soon.'

Brigid then smiled at Jessop, 'Well met, bellfounder, I have no doubt we shall meet again. Fare thee well.' And with that she turned and walked out of the foundry. Gravity returned to normal and Jessop sat down suddenly on the floor, falling onto his backside and landing as hard as a dropped sack of flour. All the strength had momentarily drained from his legs. Christopher reached down and helped him back to his feet.

159

'I know how you feel,' he said. 'She takes me like that every time I meet her. When she's in the room the whole world goes all topsy-turvy. It's like everything starts mafficking about and having a party, you know? And there she is, right in the middle of it all, calm as a millpond. When she's in the room I feel as if I'm looking at myself through the wrong end of a telescope, do you know what I mean?'

Jessop rubbed at his rump and groaned, 'I don't know about any telescope, mate, Agatha won't need any telescope to think I've been kicked by a horse! How am I going to explain the bruise on my backside to my missus?'

'You won't,' said Christopher, still gazing towards the foundry doors through which Brigid had disappeared. 'That's the thing; as you'll soon see. You won't be able to talk about the Lady with anyone else, not unless they've met her too. It's like a secret club that only the members can talk about. Yes, you'll see. It's like the words dry up in your mouth and won't come out.'

'Yeah, I can see that right enough. And anyway, if I tried explaining what's been going on here to anyone they'd be after me with a net. They'd be sure to take us to a nice soft cell where we won't be able to hurt ourselves or anyone else. Come on, I think we're done for the day. You owe me a beer, matey, no, make that two. And I could go for a hot mutton pie and peas to wash it down with. I ask you, what a way to end a day, eh? What a day!'

Standing on the stone platform at the heart of the reservoir Penelope could feel magical energy growing closer in much the same way as you might hear a Salvation Army brass band long before you see it. But in this case, only if the instruments were being played by angels. She had also sensed the lethal, razor-edged essence of the Vadhaka as he approached, and she had hidden from him. This energy was different but she couldn't find a word to describe it.

Whoever – or whatever – was drawing near that evening was decidedly female. She brought the blended essence of the seagulls' cry and salt winds blowing across the marshes, fresh and wild at sunrise. She brought the tempest and the tides. She brought the beauty of lightning and the majesty of the distant horizon, wide as the Earth itself.

Brigid had decided not to keep to her disguise as a human girl while visiting the great reservoir home of the Epimeliad Queen of London. She stepped out from the maze of tunnels and crossed the bridge to the central platform with all her true poise and majesty. Amphitrite approached Penelope holding the stave out before her like a sceptre.

The seas surround every land on Earth and touch every nation. In her true form Amphitrite reflected the diversity of all humankind. Her skin was black as a Nubian's, her hair blond as a Scandinavian's. Her eyes were green as a red-headed Celt, and tilted at the corners like a Mongolian from the Steppes. She was both the living personification of all races, and completely unique.

Penelope chose to welcome her visitor arrayed in her true colours as Queen of her clan. She was cloaked in the russet shades of autumn, her hazel eyes flashing with shards of bright emerald, and her chestnut hair alive in an errant breeze that no other could feel. Together they were a sight as would break the heart of any mortal, and in them Shakespeare would have found the truth of his words, 'O brave new world, that has such people in 't!'

Penelope performed an elegant curtsey, 'My Lady,' she said.

Amphitrite bowed, her mouth curved into a smile, 'My Lady,' she echoed. 'It has been too long. May I kiss you?'

'As the sea kisses the shore, and welcome.'

Amphitrite chuckled, 'As a sister kisses a sister, I think.' And they embraced. It was only then that Penelope glanced at the finished stave and placed her palm on its surface.

She gasped and snatched her fingers way, 'It feels like bottled lightning! This is so much more than the staff Kingswraith first gave to Jeremiah Taylor. I fancy you have had some influence on its manufacture, my Lady.'

'Please call me Brigid, and I shall call you Penelope if I may. Yes, Christopher began the craft and I finished his beautiful work. But now we must get the stave to Kingswraith, there is no time to lose. He is on his way into the Thames Estuary on a barge called Nova. Can you speak with the Doggerland folk who live there and ask them to pass on a message for me?'

27

The Vadhaka regarded the second dead policeman slumped on the floor of Owl's Tower. The man's head was twisted into an impossible position, facing back between his shoulders. The Vadhaka realised he was building quite a collection of corpses. He briefly considered carrying them both to the door of the stairwell and throwing them down to the cellar bathroom, but rejected the idea. His first victim had bled so much that there was precious little point in trying to tidy up.

They could both stay where they were, surrounded by a growling cloud of feasting black flies. Flies liked the Vadhaka, he was a good provider. He had snapped the second policeman's neck with a single stroke in the very next instant after the man had tapped him on the shoulder with his truncheon and demanded, 'Ere, what are you a' doing of, fiddling about at the Professor's front door?'

The Vadhaka had propped the dead man against the door surround with one hand, opened the door with the other, then dropped the officer's limp body on top of his colleague's headless corpse. There was no sound of alarm from the empty streets. Good, he liked that. It was almost inspirational the way the neighbours in Cheyne Row turned a blind eye and a deaf ear to everything around them.

An assassin appreciates a little discretion while he works, and the denizens at the outskirts of Chelsea were proving ideal neighbours. Once he had concluded his business with Kingswraith he might even stay on for a while. The rank, metallic reek of blood had never bothered him, nor did the stench of death which was filling the house with its sweet, meaty odour. Such things were an everyday part of his assassin environment.

Death was the coin of his realm. If he'd ever had such a thing as a motto, it should have been 'Et capitibus vincere, ut huc illucque discurrerent ... perdet caput vestrum', 'Heads I win. Tails... you lose your head'. He always won. He wasn't vain or arrogant about his skill as a killer, any more than a shark or a tiger would be. But, just like the shark, he was perfectly designed to do what he did. And he did it superbly, deriving great artistic pleasure from it.

Kingswraith's scent was also strong in that house. This was the boy's home, his nest, his lair. The scarlet-eyed killer climbed up to the dining room and kitchen. He found some raw meat in the cold store and chewed at it while he ascended to the next floor. The meat's blood smeared his lips and teeth. Here he found two bedrooms and another bathroom. One bedroom was perfumed with a woman's scent and a neutral male musk.

The other bedroom, however, was saturated with Kingswraith's odour; young and fresh. The Vadhaka could taste the bright magic bleeding from the young man as intensely as he could taste the blood oozing from the raw hunk of meat between his teeth. He dropped the remains of his meal on the floor, drank some water from the wash basin, then lay down on the bed and breathed deeply, inviting his prey's essence to permeate all his senses at once.

He wanted Kingswraith's scent to be the last thing he could smell before slumber claimed him, and the first thing he would taste on rousing in the morning. And then he would go out into the city and find the boy. Nothing would mask him this time, nothing. The wizard and his household had been lucky so far; but their luck, like the sand in their hourglasses, was running out. There would be no escape.

He slept, and he dreamed of the girl Brigid at Taylor the silversmith's forge. He had recognised the power flowing from her and instinctively knew that attempting anything with her would have been like pulling stones from the bottom of a dam and then standing under the collapsing wall waiting for the deluge. She may be a watery creature, but, in her core, he had sensed the wild force of the tsunami.

His sleeping mind then circled around Kingswraith. He hadn't as yet seen the young man but he had the taste of him now, his flesh, his sinew and bone. In his dreams the Vadhaka was the wolf bringing down a mountain goat that smelled of Kingswraith. The fantasy goat pleaded with a human voice while the wolf delicately flensed the hide from its bloody ribs. All the while he was sipping at the elegant agony of the creature's torment, tasting it raw and red, sweet and gamey. Delicious.

He imagined the slow poetry of the young wizard's mind as it slid inevitably from hope to despair to acceptance, and finally found peace. It was so beautiful, that musical transition of the soul from the victim's first wretched struggles to that final embrace. He would use all his art to teach Kingswraith how to accept death as a release, show him how to succumb to the tomb with open arms and joy.

The policemen in the hall were a different matter. They had been shocked into death. It was as if he had pushed them through the icy door of mortality and slammed it shut behind them. They had been made to endure swift, brutish ends; unfit work for an artisan killer like the Vadhaka. He regretted his haste, and hoped they might forgive him.

It was like death under the axe blade, an execution. One instant the heart was beating and the mind planning for the future, the next they were gone, leaving behind nothing of value, just so much meat and bone. All vitality vanished in an instant. What a waste! As he always did when he was sleeping, he allowed his thoughts to drift from subject to subject until he became lost in dreams and idle speculation

He wondered if the living could ever truly comprehend the utter finality of death? While their heart was still beating could they imagine what it meant to end, to reach the quietus? To cease to be? But in the same way, he wondered, how could a fabricated, soulless creature like himself ever truly appreciate the mortal fight for survival?

He had witnessed it often enough, but how could he ever begin to understand that desperate fight for light and life that inspires the meanest soul to cling to every last second of existence, to struggle for life until their final feeble breath is gasped away?

And yet, and yet. The soulless creature who had climbed out of the necromancer's crucible in that long-ago place had, over the centuries, wrapped itself in borrowed shreds of humanity, and he had developed a soul of sorts. But would it be enough for him face judgement when the time came? The Vadhaka might survive to be the last living thing on Earth at the end of days. If he eventually passed away on an airless, frigid ball of rock he must surely meet just retribution, at last.

But what retribution would be fit for an amoral entity who had been fashioned to be the ultimate assassin? How do you judge a living blade who creates razor-sharp knives from thin air, and who had never once failed his commission? It might prove a delicate question for the jury. Should the Vadhaka be punished for his endless lifetime of slaughter? Or should he be congratulated for doing such a wonderful job?

The souls he had subjected to so many refined hours of unendurable torture, they might actually be sitting in the court when his case was heard. They would certainly have an opinion about it, but they might not be sophisticated enough to answer such a unique question. Would anyone? Could anyone? The vault of his mind echoed with wild laughter.

Truth be known the Vadhaka's long years of loneliness and the endless killing of the wicked and the innocent alike had driven him quite insane. In a human court his lawyers might claim mitigating circumstances, diminished responsibility, a disturbed mind. But would that defence be heard in the court of celestial judgement?

That was when the Vadhaka came instantly awake, all his senses alert. He heard shouting and the clattering of heavy boots down on the ground floor. There were cries of horror and rage. He heard a few choice epithets and then the sounds of feet pounding up the stairs. He bounded from the bed, pressed his hat onto his head, and dashed out onto the landing just in time for a uniformed policeman to cry out, 'Halt, in the name of the law. I see you, you stay right there, matey!'

The policeman paused and stared at the vision in scarlet confronting him; from its broad brimmed hat to its bloody eyes and its Spanish heeled boots, 'In the name of all that's holy, what the f...'

The Vadhaka launched a force blade at the man which sliced through his thigh before gouging a groove from the stairwell's plasterwork. The policeman's leg buckled; his muscle slashed to the bone. His wound spurted streams of bright arterial blood up the wall. He screamed and fell back into a knot of his colleagues and they tumbled in a helpless cluster of arms, legs and helmeted heads, crunching and bouncing together in a series of bruising collisions down the narrow stairwell.

In the confusion the Vadhaka leapt up the stairs to the next landing, looking to make his escape. When he reached the study, he simply tore away the door that was leaning in its frame and flung it at the dark blue mass of bodies pressing up towards him, then he dashed into the room. The Professor's study glowed with a soft pink light cast up from the street lamps outside, and heavy rain pounded on the skylights with rattling timpani.

From out on the landing a commanding voice boomed, 'There's no escape. Come quietly like a sensible gentleman and you'll not be hurt. Don't be silly, come on now.'

The Vadhaka glanced around the study and then threw himself at the heavy bookshelves. He began scaling the shelves as if they were the rungs of a ladder. Even as the bookshelf began to topple away from the wall and threatened to crush him, he reached the top and sprang towards the nearest skylight, just managing to take a grip on the long lever that opened it to the sky. Rain poured onto his upturned face.

A shot rang out and the slug shattered the window by his head, spraying him with dagger like shards of glass. But he was already rolling through the air, nimble as a trapeze artist and to the police below who were wildly scattering away from the falling bookshelf, he seemed to have vanished into the night. Sergeant Charlton pocketed his Webley Bulldog revolver and dashed back down to the second floor where he threw open a window overlooking the street.

He called to the officers clustered around the horse-drawn black Marias in the road, 'He's on the roof! The bugger's up on the roof. You blokes with rifles, take a bead and shoot him. Aim to kill, shoot at anything red, that's red! You hear me?'

Two military trained police marksmen pressed the butts of their Martini-Henry breech loading carbines to their shoulders, and squinted up into the rain-soaked night. One of them spotted a scarlet blur and fired, the other followed his lead and released his shot. By then his colleague had already reloaded and was tracking along the roofs of the terraced houses.

'There's nothing but bleedin' chimbleys and railings up there,' he muttered. 'Who needs railings on a bleedin' roof? He could be anywhere by now. Can you see 'im?'

'I can't see anything in all this bloody rain. What a brilliant night for bleedin' ducks! Wait, hang on, wait, what's that? Look, up there!'

They fired in unison at a capering figure that appeared to be dancing on the roof of one of the houses further along Cheyne Row. They levered the spent cartridges out of their rifles' blocks and pressed fresh shells into the spout. Reloading took just three seconds, but in that time the figure had vanished once more and the squally rain had redoubled in strength. All sight of the roofs was drowned in the deluge.

166

'This is stupid,' said the first rifleman, 'In this flippin' downpour I couldn't find me own dick if I needed a piss. We're wasting time 'ere, he's well gone.'

A stocky figure barrelled towards them from the steps of Owl's Tower. Sergeant Charlton hated rain as much as the next man, but he was too angry to notice that he was soaked to the skin. He was quivering with fury as he approached, water cascading from his thick eyebrows.

'Did you get the bastard?'

'Can't be sure, Sergeant. We took a couple of pot shots at 'im on that roof there,' the marksman indicated up into the silvery midnight murk. 'Well, the roof of that house there anyway. Couldn't say if we 'it 'im, but it was a clear shot. Thing is, see, that roof is about five or six hundred yards away. I could put a slug through a sixpence at four hundred yards, but in this weather, and at that distance, you can't say... What's 'e done anyway?'

His voice trailed away in the face of Charlton's furious glare. The Sergeant growled, 'Well, where shall I start? That maniac has had Cooper's head clean off his shoulders, and he's broke Whitey's neck like he was snapping a twig. He stabbed Gregg in the thigh with something or other, poor sod has lost a lot of blood. As if that wasn't enough, he threw a door at a bunch of our lads that caved in Potter's chest. He's dead too. A bloody door! I ask you, is that enough to be going on with?'

He pointed, 'He was up on that house over there, you say? Right, right then, let's go wake 'em up and see what we can find. I tell you I want him; I want him to swing. That is, unless you can save the hangman's hemp with a well-aimed bullet. Either will do it for me, I don't care whichever happens first, I want him dead.'

28

As Brigid had promised the night remained dry for the crew of the Nova, but the air was chill and the starless sky black as pitch. They had sailed beyond Erith with Lucas in the bow searching for ribbons of luminous foam that might indicate a sandbank. Even a flat-bottomed barge could run aground if the bank was high enough. Lucas indicated the path to clear water and Mirte passed on the information to Kingswraith at the tiller. It was a silent conversation consisting of simple gestures.

The air was cold but it was also fresh and clean and Kingswraith could feel the vast open space around him, even though he couldn't see anything beyond the lamps on the barge, green on the starboard side, red to portside, and white on the masthead. Going out to sea at night meant navigating into busy waters, and Lucas had explained that he wanted to make sure that any fast-moving steamship could see him at a distance.

'They say "sail before steam" because a big steamship can turn faster than a little sailing barge like the Nova. But we have to hope the watchman is awake and sober, which isn't always the case. A big ship would roll over us like a cartwheel over a rabbit, it wouldn't even feel the bump. Yes, it looks like a big empty sea at the mouth of the estuary, but we must be sure to keep our eyes open.'

The plan was to moor for the night at Southend and the next morning take a day trip into the North Sea. The Bakkers said they had netted a good crop of fat eels and some fine crayfish during their last foray, so they could afford a little holiday with a guest. And they knew a clean tavern in Southend where they could enjoy good fish and chips and excellent beer. This last sounded wonderful, the sea air had given Kingswraith a keen appetite.

His stomach growled while he dreamed about hot and fresh fried fish, and he was also concentrating on following Mirte's gestures to left and right, so it took him a while to notice the blue phosphorescence that was building around the Nova's hull, specifically around the stern. He was about to call out and ask if the Bakkers knew what might cause this odd phenomenon when a pair of slender bodies hurtled up out of the sea, grabbed him by the arms, and dragged him overboard.

His sudden descent into the icy sea shocked a gasp of horror from his lips, and he sucked a painful mouthful of frigid saltwater into his lungs. His body convulsed and he fought furiously against his captors, but they held him with irresistible strength. The sea all around him was fluorescing with that strange blue light, but he saw darkness creeping inwards from the edges of his vision.

His eyes closed and he became calm and warm. He didn't know why but he knew he was drowning and there was nothing he could do about it. He felt his mind slipping away into the night. That was when he felt cool fingers on his cheeks and firm lips press against his mouth. A long tongue wormed its way between his teeth in a fashion that reminded him of his oddly erotic encounters with Penelope Epimeliad.

The tongue stiffened, there was a sharp sting at the back of his throat, and suddenly he could breathe as easily as if he was back on the Nova's deck. Warm energy bloomed along every sinew of his body. He came wide awake and his eyes flew open.

He found himself looking into the bright green eyes of a blue-skinned girl. Her indigo hair swirled around her elfin features, and he could clearly see the uptilted curve of her pointed ears. As she pulled away, he saw she was almost naked, wearing little more than diaphanous wisps of filmy fabric around her breasts and hips, barely enough to preserve her modesty. Apart from her colouring and scanty wardrobe she might almost have been Penelope's twin.

'I know who you are,' he blurted. 'You're the tree Sprites of Doggerland! You're the spirits of the drowned forests. Penelope Epimeliad told me about you.'

The girl nodded and laughed silently but with complete abandon, which did things to her body that Kingswraith found both embarrassing and utterly fascinating until his good breeding forced him to look away. That was when he became aware that a group of male Sprites were also floating around him, their faces alive with curiosity.

He remembered Lucas saying something about mermaids, which he had thought at the time must be a seafarer's joke. Well, now he found himself in the centre of a ring of mer-people and he believed he knew where those tales had started. And yet there wasn't a single fishtail to be seen amongst the whole group.

They floated and flowed around him with the confidence of creatures born to their watery element, moving with the grace of dancers freed from the strictures of gravity. They seemed to perform an aerial ballet. From out of the dark ocean a sleek shape entered the globe of blue light that surrounded the sea Sprites and nudged itself closer to Kingswraith. A dolphin! The wizard had hoped to see a dolphin but he had never expected to get this close to one.

The girl used gestures to urge him to grasp the creature's dorsal fin with both hands. He was completely enchanted by this unexpected turn of events, but he thought guiltily of the Bakkers who must be frantic about his sudden disappearance.

He pointed upwards and back towards their boat, 'I have to tell my friends that I'm safe,' he explained. 'They must be very worried about me. I need to tell them that I'm alright, you understand? Brigid told them to look after me, they'll be worried and I need to tell them that I'm safe.'

The girl nodded, then repeated her instruction that he should grasp the dolphin's dorsal fin. He acceded to her demand, and as soon as he had taken a firm hold, he found himself gliding through the water, almost at one with the smiling marine mammal. He broke the waves hard by Nova's bow and found himself gazing up into Lucas and Mirte's astounded faces, their eyes and mouths wide with shock and formed into almost comical circles.

Kingswraith coughed out a mouthful of salt water then shouted, 'Don't worry, I'm with friends. Carry on to Southend, I'll catch up with you as soon as I can. Sorry, Lucas, I've got your clothes a bit wet, but I'll see you soon, alright?'

Lucas howled with glee, 'Look at you with your dolphin! And I thought we were teaching you about the sea. We look forward to hearing about all this. See you soon, we hope.'

They waved and the waters closed over Kingswraith's head once more. He saw that the globe of the Sprites' blue glow, which he supposed to be a form of pneuma, was vanishing into the distance. His dolphin flexed its body and he was soon racing after the ball of light at breathtaking speed. Kingswraith felt the sea slide frictionlessly over him as if he was a torpedo slicing towards its target.

A jolt of exhilaration set his senses on fire; he had never felt more alive. He was in an alien environment riding a dolphin while following a mythical people towards an unknown destination. He should have been in a state of abject terror but instead his mind effervesced with joy. The bubbles streaming in his wake merely reflected his pure pleasure in being released into such an exhilarating land.

That was when the petrified ghosts of trees began to flash past him in the darkness. They seemed to bow towards him in mute supplication; arboreal souls pleading to be returned to life. They had once flourished under an open sky, their roots dug deep into the rich loam of the rolling hills. The poignancy of those phantom forests stripped away some of his joy, and he mourned their loss of light and life, briefly closing his eyes in respect for the dead.

He opened his eyes once more. The blue globe was drawing closer now and his dolphin began to slow. Kingswraith blinked and emitted an involuntary cry of wonder at what was emerging before him. The light had settled into the branches of a great silver tree. It was heartbreakingly beautiful; its delicate pale branches creating a perfect globe that crowned a soaring trunk of botanically impossible yet elegantly charming symmetry.

It looked like an image stolen from the pages of a book of hours, a masterpiece of mediaeval illumination made real. The sea Sprites darted through its boughs like birds around their nest. Kingswraith wondered how that jewel of a tree had survived the great flood that had swept in and drowned its legion of forests? At the heart of the tree's canopy the girl now floated with all the majesty of an enthroned Queen in her audience chamber. She beckoned for him to join her.

He stroked and patted the muscular flank of his dolphin steed in thanks for the glorious ride, and it smiled at him, its body flexing in a bobbing caricature of a human bow. It was a gesture that seemed to say, 'You're very welcome, I enjoyed it too.' Then it flicked its tail and vanished in the blink of an eye.

Kingswraith had been a strong swimmer ever since he had learned the skill in the local river during his childhood, but in his present company he seemed to have been leant wings. He flowed into the presence of the girl with effortless grace, then remained poised before her with his arms out and stroking at the water in a cruciform pose, his feet gently cycling to hold his position.

She parroted his posture for a brief second, smiled, then brought her hands together. Like striking snakes, the branches of the tree whipped inwards and wrapped themselves around the wizard, holding him in a grip of unbreakable strength. He automatically drew on his magical power to shatter his bonds and release himself from what he thought must surely be a trap; but before he could do so a musical voice broke into his mind.

'Can you hear me, Lord Kingswraith? I am Lorelei of the Selkie folk and we mean you no harm. This is our communications tree and it had to wrap you in its branches for a moment so you could hear us. Please, do not fear me, or it. We have heard tell of you, and we are proud to make your acquaintance at last. Our tree welcomes you. You are already adopted by the family of Epimeliad? So then now you have also become a brother of the Selkie clan.'

As she made her declaration Kingswraith heard the sound of an immense bell, its peal resonating through the body of the ocean like a hammer. It pounded in his heart so powerfully that he almost fainted. The tree's branches had uncoiled from his body and left him floating free in the water, but he could still feel the thrum of the bell tingling along his nerve endings. It was an ancient and powerful reverberation that somehow reminded him of a beautiful psalm he had once heard sung in St Paul's Cathedral.

The girl was like Penelope, both Queen and priestess, and he bowed to her. He answered formally, 'Lorelei of the Selkie, I am honoured to meet you and your clan, and I am proud to be adopted as a brother of your family. I accept with all my heart. But I must also ask, why have you brought me here? I am in hiding from a cruel and dangerous creature called the Vadhaka. Truth be told, bringing me here might place you all in peril.'

Lorelei returned a fluent curtsey, then raised her green eyes to his hazel ones, 'We brought you to this, the communications tree, because with its blessing we can converse with each other, no matter what language we use. From here we can also talk to any of our families, anywhere around the world.'

Her eyes flashed with brilliant green light like pure cut emeralds caught in the sun, and she added, 'Penelope says she will explain everything when you see her.'

Kingswraith replied, 'But that mustn't happen! Not yet, not until I have dealt with my enemy. I am waiting until a special device has been completed, and I it won't be ready until the day after tomorrow. I dare do nothing until then...'

His words tailed away when he heard a familiar chuckle and sensed delicate fingers that somehow stroked his cheek. Penelope's voice spoke from the ether, 'No, my Lord Kingswraith, there's no need to wait. You must come to me now, come as fast as you can. Your wonderful stave is ready, and I have important news for you. Very important news. Don't delay.'

29

The Vadhaka had been hit squarely in the chest by one of the police marksmen's bullets. It would have killed an ordinary man but the slug was only soft lead, and the assassin was no ordinary man. The shot had caught him when the heel of one of his Spanish boots had clipped some wrought iron ornamentation between two houses and nearly toppled him down the slippery tiles of the Mansard roof. Even a cat would have lost its footing in that weather.

He had recovered his balance by pinwheeling his arms and writhing his body, which the marksman had seen as 'capering' before taking his shot. The lead slug had smashed the Vadhaka against the sooty brickwork stack of a chimney, and in his fury, he had sliced it clean away with two force blades.

He was a magical entity, which made him deeply allergic to iron. Lead could hurt him, gold could bruise him and silver might break his bones, but it would only be temporary. They wouldn't kill him, or even appreciably slow him down. With the police slug still embedded in his chest the scarlet killer made his escape, leaping from rooftop to rooftop until he could launch himself into the branches of a tree from which he climbed down to the pavement and sprinted away into the night.

In Cheyne Row the pounding of hefty fists on the street door of the house on the roof of which the Vadhaka had been shot was finally answered by a grumbling housekeeper who was wrapped in a pink candlewick housecoat and wore an old-fashioned floppy linen mob cap tied around her head by a black ribbon. She raised her candle to squint at the officers and her mouth fell open in shocked surprise.

'Lord save us,' she groaned. 'Will you look at this lot. It's raining cats, dogs and mutton shunters. What do you bleedin' lot want on a foul night like this? Can't a respectable woman lie asleep in her bed without you knocking her up at all hours? What do you want then?'

The burliest constables pushed past her and clattered up the stairs, and she shouted after their vanishing backs, ''Ere now, where are you lot orf too? The master will 'ave my month's wages in me 'and, and see me walking the streets before breakfast.' She turned on Charlton, 'Right then, are you going to tell me why your great brutes are tramping mud through the 'ouse and getting me fired, or am I going to start screaming for 'elp?'

Charlton's mind was still filled with brutal images of his murdered officers and he had little sympathy for hysterical women. He chose to be blunt, 'Madam, we have reason to believe that you have a dangerous killer on your roof, and if we don't apprehend him, he might well murder all of you in your beds. What would you have us do? Leave him to cut your throats like pigs to the slaughter? Or should we capture the devil and take him away in irons? Which would you prefer we do, eh?'

She pulled her housecoat tighter around her scrawny frame, 'Murder, is it? Well, that's a bit of a rum do, ain't it? If you lot, you officers of the law did your jobs proper like, there wouldn't be any villains runnin' abaht on respectable people's roofs, now would there? Fair get away with murder they do.' She repeated the word with venom in her voice, 'Murder!'

There was a clatter behind her and the two constables reappeared at the bottom of the stairs. The larger one said, 'He was up there alright, but there's no blood to speak of. If there was this bloody rain would have washed it away by now. I swear I've been dryer in me bath.'

Charlton asked, 'Then how do you know he was there?'

'Cause he's taken the 'ump with the chimbly, sarge.' He turned to the housekeeper, 'When you're lighting the fires in the morning they might not draw very well, your chimbly's gone a bit short, well, half of it is gone, love. And the rain might have got in too. You'll have to get a man in, I'm afraid. That bloke has chopped it clean through the brickwork, neat job too. I've never seen anything like it, and I've seen a few things in my time.'

The housekeeper's candle blew out in a gust of wind and she emitted a strangled little squeak, the brief, final sound a mouse might make as it vanished under a steamroller's wheel.

'The master will 'ave something to say about this, you mark my words. He's not a man to sit still while murderers are smashing up his chimblies and mutton shunters are walking muck through the house like it was Piccadilly Circus. I'll wish you gentlemen good night and ask you to get orf my doorstep sharpish. I'm back orf to bed. I've got an early mornin' dealing with chimblies by the sound of it. What's the world coming to, eh? I ask you.'

The door slammed shut on her disgruntled features and the officers descended to the pavement. They looked at each other. The shorter constable took off his helmet and vigorously scratched at his scalp, then rotated his right forefinger in his ear with a pronounced squeaking sound.

He pulled a face, 'Well, that's put a flea in our ears. We've been told good and proper and no mistake. She can look after her own murderers from now on, and Gawd help 'em I say.'

The tallest constable shook his head, 'I'll never understand women like her. Fact is, I'll never understand women; never have, never will. You'd think she'd be happier waking up with her skinny throat cut and her blood all up the wall. That would teach her a lesson.'

Charlton squinted at the sky. There were streaks of moonlight breaking through the cloud and the rain seemed to be subsiding at last. 'Well, she might be off to bed but we've a crime scene to investigate. Barker, Willis, can you boys cut off to the Yard and fetch the night duty medical examiner? The rest of you join me back in Owl's Tower. Our man might have got away for now, but let's see what clues he's left behind. I hear Sherlock Holmes is busy so we thick-witted mutton shunters will have to manage on our own. Go on, get busy then.'

As the group headed back towards the Professor's house one of the constables asked Charlton, 'Speaking of detectives, sarge, but why isn't Detective Inspector Chandler here? He's the one that set Cooper and White to look after his mate's house while he was away. So, what I mean to say, he's the reason they met that murdering lunatic. He should be here.'

'Ours not to judge our betters, Pugh. Remember that. Fact is that DI Chandler's got enough on his plate with detectoring those faceless men what woke up and set about us down in the bone cellar. If it wasn't for the Professor, I dread to think what might have happened. Fair put the willies up me it did. And there's people going missing over Richmond way. I tell you, this ain't Conan Doyle's cup of cocoa. Holmes is a smart bloke, he'd have it away on his toes with Watson close at his heels, and I wouldn't blame him one little bit.'

He raised his voice, 'Alright lads, listen up now. Fingertip search, keep your eyes peeled. I know you will but be careful in there, don't go moving things about. If you see something interesting don't touch it, come and find me. Wilkins, get up into that top room and see what you can do about that broken skylight. This is a nice house and the owner won't thank us if he came home and found it flooded, what with all this rain coming in.'

Meanwhile the Vadhaka had swiftly made his way down to the river and was jogging along the Chelsea Embankment towards Westminster. For all his speed he was limping slightly and holding his arms tight to his ribs. He was in a lot of pain and needed to find somewhere quiet where he could extract the rifle slug from his body; somewhere out of the public eye.

Before him the needle-sharp towers of Parliament rose up into the dank night. Facing it loomed a mighty Gothic bulk. Westminster Abbey, perfect, he thought, and accelerated his pace. He leapt towards the Abbey.

Unlike Kingswraith the Vadhaka could not fly. His progress through the air was more like a series of mighty leaps and bounds, and he crashed violently into the ground on landing because he had no brakes and no way to slow down. He struck the Abbey's leaded Henry VII Triforium roof like a missile; smashing through it and clattering into the cluttered, vaulted gallery below.

He rolled along the floor knocking chairs and boxes flying until a stone sarcophagus broke his progress just before he could burst through one of the gallery's delicate circular windows set into a pointed arch. A lesser man might have groaned and lay smashed and broken on the stone flags of the Abbey's hidden gallery, but the assassin had no time for such luxuries. He needed to take that lead slug out of his body before he could begin his healing process.

He peeled off his scarlet coat, placed it carefully on the lid of the sarcophagus, then took off his hat and put it on top of his coat. His bloodied shirt followed. The blood was actually a blueish purple colour but it looked black in the darkness. What little light there was exposed the many centuries of scars that laced the Vadhaka's well-muscled torso, each a memento from the times his victims had fought back. Every scar had a story to tell.

The Vadhaka's art required skills similar to those of a surgeon, and after placing himself into a beam of brightening moonlight he used one of his finest force blades to cut into his body until he had exposed the flattened marksman's bullet. His nerves screamed with pain, but he embraced it, reminding himself that pain was life. After all, the dead could feel nothing at all.

The slug fell into his lap and he lifted it up to his eyes and smiled, a cold white crescent of teeth. He squeezed the lead between his fingers and thumb as if it was wet clay until it became a little dish shaped disc, the patterns of his finger and thumbprints embossed into the grey metal. He looked up when the yellow light of a lamp bloomed into the gallery, and behind it saw the shadowy bulk of a watchman approaching carefully.

The watchman didn't want to be up there but the Vadhaka's entrance had made so much racket that the reluctant man had no choice but to investigate. At worst the watchman expected to find a wild bird had got into the Triforium, and that meant catching it and setting it free, or breaking its neck and putting it with the other rubbish.

What he didn't expect to see was the half-naked figure of a man framed by moonlight, standing with his arm drawn back like a javelin thrower. The watchman had barely framed the word 'Who?' when the stranger's arm whipped forward so fast it was just a line of light in the glow of his lamp.

The lead slug that had failed to take the Vadhaka's life struck through the watchman's chest and ripped into his heart. He died instantly with an expression of surprise on his puffy, pale features, falling backwards in a heap. His Marsaut lamp automatically snuffed out when it was dropped, and the gallery was lost to darkness once more.

The Vadhaka sat cross-legged on the stone floor and began his damaged body's healing process. Once again, he regretted his haste. He didn't have enough time to tease the life from the watchman, and he silently apologised to the mound of human flesh in the centre of its growing puddle of blood. The dead man's corpse wheezed out a posthumous breath, but his soul had already departed and was swiftly travelling along the corridor of light towards the halls of the dead.

The Spiritus Iudicii in its featureless plain ignored the fresh soul passing overhead as a thing of little interest, but Garth found the confused watchman's story extremely interesting. After hearing it he waited eagerly for Kingswraith's next visit so he could share his news.

30

If Kingswraith had known anything about the bends, also known as aerobullosis or decompression sickness, he might have been more careful about returning to the Nova at high speed while clinging to the dorsal fin of a dolphin. But because his body had been modified by the Selkie clan he could fly through the water like a bird and remain unaffected by deadly pressure changes that would have turned any other man's body fluids to soda water.

As it was, he burst from the sea as slick as a penguin and appeared on the Schuyt's deck like a jack bursting from its box, causing the Bakkers to cry out in alarm. His clothes were wringing wet so he used a trick Penelope had taught him to spin the water away from the fabric using natural electrical fluid.

As before he felt his hair stand away from his head in a comical parody of a dandelion clock, which he cured by leaning over the gunwales and touching the sea. The resultant streak of lightning skittered away from his fingertips like a white-hot rip in the fabric of the Earth. The Dutch couple watched his antics in open mouthed amazement. Kingswraith ran his hands through his hair, grinned at them and said, 'Hello, I'm back.'

The couple ran to his side and touched him with tentative fingers, as if worried he might explode or vanish in a puff of smoke. 'Is it really you?' asked Lucas, his eyes round as sovereigns. 'What happened to you? What was that streak of light?'

'Yes, it's really me. Sorry about all the fuss just now but I needed to dry your clothes before changing back into my own, and that was the only way I knew how to do it in a hurry. It's a trick I learned from a good friend. She's a lot like Brigid, you'd like her.'

Mirte said something to her husband and he nodded his head before asking, 'So, right then. Can we go to Southend for fish and chips now? My wife is very hungry, and we want to hear all about whatever you did down there in the sea. You're a very surprising young man, my friend, but then I think you knew that already.'

'Yes, please, set sail for the moorings and your dinner. But I'm afraid my story will have to wait. I must get back into my own clothes and then I'm for London. I've been asked to return. Things are happening, important things, and they need me there straight away. I promise I'll see you again and I'll explain everything if you'd let me. One day I'd love to help you with your eels, and to join you for fish and chips in Southend, but first I must go to London.'

Mirte took the tiller and Lucas followed the wizard down into the neat cabin. While Kingswraith got changed back into his accustomed garb, the Netherlander explained that there was little point in even trying to sail back up the Thames until the morning. The tide and the winds were against them. And anyway, he said, changing his clothes before they were in sight of the great Pool of the city and heading for the moorings would be pointless.

Kingswraith listened quietly, buttoned his coat against the evening chill, and then took Lucas's hand in both of his, 'Lucas, I can't tell you how wonderful it has been to make two such firm friends so quickly. And I can't thank you enough for making a complete stranger so welcome. Now you're about to see something else that you must keep under that Rembrandt hat of yours; that's if you and Mirte will be good enough to keep yet another secret for me?'

Lucas followed him back out onto the deck, protesting that he would of course keep any secret as would his wife. But even a magician like Kingswraith couldn't turn the tides, any more than could the famous King Cnut. It couldn't be done.

Kingswraith smiled, then went to the tiller and hugged Mirte before kissing her on both cheeks. The woman became quite flustered and uttered an embarrassed and quite girlish giggle. Then the wizard took Luca's hand once more and grinned at the eel fisherman's evident confusion.

'Old Cnut was just proving a point,' he said, 'and you're right, we can't turn the tides. We can't change the direction of the wind either, although I suspect that Brigid might manage it if she wanted to. She is an exceptional soul. I haven't an ounce of her power. But then I don't need it. I'll see you soon, and thank-you, thank-you again.'

He saluted them, flexed his knees for a moment, then rocketed away into the evening sky. Within seconds he was a black speck against the clouds, then a shaft of moonlight caught him, and they watched until he flew out of sight, heading back up the Thames towards the capital. Mirte gasped, sucking air deep into her lungs; for a moment she had forgotten to breathe. She crossed herself and said in a quiet voice, 'Is hij ook een vogel?'

Lucas answered in English, 'Is he a bird, you ask? My love, I don't know what he is, perhaps he's some sort of angel? But whatever he is I feel blessed for having met him. I pray he remains safe and we see him again when his work is completed; I do hope so. But for now,' he patted his stomach, 'we go to Southend. We've an appointment with a plateful of fresh fried haddock and some fried potatoes. I'm starving.'

Far overhead and increasingly far away, Kingswraith's first attempt at flying out in the open air was proving troublesome, he became disoriented by shifting breezes that seemed hellbent on drifting him off-course. Then he remembered Lucas's explanation of 'leeway' and the purpose of the spoon-shaped leeboards on the barge.

He began to experiment by moving his arms with his hands cupped, almost sculling into the air-flow like a man at the oars. He discovered that the most effective technique was to treat his arms as wings, to emulate the birds. He had no need to flap his arms, but he could use them as rudders to steer himself along, following the glittering highway of the Thames until he could smell the smoky metropolis drawing closer.

His nose picked up the scent sooner than his eyes spotted the glow of gas lamps which traced the intricate tapestry of London's streets like the yellow veins of a vast slumbering monster. There was certainly a monstrous enough smell. His time out on the barge in the estuary had washed his senses clean of the old familiar stink, and now he felt as if he was entering the redolent lair of a filthy and flatulent behemoth.

It was difficult to breathe in that thick miasma, and just as hard to make out landmarks in the smoky darkness and mist, but he kept following the river until he spotted the unmistakeable silhouette of the great Tower alongside the riot of masts and hulls that made up the Pool of London. It had taken most of a day to sail to the Estuary, it had taken little more than an exhilarating half hour to return by air.

Kingswraith sought out the darkest shadowed area to make his landing close to the Tower's outer wall. And then he made his way on foot to Candlewick and the familiar paving slab by the bulk of St Mary church. The foul reek of the sewer had been slightly mitigated by the evening's rain but he gagged as he climbed down the stone steps, desperately trying to hold his breath until he had reached the safety of the secret door into the Epimeliad tunnels.

He took a deep lungful of the sweet, green scented air in the tunnel after the door swung closed behind him. How the tunnel filtered away the sewer's stench so quickly was a mystery, but he was happy to take advantage of it. He also didn't know how he could fly, or, more recently, how he could swim like a fish and breathe salt water, but he was willing to accept his talents with ignorant gratitude rather than reject them because he didn't understand the science. Maybe they were nothing to do with science, who knows?

Do you need to know how your eyes work to enjoy the sunrise, or how your ears work to appreciate birdsong? No, any more than you need to understand what excites you while taking pleasure from a kiss, or why you appreciate the salt crispness of the open sea air, or why your mouth waters at the satisfying aromas of a good meal after a long and hungry day. All of these are gifts of nature; Kingswraith had merely added his own very individual treats to the simple joys that everyone else could appreciate.

He followed the pneuma along the tunnels, thinking that being able to see the pale blue glow lighting his path was yet another novelty in his sensory palette. It was a thoughtful young man who stepped out onto the familiar, arrow straight bridge stretching across the black waters of the Roman reservoir. He was absorbed in his contemplations as he made his way towards the stone platform at its heart, for all that he was keen to see Penelope once more, and curious to hear her news. But he almost came to a halt as he drew closer and looked up.

There were two figures on the platform. One was Penelope in her familiar mature guise, but the other was a stranger; an exotic, dark-skinned creature with a fine mane of blond hair. She stood at Penelope's shoulder, smiling at him. Her green eyes smouldered like shafts of sunlight piercing the sea and her body was sleek and slender as a fish. Her robe was simple and elegant, the fabric finely woven and white as the feathers of an albatross.

Kingswraith wondered why such specific marine concepts had sprung to his mind, and then he burst into a delighted shout of laughter. 'Brigid? Is that you? My word you are a surprise. So then, tell me, both of you, are these aspects the mask or your true faces? I would say such beauty must be honest. Look at you both, if the stones had mouths, you would incite them to poetry. Where is master Shakespeare when you need him?'

Penelope stepped forward and spoke formally, 'Lord Kingswraith, this is the true physical aspect of Amphitrite. She is the spirit of the sea and she can also appear as Brigid, a young Celt, when she walks amongst men. As you know, I also walk as a street Arab when in the human world, but we both greet you in our true forms, last scion of the line of Pendragon.'

Amphitrite asked, 'What of my friends the Bakkers? Are they well?'

Kingswraith chuckled, 'They've had an interesting day, I'm sure they'll agree to that. Their guest has been abducted by sea nymphs, reappeared as if by magic, set lightning across the mouth of the Thames and then flew off like a Chinese rocket. When last I saw them, they were on course for fish and chips in a Southend tavern. Wonderful people, salt of the sea and hearts as big as the ocean. But tell me, what is your wonderful, important news?'

Penelope passed a questioning glance at Amphitrite who nodded. Kingswraith realised his Sprite mentor was seeking permission to speak first, something he had never imagined her doing. He decided it was best to tread very carefully regarding these two women. As a junior member of the British aristocracy, he was very aware of the importance of recognising one's place in the social strata.

Penelope continued, 'First, my Lord, call your stave. We must see how it reacts to you. Much as you have been adding interesting new gifts to your portfolio of talents, your stave has become a very rare device indeed. Call it, my Lord. Hold out your hand as you would to a beloved hawk. Call it, and we shall see if it still knows you.'

The wizard held out his right hand, palm open. He whispered, 'To me' and felt the same surge of tingling excitement he had experienced when the staff had first chosen him and leapt from Penelope's grasp those scant days earlier. He reached out with every ounce of his being, he reached out with an emotion close to love. Every fibre of his body was vibrating, calling, willing the stave to respond.

He was answered. He felt himself suddenly bathed in an explosion of joy, as if a previously unknown gap in his being had been filled and he was complete at last. Penelope's cave of woven roots burst open, radiating a halo of light and the stave flew out. It winged towards him, tumbling end over end, then smacked hard into his palm with a resounding slap!

A blinding effulgence erupted from its tip, spreading out in bright streamers to every corner of the vast reservoir. Penelope and even Amphitrite staggered back, awed by the brilliant display. But Kingswraith didn't see them. His eyes had snapped shut and he was listening to a sonorous voice that only he could hear.

It sounded vast as if a god was addressing him. It was if the Earth itself had found its tongue and was speaking exclusively to him. He felt uplifted and diminished at the same time, a tiny mote adrift in a tremendous place, but he listened without fear.

'Your time has come at last, my son. Welcome and well met. I shall guide your hand when you tear down the walls of deception and evil. Yours is the bloodline of the children of the Way, the first true man to bring love, goodness and faith to the hearts of humanity. But in the bloodline of your enemies flows the black blood of the Word. Their blood is poisoned with treachery, they can only thrive in the shadows. They are half-made things, unfinished. But even so be warned, they are powerful.'

The voice paused as if its owner had been lost in thought for a moment, then it continued. "Know me, my son, I am the Draco Terrae. And know these my children of whom I am justly proud. They are souls you can trust. The time has come for us to rise against evil and end it. Once the vile blood of the Word has been cleansed away – and perhaps only then – will humanity finally find its true path back to redemption.'

31

Blood trickled from the oddly pink lips and down the crystalline chin of Makrut Wyndsyster and she wiped it away with the back of an elegant hand, then she licked her hand clean. She and Cymbeline Fleischer had feasted on the flesh of an angler they had discovered down by the river in their grounds, and after they had finished their meal, the dark enzymes carried in Makrut's saliva had reanimated the corpse's body. It had climbed back to its feet and trotted nimbly after them when they returned to the house.

The wine cellar already held a number of faceless men and women, all standing in a series of torpid circles while waiting for their mistress to command them. The fisherman descended to the cellar and joined the undead horde of manus mortuus. They were blind and soulless; in death they had become mindless slaves to Makrut's will. Except for the odd times when they would rotate slowly around a central point like donkeys turning a millstone. Makrut didn't know why they did it, but then, thanks to her towering arrogance, she didn't care.

It was probably Makrut, hunting from her home in the mountains of the eastern Austro-Hungarian empire, who had first inspired nightmares about vampires. Her deadly bite created undead vassals who followed her every command. Bullets and blades had little effect on them; after all, how can you kill that which is already dead? The only way to stop them was to burn them or tear them apart.

The manus mortuus did nothing unless they had been ordered to, except when the scent of white magical practitioners filled them with a dreadful hunger. They would attack any but the darkest adepts. Makrut had sent three of her manus mortuus into a death-like sleep to be used as traps, hoping to catch their white wizard enemies unaware. She realised they must have failed; but the growing horde in the cellar were both tasty treats and weapons she would use if and when they were needed.

Until the day she had arrived at Arcadia House with Cymbeline and Frossard, she had sent her victims to sit quietly in the silt at the bottom of the deepest part of the river Thames. Some of the faceless ones in the cellar of the house still stank of river water and raw effluent, and were developing a fine coating of mould. Their own mothers wouldn't have recognised them, in fact they would have run screaming at the sight of them.

Cymbeline's ape-like servants were almost as mindless, but they were different in two major ways. First, they were alive, albeit a miserable life in thrall to a cold, evil mind. Second, they were hierodules. They were totally dedicated to Cymbeline and worshipped her as if she was a goddess. They were capable of independent thought when required, but if Cymbeline had ordered them to, they would have flung themselves to their deaths without a moment's hesitation.

Cymbeline turned to her 'sister', 'Your little toys in the cellar were very agitated yesterday evening when that rain came down. Why was that? They're safe enough in the dry, and anyway it's not as if they can drown, is it? They can't be prone to water damage? After all some of them spent days in the river, and apart from the mould and the smell they seem fine.'

The crystal woman snickered, a brittle chiming sound like someone tapping a spoon against a lead crystal glass. 'No, no, my heart. Water can't hurt them. It was the nature of the rain that "agitated" them as you say. It was unnatural. Couldn't you sense the magic in it? I'm certain that a white practitioner must have deliberately steered that storm in this direction for some reason.'

She sneered with patent derision, 'Perhaps it was diverted from its original course to fill the rivers or cleanse the sewers; but whatever the reason it was for a "good cause". My "toys" simply wanted to find the good white hand that had directed that tempest towards us and rip it from its owner's arm, rapidly followed by tearing off their head and eating it.'

Cymbeline chuckled, 'I do envy you your bite. That is such a sweet gift you have, my dear. I have to rummage around in my devotees' brains and weave them to my will, which can be quite tedious, you know. Hierodules have such shallow, animal minds. I have to pick through so much rubbish to find anything of value. They are a poor meal with no nourishment.'

She mimed biting and grinned, 'You, ah, it's so simple! You take your pound of flesh and there they are, a flock of devoted chattels ready to follow your every order until the meat falls from their bones and their sinews rot away from their joints.'

'Yes, I wish I could say the same about our tame assassin. It's been two days now and no news. I thought we'd sent out a wolf to bring down the spring lamb

186

but there's not been so much as a peep from him. He had his ransom in advance, so then, where's our prize?'

'Careful what you say, Makrut, he might be in earshot. Remember there's nothing tame about the Vadhaka. We don't want to anger him. I heard tell about one of his clients who paid him his due but then made sport of our scarlet-eyed friend while stupidly trying to impress his female friends. It was a profoundly idiotic thing to do. The Vadhaka completed his mission well enough, his target died in exquisite pain. But the client couldn't celebrate because his head and his body had parted company, snick!'

Makrut put her hand to her throat, 'And I have a little neck, as a queen might say.'

'You have indeed, my lady.' The Vadhaka emerged from the shadow of a tall hedge and stepped towards the two Umbra women with an insouciant air. 'I was curious to hear what you might have to say about me, so I held my breath and waited. But please, don't be afraid. I'm not so quick to anger as some might have you believe. Any display of emotion is a waste of energy unless it is channelled properly. Nevertheless, I have come to report.'

He told the pair everything that had happened over the previous few days, the reservoir, the smithy, the house in Chelsea, the police, and the killings. He spoke at length about the girl protecting the goldsmith.

'You told me that we face powerful talents. Well, I have faced the powerful before and I am still here. But that quiet little girl... she was something else altogether. She was a true force of nature. My dear ladies, I must warn you that your enemy has formidable friends. I learned to think of humans as little more than sheep for the slaughter, they are nothing to fear. But this girl was so much more. Humans may be sheep, but I believe we are now faced by their shepherds.'

Makrut sneered, 'Wait, what is this? Are you saying that you can't fulfil your part of the bargain after you received your payment in full? Is that it? And look, is that blood on your shirt? It looks torn! Have you been wounded? Well, well. So much for the legend of the Vadhaka. I must say, I'm very disappointed. We call for a wolf and we get a lap dog. And are you really afraid that these dangerous "shepherds" might harm us? I think not!'

She flinched at his lupine grin. He growled, 'Strong words from a woman with such a little neck. No, my lady, I did not say that I couldn't get my job

187

done, never think that. But I am warning you that your wizard's friends might take exception to his death and come after you. So, accept my warning you'll need to be prepared.'

He stepped closer until they could smell his feral odour, 'Could they harm you? Yes, they probably could. I know I could. I know I could kill both of you in a second if you gave me enough cause. But even I would be careful going up against those standing at the boy wizard's shoulder. So, listen closely to what I say, be warned!'

Makrut drew herself up to her full height and raked the assassin with her haughtiest glare, 'We have our own talents and our own defences. You do your job and let us worry about the repercussions. We have power enough to hold back an army, let alone a few sheep herders. You can't scare us, we're not such easy meat.'

The Vadhaka reached into his pocket and fetched out a small bag which he handed to Cymbeline. She opened it cautiously and gazed inside, then poured some of the contents into her hand, 'Ash,' she said, flatly. 'Why have you given me a bag of ash? Is this an odd joke?'

He pointed at the bag, 'I found that in a box in the study of the Kingswraith's house and I thought you might want it back. I believe it to be the remains of the fellow you sent to Chelsea before me, there was very little else left to identify him. And that place reeked of magic, there must be more than just one practitioner. It was a hive of the devils. I aim to kill but one, Kingswraith, unless the others force me to defend myself. I'll warrant your ashen friend here was just as confident as you are. No doubt that was his downfall.'

Cymbeline flung the bag away and rubbed her hands together as if they had touched poison, 'Very well, sir. You have reported and we are grateful. Now you must return to your duty and we shall prepare for whatever repercussions might be inspired by your complete success. If they send the wind, we shall respond with a whirlwind. If the earth itself rises against us we shall overcome and strike it flat. To your work, sir, and may God be with you.'

'God? You would have Him gazing over my shoulder? God is never with me, my lady, any more than He is with you. But He might be with the foe, bear that in mind. Fare thee well.'

In a blur he was gone, leaving the two Umbra females to recover their composure. Makrut emitted a heavy sigh, 'I will admit that fellow knows how to make a good exit; and he has the art of the entrance at his fingertips. I wonder he isn't on the stage.'

'I'd hesitate to guess at the audience that would appreciate his performance. You saw what he did to that Sprite boy. Enthusiasm for one's work is admirable, but really; what stomach could endure his art? His is a performance that God himself would turn away from? But he is right, the Lord is no more with us than He is with him. We must look to our defences. If he succeeds, and if he's right, we'd best be prepared.'

'What about Frossard's ashes? What shall we do with him?'

'Leave him where he lies. He might do some good for the garden. He's little more than compost now. He never was much of a conversationalist at the best of times, let him listen to the grass growing.'

They walked back towards the house. Makrut mused, 'Do you really think he could kill both of us in a second? Personally, I think he would find it very difficult. Would a lap dog threaten a lion? Surely, he doesn't know what we are. I wonder if he can imagine what he would be dealing with.'

'He's an arrogant devil, isn't he? And the way he smells, he's like something from the jungle.' Cymbeline paused and looked at the house, 'What on earth?'

They heard the wet, gurgling, shrieking sounds that a host of lipless and tongueless mouths would make if they were all sounding at once. Cymbeline looked at the sky and then turned to study the horizon. Her eyes narrowed to slits.

'You say your toys become agitated in the presence of white magic? Well, listen to them! Get them out here, I think we're about to meet some of the Vadhaka's shepherds. I do hope your faceless lovelies are hungry, I think dinner is close.'

The undead spilled out onto the drive in their dozens and formed a defensive ring around the Umbra women, their ruined faces turned up and gazing blindly towards the sky. Behind them came the small army of hierodules. The ape-like creatures had armed themselves with anything that could hack, pierce, slice or pound their attackers. They formed an inner ring.

Makrut jeered up at the sky, 'Come on you little sheep herders, we're waiting. You're facing the real thing now. You'd better make your peace with your God! No, no need, just wait just a few minutes and you'll be able to do it in person. I don't think you'll need an appointment; He'll be expecting you.'

189

32

The minutes ticked by but no invading army of white wizards made their appearance. Instead, Cymbeline squinted down the drive and pointed at a single, bowed, broad-shouldered figure walking steadily, almost jauntily, towards them.

Cymbeline was confused, 'What's this?'

All around them the circle of manus mortuus howled and jittered, eager as a pack of hounds straining at the leash and filled with an insatiable bloodlust. Their exposed teeth clashed and chattered madly and their fleshless hands reached out like claws as if eager to rend everything within reach.

Makrut crowed, 'See? They're maddened for it. See, see! They can smell the reek of white magic coming off this one. Look at them, they're like dogs hungry for meat. Shall I release them? Or shall I bite him and make him mine?'

The man walking up the drive removed his hat and held it in both hands. He smiled as he drew closer, his calm features, grizzled grey hair and very dark skin surprised the Umbra sisters. Cymbeline shook her head, 'No, not yet. Let's see what he wants before you kill him. I have to admit I'm curious to find out what he has to say, aren't you?'

Makrut sneered, 'Do we care what a human has to say? He probably wants to beg for his friends' lives while he still can. But, very well, perhaps you're right. His coat might have been cut by a different tailor and today I need to be entertained. We'll allow him to tinkle in our pot until he bores me, then we'll let my toys rip him to pieces. Our assassin's insolence has left me with a bitter taste in my mouth, and this fool's blood might help wash it away.'

'I don't know. Look, my heart, look at your creatures. Some are watching this black fellow like blind hawks, but most are looking up towards the clouds. I've got a very strange feeling about this. We must be careful, Makrut, after all the Vadhaka warned us.'

The black man stopped just beyond the reach of the manus mortuus and gave the two females a pleasant wave. Makrut glared at him down her slender nose while Cymbeline continued to scan the horizon. She was certain their new visitor was a diversion and she refused to be caught by surprise twice in one day. The Vadhaka popping up from nowhere was enough. But his warning had seemed genuine. What, she wondered, would a shepherd look like?

'My name is Jeremiah Taylor,' the man's voice was deep, clear and respectful. 'You don't need these poor unfortunate guardians of yours. I mean you no harm. They'd be better resting in the ground where they belong rather than walking around up here. Anyway, ladies of the clan of shadows, I bring you a message from the Lady Brigid. She would have brought it herself, but she didn't want to scare you, she's very considerate like that.'

His face crumpled and he turned his pitying eyes on the faceless horde, 'I promised her I would say nothing about your wickedness, but look at them, poor souls. What kind of dark heart would dare do this to God's creatures? This is a shameful act. Shameful.'

Makrut's voice was filled with withering scorn, 'Your opinion is neither welcome nor asked for, fellow. We don't know any Lady Brigid. Tell me, are you shepherd, or sheep?'

Cymbeline took her gaze from the clouds and studied Jeremiah with curiosity. He answered Makrut with a sigh, 'Who would answer a question that brings no honour to the questioner nor the recipient? Who would ask it? I am a silversmith, a simple practitioner of an ancient and noble craft. My Lady bade me offer you the gift of her message. If you choose to refuse her gift, very well, then I shall bid you good-day.'

The crystalline Umbra cackled at this, but Cymbeline stepped forward, 'I would hear this message, silversmith. Pray, deliver your Lady's gift.'

'The message is this; my Lady gives you permission to leave and never return. She says that you are not wanted in Albion. If you remain, your mortal souls shall be forfeit. This will be your fate and the fate of all your kind unless you stay away from our sacred shores. She asks me to tell you that this message is neither warning nor threat, but a promise. It will happen as night follows day and day follows night. Your evil will no longer be permitted here. That is her message and her gift.'

Jeremiah replaced his hat on his woolly grey thatch, nodded curtly, and once more examined the howling circle of mangled faces and fleshless hands. 'A shameful waste of so many lives. Retribution shall be mine sayeth the Lord, and when it comes it shall be as a pillar of fire and it shall purge wickedness from the land.'

Makrut giggled, a girlish sound that rang oddly from her pink mouth, 'You speak very bravely for a man who comes here all alone. My creatures could tear you apart, rip you screaming limb from limb. What about that? Or I could turn you into one of them, and you would do my bidding like a blind puppet. I think you have bored me long enough, little sheep. So, then, what shall I do with you now?'

Jeremiah looked straight at her with sorrow in his eyes, 'What has time done to you to make you so vile? And what makes you think that I came here alone? My Lord is with me always, yea, though I walk in the valley of the shadow, he is with me.' And with that he turned on his heel and began making his way back towards the distant gate.

In the hissing tones of a snake Makrut urged her undead slaves on, 'Take him, he is yours. Use him as you will. Make him pay for his insolence. Make him scream for mercy, make him suffer. Entertain me, do your worst.'

The pack of manus mortuus needed no further urging. They leapt away, snarling like maddened hyenas, and raced after the silversmith. Their jaws opened impossibly wide showing bone white teeth, and their skeletal hands stretched out to rend and tear.

But they never reached their prey. Those closest to Jeremiah Taylor suddenly erupted into gouts of yellow fire and hissing jets of oily black smoke. It was as if there was an invisible barrier around the walking man. When the faceless horde ran into it, they instantly burst into flame. The incineration of their fellows seemed to drive the remaining undead into a frenzy. Makrut began shrieking at them trying to call her creations back to her side, but they were out of control. They started climbing over each other as if desperate to reach whatever was turning them into flaming torches. They leapt into the pyre in a maddened frenzy.

The silversmith did not turn around to watch the slaughter. He maintained his steady pace away from Arcadia House and the conflagration of faceless undead. Before he reached the gate, every single body had been rendered down to a burnt and twisted ruin. The stink of charred meat was intense.

Makrut screamed with rage and threw a lethal carmini after Jeremiah's vanishing back. Cymbeline matched it with one of her own. Nothing could have survived that brace of powerful killing curses; they had enough force to stop a tiger in mid-leap or bring down a charging elephant. Each meant certain death, together they should have pulverised the man. But nothing happened.

Jeremiah reached the gate unscathed and turned left into the tranquil street. He didn't so much as deign to glance back at the carnage he had left in his wake. The faceless dead had been reduced to a swathe of blackened bone and seared flesh smeared across the drive. The lush green lawns had been scorched yellow wherever they had fallen and burned.

Makrut screamed in fury, 'Cymbeline, get that scarlet buffoon back here. I want him to kill these vermin wizards, I want them tortured until the last breath has been wrenched from the last body. I want them dead; I want all of them dead, and I want to see them burn! Whatever it costs I want them dead. They insult us! They treat us like idiots, and now they must pay.'

Cymbeline was quiet, her eyes hooded in deep thought. Makrut finally screamed herself into something resembling her usual composure before she realised that her clan sister was ignoring her and completely lost in deep contemplation. Cymbeline's gaze was fixed on the gate through which the silversmith had vanished, a gate almost hidden behind the curtain of smoke billowing from the cremated dead. Her lips formed a silent question; she kept repeating the single word 'Why?'

Makrut touched her shoulder making Cymbeline jump. The crystalline Umbra asked, 'What is it? What has you so concerned, my heart? Is it that silversmith? Forget him, we have dealt with his sort before and we've never lost. But I'm concerned to see you so apprehensive. Come, tell me, are you afraid? Do you think we face real danger? Surely not?'

Her sister shook her dark mane of silky hair, 'Afraid? No, never. Nothing born of Earth can frighten me. But I am confused. What just happened here made no sense to me. Can't you see it too? Look at this carnage and consider the power it takes to do that, and to shrug off our killing carmini as if they were merely a shower of rose petals. That takes profound control, such control as I've only ever witnessed before within the circle of our own clan.'

'Wait, are you saying we've been attacked by one of us? Are you saying that that was caused by one of the Viventem Nominis Umbra? Yes, I can see it now, Flight or Chambers would do something like this. Bastards! I'll have their eyes for this!'

Cymbeline chuckled, 'I hadn't thought of that, you could be right. But no, what I was wondering is this. Why put on such a demonstration of force but leave us completely untouched? Whoever did that could have challenged us, it might even have singed our eyebrows to prove a point, but it did nothing. The old man delivered his message and everything that happened after that was purely defensive. They made no aggressive moves at all, none. Why is that?'

'Then that rules out Flight and Chambers. It rules out all of them. Our fellows would attack at the first sign of a threat, they would attack if they so much as thought there might be a threat. Strike first without mercy, strike fast without quarter. Leave none alive for another day. The dead are no threat to us, they are finished, unless we have them to serve us.'

'You are right of course. Do unto others before they even think of doing unto you. So then, what are we facing here? What is it that is afraid to strike except in self-defence? It certainly isn't that silversmith; he couldn't wrestle the skin off a custard. So, who or what was here protecting him but left us unscathed? That's my question.'

Jeremiah Taylor had a similar question for Kingswraith when the young wizard appeared by his side. 'I knew you were there,' he said, 'I could feel your stave in my bones. You were drawing those poor dead creatures away from me like filings to a magnet. I don't know what you did to the wretched things but at least they are now at peace. But why didn't you also punish those wicked women who did that terrible thing? Were you not angry? I was.'

The young man's expression was bleak, 'I ask you, is it for me to punish the wicked or is it for God? I hurt nothing back there, Jeremiah. Those poor faceless people were already victims of the Umbra. They were already dead and I released them with fire. Those women tried to kill you, my friend, but I wouldn't allow it. Must I now stoop to their level? Must I?'

Taylor took off his hat and rubbed at his grizzled scalp, 'But what if they attempt to inflict more of their evil on the innocent? What if they ignore the message and remain here to spread their foulness on the soil of Albion? What then?'

Kingswraith's looked back the way they'd come, 'Then perhaps that will be the time when I discover the answer to my questions. Perhaps I will be forced to stoop to their level; perhaps I won't have any choice. We shall see, yes, we shall see.'

33

The second day after their arrival at Whitekirk Hall the Professor and Clare were down in his family's laboratory practicing defensive thaumaturgy. Clare's wild talent could be allowed free rein within the strong stone walls of the thirteenth century crypt that housed the lab, where even her most dangerous carmini could do little more than scorch sooty streaks on the walls and ceiling. She was creating magic that the Professor had never seen before.

The lab was the secret place at the bottom of the flight of stairs behind the bookshelf in the priest hole that the Professor had intended to show her before accidently ridding the house of all its eight-legged occupants and their webs. Now that they had enough time to continue Clare's tuition in the white arts, he wanted to test her mettle with his new stave, and she was proving a keen and powerful student.

Meanwhile Mrs Vermont, Jenny, and Millicent, were in the kitchen planning that evening's dinner. Shelagh had been helping them to begin with, but when Jenny had bemoaned the lack of a full-time gamesman to stock her larder with rabbits, pheasants, and grouse, which were plentiful in the grounds.

According to Jenny the game animals were, 'Going to waste just flying around and breeding like, well, rabbits.'

The little housemaid became thoughtful, and shortly afterwards, in one of the rambling outbuildings by the stables, Wills and Marple found themselves confronted by Shelagh and listened to her with bemused curiosity.

Wills folded his powerful arms and furrowed his brow, 'So what you're asking, if'n I'm understanding you right, is for us to make you a leather shepherd's pouch sling and some iron shot for you to fire from it. Is that right? That's what you're asking us, eh?'

Marple shook his head, 'I've seen poachers using a sling to bring down a hare, but they use smooth river stones and pebbles. Why should you need to use iron shot? It seems mighty peculiar. And what would a jot of a thing like you know about shepherd's slings anyhow? There's an art to it, a man's art. Who says you could use one? You'd probably clout yourself on the head and do yourself an injury. I say best leave well enough alone.'

Wills disagreed, 'That ain't it, Mr Marple. Shelagh has her own way of doing things. If she says she can use a sling I believe her. She ain't foolish and she don't waste a person's time on folderols. I'd just like to know what she's intending if she wants us making iron slugs. What's the idea, missy? Are you going to tell us? Or is this another of your secrets?'

Shelagh could have told them the truth, that iron was the only effective metal when dealing with magical creatures, but she had promised Kingswraith she would hold her tongue until he rejoined the household. She felt strangely hollow inside while he was away, as if part of her was with him, wherever he was. She was still very confused about how she felt about him. Nobody had ever made her feel like that before, a sense of belonging.

Even so she smiled brightly at her companions, and basked in the warm smiles she got in return. It was only recently that she had become aware of the effect she was having on the male of the species, and was still learning the art of using her feminine wiles to get her own way. She wouldn't tell them the truth, she decided, but she would come close.

'You see it's like this; as what the young master was saying before we left him back in London. He says that there's something properly nasty that might be after us, a right wicked bugger, and that's why we've come out here. Being here is nice an' all, that's true enough, but we still have to be careful as baby birdlings when there's a cuckoo about or we'll be tipped right out the nest. See?'

The smile on Marple's face froze while he tried to sift through what he had just heard. Wills was more accustomed to Shelagh's unique slant on the English language so he just nodded and said, 'Right, yes, and so?'

Shelagh continued, 'And so, you men can use shotguns or cutlasses or pitchforks to skewer any wrong uns as come up 'ere. Big strong chaps like you would give them a taste of the martial conversation and they'd be best away on their toes before you shove their faces up their backsides and roll 'em across the lawn like hoops and they'd holler like redskins on the warpath. You could do that, see? But I can't, can I? Cause I've too delicate a constitution.'

Wills grinned, 'Right again, but hopefully that "martial conversation" won't be needed out here in the sticks. But where does the sling come into the story? You any good with a sling?'

196

'We didn't never go hungry when I was still livin' with me mam by the pond. So, if 'e makes me the shepherd's sling and the iron slugs proper and round like, I'll bring 'e a few brace o' coneys for supper, sweet as Pretty Polly Perkins. Jenny was saying as how her larder is empty of game, and that she misses it. With a sling I can put some good meat in the pot. And with iron I can clout a wrong un upside his head. So, we got a shake on that?'

Marple asked, 'I can make the iron slugs using wax resist in the farrier's shed. All the kit is still there including fine sand; and we'll have wax in the store. If Wills is willing to make the sling, I'll make your iron-wear. Lead would be a lot easier, are you sure it must be iron, miss Shelagh? And what size and shape d'you need?'

'Iron it must be, and that's a fact. Lead won't butter no parsnips with them wicked buggers as what we'll be a doin' of. And the slugs best be the size and shape of a single gentleman's trouser marble, as what I've never shaken hands with, being a maid and raised proper. But I knows the size of 'em cause I ain't blind neither. Now, I must go and see if the missus needs me with my hands busy around the house. I'll thankee gentlemen, and I'll be letting you off and about your business. Time don't never wait for ones such as we, do it.'

She bustled off towards the big house leaving a blank-faced Marple in her wake. Beside him Wills was fighting to hold back his laughter. His eyes shone with tears and his shoulders shook. He strongly believed that Shelagh's turn of phrase belonged in the music hall, and wondered if even she could hear what she was saying, sometimes.

Marple turned on him, 'You seem to understand the little lady, Wills. But I'm afraid I'm flummoxed every time she opens her mouth. What does she mean by a "gentleman's trouser marble"? Does she mean a pocket marble like a cat's eye, or a bonker perhaps? Or is she talking about a cosher, masher, or a plumper? I was quite the devil at marbles in my time, I know my sack of round treasures very well. But I don't know what she means. Do you?'

The big man couldn't contain his mirth for another second, he roared with laughter and became completely incoherent for several minutes, slapping at his thighs with his fists.

Marple's round cheeks reddened and he huffed with annoyance, 'Well, I'm blowed. Is this right? Is it polite to make merry of a colleague? I just want to make sure the lass gets what she's asking for, the right size and shape. Is that so very funny? Come on, man, what's this gentleman's trouser marble she's...'

As he spoke it was as if a light had flashed on in the steward's head and the words died on his lips. At that moment he had pictured exactly what Shelagh was talking about, and he coloured crimson from his cravat to his collar stud. His hand drifted towards his groin.

This set Wills off howling with laughter again, but he finally recovered himself enough to gasp out, 'That's right my old chum, I can see you've got it. She's talking about them what makes the difference between a stud champion and a gelding. Reckon that'll be about the same size as your old bonker, don't you?' And he roared with amusement once more.

The scarlet-faced steward stormed away to the farrier's shed, gathering the shreds of his dignity around his rotund form before searching out his metalworking tools. Wills finally recovered enough of his wits to head for the kitchen and discover if Jenny could find him some of the soft leather he'd need to fashion Shelagh's weapon. Life, he decided, was rarely boring with that little maid around.

Rather than head back to the kitchen and resume her duties, Shelagh had fetched a sack from the cellar beside the kitchen which held stores of apples, pears and root vegetables. Marple had been right about river pebbles. Water smoothed stones were perfect for game.

If needed she could walk through the woods to the river Thames which bordered the estate to the east, but first she would investigate the pebbles in the stream that ran from the pool of the Virgin's spring in the Hall's walled kitchen garden. It flowed under an arch in the east wall, and then down the mile or so until it reached the great river, threading its path through the meadows and the forest.

Millicent had shown her the walled garden and explained that the spring was the reason the Hall had been built on that site. Its name derived from the time when the Virgin Mary had stopped there while travelling through England with Joseph of Arimathea. They had both been parched by the dusty road and the spring had appeared as if by a miracle, welling up in the Virgin's footprint. It was still flowing with sweet water two thousand years later.

Millicent had even pointed out where you could still see the footprint in the stone by the head of the pool, and Shelagh had agreed that yes, there it was.

She could see it clear as the newt swimming under its little waterfall. Millicent said she had heard that newts were proof that water was sweet and pure, but when Millicent urged Shelagh to try it, she had only cupped water from the point on the stone where the spring welled up from that footprint.

She didn't agree with live animals swimming about in her drinking water, she thought it dirty. The frogs didn't look as if they'd washed their feet before diving in neither, and there were fine fat fish nosing through the weeds; in fact, the pool was swarming with livestock. The water had been delicious, cold and flinty, and she had traced the outline of the Virgin's footprint hoping to sense the energy of that ancient miracle. But she had only felt the water smoothed rock and the slick, hairlike algae.

Her stone hunt took her through the lush, late autumn meadows. Giant yellow hyssop peppered the slender wheatgrass with colour, while drooping poppies still splashed bright as blood against the green. The delicate white campion fluttered in the slightest breeze. Shelagh felt as if her soul had expanded to touch the fair-weather clouds in the sky. The grasses were still damp and springy, but they soon gave way to brown pine needles and red maple leaves.

She paused at the treeline of the ancient wild woodland. It was dense and fenced with thorny blackberry bushes, some still laden with fruit. But she knew not to eat them because her mother had warned her that this late in the year the Devil would have peed on them.

Following the stream deeper into the bosky shadows Shelagh pressed forward until, under the shade of a wych elm by a clump of box shrubbery, she found the perfect place in the stream to peel off her boots, hitch up her skirts, and wade out into the icy flow. The shallow stream was wider and deeper there and she could see that its bed was cobbled with perfect sling stones. She could already taste the game they would soon have for dinner.

With her skirts bundled up and tied in a knot at her hips she started filling her sack with stones, carefully choosing the prize specimens. She got a fine selection but after several minutes, during which her feet began to ache with cold, she heard a rustling sound in the box hedge. Her heart in her mouth she looked up, straight into the bright green eyes of a beautiful woman. The woman smiled. 'You must be Shelagh,' she said.

34

'Her name's Eurynome, she said, and she's sister to the young master's friend Penelope who is in London by a tree. They can talk, the trees can, well the people can talk through the trees. I don't know if trees talk, but I sometimes think I can hear them whispering to each other when I'm on my own, don't you? Anyhow, Eurynome told me as how young master Kingswraith is on his way here, and that we should be ready for guests.'

Jenny and Mrs Vermont had been astonished by the sudden appearance of a bedraggled and barelegged Shelagh. The little maid had burst into the kitchen with her skirts tied in a knot at her hip and scurried towards them leaving damp footprints on the flagstones.

Before letting her say anything Mrs Vermont had insisted that she get herself at least halfway decent. She had made her dry her feet, untie and smooth her bunched up skirts, and pull her boots back on. Jenny had fetched them all some tea.

But they could do nothing about the wild state of the girl's hair and the scratches on her face, arms and legs until they had listened to her news. If they made her wait any longer, she told them, she'd have blowed her lid clean across the room like a kettle when the steam can't get out. Words spilled from her tongue in a frantic rush.

Jenny left the questioning to Mrs Vermont. She thought it best because 'Eth' knew the odd little maid that much better, and might be able to separate the wheat from the chaff during Shelagh's stream of very individual sentences.

But she wanted to know one thing, 'This Yury-whatsit woman, is she camping in our woods? I'll have Marple onto her. This is private land, this is. She'll be with the gypsies I'll warrant. They can't just move onto our land like they own it! I'll set the constable on them and he'll see them off, you see if I don't.'

'I'm afraid you won't, miss Jenny. Her name is Eurynome and those woods have been her home since long before the first Lord Whitekirk laid the first foundation stone of the great hall. Good to see you again, Mrs Vermont. Hello, Shelagh, have you been in the wars?'

All three women leapt to their feet when Kingswraith strode into the kitchen. His presence filled the room like warmth from a blazing fire. Shelagh made a strangled sound, threw herself at him and wrapped her arms around his ribs, pressing her face to his chest. She almost wept with joy, a broad smile creasing her pretty face.

'She said you was coming, and I was so pleased I ran all the way back here to tell un all the good news. And here you are, you're here, and so fine you look there ain't enough words in the thickest book on the shelf to say how fine and noble you are. I tell you I could lay a clutch of eggs and quack like a duck. Oh, I don't know what I'm saying, I don't an all!'

Mrs Vermont was tutting over the girl's excited demonstration of affection. The maid had clearly forgotten her station in life. Behaving in such an over-familiar fashion would have seen her instantly dismissed from any other household. Jenny was just as astonished at Shelagh's behaviour, but she was more shocked by the changes to Lord Henry's ward. He was barely recognisable as the shy youth she had last seen over seven years before.

The young man pushed Shelagh away and hunkered down until he was face-to-face with her, holding her by the elbows. She wriggled like a puppy in his grasp. He said, 'Penelope told me she had sent a message to Eurynome. I thought she'd have told the guvnor or Clare, or sent one of the Clan with a message to the Hall, but she told you. Did she say anything else? Can you remember?'

The little maid finally calmed her breathing until she had hiccoughed her way into something resembling a sensible state. If she was embarrassed, she didn't show it. Her hazel eyes glittered with bright emerald sparks, and that signified a welling up of magical talent far greater than anything Kingswraith had ever seen there before. Everyone else thought of Shelagh as a conundrum, but the young wizard thought he was beginning to understand at least the bare kernel of the truth.

'It was something she said,' the girl admitted, 'she said when the thing was done, I was welcome back in the forest, back there where I found my sling stones as what are in my sack, over there.' She pointed, 'She said, as there are some as are neither rabbit nor hare. She said that you would know the difference. She said that I could live on hearth or heath, and be happy at either, but that I must be true to my nature or live a lie. She gave me summat too.'

Shelagh pulled her sack off the floor and dug around amongst the stones, 'Ah, see, here it is. Pretty as anything, ain't it? I told her, I said, no, course not, it's much too fine for I. But she said no, 'twas mine. If I touched it and it liked me then I could keep it, it's like a responsibility. See, sir, it's a lot like that ring you've been wearing, see there, see the snake biting its own arse?'

It was a silver amulet chased with a circular design of a dragon biting its tail. It flowed around the metal like rippling water and seemed alive when the light caught it. He studied the amulet and compared it with his ring. They must have been made by the same skilled hand, he thought, and Eurynome had given it to Shelagh?

He touched the amulet with his fingertips and as he did so he heard once more that great voice that had spoken to him in the reservoir when he had received his completed stave. It simply said, 'Good, well met, son and daughter of the Way. This was foretold.'

Shelagh jumped and looked around wildly, 'Where is he? Who said that?' She gazed at Kingswraith with eyes so huge and so brilliantly green that they cast emerald light into the room. The scales fell from the young wizard's eyes and he suddenly really saw her for the first time. He recognised the familiar lines of a beloved face, an echo of a forgotten memory, bone deep and from a time many centuries before he was born.

How had Eurynome found that amulet? How had she known to give it to Shelagh? What was happening here? The voice spoke again, 'There is a silver chain in your mother's box, it was a gift from your father. You must fetch it, thread it through the amulet, and then put it around my daughter's neck. Only then will you begin to understand all. You must do it now.'

Mrs Vermont and Jenny felt as if they were the audience at a play without a script; that the players were making the thing up as they went along.

Kingswraith said, 'Wait here, all of you.' Then he dashed out of the kitchen and bounded up to his old bedroom, the Bedouin tent room with its silk ropes, canopied ceiling, and striped walls. He had loved that room on the rare times he had visited the manor in his youth, and had left his treasures there for whenever he returned.

His mother's box was in his bureau where he had left it. He unlocked it for the first time in his short life, and was startled to find a photograph of his parents standing together and smiling at him. They looked so happy, and he missed them so much that his breath caught in his throat. Then he lifted out the upper tray and underneath it the glitter of silver caught his eye. A bright chain almost leapt into his hand. This must be it, he thought, so, now what?

He put the photograph in his pocket, locked the box once more and put it away, then hurried out of the bedroom and back down to the warmth of the kitchen. It was a big space down there but when he reached it, he found it had become crowded with the entire household. The Professor and Clare welcomed him as if they hadn't seen him in a year rather than a few days. Wills shook his hand with enthusiasm while Marple seemed wordless, as if stupefied to see him.

He accepted the hugs and the handshakes, but all the while he was looking at Shelagh, who seemed to have become distanced from the group and to have edged away from all the attention. She looked uncomfortable.

Kingswraith said, 'It's wonderful to see everyone looking so well, but first, please, there's something I must do. Shelagh, please, may I have your gift, just for a moment?'

She was shivering as she stepped forward. She said, 'Jenny said I must have found it somewhere and it din't belong to I, but when she tried to take it away to look at it, it burned her fingers. She said it must be a proper wicked thing, and I should throw it away. But I'll gladly give it to e, sir, if'n it doesn't burn e, for I wouldn't have that. Here you are.'

With trembling hands, she held out the amulet. He took it firmly. A jolt of pure energy arced from the amulet to his ring, and he felt the chain grow warm in his clenched fist. The Professor and Clare both stepped a little closer, their eyes wide with curiosity. Kingswraith wondered what explanation his guvnor might come up with, for what was about to happen. He didn't know himself, but he felt as if he was teetering on the brink of a precipice. He carefully threaded his mother's chain through the hole at the top of the amulet.

The voice told him, 'Tie it tight. Once this is around my daughter's neck only death may loosen it.' Following precise instructions Kingswraith knotted the chain fast to the disc, and then he beckoned Shelagh to step forward. But she shook her head and drew further away. He could feel Jenny's narrow eyes boring into his shoulders, sharp as a carpenter's awl. The atmosphere in that kitchen was so thick it was becoming hard to breathe.

He pursued Shelagh until she fetched up against a bench, 'Please,' he said, his voice gentle. 'Please, Shelagh, turn around for me.' She whimpered as she shuffled round to face the corner of the room. He heard affronted intakes of breath from Jenny and Marple, and a murmured conversation between the Professor and Clare. He leaned forward and whispered so that only Shelagh could hear him, 'Please, trust me.'

She turned to look at him over her shoulder, 'By my life,' she whispered back, 'always.'

He smiled at her, 'Can you lift your hair for me, please?' She used both hands to pile the wild and heavy mass of midnight curls on top of her head and balance it there, exposing the smooth white column of her neck. Jenny emitted a scandalised hiss, but Kingswraith heard his guvnor's gentle reprimand and she quieted.

He could feel the heat of suspicion in the housekeeper's gaze burning his back. This must look like a scene from a Penny Dreadful, he thought, wicked aristocrat seduces innocent housemaid. What a scandal!

He looped the chain around Shelagh's neck, and then screwed the clasp closed until it made a satisfying 'click'. The girl gasped as if she had been doused with ice water, her shoulders rose and she collapsed backwards into Kingswraith's embrace. She spun to face him, gripping his arms so hard her knuckles were white. Her expression was a mixture of wonder, terror, and shock. Her mouth worked as she fought to find words.

She gasped 'What is this? What's happening to me? What is this? I've never felt anything like this before. Sir, oh sir, what have you done? Oh, my love, my love.'

Around her neck the dragon motif on the amulet began glowing with a blue pneuma light which formed bright beads that raced up and around the chain, on which Kingswraith could now see the dragon which was woven from link to link, performing an intricate dance. He felt the heat of the ring on his finger and held up his hand to see the same blue light flickering from the dragon's head to its tail, round and round.

The group huddled silently at the other end of the kitchen saw the blue light flare, and then the green shafts of intense brilliance that ignited in the couple's eyes. The light exploded into a blinding halo when they kissed for the first time.

Even Jenny was awed at the sight. She gasped, her voice raw with emotion, 'Have you ever seen anything so beautiful in your life? What's going on here, what's happening?'

Mrs Vermont said, 'Well, I'll be blowed. Never in my life...'

The Professor and Clare put their heads together. Clare muttered, 'She said, "my love". You heard her?'

The Professor nodded. He replied, 'As soon as you can, try to get the girl somewhere on her own for a friendly chat. I'll take Martin for a walk. Let's see if you can get some clue about what's happening to them and I'll do the same. Agreed?'

Kingswraith and Shelagh heard only one voice. With soft tones sounding vast as an ocean the Draco Terrae said, 'It is done, and I see that it is good. So be it, my children, so be it.'

35

‘ The house was a mess, guvnor. I went there to see what was what and ran into a crowd of police officers. There was a glazier, and some professional cleaning bods that Inspector Chandler had organised. Mrs Vermont would have had kittens if she'd seen the state of the place. That was bad enough but I can't help but think of those poor constables. They didn't stand a chance when they ran into that Vadhaka demon the Umbra sent after us. One's been decapitated and the other's neck was snapped like a stick of kindling.'

The Professor had been listening to Kingswraith's adventures, including his incineration of a pack of faceless men and women. He said, 'What about those poor mangled people? Was there truly nothing else you could do? Could they have been saved?' He thought he knew the answer, remembering the faceless men Clare and he had met at Scotland Yard.

'No, sir. They were already dead, poor souls. Brigid tells me that the Umbra necromancer who did it has come here from the Carpathian Mountains. She says she's quite the legend; and she's been at it for ages. They use her name to frighten naughty children. She only eats exposed flesh and her bite enslaves her victims. We thought Haven Slighe was bad enough, but this one's a nightmare. Makrut Wyndsyster she's called, a truly horrible creature.'

'But, are they even human? You called her a woman, but are they like us? And you say they're coming here. Can you really be so sure?'

'I'd put my shirt on it, guvnor. The Vadhaka can smell magic, and Brigid tells me he's got my scent like a hunting hound. And I think Clare's been burning up the cellars here, hasn't she? Even I could sense what she was doing while I was still back in London. She's a powerful beacon, so yes, they'll find us alright. That's why I'm here. We've got the choice of running further away or staying put here and fighting. I say we fight. I say it's time.'

'I'm with you, old lad, but I think we'd best get the household out of it first, don't you? We'll get them to a guest house or an hotel in Wallingford, somewhere safe until this is finished one way or another. But I've got to ask, what's going on between you and Shelagh? She's a pretty little thing I can see that, but you're not the sort to take advantage of a besotted housemaid, I know you too well to believe that. So, then old lad, what's afoot, can you tell me what's going on?'

'When we have more time, I'd be pleased to, guvnor. But for now, please trust me that what's happening between us is as much a surprise for me and her as it is for you. It seems it was foretold that we should be together, in fact it has to do with events that go back to a time long before the Egyptians. It makes one heck of a bedtime story, but the fact is that Shelagh's no more a besotted housemaid than I'm the mooncalf boy of a chimneysweep. I promise I'll tell you everything once we've got the others safe, agreed?'

Meanwhile, Clare was standing with Shelagh by a fence next to the stables. They were placing spoiled apples along the fence so that Shelagh could practice with her new shepherd's sling. It was a beautifully crafted device with a generous leather pouch carefully sewn between two long leather braids. Wills had presented it to her after the extraordinary events in the kitchen. He'd stumbled over his words as he held it out to the girl whom he had so recently thought of as almost a daughter, but who suddenly seemed so very much a stranger.

'Shelagh, I don't, you see...' He gave up, 'Well, anyway, 'ere it is.' The housemaid now had a glamour about her that he'd never experienced before, and he found something very unsettling about the way her eyes seem to glitter brighter than emeralds, while her face glowed golden in the half light of the kitchen. Literally glowed, as if she carried an inner light. When she had gasped and hugged him, thanking him for his gift his mouth had gone completely dry.

Out by the stable Shelagh hefted one of her stones in the sling. She asked Clare to stand well away and to one side, explaining that, 'Things do sometimes go wrong and the stones go astray. It's passing rare, but even so, better safe than a rock in the head, that's what I say.'

Clare had had no chance to ask her about Kingswraith. Shelagh was too eager to try out what Clare thought of as her 'new toy' to engage in intelligent conversation. As a result, she was on hand to witness what happened next, and she felt the energy of Shelagh's wild carmini emanating from the little maid's lithe body.

Shelagh placed one foot firmly before the other, both pointing towards her targets. She fixed her eye on an apple that Clare estimated to be at least sixty feet away, then stood still as any sculpture. She looked frozen into place. To

Clare the shot seemed impossible. It would have been difficult with a pistol. The apples seemed too small and far away. Then Shelagh moved like an athlete, fluidly whipping the sling above her head just once, and she released.

The apple on the far left of the row exploded. Shelagh picked up three more stones, one after the other, and one after the other three more apples vanished in a shower of juice, red skins, and pale flesh. The girl's face had become a mask of pure concentration; her expression stern and cold as the stones she was aiming with unerring accuracy. She paused and took several steps further away from the remaining apples.

Clare had originally thought the sling to be trifle, a plaything created on a whim, but Shelagh's lethal demonstration clearly proved otherwise. Even from the greater distance Shelagh continued destroying her targets as effectively as a marksman with a rifle, and she did so with exquisite poise and elegance. Every movement was beautifully contained, almost balletic. And all the while Clare felt that wild magic at work. Evidently so had the Professor and Kingswraith. Clare jumped when her husband placed his hand on her shoulder.

He nodded at Shelagh and said, 'She is quite the fifteen-puzzle isn't she; and something much more. Martin tells me the story is as old as the Earth itself, which is intriguing I'll admit. But first we must get our people away to safety and prepare to defend ourselves. I should prefer it if you took Shelagh with you. I fear this will soon be no place for women.'

It took a moment for his words to sink in, then Clare turned on him in a fury, 'How dare you treat me like some silly little housewife! How dare you! Have I been practicing defensive carmini just so I can sneak off with my tail between my legs at the first sniff of trouble? Must poor little wifey leave her brave boys to fight alone? I don't think so. I'm still getting used to being married to you, Professor Henry Whitekirk, and I've no intention of getting used to being your widow! Not for a long, long while.'

Another voice sounded from nearby. They looked up and found Mrs Vermont and Jenny standing between Wills and Marple. Mrs Vermont repeated her statement, her voice brooking no argument, 'I'm sorry about this but we won't be sent away. Millicent is frightened, that's true enough, but Mr Marple has said he will go with her to the rooming house in Wallingford and look after her. He says it's not right for a woman to be a' wandering on her own. But Wills and I are staying to help, and Jenny has something to say too.'

208

'I do, yes, yes, I do. This here is my home and the Whitekirk people are like family to me. I'm staying. Whatever happens I can help look after things. Don't worry, I won't be a burden. I learned how to load a rifle, pistols and shotguns when I've been on the shoot with the old master. I stayed with him and I'll stay on with the new one too, thanking you all the same.'

Marple stepped forward, 'I'd stay, too, sir, I'm a decent shot. But I couldn't countenance young Millicent going off on her own. We can stay at the Green House on the London Road; I know Mrs Campbell there very well. It's a quiet time so she's sure to have rooms at this time of year. I'll take Millicent in the dog cart, with your permission, sir? We can wait there until we hear as how things are safe again. If that's alright with you, sir?'

The Professor sighed, 'I'm glad somebody sees sense in this madhouse. Tell me, is there room on this dog cart for Shelagh? We can at least get both the young ladies to safety.'

Marple jumped, 'Yes, sorry, yes, and that reminds me. Miss Shelagh, I have your iron trouser marbles in this bag. I made ten of them, I hope that's enough? If you catch a rabbit, you can recover the marble, can't you, yes? They're pure, unadulterated iron as you asked, and I believe they will prove to be the exact right size. I, hmm, checked.'

He shuffled to Shelagh and handed her a small jute sack that looked heavy for its size. The girl cautiously reached her hand into its neck and withdrew it much faster, wincing with pain as if she had just been burned.

'Yes, Mr Marple, they be right as right can be for I. I see I'll need gloves to touch them at all. They'll be perfect to bring down the wickedest coney in the field and no mistake. You're a right good 'un, Mr Marple, a proper gemmun who knows his marbles well, I'll warrant.'

She fetched a large white handkerchief from her sleeve and used it to protect her fingers from the touch of the metal while she dropped one of the iron slugs into her sling's pouch. Then she faced the fence on which was balanced her last apple. She was now standing at least one hundred and fifty feet from her target. The iron flew and the last apple disintegrated.

The little markswoman jigged with satisfaction while her audience stared open-mouthed at the space where the apple had been. She shrugged, 'I know, they ain't moving about like a rabbit or a pheasant would be, which makes it all simple as bobbin' in a barrel. But it proves Mr Marple has made some proper good slugs and Wills fashioned a sling old David would have been made up for. Best I've ever owned, coneys won't know what hit 'em. I'd better get that iron shot back in the bag though, sounds to me as if we might need it and soon.'

She took a few steps towards the fence, and then looked back over her shoulder at Kingswraith. He thought it was one of the most artlessly beautiful poses he had ever seen, showing off her long neck and perfect face framed by her tangled nest of hair, still in disarray after her encounter with brambles in the forest.

She smiled, 'My lord, my love, while I find Marple's marble can you explain to allus here why I'm not going near any Green House in any dog cart? My place is here with e, and if'n I can't be here with e, and thee with I, then all the sky will fall down and the seas shall rise and the mountains tumble and that will make a mighty commotion as will upset the neighbours. That big voice said as much. You tell 'em.'

Everyone watched her walk to the fence, climb through its bars, and begin her hunt for her iron slug. Then they turned expectantly to Kingswraith.

He coloured and grinned, 'Look, I'm sorry but I'm still trying to get used to this too. I've never been "foretold" before, and I've never been called "my love" before either, but I feel it to be true in my bones. She's right, my place is with Shelagh, and her place is at my side. And she'll obviously be useful in a fight if the bad lot are throwing apples at us. In fact, after seeing what she did to that poor pippin, they'd be best to turn up in armour, don't you think?'

36

Marple and Millicent departed for the Green House, while Shelagh had proved as good as her word by going out into the fields with Kingswraith and returning with four fat rabbits, each killed by a single strike from her sling. They were gutted by Jenny, then skinned and quartered and dredged in seasoned flour to be fried then boiled with beef stock, onions, wild garlic and vegetables for that evening's meal. Most game would have been left hanging from black metal hooks in the game larder, but rabbits were best eaten fresh or they spoil.

Wills was on watch to the rear of the house, the Professor at the front. Kingswraith was floating a few inches above his bed in the Bedouin tent room. He was spirit travelling to visit Garth and gather the latest news about the movements of their enemies.

Clare was in the dining room helping Mrs Vermont load some fine Purdey over-and-under shotguns plus a number of revolvers and breech loading rifles. Defensive spells were fine and dandy, but a loaded rifle at your shoulder offers a greater degree of confidence in any martial conflict. The locked walk-in firearms safe Jenny had opened for them contained sufficient arms and ammunition to fight off a small army, which was what they feared was coming.

Shelagh had found herself pulled back to where the stream flowed out beyond the walled garden. Something had been calling to her, and as the sun slowly settled down towards the horizon in the west and the sky took on the silvery glow of a late autumn afternoon, her eyes were drawn to the forests.

They seemed to step out of thin air. One moment there was nothing, and the next she saw a group of a dozen or so black-clad urchins appear before the tree-line and stride across the meadows towards her. As they drew closer their leader swiped the tattered hat off his head and bowed.

'Evening, miss. I'm Porewit, see, and we're the Boss's companions come up from London. We're meant to be hiding down in the woods, but it doesn't seem right to leave the Boss on his own, what with what's going on around here. So, we've come to stand with him. You're his special friend with the shepherd's sling, aren't you? Pleased to meet you, miss.'

Shelagh reached out, lifted a lock of curly hair at the side of Porewit's head and touched his pointed ear. 'My pa was like you. He was taller and looked older, and he was more of a man than a boy, but he looked like you. My mam and he never took no vows, they had no reckoning of it, but she always loved him. They were like billy coo, like pigeons and such. Love. Never knew what it meant before, but I do now. It feels like someone's playing music in your bones and moths are dancing in your belly. He's in his room, shall I go fetch him?'

Kingswraith appeared around the wall at that precise moment, 'No need, my love, I'm here, I felt them too. It's wonderful to see you all again, my dear friends. Garth told me you were coming. He also said that the Umbra women are on their way here by boat with an armed gang of hierodules. Thank God there are no more of the faceless undead; but the hierodules are almost as bad. What about you, lads? I could fetch you some knives or swords from the house, there's plenty for all.'

Porewit reached behind him and from thin air he plucked a fine short recurve bow that a mediaeval Mongolian horseman would have recognised, and then a full quiver of arrows, as did his companions.

'Thank-you but we'll say no to iron and steel, Boss. 'Tis the vampire metal and not to our taste. We'll be right with our hunting bows and flint-tipped arrows, sharp as a razor. Your lady here has her iron shot and you've got your fine staff. Your people have their guns and axes and all, I reckon that's enough iron to be getting along with. Truly, I feel sorry for any army coming here today. They'd best be ready to meet their maker, eh?'

Kingswraith glanced at Shelagh, 'Personally I would rather face these creatures on my own, but I can't force anyone to leave who won't go. Now, lads, listen to me, this is important. There is a man with them. He's called the Vadhaka. He has red eyes, red hair and he dresses in red. Do not approach him. Don't tangle with him, whatever you do. You must leave him to me. He's incredibly dangerous. Do your best to keep the Umbra and their hierodules away while I deal with him. Is that understood?'

Yarrow stepped forward, 'We'll not let you face him alone. The Lady Penelope would skin us alive if we did that, is that not right, lads? We'd never be allowed back home, she'd exile us all from London, sure enough. So then, we're there at your side come hellfire and the red-eyed devil himself.'

'No, Yarrow, the lady wouldn't skin you, you know that. But this "man" if that's what he is, certainly would. He would do it without a second thought. It was him who tortured and killed Okeanus. It was because of him that Penelope sent you away from London and I had to hide away on a barge. He looks human enough but he was fashioned thousands of years ago to do one single thing – kill – and he's very, very, good at it. Don't go near him, promise me? He's far worse than any demon from Hell.'

The Sprites looked shifty for a moment, then Yarrow said, 'You're the Boss, Boss. What you say is carved in stone with us, you know that. But when the storytellers recount this in a hundred years' time we won't have them saying that the noble lord Kingswraith faced the red-eyed bugger all by himself, while his companions hid behind a tree and waited for the bad people to go away. That's not much of a legend for the feast, now, is it?'

'No-one doubts your courage my brave lads. You'll have enough to do protecting the Lady Shelagh here, and the women of the house. They'll sing of your deeds as guardians of the innocent, and remember your names with pride. While I try to bring down the red bugger, the Umbra females and their horde will be attacking everyone else and I might be too busy to help. You must stand with the Professor and his man Wills; they'll need your help.'

Porewit grinned, 'Protecting the innocent, is it? We're the very lads for that,' he paused, 'but may I just point out that the Lady Shelagh is of warrior blood and I think she might be standing with us too.'

He held his hand up, 'Now, don't look at me like that, Boss, I'm just saying what we all can see clear as any day. She's a brave wee lassie as they'd say in the mountains of Hibernia, a she-wolf. And you don't lock a she-wolf in the barn for fear it might be hurt by a pack of wild dogs. If the dogs attack, you'd best let the she-wolf loose to do her thing.'

Kingswraith's head was spinning. He needed time to think, at least long enough to understand what was happening to him. He wanted to know how Shelagh had smitten him so deeply during that strange time in the kitchen during that business with the amulet and his mother's chain. He had heard nothing more from the Earth Dragon since. On top of that he felt bowed under the weight of too much responsibility. Too many people were looking to him to make the right decisions, when the wrong ones, might see them all killed.

If he failed, he would die, but everyone else would die too. Everyone who mattered to him would be slaughtered by the Vadhaka and the hierodules would put any survivors to the sword. The Umbra wanted them all dead, Garth had said so. He gazed towards the river. A small army was coming and they would be armed to the teeth and have blood in their eyes, red as the Vadhaka's.

His heart quivered in his chest. Was it fair that all this responsibility had fallen onto his shoulders? Surely, he was too young for this? He had always looked to his father or the Professor to make tough choices, why must it be him all of a sudden? Why must he make these life-or-death decisions now? Couldn't someone else take charge? Wills, the Professor? But no, the chalice had been passed to him and he must drink deep of it.

It wasn't the thought of his own death that was twisting his bowels into a knot. He knew he led a privileged life and now he had Shelagh he had so much to live for. But, in truth, the shadow of death held no sting for him. He knew there was an afterlife, he'd been there. Death would be a continuation of life but in a new landscape.

But Shelagh? She was still so fresh and vital in her new role. What wonders would the future hold for her if she lived? Just finding out what happens to her and what she does next was a great reason to stay alive. And then there was the household from Owl's Tower; Mrs Vermont and Wills, the Professor and Clare. There was Jenny, and these urchin Sprites who were willing to face anything to be with him. What would happen to them if he failed? He was responsible for all of them. Surely it would be best if he fought alone?

Shelagh must have seen something of the conflict chasing these thoughts around in his head. She reached out, took his hand, and stood on tiptoe to touch her cheek to his.

She murmured, 'They say this red man was fashioned as a murderer. Well, says I, if 'e was born like a wolf for killing the flock like, well then, someone else must be born to stop him. The flock needs its shepherd, and old shepherds used slings like mine to kill wolves. That David killed the monster Goliath with one of these, for all 'e 'ad no clothes on. We're the shepherds now, and the wolves are coming. We got our job to do, says I, and we will, an all.'

Kingswraith remembered the Derby figurine of a shepherdess that his mother treasured and he hadn't been allowed to touch as a child. That figurine was all bows and flounces with buckled shoes and an enormous hat on which three sheep could have grazed the fancy flowers without falling off. In his mind's eye he compared that porcelain fancy with the lady by his side. One would have ended up as a wolf's dinner for sure, but he didn't rate the wolf's chances against Shelagh.

She was still wearing her black maid's frock under which were a pair of heavy boots that made his own highly polished hand-made Church footwear look dainty. Her hair was a tangled mess around her pert little face with its haunting eyes and cupid's bow mouth. Unlike Penelope, Shelagh had no choice about how she looked. She couldn't switch between street Arab adolescence and striking mature beauty. She was who she was. Perhaps that's why...

Porewit broke into his chain of thought, 'Now see here! We might be fighting monsters but we ain't taking our clothes off to do it. And if your mate David was here, miss, I'd ask him to at least put a pair of pants on. It ain't decent running around in your skin. There are some things as are only between me and my bathday and that's an end to it.'

The other Sprites agreed that they would fight to the death, but only while wearing the clothes they stood up in, although Yarrow said he would take his coat off and roll up his sleeves if the young lady thought it might help.

Shelagh pouted, 'You are right. I don't think my mam would think it proper for I to be running about without my drawers on in company, and outside the house too like a heathen savage. It doesn't sound the thing at all. And I'm keeping my boots on. Bare feet on cobbles ain't no good for I, there's that said an all.'

It took a few minutes for Kingswraith to assure everyone that they could maintain their decorum in the heat of battle, and that David was a long time ago and somewhere a lot warmer than Oxfordshire. So, clothes were the order of the day. He then led the group to the stableyard where Wills and the Professor were building a redoubt from an old cart, barrels, hay bales and anything else they could find. The Sprites were made welcome and joined in with gusto. The sound of hammering filled the air.

The sunset was red as blood and filled the west with fire. It was a heavenly evening. Jenny and Mrs Vermont brought out trays of bowls filled with the rabbit and vegetable stew, and slabs of good buttered white bread on the side. Everyone sat where they could to enjoy their meal. Kingswraith sat beside Shelagh, surrounded by his companions.

It was a convivial company. They were taking what pleasure they could from each other while appreciating the peace. Even so, their voices were muted and there was little laughter. They were waiting. Once the meal was finished the bowls were collected and carried back to the kitchen, while Wills and Kingswraith joined the Professor in checking their defences.

The night was cloudless and the moon was bright. The meadows became a monochrome landscape of light and shadow pricked by a host of stars and planets. The company made its final preparations, checking the rifles and swords they had stacked in the redoubt for the fourth or fifth time. Then there was nothing else to do but wait.

It was just after nine o'clock when Kingswraith whispered, 'They're here. Get ready.' And he vanished from their sight.

37

The defenders crouching down in their redoubt first heard the strange ululation of the hierodules, a sound very like the howling of hyenas, then they saw them moving forward like a great shrewdness of apes, advancing across the meadow. The Umbra had wisely skirted the woods to avoid meeting any Sprite warriors. They wanted to reach the people of Whitekirk Hall as quickly as possible and destroy them without any distractions. They had planned for the fight to be brief and brutal, they believed they had many more fighters than they needed.

A streak of light fell from the heavens and crashed into the meadow, hurling a spume of soil dozens of feet into the air and blasting a large crater just before the first line of attackers. A scarlet clad man rose up from the crater, dusting down his freshly cleaned and carefully repaired costume. The Vadhaka took his place at the head of the Umbras' pack, pulling his wide brimmed hat down over his bloody orbs. The hierodules screeched and chattered with their eagerness to reach the enemy and tear them apart, but the red man remained silent.

As he walked, he moved his hands in the air like a dancer caressing an invisible partner. Then he squared his broad shoulders and breathed deeply. He knew that at last the chase was nearly over, he could smell his prey. Kingswraith was close, very close. Afterwards there would be others. He could sense other practitioners who might also warrant his attention, but Kingswraith must come first. He had led him around in a merry dance but the music was finally finished. The game was done. It was time for his quarry to die.

This was the reason the scarlet man had climbed out of that crucible in that long-lost workshop in a forgotten city. He had since killed Kings and Emperors, Princes and Queens. He had walked through an army camp and killed their General leaving no trace behind him except the man's bloody corpse. He had slaughtered bishops and book-keepers, husbands and wives. He never asked why, he just took his bounty and did his work. And he had never failed. Never.

He strode swiftly forward at the head of the Umbra pack because he must reach the victims first and carry his chosen game away from the conflict to kill him slowly, with all the respect due to a worthy opponent. Kingswraith must welcome his end as the release it would surely be after the artist of pain had carved another of his masterpieces into his victim's agonised flesh. The Vadhaka imagined himself plucking at Kingswraith's nerves, playing a melody, a duet that only they would hear. Such pain; such pleasure.

The Professor and Wills were looking along the sights of their rifles at the mass of moving shadows. Beside them Clare held the stave in her right hand. Behind them Mrs Vermont and Jenny stood ready to reload their guns and hand up fresh weapons. Kingswraith had vanished into the ether and his companions had dispersed to God only knew where.

Meanwhile Shelagh had moved away from the redoubt to the deep shadows beside the stables and outhouses. She needed enough room to whirl her shepherd's sling at its full length to ensure the maximum lethal impact when her shot found its target, and the redoubt was far too cramped for such work. She was more likely to crown a friend than bring down a foe.

She was desperately worried, not just because she didn't know where Kingswraith had vanished to, but also about his companion Sprites who seemed to have melted away into the night like ghosts. She knew that they hadn't run away, she was certain that neither she nor the little group in the redoubt had been abandoned, but she felt afraid and very alone all the same.

The horde of noisy, ape-like creatures was getting closer. She caught glimpses of a man in a broad brimmed hat marching at their head. There was magic there under that hat, she could feel the force of it, and somewhere in the mass of figures was a tremendous source of dark power, but the ape-men themselves were simple flesh for all their odd looks. She would only need the smooth river stones to stop them. She would save her iron for the true enemies, if she could see them. It was so dark and comfortless.

A burst of light jolted her out of her revery. From somewhere to the right of the attackers roared a thick tongue of flame, right into their midst. By the fire's light Shelagh also saw the flicker of arrow shafts pouring into the horde like lethal rain. The ape-men were falling and burning alive, but the light also showed how many of them had arrived at the Whitekirk estate, eager to kill Kingswraith and his friends. Too many to count, her heart sank.

Her carefully collected pile of smooth river stones suddenly seemed pathetic. She might as well try to stop a charging elephant with a blade of grass. She could also see the red costume of the man in front, and was amazed by the way he suddenly ran at the redoubt, never moving in a straight line for longer than a few seconds. He was shifting effortlessly from one place to another making a difficult target for the guns. And all the while his hands wove a strong web, as if he was throwing things at Clare, the Professor and Wills, invisible darts of energy.

Bits of the redoubt flew up into the air, exposing the defenders who instantly dropped to the ground, covering their heads. Without thinking Shelagh grabbed one of her iron slugs, burning her fingers, and she used her sling to hurl it at the scarlet man. She followed it with another just moments later.

In truth she didn't know what to expect when her slugs hit the scarlet man, she just wanted to stop him from hurting her friends. The man paused for a moment and shook his head as if he had suddenly remembered something or heard an unexpected noise, then he slowly and deliberately turned his face to his left.

She followed his gaze and saw Kingswraith step forward from the shadows under a tree, his stave held across his chest like a barrier. The scarlet man snarled and sprinted at the young wizard, hands outstretched ready to snatch his prey off his feet and carry him away for the agonising poetry of the long kill. Shelagh's iron slugs had obviously done nothing to slow him down and he grinned with vulpine triumph. At last!

Shelagh whimpered with despair and abject horror. To have found her only true love and to lose him so soon afterwards, that must be the darkest and cruellest irony. The gods were mocking her, and she thought, when a fool makes a plan, the fates laugh.

Without the deadly fusillade from the Vadhaka to pin them down the Professor and Wills were up and firing into the horde with shotguns, rifles, pistols, anything the two women at the redoubt's rear could reload and hand forward. Clare was rolling 'sticky' fire balls at the ape-men, a carmini she had discovered by accident in the cellar laboratory. The ball sped along the ground then climbed and engulfed the first thing it met. Meanwhile Shelagh was using up her supply of river stones in a lethal barrage, but all the while she was watching Kingswraith.

The Vadhaka was jarred when the iron tip of Kingswraith's stave was thrust into his chest, and when he grabbed at the rod to pull it out of its owner's grasp, his hands had bloomed into bright yellow flame. He pulled away and beat the flames out on the ground, then he flung force blades at his quarry. No time for subtlety, no poetry, it was time to kill, and kill quickly.

The blades caught at the young man's clothing, tearing away strips of the cloth, and the Vadhaka expected to see Kingswraith cut down, bleeding from deep wounds, his limbs carved away in a welter of blood. But such was not the case, instead, the young wizard blurred into action and his staff spun. The web of force blades struck sparks as they were deflected away from their target and spun into the night. The Vadhaka snarled and threw more, but always with the same result. Then the young wizard aimed his staff at the assassin and cried Mori his face a mask of fury.

The scarlet man spat in contempt; such pathetic incanto had no effect on him. He reared back and prepared to fire his ultimate weapon, a force spear that could penetrate any defence and would melt his target's vitals into a bloody pulp.

He hissed, 'Try to stop this, boy!'

But instead of unleashing his spear the Vadhaka suddenly staggered backwards. He reeled away in confusion as a relentless wave of agony crashed through him, wrenching at his nerves with a pain so intense that it felt as if a great hot knife had sliced into him and ripped him open from chest to belly. His spine twisted uncontrollably as his muscles tried to find release from the excruciating torment but found no release.

This was not pain as he thought of it. This was no art form; this was nothing like his carefully crafted melody of death. Instead, it was a crescendo of anguish, it played with him as if every nerve shredding ounce of torment he had ever inflicted on his targets, every exquisite moment of torture he had ever wreaked on so many victims over the long millennia, all of it had been focused and drilled deep into his flesh in one endless unendurable moment.

He screamed and fell to his knees, clutching at himself with his blackened fingers. What was this? Then his hands felt the places where two iron slugs had been fired into his vitals by Shelagh's sling. The vampire metal had been sucking his strength out of his body, stealing away the binding weave of necromantic feral magic that had held him together since before history began. He felt everything draining away, and weakness flooding his tissues.

Kingswraith's death curse had only accelerated a process that was already in motion.

The young wizard approached the assassin with caution, but the scarlet man seemed to be shrinking into his clothes, shrivelling away. Kingswraith could see the torment etched deep into the man's face and felt a brief pang of pity. He touched the Vadhaka with the tip of his stave and barked Mori once more, intending to put the devil creature out of its misery. The carmini worked, but with a far greater and more devastating effect than he had expected.

In front of Kingswraith's astonished eyes the scarlet man deflated like a burst balloon – and then he exploded in a wet sounding eruption of bloody shreds.

Kingswraith automatically warded off the Vadhaka's gory fragments by using the same simple carmini he sometimes used to deflect rain. He had not expected such a violent outcome and was momentarily stupified by what he had done.

But then he saw the two iron slugs that had tumbled to the ground, released from the Vadhaka's shattered body. Shelagh must have got him with her sling, he realised, the she-wolf had killed the wild dog after all. He looked up to find the girl and saw her standing in front of the stables, gazing back at him.

It was only then that he became aware of the melee surrounding the defenders. Wills and the Professor had exhausted their ammunition and had resorted to axes to drive back the Hierodules. Clare was hurling fire balls from her stave and Shelagh had begun gouging up loose cobbles to throw from her sling. There was no sign of Jenny, but Mrs Vermont was desperately thrusting at the ape-men with a pitchfork. He couldn't see his Sprite companions at all and he feared them lost.

He ran at the horde, blasting them with flame and his Cultro carmini. The front lines instantly fell back, but those behind clambered forward over their fallen comrades. That was when the horde opened and he saw the two women at their heart. They were the same Umbra he had seen at Arcadia House. One of the women cast a spell at Shelagh; there followed a flash of blue light and he saw his girl crumple to the ground.

He shrieked, 'No!' and in a savage rage he began to blast at the hierodules and their mistresses with every destructive force he could muster. He was filled with so much hatred and agonised fear – certain in his bones that Shelagh must have been killed – that it threatened to tilt his mind into madness. A heart that can love will die to protect the subject of that love; it will also kill to avenge it.

This was not fair! The monstrous Vadhaka had been vanquished, this nightmare should have ended with his death; but the Umbra still lived and insisted on pursuing their relentless campaign of vindictive horror without their champion. Very well, he thought, they must pay for this. They had killed Shelagh!

But with a start he realised, something new was happening. The complexion of the ape-men's onslaught was changing from its thrusting, mindless attack to a stuttering melee. Kingswraith fired a burst of flame into the Umbra's horde and almost whooped with joy at what he saw. Clouds of arrows were decimating the throng from behind. Kingswraith heard commanding voices and shouts of elation. The hierodules lost all sense of order, in terrified ranks they began to break away and scatter in all directions.

Away behind the panicking crowd he saw rows of mature Sprites releasing a rain of arrows into the ape-men with uncanny precision, until only the Umbra women remained standing, left exposed and alone, their army dissolved around them. The women ducked down and ran away from the fight and back towards the river, making their panicked escape.

The battle of Whitekirk may be lost but the war was not yet won. Another day would provide fresh opportunities; they need only live to gather greater forces and return to defeat the enemy. They believed that nothing could stop them.

Kingswraith hesitated for long seconds. He wanted to get to Shelagh, to see how she fared, even though he suspected the worst. She had gone down with a boneless finality and he ached to run to her side. But at the same time, he couldn't let those vile creatures who had killed her escape to plan something new.

When he spotted Clare rushing from the redoubt to gather up the little maid's inert form, that decided him, he would exact his revenge. With a hot heart and cold resolve, he launched himself into the air and called on his pneuma light to illuminate the ground beneath.

The Umbra could not fly, that much was obvious, but they could glide across the meadow almost as fast as he could speed through the air. He caught up with them just in time to see them both dive into the Thames. He rocketed down and plunged into the river close behind them. The women could move very fast through the water and were already vanishing away into the murk. He idly thought that a dolphin would have proved very useful at that moment.

He thrust his stave forward and cried Lux! Blue light bloomed from its tip and threw the two women into sharp relief. They were closer than he thought. The crystalline woman who had cursed Shelagh turned and drew her arm back as if preparing to attack him. The dark-haired one also prepared to fight. They hung poised in the water before him.

With a swipe of his stave, he yelled Stupefaciunt! He needed them at his mercy and they were too dangerous to leave conscious. They had both already released their killing curses, but those were easily deflected. The women were not so lucky, his stun carmini had left both of them floating helplessly in the current. What Kingswraith did next would haunt him for the rest of his life. He swam to the unconscious crystal Umbra, touched her with his staff, and barked Mori! The word exploded from his mouth in a cloud of bubbles.

Red streaks of glowing light raced across her glass-like features, her fists clenched and her mouth and eyes flew open in shock. She imploded and shattered into fine shards. Her empty dress floated to the riverbed amidst a cloud of glittering fragments. As if jolted awake by her sister's sudden death the dark-haired Umbra lurched back to her senses and howled at him, an animal sound filled with fear, confusion, and rage, all trace of civilisation scattered.

Cymbeline spun in the murky water, frantically searching for some sign of Makrut. But with sickening certainty she realised her sister Umbra was gone, and deep within her dark, hollowed out soul, she knew that she was all alone and facing Kingswraith. This boy was the bane of all their plans, how could this be? She squinted into the water's murk looking to see if a true adept was lurking there, mocking her. Nothing.

She had to get away, and Cymbeline began making imploring gestures, as if pleading to be allowed to leave. If she could only get back to her Viventem Nominis Umbra family she could return in force and totally destroy this upstart wizard. Whatever defences and friends the boy might have, she thought, surely, he could not overcome the concerted power of seven living shadows facing him all at once?

He was just a human, a weak creature. How had the Vadhaka described him? A shepherd? So be it, despite his victory that day he was just a pathetic sheep herder, against the ancient power of the Umbra he must be brought to his knees. He must fail.

Kingswraith watched Cymbeline's performance with a cold heart. For all her begging gestures she couldn't disguise the cruel arrogance stamped firmly across her features, nor the sly glint in her eye. She could no more act the terrified penitent than he could be the callous killer that wisdom told him he needed to be. He was tired of her evil, he wished her gone. All he wanted to do was return to the crumpled form of Shelagh back at Whitekirk Hall.

'Very well,' he said, his voice clear in the water. 'Leave now and never return. Leave and you can live. You are not welcome in Albion, leave or your soul will be forfeit.'

He turned away from her and prepared to swim back upstream. Cymbeline regarded his unprotected back and realised that he was indeed, every inch the weak and foolish sheep herder she had thought him to be. She drew on her deepest reserves of dark magical energy and prepared to throw the most lethal killing curse she had ever fashioned.

She hissed, 'Die you fool!' And her face lit up with a blaze of triumphant venom. The curse lanced towards the young wizard with a force that split the river like a razor-sharp blade, flying straight at the young man. It would rend his flesh from his bones in an instant.

Kingswraith had felt her building her magical force. He looked back over his shoulder and gently reflected her own curse back into her grinning features, then followed it with a sharp command, Mori! Cymbeline's last expression was one of surprise. She was the powerful one, the pinnacle of magical perfection, and yet, in her final brief moments, she felt her own charm flay the flesh from her bones, tearing the skin from her face and hands, as Makrut had done to her faceless slaves.

The young wizard took great satisfaction in watching her bloody corpse drift silently down towards the silty riverbed. It seemed apt somehow. Then he took a deep breath and turned towards Whitekirk Hall, towards the tragedy he knew he would find there.

I avenged you, my love, he thought, Shelagh's lovely face haunting his mind's eye clear as a picture, I avenged you. I avenged you, my girl, but it won't bring you back to me.

And as he swam his tears left a faint trail of salt in his wake.

38

The Spiritus Iudicii ignored the odd little soul that had once been the Vadhaka. It was a poor and innocent thing, confused by its death and terrified by its new status as a ragged spirit bowling along a tunnel of light towards the Halls of the Dead. It remembered power, it remembered pain, it remembered so many things, but it no longer understood any of them. In many ways it was a baby for whom everything was brand new, frightening and strange.

Makrut Wyndsyster, however, was not so fortunate. She was snagged from the flying stream of the dead like a salmon hooked from the brook, and found herself pinned helplessly to the colourless soil of the dimension between worlds by a child-like foot. Her captor looked small, malformed and cadaverous, but she could no more wriggle free from its grip than she could understand what it was, or where she was being held captive.

She began to protest in a wheedling tone. She had passed through the veil before and had always been reborn with all her powers and memories. This was different, and she had a very bad feeling about what was going to happen next. The child kept its black eyes pinned to the glowing river of souls above its head and ignored her. It has not hurt me yet, thought Makrut, was that a good sign? Was this just some strange diversion on her journey to reincarnation?

But then she remembered Frossard and Haven Slighe. They had both vanished from the ether, been eradicated as if they had never existed. Something had plucked them out of the universal essence, and wiped their slates completely clean. Was this it? Had this child-like thing taken them? If so, where were they? Where were their remains? She strained her neck trying to spot some clue in the bleak, featureless landscape, but nothing caught her eye.

Like a fisherman reeling in his line the Spiritus Iudicii reached up and plucked another soul from the ceaseless torrent of chattering dead. He dragged the struggling Cymbeline Fleischer down into his shadowless domain, and he held her in his hands with the ease of an infant cradling a doll. Pinned under his foot Makrut watched in nauseated horror as he began to eat Cymbeline's body with greedy relish. He savoured every bite, each nibble with his knife-like teeth, starting with her toes.

In a place where time held little sway the nightmare took an age to end. All the while the only sounds were those of methodical chewing, the grind of the child's teeth splintering through bone and sucking on flesh. Over all there came the agonised, inhuman shrieks and bubbling sounds her Umbra sister made as she was devoured. It seemed impossible, but the screams didn't stop until the child had ripped out and swallowed her larynx.

Makrut could see Cymbeline's terrified eyes still swivelling in insane horror while the creature tore out her writhing tongue and played with it for a while before stuffing it into his gaping maw. He swallowed the tongue as if it was a tender delicacy, then he reached out and prised the frantically rotating orbs from their sockets and slurped them down.

He finally crunched through all that was left of Cymbeline's head until the only part of the Umbra that remained was her mane of silky dark hair, and even that seemed somehow alive, coiling around her tormentor's fist. He opened his hand and blew on it, and in a cloud of white flame the hair vanished like mist under the sunless sky.

The child belched, smiled with satisfaction, and then he reached down to take Makrut by her ankles. Because he was no longer desperately hungry, he decided to take his time with this second feast, slowly savouring every morsel. For Makrut the torment seemed to last an eternity. By the time he was nibbling at her lungs and lapping the marrow from her shattered bones she was completely insane and gibbering for forgiveness and mercy. She received neither, not until the child took his last bite and finally granted her total oblivion.

…

'She's alive. She's shaken and bruised but she's alive. That amulet thing she was given by the Sprite woman had some kind of protective shield built into it. The killing carmini couldn't penetrate far enough to do much damage beyond scaring her and knocking her out cold. More's the pity, Jenny had no such protection. She's badly hurt. We don't know...'

Clare had rushed to meet Kingswraith in the entrance hallway and had quickly summed up the agitated state of the young wizard. She had hastened to tell him the good news – and the bad. At first his face had brightened at her words, and then darkened when she told him about Jenny. He looked around.

He said, 'Are any of my companions here?'

The answer floated up from the stairs leading down to the kitchen. Porewit called out, his voice muffled by his mouthful of food.

He said, 'Course we are, Boss, just having a little nosh after all the excitement. Nothing gives a fellow an appetite like facing up to mortal peril, and overwhelming odds, does it, eh, lads? Mortal peril I said, and mortal peril it was.'

The enthusiastic answers were hampered by bread and cheese, apples, and carrots. Kingswraith asked, 'Is everyone alright? You did a brilliant job with those arrows, by the way. We couldn't have managed without you.'

Porewit shook his head, 'No Boss, it was you tearing into them like a berserker on a spree that did it, and Eurynome's clan deciding to step in and support us, that's what won the day. Us, we did what we could, but we ran out of arrows after the first few minutes. Penelope said it was a small army, but it wasn't that small. Our only injury was Melsh there; he caught his thumb with his bowstring, bruised it black. But he always was clumsy, even as a puppy.'

An affronted, food obstructed voice cried out, 'Oi!'

Kingswraith took Porewit by the shoulder and grinned, 'They'll still be singing about this in a thousand-years-time. But I have to ask, have you any of the Lady's elixir with you? One of our friends is badly hurt, it's Jenny. It might be her only hope.'

Porewit fetched a silver flask out of the mysterious depths of his shabby coat and shook it to test how much it contained. It sounded full.

He looked worried, 'One of the ordinary human folk? Someone from about here, is it? Right then, best be careful with this, don't use no more than a capful. That's powerful stuff that is, and it might do more harm than good. And another thing, you'll have to share some of your energy with her, some of your essence. Touch her with your staff and say, "Sap from me to you". That's all.'

'Will it work?'

'Can't think of anything else just now. It's worth a try anyhow, wouldn't you say?'

Kingswraith took the flask and turned to Clare, 'Can you take me to Jenny, please?'

'What about Shelagh?'

'You say she's alright? That's good, we've got the rest of our lives to hold hands. Let's see what we can do for Jenny first. Maybe we can gift her some of the years she deserves to enjoy, give her back her life. She has a brave heart, eh? We must try.'

The woman in the bed was pale and looked on the point of death. Only her faint breathing told Kingswraith that he still had a little time to act, but it would be touch and go. He poured a capful of the sparkling liquid and pressed it to her lips, careful not to choke her. Clare watched everything with intense curiosity. Jenny's eyes fluttered open. Then Kingswraith touched her with his stave and muttered 'Sap from me to you.'

The reaction was instantaneous. Jenny arched her back and screamed through gritted teeth. Kingswraith jerked away from the bedside in horror as she rolled from side-to-side, panting like an overheated dog. She clawed at her chest and stomach, trying to tear the bedclothes away to reach her wounds. Kingswraith threw himself across her, clinging to her wrists.

He leaned close and gasped into her tormented face, 'Jenny, Jenny, what is it? What's happening? What's happening to you?'

She screamed, 'It hurts, it hurts so bad! It hurts.' She fell back in a faint, her eyes rolled up in their sockets until they were little more than twitching white crescents. Her hands twisted and plucked at the counterpane, and her groans dwindled away until they were little more than a keening sound; like a hacksaw blade ripping through wet wood.

Clare turned on Kingswraith, her eyes blazing, 'What have you done to her? After everything that's happened to her do you have to torment the poor woman to death? Get out of here, Martin! Just leave her in peace, will you? Get out.'

He almost ran from the room, tormented by the sounds of Jenny's agonised distress and the fury in Clare's eyes. He had never seen her angry like that before, and after the traumatic events of the evening he felt crushed. He couldn't take any more. Too much killing, too much pain. He was exhausted. So much for the noble hero, he thought. Hail the fool who kills foe and friend alike. He fought and failed to hold back his tears.

His Sprite companions joined him on the stairs. Yarrow studied him closely with concern writ large on his usually impish features.

He said, 'We heard the screaming, Boss. Is your friend alright? Are you alright?'

Kingswraith shook his head, 'No, no, I'm not. Jenny was dying peacefully and you know I tried to help? But all I've done is fill her with pain. Thanks to me her last moments are lost to torture and despair.'

He slumped onto a step with his stave across his lap and buried his head in his hands. His voice was choked 'It's my fault, I didn't know what I was doing and I shouldn't have tried. I'm not Penelope, I'm an idiot, and I've only made things worse.' He sniffed loudly, a child-like snort.

Behind him the sounds from Jenny's room had died away to little more than a cat-like mewling whine. In a way that was worse, she sounded exhausted and close to the end.

Porewit put his arm around Kingswraith's shoulders and patted his hand.

'No, Boss,' he said, 'you're wrong. You did alright, you did. I should have told you it was going to hurt her. You should have heard the racket you made when we got you back from Piccadilly that time after the fire. We thought the whole roof was going to come down on the reservoir, didn't we lads?'

Kingswraith looked up, his eyes glittering with salty moisture, 'What do you mean?'

Porewit nodded at him, 'The elixir is strong, and the charm lends some of your magic to your patient, see. Penelope did that for you too, we all did a bit, all of us. So, what I'm saying is, your friend Jenny is beginning to knit, and that's like, well, like darning a sock. Think what it feels like for the sock to be strung together across two needles, can't be comfortable, can it? Clackity clack, an' all. That's going to hurt, it must do, see.'

The young wizard was confused and wiped the back of his hand across his nose. It smelled of river water and something alien, something sharp, like some strange cooked meat. With a gasp of horror he recoiled, realising that his hands still smelled of the Vadhaka's burned flesh. At that moment, the realisation came crashing down on him. He was a killer.

He had killed them all! The Umbra, the Vadhaka, the Hierodules. Before that he had cut Frossard's head off, turning him to ashes, and he had burned the mob of manus mortuus, the faceless ones, to a pile of greasy black soot. Thanks to him Haven Slighe had died in the furnace heat of his London home. So many lives stripped away.

He was a killer! He'd talked nobly enough to Jeremiah about not stooping to their level, but look at what he'd done. He'd slashed and burned his way through his enemies as if they were vermin who deserved to die. He'd shattered the crystal woman and sent the dark one to the silty river bed with a smile on his face. Noble? No, he was no better than the terrible creatures he had slaughtered. He was a cold killer, no better than the Vadhaka.

A slight dark figure sat on the step by his side, his companions moved to give her space.

She said, 'I think that wood spirit lady is like a Queen. She and her soldiers came to help. But I see what you done, I saw what you did before they clouted I, then I was down like a poleaxed calf. What I hear is that without you we'd a' been in a deep bucket full of trouble before the Queen ever got here. You killed they wrong-uns before they killed us. You had no druthers, and that's a fact.'

Shelagh pushed her arm around his shoulders, she continued, 'They came here and they hadn't been invited. We didn't go after them; we didn't walk up to their house with swords and knives and faces like angry badgers. They came here after us. They would a killed us all and laughed about it afterwards, ha, ha they buggers would. It's true, they would, an all.'

He looked into her earnest little face, 'I killed them, Shelagh. What does that make me?'

She didn't smile when she answered, 'It makes you the man who saved everyone's life. That wicked bugger in the red coat, he was running at Wills and the Professor and Mrs Clare and the missus. He was after chopping them all to bits like kindling. Those monkey men, they would have chopped us all up to bits and probably ate us up like coneys but without the stew pot. You stopped them. I tried to help but when I slung iron slugs at that red bugger nothing happened. Bugger didn't even take notice. I should have thrown feathers for all it mattered.'

Kingswraith smiled for the first time since running from Jenny's room. He reached into his pocket and carefully pulled out the two iron slugs he had found on the ground after the Vadhaka had been destroyed.

'No, my love. These are what stopped him, that "red bugger". I spelled him but these are what stopped him. He was already coming apart from the inside, and that was because of you. You've saved my life twice, you know that?'

She smiled then, and it was like the sun had risen to warm Kingswraith's heart. Melsh sobbed, 'This is like something come alive from a tapestry. I can't wait to hear the story told proper by the poets, not if I have to wait another thousand years 'til they get it right.'

Kingswraith said, 'Wait here, I'll not be long.' He leapt up the stairs and along the landing to his room. He fetched his mother's box and lifted out the upper tray, found what he was looking for, put the box away and hastened back to the stairs. Clare appeared in Jenny's bedroom doorway as he approached and held up her hand to attract his attention. He ignored her, and descended back to his place at Shelagh's side.

He took her left hand and kissed it, then slid his mother's engagement ring onto her finger. 'If I need you to save my life again it might be best if I have you by my side all the time. What do you say?'

She protested, 'Oooh, no, look at that. That be too posh and proper for my red old hand. What are you saying? I can't clean house with this on, can I? That might ruin it! No, it's too nice. Ooh, but isn't it lovely.' She held her hand up, fingers splayed, and let the light catch the diamonds and emeralds set in white gold. The ring sparkled almost as bright as the emerald shards glinting in her dark eyes. Then she went to take it off.

Kingswraith stopped her, 'What I'm saying is, Shelagh, will you marry me?'

Melsh was sniffing and swiping at his eyes, making odd snuffling sounds. The other Sprites had adopted soft expressions, the kind of faces a child might make at the sight of a puppy, or a spring lamb bouncing across the fields.

From the top of the stairs behind them a familiar strong voice said, 'If this isn't the strangest day I've ever lived, I don't know what is, and my name isn't Jenny Maitland. And that's the truth of it.'

Porewit grinned, 'Looks like your sock's all darned and ready, Boss. Knit up nicely too, better than ever. Can't say I didn't tell you. The day's turned out nice after all.'

Shelagh looked radiantly happy. At that moment Kingswraith thought her the most beautiful creature on God's Earth, the breath caught in his chest. She answered, low and quiet, 'I am for thee, as thou art for me. I say yes, and yes, and yes again.'

She giggled, 'Mam will have a litter of stripy kittens when I tell her, she will an all!'

39

When Millicent and Marple returned to the Hall the following day, they couldn't get over the change in the household. Jenny was bursting with energy and looked ten years younger. The little maid Shelagh and the young master had become inseparable, and Millicent noted the ring on the girl's finger with a warm spurt of envy. She could tell that the ring wasn't paste, and thought it must have cost at least a lifetime of anyone's wages to buy; probably more, probably much more.

The Professor Lord Whitekirk and his bride seemed distant, haunted. Lady Whitekirk kept stealing glances at young master Kingswraith as if she had discovered something odd about him, something difficult to swallow. Millicent thought it likely that the young master's new relationship with the little maid was enough to make anyone's hair curl. It cut through every status barrier she had ever known. And yet... They looked so right together. They glowed!

The previously friendly Mrs Vermont now kept herself to herself. She kept gazing out of the kitchen window towards the stableyard. Marple recognised that look. He had been with the quartermaster's corp in the army during the Crimean war. He had seen soldiers return from the front with that same expression. It was the face of someone who had felt the breath of the tomb on their faces; a survivor who couldn't yet believe they were still alive. It took some people like that.

Wills was quiet and remained close by his wife's side, his big honest face creased with concern and confusion. His wife had always been the one in charge, she had always ruled the Vermont roost. He didn't know what to make of the muted woman who had spent the night huddled against his chest, quivering at every sound on the night air. Wills had very little imagination, but now he thought his Ethel might be suffering from a little too much. A surfeit of bad dreams.

After putting the dog cart under cover and stabling and currying the horse, Marple had sought out the Lord Whitekirk to share an urgent observation.

'Sir,' he said, 'I have to say that the grounds are alive with what looks like street Arabs and gypsy folk. I believe they've set up camp by the woods. Shall I fetch the constable, sir? There's a fair number of them.'

The Professor offered a bleak smile, 'Thank-you, Marple, but no. They are friends. We had quite a time of it yesterday evening. It was touch-and-go for a while. Those "street Arabs and gypsy folk" as you call them saved our bacon, alongside young Martin who was quite astonishing. They're helping us tidy up the mess. Best leave them to it. They're having to do things as might turn your stomach, old friend. Yes, leave them to it, that's best.'

Very few of the hierodules had escaped the combination of fire and steel from the redoubt, along with Shelagh's sling, Kingswraith's furious assault, and the hail of stone tipped arrows released by Kingswraith's companions and Eurynome's Sagittarii. Many ape-men had been burned to ash by Kingswraith's stave, but those riddled by arrows, blasted by shotgun, skewered by pitchfork or hewed by axe, had to be cleared and cremated before they rotted and released the foul stink of decay and contagion to the air.

After clearing them away from the house and the forests, tens of dozens of bodies had been stacked like cordwood in a freshly dug shallow pit. Kingswraith was called. With Shelagh at his side and his companions in tow he slowly approached the great mound of mangled corpses, piled at the centre of a circle of Eurynome's Sprites. A dense, ever moving cloud of flies were already feasting, filling the air with the grinding drone of wings.

A sombre Eurynome came to Shelagh who was staring at the heap of dead with an expression of nauseated horror.

The Sprite Queen took her hands and said, 'You should not be here, my Lady. Such things open our souls to nightmare. We killed these creatures and now, to heal ourselves, we must honour their passing. You are innocent of this slaughter. You need not witness this act as we must in order to guide our souls towards peace. Go back to the house, my Lady, wait there until this thing is over.'

Shelagh shook her head, 'No, I did it too. I killed as many as I had smooth stones. You saw how many stones I collected when we met by the stream, and that's how many I killed an' all. I knew what I were doing, like David with Goliath. I were the shepherd and they were the wolves; but I never knew they were so many in the pack. They seemed so big yesterday, but look at them now, all piled up higgledy-piggledy. Don't they look small.'

Eurynome regarded the girl with new respect. She replied, 'Forgive me, my Lady, you must do as you see fit.'

She turned towards the young wizard, 'My Lord Kingswraith, we ask if you would honour these dead and bring grace to the living. Will you accept this sad duty?'

He nodded and offered Eurynome a slight bow, 'It is both my burden and my obligation. I brought these creatures here. Their path to this place was laid down by my actions over a year ago. Their blood is on my hands. But first, what are they? Are they men or beasts? I've never seen their like before, not in life nor in any book.'

'Neither, and yet, perhaps both. They are hierodules, were-men, thralls. They are creatures twisted from their origins in the wild, great apes pressed into service. They lived and died as slaves, bound to the will of a mistress they worshipped as a goddess. For them to find peace is to find release. Mourn them, but do not pity them. We have broken them free from their bonds; so, now, my Lord, it is time to set them free from their tainted flesh.'

The Sprites, including the Queen and Kingswraith's companions, began a low song, so deep it vibrated in Shelagh's stomach. Kingswraith took his stave in both hands and pointed it at the mound. He gazed at the tangle of arms and legs, hands and feet. He saw brutish faces, some still snarling, mouths open, teeth bared, eyes wide. Others just looked surprised, as if they had been caught unawares at the moment of death.

He closed his eyes and prayed, 'Forgive me, Father, for what I must do, and for what I have done.'

Then he opened his eyes. Without uttering another word to produce his carmini, he sensed the power rising up within him. The sheer strength of it forced a groan from his lips. It built and built until he felt as if he was about to burst, and then it flowed through him and into his stave, unleashing a torrent of blinding fury.

The Sprites reeled away in shock as the hierodule corpses were enveloped in an actinic bloom of light. They were not burning, there was no stench of roasting meat, but instead their tissues began undergoing an alchemical change. The molecules binding their flesh and bone together were breaking apart and floating free. The light flared brighter and brighter, and all the while the mound was diminishing, slumping down into the shallow pit.

Kingswraith realised he was not the source of the energy, it was too much, even for him. It was flowing through him not from him, but he felt himself drained by the sheer force of the outpouring, as if he was too weak a vessel to contain so much power. He was shaking. His hands began vibrating, he tasted tin in his mouth and his sight was dazzled.

Blue and pink dots floated before his watering eyes and all cogent thought had ceased. He had become the mindless conduit for violent forces he had never experienced before. When it finally ended it caught him by surprise and he crumpled to his knees. It took him a few moments to gather his wits and try to catch his breath. Shocked silence filled the air.

Some of the Sprites were lying on the ground, others were kneeling or crouching down. All were gazing from him to the empty trench. A few sparkles of crystalline light glittered above the freshly turned earth and then were gone. No trace of the corpses remained, not so much as a hank of hair or a broken bone. They had dissolved, vanished completely away.

He didn't know it, and he would never find out, but the few ape-men who had escaped the slaughter had also been dispersed. Lost and confused, their world shaken apart by the death of their goddess, their minds set adrift without guide or direction, Kingswraith's intense outpouring of energy had also sought them out and given them peace.

Distant shouting, voices raised in alarm. Across the meadows they saw the Professor and Clare sprinting towards them, their faces pale with apprehension. Kingswraith climbed back to his feet as did the Sprites. Some of the forest people started a whispered conversation, most gazed at the young wizard with a strange and knowing light in their eyes.

The Professor reached his ward and grabbed him by the shoulders, 'Martin,' he gasped, 'are you alright? What happened here? We heard, we felt, something. It was like a whirlwind, an eruption, like the end of the world! It was coming from over here; what was it? The servants couldn't feel anything, well, Jenny thought she was getting a migraine, but the others felt nothing, so, we guessed it had to be magical. The Thaumatograph must be spinning off its spindles back in Chelsea? What on earth was it?'

Eurynome joined them, 'My Lord Whitekirk, what you felt was the breath of the Draco Terrae as it cleansed the world of the hierodules. The Lord Kingswraith was made the vessel for that cleansing, as the Draco is ultimately the vessel for God. The Draco still resides here on Earth. His body sleeps under the stones of Albion, but his soul is awake and he cares for the children of the Way. He loves us.'

She indicated the young wizard, who was quivering in his patron's grip. 'Sometimes, very rarely, he chooses one of us to be his emissary. It is a heavy burden that only the best of us can bear. This time he has chosen the Lord Kingswraith to be his plenipotentiary and to wield his power for the good of all. It will prove both a blessing and a curse.'

Wordlessly Kingswraith plucked his patron's hands from his shoulders, looked around, and hurried to where Shelagh was still lying on the grass. As he drew closer her eyes grew huge and she drew back in fear, but he held out his hand to her and smiled. He helped her to her feet, brushed the soil and grass from her dress, put his arms around her shoulders, bent forward, and tenderly kissed her on the mouth.

At first, she seemed frozen to the spot, then she melted into his embrace and returned his kiss with a warmth that startled and excited him. They held their caress for long seconds that swept them away from everything dark and ugly in the world, then Shelagh took a breath.

She whispered, 'I think as there might be people watching just now, don't you? I'm not saying I don't like it. I like it a lot, and I want to do it again, but I think doing it where there's just thee and me might be favourite. And I truly want to know who you are. I've never seen nothing like what you just did there; it was like summat from Moses.'

They sheepishly turned to face the group still clustered around the shallow trench. Kingswraith's companions were proudly beaming at them as if they had just performed a clever circus trick, the Professor and Clare were pretending to examine the trench while talking with Eurynome. The forest Sprites were performing weaving motions over the raw soil of the trench, and even as the couple watched, fresh grass began to sprout there.

By the time they rejoined the company it looked as if the meadow had never been disturbed. In less than twenty-four hours all trace of the Umbras' attack on the Whitekirk estate had been erased, except in the hearts and memories of those who had fought there.

Shelagh broke away from Kingswraith and hopped across to confront the Sprite Queen.

She said, 'I did hear what you said about the Draco an' all and it sounds marvellous like a picture book to I. But what I want to know is, who are they, the children of the Way?'

Eurynome smiled charmingly, 'Why, my Lady Shelagh, you are, we are, all of us here. Didn't you know? It is quite the famous story.'

40

Two months later, with Christmas looming and the skies leaden with dense cloud, the young couple were married in the Wallingford church of St Leonard's. It was a quaint little church and the oldest place of worship in the town, so long as you ignored every form of worship older than Christianity. St Leonard's sixth century Saxon stonework underpinned the post-civil-war restoration required after parliamentarian troops had used the place as a barracks and 'knocked it about a bit'. More recently it had been spruced up in the blandly ubiquitous Gothic revivalist style favoured by too many Victorian architects.

Shelagh thought it 'pretty' but Kingswraith sensed something else beneath the Christian flagstones; something primeval and more organic. His best man, the Professor, agreed. As they stood in front of the altar and waited for the bride to arrive with her attendant matron of honour, Mrs Vermont, and bridesmaid, Millicent, the friends chatted about the old religions.

The Professor warmed to his subject, 'The English landscape is littered with sites of ancient veneration; henges, sacred glades, barrows of rebirth. The church of Rome's eagerness to smother them with fresh chapels, prayers and popery saw priests arriving by the boatload, and the people had little option but to accept their Christening into the new church.'

He smiled, 'It didn't work, of course. We still have our Maypoles, the Green Man, Morris dancers, Christmas, and Easter. The Sun and the Moon are still worshipped and the solstices celebrated. The further you travel away from the towns and into the countryside the more likely you are to find Celtic Triskelions carved into out-of-the-way earth-banks, and phalluses whittled into the living wood of old wych elms. These are all celebrations of fertility of course; asking the gods for a fecund wife, a good harvest, and fair weather.'

Kingswraith had been feeling nervous before, but all the Professor's talk about fertility and phalluses was making him feel worse. He thought about the urgent reasons that Shelagh and he had decided it would be best to marry sooner rather than later.

They knew how they felt about each other, the wedding ceremony was merely a ritual to formalise a marriage that was already firmly established in their hearts, if not yet consummated. It was that consummation that was playing on Kingswraith's mind. He was completely naive about such things.

The reaction of his ring to the amulet Shelagh was wearing, had already plighted their troth in the eyes of the Sprites, who simply couldn't understand what was holding them back from their marriage bed. When Kingswraith spoke about posting the banns and the need to observe common decency, Porewit told him that in the old days all the couple needed to do was to jump over a fire three times and say 'I marry you' which each jump. There was none of this banns nonsense.

'Why wait?' Porewit had wondered, and shrugged.

Kingswraith realised that his fiancée was changing, maturing, becoming more confident and lovelier every day as the wedding drew closer. Even her antic language seemed less eccentric. Freed from her household duties Shelagh had also begun spending more of her daylight hours down in the woods with Eurynome. When he asked her what they were doing out there all day she blushed.

She said, 'There are things a woman needs to know before she gets married. That's all I'm saying. And it's not all about birds, bees, and acorns neither. I know some of it, I can cook, clean house, and I know what to do with laundry and such; but I reckon there's more to a marriage than just holding hands and looking into each other's eyes, if you see what I mean?'

He was all too afraid that he did. He had also met Shelagh's mother. She had walked out of the woods one morning searching for her daughter, and insisted on meeting the Professor and the boy she described as, 'My girl's heartstring on legs what has got the blessed creature into a proper pother, and all unnecessarily fussed about in her wits, all turned about and about 'til she doesn't know the day of the week from her elbow. Where is this mortal paragon of male beauty? Shall I set me eyes upon him?'

Kingswraith quickly realised who Shelagh had inherited her very individual use of English from. The Professor was fascinated to discover that the woman's name was Kee-va Pridia, which sounded very old English to him, perhaps pre-Roman. When he asked her to write it down for him, he was surprised to learn that her Christian name was actually spelt C A O I M H E which looked like a true Celtic tongue-twister, but for some arcane reason was pronounced simply, 'Kee-va'.

When he asked her if she could explain the difference between the spelling and the spoken word, she merely smiled enigmatically and said, 'It must have got mixed up with something on the swim over from Eire to Cornwall. You'd have to ask me great, great, great grand dam if ever you meet her. And even she might not know.'

He invited her to stay at the Hall, but she declined, almost running to the door as she answered, 'No, I only wanted to meet the darling boy and give him my blessing. I can sense they'll be bumps in the road ahead, but they'll manage. I never thought my Shelagh'd meet her match, but I'm glad she has before she's too stricken in years. I met my man when I had fourteen summers, and Shelagh saw her sixteenth this year, she's nearly an old maid.'

She sighed and smiled, 'They do look fine together though, don't they? Like ripe pears on the branch. He'll soon find my girl has more layers to her than a tin mine, so he'll never be bored. He looks more the sort to use the kiss rather than the paddle, and that's the secret to a happy life.'

She didn't look old enough to be Shelagh's mother. Dimpled and auburn-haired with a merry light to her chestnut eyes, Kingswraith could see what had attracted her daughter's Sprite father to her in the first place. She was buxom but not fat, and looked more comfortable outside in the open air than closeted in a room. The world had rubbed roses into her cheeks and lent a golden glow to her freckled features, Caoimhe was clearly born to be a woman of the earth.

She left in the late afternoon of the same day she had arrived, and Shelagh walked with her into the woods. It was two days before the little maid returned, and when she did, she sparkled with a fresh vitality that lit the emerald shards in her eyes and brought colour to her cheek. She carried with her the scent of flowers, cut grasses, and fresh herbs. Even the birds seemed to sing louder and more brightly when she drew near, and everywhere she went her enchanted happiness captivated everyone around her.

No, not quite everyone. Clare was the sole member of the household able to resist the girl's charm. Everyone else smiled, laughed, walked with a lighter step and seemed to share in the sheer pleasure in life that Shelagh exuded like a fresh perfume. She was music made flesh and she danced through the days leading up to her wedding, but Clare couldn't hear the tune. Her head was caught up with questions and the girl's fifteen-puzzle mysteries.

She wondered what sort of surname 'Pridia' might be. It sounded foreign. And for all that she tried hard to accept the little maid's new standing she couldn't quite stomach such a major change to the status quo. She also couldn't explain why she had become so discomforted by Shelagh's presence, but she was. The little maid threw up more questions than anyone could answer, but nobody else seemed to be asking them. Why?

Perhaps Clare's wild magical talent was fighting Shelagh's blossoming natural glamour, an intoxicating form of praeternatural fascination that reached out with subtle energy and enraptured everyone touched by her presence. Clare had never let anyone tell her what to do and she resisted Shelagh's magical persuasion with all her prodigious willpower.

She thought she had kept her aversion to the little maid a close secret, closeted away behind her civility, grace, and good breeding. But in truth the only person not aware of the friction between Clare and the girl was Shelagh herself. She was so wrapped up in joy that she couldn't find fault with anyone or anything. She was blind and deaf to the snippy little darts that Lady Clare Whitekirk flung her way at every opportunity.

The day arrived and before the altar of St Leonard's, the Professor paused in his monologue regarding the old religions, looked back down the nave, and said, 'Here they are,' bringing Kingswraith back from his brooding to the here and now of his wedding.

The organist struck up Felix Mendelssohn's Wedding March. The piece had been written over forty years previously for a performance of Shakespeare's play A Midsummer Night's Dream, a fantastic drama originally written for a wedding. Its plot involved fairies, Sprites and magic, which seemed apt. For all the Christian values the vicar represented with his high church wine and wafers, the 'bringing together of this man and this woman' could just as easily have taken place in a forest glade before a congregation of wildlife.

When Shelagh fetched up at his elbow her sweet figure was lost under layers of white lace, clouds of linen roses, and fine embroidery finished with seed pearls. The dress had been the Professor's mother's wedding gown and the ladies of Whitekirk Hall, sans Clare, had adjusted it to fit the much smaller bride to be. It was a thing of elegant beauty, and almost made a stranger of the little maid, until he heard her unmistakeable giggle.

241

Kingswraith felt his heart pounding in his throat when she tilted her head up towards him and lifted her veil. Her innocent beauty shone bright in the cool grey light of the chapel. Kingswraith's breath caught in his throat and the world roared in his ears. He felt dizzy and almost drunk on her loveliness. The vicar had to cough and tap him on the shoulder to bring him back to earth before they could start the ceremony.

The church was more than half full of locals who wanted to see a posh wedding – and friends of the Whitekirk family – but not a single Sprite had attended. They found churches claustrophobic, places of sombre piety that sucked the air from their lungs. Yet Brigid was there. Wearing her younger guise, she was sitting near the front of the groom's party. Next to her sat Lucas and Mirte Bakker looking uncomfortable in their Sunday best.

Jeremiah Taylor sat behind them accompanied by his wife and son. The silversmith wore an expression of pride on his broadly smiling face, and there was no mistaking his sonorous voice during the hymns. Even William Cosgrave, solicitor for both the Professor and Kingswraith, had accepted his invitation to celebrate the wedding and sat beaming at the bride and groom. Next to him was a charming woman Kingswraith presumed to be his wife.

Kingswraith was already wearing his dragon ring on his left hand, so it was just the single fine golden ring that Jeremiah had been commissioned to fashion for Shelagh that the Professor fished from his waistcoat pocket and placed on the open book in the vicar's hands. Around its circumference the dragon chased its tail and glittered as if it was alive.

They took their vows, and when the vicar finally intoned, 'By the power vested in me, I now pronounce you husband and wife. You may kiss the bride,' bright sunlight poured through the arched windows and flooded the nave. Kingswraith cast a quick glance back at Brigid who grinned archly at him and winked.

Shelagh whispered to him, 'We should always bring a goddess to our weddings.'

He replied, 'Once is enough, wife. This one is for life. I love you.' And they kissed.

The church exploded with applause and handkerchiefs were flourished to dab at damp eyes. And a great voice that only the newlyweds could hear spoke to them, 'May the blessings of the Lord be upon this union. Amen.'

Goddesses and dragons, thought Kingswraith. Goddesses and dragons. They say some marriages are made in heaven, but what would the vicar make of this one if he knew?

When they left the church a crowd of familiar looking street urchins clustered around to shower them with freshly picked leaves and seasonal flowers. The only girl in the group strode up to the new Mrs Kingswraith, bowed, and then hugged her like a sister. They both looked at the freshly minted husband with knowing glances.

Eurynome, took his hand, 'You're a very lucky man, you know that?'

He grinned, 'I'm still finding out just how lucky I am, but yes.'

'May your voyage of discovery be long and fruitful. You've married an interesting woman, perhaps more interesting than you know. Now then, my Lady Shelagh, time to throw the bouquet, the ladies are waiting.'

Millicent caught it.

Much later, after the toasts were finally done and the excellent food applauded, the last glasses of wine drunk and the guests departed into the chill evening with promises to return for breakfast the following morning, Kingswraith and his wife retired to the Bedouin tent room. Neither had ever shared a bed with another person before, but they managed to get to sleep. Eventually.

The last thing he asked her was whether she liked fish and chips. She said that she did. He told her his friends the Bakkers had a boat and they knew a lovely place for fish and chips, she breathed, 'that's nice,' yawned, and was asleep. He kissed her and settled down himself.

At a time somewhere between midnight and dawn, Kingswraith roused from a strange dream in which a beautiful woman was sharing his bed, and found it to be true. The moon shone through the window and splashed silver light onto the tangle of curls, tousled and black as a raven's wing, that framed the lovely face of his new wife. Even in sleep she demanded all his attention.

He desperately wanted to stroke her cheek but held back for fear he might disturb her slumber. He gazed down at her smiling mouth, the long curve of her eyelashes, the perfect symmetry of her eyebrows, the sweet dimple in her cheek, and he felt a surge of fear bubble through his body. What if he was to lose her? What if something happened to take her away from him? Could he survive? It must never be allowed to happen.

Six of the Umbra are left, he remembered. Six of them and their cohorts. And he vowed he would kill every single one of them if they came anywhere near his wife. He would destroy them all, whatever it took, even at the cost of everyone else. Shelagh must survive. If it meant his own death she must survive. No-one who saw his grim face in that dark hour before dawn would have recognised him, but they would have feared him.

41

‘ Makrut Wyndsyster chose to join Cymbeline on her little adventure to Albion, as did Frossard. They made their choices and they died. Perhaps they were foolish, perhaps they were careless, we can't say which.' The cool voice whined with exasperation, 'This is ridiculous! Has anyone received any kind of intelligence from that damnable place? Are we saying we know nothing at all about what happened there? Nothing? How is that possible?'

The pale, angular face of Titres Chambers glared around at his five remaining companions. All six were standing within the carefully drawn circle in the six-hundred-foot-long, boat-shaped depression on that Turkish mountainside. The Umbra eyed each other warily. There was not enough trust between them to fill a thimble, but all they had was each other.

Emmanuel Flight rumbled the words that the others dared not utter, 'It is foolish to believe that some upstart white wizard has got the better of four of us. A human? I would rather believe that one of us, one of you, is behind this impossibility. It is not me, so then, why can't the guilty one step forward and lay claim to their culpability? Let's have done with it. We are six now, three female, and three males. The balance is restored. We are wise and we are powerful. Surely, we can work together? The world is big enough for all of us.'

This brought an uproar of disagreement from the group, a sound that was picked up by the shadowed throng of motley vassals the six had brought with them as bodyguards. Much like Cymbeline's hierodules they were very sensitive to their masters' and mistresses' moods. The slightest insult to their godlike rulers would normally be met by immediate and savage retaliation. But that night there were six gods in that place, gods they were forbidden to touch. The thralls were confused, so they vented their frustration in howls of baffled fury.

Fiorina Chrysas barked at her minions to be still, and then turned her attention on Flight, 'It is always true that the first to deny anything is the culprit; that's basic schoolyard logic. But in this case, I believe you are being truthful. You claim it is not you who has been scouring our conflagration of shadows? I believe you. Personally, I would not even know how to remove one of us from the ether. They are not simply dead, Emmanuel, they have not passed through the veil, they are gone! Completely gone. Could any one of us do that? I couldn't!'

She got nods of approval from everyone. All around them the thralls made satisfied chuffing sounds, their heads bobbing up and down, mindlessly and unconsciously aping their lords and ladies. Fiorina sometimes suspected that her minions might actually be ridiculing their betters, but no, that was impossible. If their brains lit lanterns that shone through their eyes, they still wouldn't have enough light to read by. If they could read.

Cho Yun Ye held his arms wide open to gather everyone's attention. He was the oriental master of the Umbra and slender as a stiletto in a silken sheath. His hair was worn in a carefully braided queue, pulled back from his plucked forehead. His high collared, jet-black robe made it appear as if his attenuated head was floating in mid-air, and his face was disturbingly hairless, marked only by a raven dark, arrowhead shaped chin tuft.

In his surprisingly pleasant sounding, sing-song voice, he said, 'There is no benefit in our infighting. Cymbeline warned us before she took her path to Albion. She warned us that we must work together to defeat our foe. Now we see that she was right. The silent Frossard has gone, as has Cymbeline and Makrut. Have they joined Haven Slighe? We do not know; we only know that four of our number have vanished from the weave of Umbra. What shall we do now? Anyone? We are losing our resources and we cannot afford to be profligate.'

'Nor can you afford to be too cautious.' This new voice echoed from amongst the throng of beastlike thralls. It was clear and chimed in the Umbras' ears with a conviction they had never experienced before. It was a voice to which they had to listen; they had no choice.

Flight answered, his speech sounding crude and unpleasant by comparison, 'Who comes to us here in this sacred place? You are most welcome, friend, but please, make yourself known to us. Come forward, share your wisdom.'

It should have been obvious that none of the Umbra were thinking clearly. They didn't ask how the speaker had made his way through their vassals without being torn apart. They didn't ask why they had received no warning that a stranger was approaching. Nor did they wonder at how easily the stranger had charmed them with his voice. Magic was at work, but it was magic of such subtle power that they didn't realise how completely they had been snared.

With the grace of a dark angel the newcomer walked out of the night and, without using an unlocking charm or a silver athame to open the circle, he stepped lightly across the eastern line of their protective zisurrû. Even this impossibility didn't disturb any of the six. They placidly accepted the stranger's entrance into their midst without question. All around them their minion host rumbled sedately, happy as a plump herd of sweet grass-fed cattle.

The man spun at the centre of the circle, taking his time to consider each of the Umbra in turn. He smiled, 'Children of the shadows, sons and daughters of the Word, I am proud to meet you at last. This happy and overdue meeting fills my heart with joy. Yes, well met, noble shadows. I know each of you. I have followed your extraordinary careers across the centuries, but now, perhaps, is the perfect time for me to join you; with your permission?'

All members of the Umbra looked around their circle, and all were nodding their approval. The stranger was very welcome to join them, they were all in agreement. He was a fine addition to the conflagration.

Fiorina Chrysas almost simpered. She was a slender golden beauty who had been celebrated throughout Tuscany for her wit and radiant charm, but before the stranger she acted like a besotted schoolgirl.

She giggled, 'Sir, you say you know us? Then please, may we be permitted to learn your name? Perhaps we have heard tell of you?'

'Of course,' he smiled and they all felt his hypnotic allure in the pit of their stomachs. 'I am called Loquelo Primo, and I am here to help you destroy a young man called Kingswraith. Once this is done the world shall be yours once more and none shall dare stand against you. We shall fight together to crush him utterly. Together we shall break him, shatter him on the anvil of your irresistible resolve. Are you with me? Well, are you, my brothers and sisters? Are you with me?'

The cheers of the Umbra and the joyful hoots of the thralls rang around the mountainside, setting small landslides in motion. Loquelo Primo had risen once more. The Word had joined his children. Darkness had found its true voice.

www.ingramcontent.com/pod-product-compliance
Lightning Source LLC
Chambersburg PA
CBHW020755250626
47155CB00003B/1082